LILLI DE JONG

The purchase of this book
was made possible
by a generous grant from
The Auen Foundation.

This Large Print Book carries the
Seal of Approval of N.A.V.H.

LILLI DE JONG

JANET BENTON

THORNDIKE PRESS
A part of Gale, Cengage Learning

GALE
CENGAGE Learning®

Farmington Hills, Mich • San Francisco • New York • Waterville, Maine
Meriden, Conn • Mason, Ohio • Chicago

GALE
CENGAGE Learning®

LIBRARY OF CONGRESS CATALOGING-IN-PUBLICATION DATA

Names: Benton, Janet, 1963– author.
Title: Lilli de Jong / by Janet Benton.
Description: Large print edition. | Waterville, Maine : Thorndike Press, a part of Gale, Cengage Learning, 2017. | Series: Thorndike Press large print peer picks
Identifiers: LCCN 2017010925| ISBN 9781432839819 (hardcover) | ISBN 1432839810 (hardcover)
Subjects: LCSH: Quaker women—Fiction. | Unmarried mothers—Fiction. | Mother and child—Fiction. | Self-actualization (Psychology) in women—Fiction. | Pennsylvania—Fiction. | Domestic fiction. | Psychological fiction. | Large type books.
Classification: LCC PS3602.E6973 L55 2017b | DDC 813/.6—dc23
LC record available at https://lccn.loc.gov/2017010925

Published in 2017 by arrangement with Nan A. Talese/Doubleday, a division of Penguin Random House, LLC

*For family, wherever one may find it,
with gratitude and love to mine*

Every other door . . . is closed to her who, unmarried, is about to become a mother. Deliberate, calculating villainy, fraud, outrage, burglary, or even murder with malice aforethought, seems to excite more sympathy, more helpful pity, more efforts for the reclamation of the transgressors than are shown towards those who, if not the victims of others, are at the worst but illustrations of human infirmity.

— annual report of the
State Hospital for Women and Infants,
Philadelphia, Pennsylvania, 1880

NOTEBOOK ONE

1883. Third Month 16

Some moments set my heart on fire, and that's when language seems the smallest. Yet precisely these bursts of feeling make me long to write. I sit now in a high-walled courtyard, amid the green smells and slanted light of early spring, with that familiar burning in my heart. I'll need to destroy these pages before returning home, but no matter; for the first time since Mother's death, words come to me.

I've lost more than I've gained since Mother died last year, when I was but twenty-two. Yet I wish to tell of some good things. This small courtyard with its carved stone bench, for instance, which fast becomes my refuge. For with spring upon us, there is such a wellness in the out of doors. Crocuses peer from the melting snow. Budding trees sweeten the air with their exhalations. If I were at home, I'd have turned the soil in our kitchen garden today, and planted radish and lettuce seeds besides. For supper, I'd have made a soup from the hardy kale and onions that survived the winter.

But I'm not at home. I'm at the Philadelphia Haven for Women and Infants. I've fled the building to this sheltered patch of ground to escape the struggles of my roommate Nancy — who till this morning slept in a bed beside mine and now moans and yells from the birthing table. Her sounds are as guttural and plaintive as those of a dog with its leg clamped in a trap. Even the stoutest girls among us have gone pale from hearing, for each will have her turn soon, and then will return from disgrace only by giving up her offspring and denying its existence ever after — as I will do.

For Gina and me, who share a room with Nancy, the anxiousness began last night with Nancy's moaning and tossing in her sleep. At dawn she awoke, her thighs and sheets wet with a watery fluid.

"No one came for me!" she wailed as Gina and I wiped her clean. She wasn't crying from bodily pain — not yet; she cried from understanding, at the age of sixteen, that her daily hope of rescue had reached its end. Her parents had sent her to domestic service in the city, and for three years they'd relied on the money she sent home to their farm. She lost her work due to her pregnancy, which arose from misplaced trust in a fellow servant, as she explained to us one whisper-filled night. Yet though she'd written many pleas, her parents had supplied no aid, made no visit, sent no letter of condolence.

Gina bent her head of dark curls to kiss Nancy's cheek. I squeezed her hand and eased her into a clean nightgown. And despite the fact that Gina and I are in our ninth months, too, we helped her down a flight of stairs and to the chamber of the Haven's matron, Delphinia Partridge. At the door, we knocked and waited while Nancy hung about our shoulders.

Soon the bleary matron emerged, clad in a worn blue dressing gown, her silver hair tucked beneath a sleeping cap. We walked to the delivery room, where she encouraged a shivering Nancy to lie upon the birthing table.

To Gina and me the matron said, "Wake up the cook. Tell her to fetch the doctor." She motioned with her head toward the door. But Nancy grabbed Gina's plump arm and held it. Her lips were pale from how hard she pressed them together.

"I can stay?" Gina asked Delphinia. She

came from Italy two years ago and speaks well for that.

Delphinia shook her head, unyielding. So we traveled the hall and woke the cook, who pulled a Mother Hubbard over her large form and ran out to fetch Dr. Stevens, a professor at the Woman's Medical College who attends to us. Then Gina and I joined the other nine pregnant occupants at breakfast, poking at our bowls of oatmeal, after which we went about our chores, with Nancy's cries punctuating our efforts.

Gina and I had kitchen duty. The cook had only turnips and onions for us to chop for the barley soup that would become our midday meal — not even canned tomatoes, since the winter's stores were gone, and neither meat nor bones. But scarce rations were not our first concern. As we wielded knives against the stubborn curves of turnips and bit stale bread to keep the onions from stinging our eyes, Gina complained at how Nancy's suffering pervaded the house. Girls in labor, she said, ought to be sent elsewhere, as it does us no good to be frightened.

The cook appeared too absorbed in preparations to bother listening. But she must have told the superintendent of this comment. For at the midday meal, Anne Pierce sat at the head of the table in a muted gown, her gray-streaked hair pinned close to her head, and reminded us why Nancy labors here. By the disgrace attending our conditions, we are barred from home, where otherwise we'd have given birth. And there exists no local institution but the Haven, Anne said, that will admit a parturient woman who isn't married — besides the city hospital at Blockley, which houses the most contagious diseases and people far rougher than us, and often discharges them in coffins.

"No one with her own bed and two pennies to rub together would consider that hospital fit for a birth," Anne said, puckering her lips as if tasting a lemon. "Besides, I see a purpose to your bearing witness." She proceeded to give a talk from her end of the table that amounted to this: "Let Nancy's suffering be an antidote to your passion."

As if passion alone explained our predicaments. Our being female and unlucky — and, in my case, a near idiot in the ways of amorous men — must be added to that. We heard Nancy call for mercy each time Anne paused and leaned her proud head to sip her tea. Though we hover constantly at the edge of being underfed, few girls had an appetite.

Since then Nancy has made slow progress and been urged along by the doctor to no avail. Her youthful hips are narrow and the baby is large. If chloral hydrate or ergot won't hasten her progress, the long forceps that Mother said can crush a baby's skull or cut its mother may have to be employed, or surgery may be called for. A meek woman named Alice, said to be carrying twins, has whispered her worrisome conviction that we'll all suffer such difficult labors because our babies are bastards.

It might fairly be asked how Lilli de Jong has come to belong in such company.

A memory answers. Bitterness is poison, yes, but I hold a flask of it to my lips and drink.

One cold night in First Month of last year, barely three weeks after Mother had passed, I awoke in a state of vexation in my slant-walled room in Germantown. I lay on my mattress, waiting for my heartbeat to slow and the tendrils of some frightening dream to evaporate into the air. My mouth was parched from panting; I rose to fetch a cup of water, only to find the pitcher on my washstand empty. So I descended the narrow stairs into our main room and headed for the kitchen. Across the planks I walked, past Father's bedroom.

Its door was ajar, its bed, empty.

Was Father staring at the embers of the kitchen fire again, too miserable to sleep without his dearest Helen? No; the kitchen was bare of life; its hearth was still and silent.

By the back window, as I ladled water from a bucket to a cup, a quick movement outside caught my eye. Something was moving in front of the outhouse. In air shimmering beneath the moon, a white shape billowed. It became recognizable as Father's first cousin, Patience. She was a spinster from Ohio who'd arrived two days prior, ostensibly to aid us in recovering from Mother's death. That woman stood in her dressing gown on the frozen ground, her pale hair loose and stippled with moonlight, her muscular arms clutching my father's torso. And he, clad in faded woolen underwear, gripped her in return. Their pelvises were pressed together, and their faces seemed joined at the lips, as if consuming one another.

I clapped a hand over my mouth and ran upstairs to the shelter of my quilts. In silence I shivered, half waiting and half dreading for the darkness to yield some noise from that unseemly pair. When they

17

did come inside, their footsteps halted on the first story, though Patience's steps should have risen to the bedroom beside mine. The door to Father's chamber clicked shut.

I knew little of such congress then. But I imagined nauseously their protuberances and indentations, their odd bits of bodies covered in curls of hair, fitting together in ways obscure and obscene. I lit a candle and stared at the cracks in my plaster ceiling, trying in vain to find the shapes that as a child I'd perceived as rabbits and mice, looking for the fissures that once had seemed to spell my name. I even picked up my book of Bible verses — but nothing took away the ghastly picture of my father, like a drowning man, grasping at a piece of flotsam.

It is many a spinster's custom to travel relative to relative, staying as long as she's needed. But in our little stone house, with its patriarch in grief, Patience had found a way to halt her wandering.

I intended to wake before dawn to prepare our meal. I wanted to witness their emergence from what had been my parents' room and thereby to impose on them the shame they ought to feel. But I was trapped by heavy sleep till sun came streaming in and overheated me. I dressed and rushed downstairs to find Father, Patience, and my brother, Peter, seated at our oak table. Father and Patience wore bland expressions. Their bodies appeared to have softened, like butter placed near the stove. His hand brushed hers in passing the canned peaches, and her thin lips opened to expose her small teeth, then eased into a dog-like smile.

Peter saw nothing amiss, for he kept his eyes on his plate, as he had at every meal since Mother died. He chewed and swallowed bite after bite determinedly, as if taking care not to choke on his own restlessness. And when Father's gangly, red-haired assistant came down from his attic room and joined our table, he greeted us as usual and fed heartily.

"Lilli," said Johan, his broad cheeks pink with anticipation, "can we haul those scraps to Rittenhouse town today?"

The bits of linen left behind from Mother's sewing and the rags too worn for use would fetch much-needed coins at the paper mill, and I'd be glad not to perform that sad errand alone. Such an outing, too, would allow Johan and me to share the fruits of our minds. On our return, freed of the sacks of cloth, we could ramble the snowy roads and stop for a sweet at the market, perhaps dangling our gloved hands near, even curling them together.

I had the freedom to accept his invitation. With Patience there, my home duties had lessened, and the students I taught at the Meeting school were on their winter vacation. So I answered Johan in the affirmative. Yet as I spoke, I felt a cramp of fear in my belly in place of my usual tingling anticipation of our heady talk. For in that kiss I'd witnessed, in the hunger that had made the bodies of my father and his cousin press hard into one another, a contagious force had come too near.

I watched as Father ate his sausage and dipped a hunk of bread in the fat, his lips and the surrounding skin growing greasy and slick. He never had been suited to Mother's refinement. Clearly, Patience was another sort of woman.

Soon that woman bundled her sturdy frame against the cold and left to buy meat at the butcher's. The three men entered their cabinet-making workshop at the side of our house. I went in as usual to straighten Father's bed, which had been clumsily assembled. And strewn upon Mother's pillow, where her chestnut hairs had always lain, was a tangled patch of Patience's yellow hairs.

I raised the familiar pillow to my face and inhaled, hoping that a trace of Mother's violet water still lingered. An odor of sweat as harsh as cat's urine penetrated my nose.

I threw the pillow to the bed, the very bed on which Mother had died three weeks before, and left the room behind.

Dear diary, that moment cut me loose of family and left me rudderless.

Mother was injured while driving our wagon filled with donated goods to a family whose house had burned. A wild dog frightened our horse and the horse bolted, dragging the wagon across a heap of rocks. Mother was tossed to the rocks, and furnishings toppled onto her.

She was mottled with bruises, swollen in her head and a dozen other places, afflicted by pains that prevented sleep and comfort. To relieve the swelling, our doctor decided she must be bled. Mother, usually outspoken, always fell to muteness in the company of medical men, and bleeding had been a more acceptable method in her youth. For our part, Father and Peter and I had no grounds for doubting. We let the doctor do his ghastly work.

She was sitting up in bed when he began it, cutting a vein in her arm and placing his collecting bowl beneath. He considered the blood loss sufficient when she fell forward, unconscious. She opened her eyes not long after but remained slumped and fragile. I fed her raspberry-leaf tea and beef juice, and by the next morning she could rise. But by then she had head and neck aches so severe that she could hardly walk.

Saying her nerves were damaged, the doctor sent her back to bed and prescribed strong-smelling decoctions to ease the pain. When these didn't help enough, Father informed him by letter, and the doctor called for increased frequency.

I'm convinced it was those medicines that poisoned and extinguished her.

The morning of her final day was warm. The golden sun was melting the latest storm's ice and snow, making the roads safer for travel. So Father sent Peter and Johan to a lumber mill with a list of supplies to buy. Watching them depart, I'd wished that I, too, could escape the misery of our house. I wanted to travel in our wagon with those relatively untroubled young men and drink in their vitality. How callous this was! When Mother had been expecting to die, had even asked for paper and pen and prepared her will. Yet none of us believed her. We thought the medicines and pain were turning her mind morbid.

As her daughter, and the nearest thing to her own flesh, I ought to have taken heed. I ought to have banished the doctor and his decoctions and sought out safer ways to ease her suffering. If only, at the very least, I had soothed her grief over dying at only forty-seven, with Peter not yet twenty and me twenty-two, and neither of us settled, and her husband sobbing in his workshop while her strength faded. If only I had found a place of calm within myself and tried, by my touch and voice, to transport her there.

By late that afternoon, Mother was vomiting often, and her mental state had worsened. She shifted from near catatonia to confusion to agitation. Father left, to buy more medicines, he said. Her last hours came soon after, and they seared me like a cattle brand.

I was walking away to fetch a cooling cloth for her forehead when a scream issued from the dearest person to me on earth. I turned to see her once-graceful body convulsing, gripped by unseeable sensations. Running to her side, I grabbed her hand. Her fingers were hot, like rods of fire, as if her remaining life was burning painfully away. Her face was scarlet. Even her eyes were changed, showing little but black. Then she began to make odd sounds I couldn't recognize as words.

I lay alongside her and curled over her slender limbs, willing her excess heat to transfer to me.

"Shush," I told her. "Rest easy. All will be well, Mother." I repeated such assurances and held her for some unmeasured span and hoped Father would come home and prayed to God for mercy as she jerked and moaned and struggled to breathe, her heart pattering quickly against mine, until she ceased to move.

The closest church bell rang seven times to mark the hour when her spirit departed and death weighed her body down. It seemed she had been pulled into a sucking void, a void that drew my spirit swiftly after, rushing and pulling and stretching me forward but never bringing me nearer.

When Father returned from the dispensary, he found me curled about her stiffening body, my wet eyes and opened mouth pressed against her neck and cheek, calling, *No, my dearest, come back, Mother.* Father pulled me off and carried me before the main hearth. He set me up with a quilt, then left to find the doctor so the dreadful fellow could declare his patient dead.

My life's order and beauty fell down flat

— as if they had been nothing more than painted scenery.

Mother's burial took place the next afternoon. Few of our kin remained in the region, having earlier sought land to the west and formed new Meetings. Yet after a silent Meeting for Worship, members swarmed the burying ground, along with dozens of neighbors and persons whom Mother had aided in her decades of charitable work. Old Hannah Purdes stood to my left. She'd been a lifelong friend to Mother's mother and a ballast to Mother when others had called her too forthright. Hannah clasped my enfeebled body to her more solid one when the coffin bearers approached and laid the heavy box on the ground, and we stared into the gap in the earth that would soon devour Mother's simple coffin. Reaching beneath my coat and shawl to my neck, I touched my gold locket, with its snippet of Mother's hair and her tintype picture inside.

In the silence I recalled Lucretia Mott's burial at Fairhill, when no one could speak until one mourner observed that the woman who'd spoken for us had died.

Two persons did speak at Mother's burial. The first was Johan. He stood opposite the

25

open grave from me and my family, the sun outlining his lanky frame, and said, "She was that rare human who loves and is loved by kin and stranger."

This was a fitting tribute. A sigh passed through the crowd. The sun that glowed behind Johan seemed to come from within him.

Then I opened my mouth, and out came words of Lucretia Mott's that Mother had admired: "If our principles are right, why should we be cowards?" A shiver passed along my spine.

The coffin was lowered; the men with shovels were at the ready. Soon Mother's body would be covered by earth. All those present walked past the hole and streamed away. Some burst into speech as soon as they left the burying ground, but Father and Peter, Johan and I walked home in silence to face the gloom.

In my narrow bed I fell to staring into the air, and at nightfall I entered a nightmare-ridden sleep.

After passing most of another day in staring, I received a knock upon my door. It was Johan, suggesting that we go to the skating pond. Despite the weight of feeling that pressed me downward, I consented — for I had always loved immoderately to skate on ice.

My outlook remained dismal as we walked to the huge pond by Tulpehocken and Wayne and pulled on our skates — until I planted my feet on the ice, took one step, and sailed away. Oh, I relished that swiftness, the gathering of warmth under my clothes, the reddening of our eager faces in the glow of the lowering sun. Johan and I raced side by side across the pond, then followed its oval perimeter, panting whenever we spoke, our feet rising and gliding, rising and gliding, carrying our willing bodies through air that stung our cheeks and froze our eyelashes. Despite losing Mother, or even more because of it, I rejoiced in that vigorous and gladdening flight.

We stopped when the light grew dim enough to threaten our safe return homeward. As we changed into our boots, Johan held my mittened hand a moment and raised it to his mouth, exhaling heated breath to warm me. At his temples, from beneath his knitted cap, sweat trickled. His lips were wide and dry.

I wondered, *Will I kiss those lips?*

I thought, *My husband.*

And then, *This foreknowledge can't be rushed. I'll live toward it till its prediction comes to pass, or doesn't.*

On that day Johan replaced Mother as my lodestar, the pinpoint of light by which I charted my path. It may be that the explanation for my unwise surrender to him lies herein, that I couldn't perceive my own guiding star, or find it in the Light everlasting.

Yet something new did grow in me after Mother died — a capacity for cynicism. What was the sense in my mother's death? Was heavenly justice no more than a fantasy? I kept my doubts and bitterness quiet in myself, but through the ensuing months I observed others to see if they held them, too. When, after silent waiting, people stood in Meeting to speak what came into their spirits, most gave forth consoling messages of love; yet others spoke of hardships, within or without, and the barriers to overcoming them. I no longer shrank from the words of these messengers.

Something else, too, was pressing to have its day. Many nights I couldn't sleep, convinced that knowledge poured through me — all the knowing Mother had released into my body when she died; in vain I searched for words to give it shape. On other nights I slept excessively, as if this growing power required added rest.

Having always been a Friend and attended twice-weekly Meetings for Worship, I was raised on insights and revelations conveyed by God through willing humans. But the person receiving this wisdom and rising from a bench to convey it had never once been me. Now a newfound force gathered during our silent waiting, inciting me to stand. On every occasion I resisted, fearful to become a channel for God's truths. The force brought on an elation so strong that I feared, if I surrendered, I might be called to the life of a traveling minister, might have to go from Meeting to Meeting to share what I was given. But what was I given? If I opened my mouth, I feared, it might emerge as an unformed ramble.

In any case, my chance expired. I never did find the words to stand and speak. Our lives were too far altered before my inner battle had its victor.

I last attended Meeting for Worship on a chilly spring morning four months after Mother's death. Peter and I sat as always on opposite sides of the crowded meeting-house, one side for women, the other, men. Perhaps Father knew what was planned, which might have explained his absence. But we were stunned when an esteemed elder rose from a facing bench and testified against our father. For soon after taking up with his first cousin, Father had begun drinking alcohol to excess. Then he'd married his cousin, who wasn't a Friend and didn't seek to become one, and married her two months after Mother's death rather than waiting the required year. All of this was out of union with our Meeting's Discipline. Father had been treated with privately, the elder told the assembly, raising his arms. He'd been counseled that he and Patience could acknowledge their errors in writing and that she could apply for membership. "Yet way did not open for Samuel de Jong," the elder said sadly to those assembled. Father had failed to repent.

In shame I rose and left my seat; Peter met me at the doors. We crossed the broad porch of the meetinghouse and stepped toward home. I reached for his hand, as I had when he was small, and he let me hold his damp palm to my own. Above us spread a blank white sky, a page cleared of its story.

Some days later we learned that Father's disownment had been approved, when old Hannah Purdes brought a letter stating his right to appeal. Hannah knew Father well; she'd even been a member of the Clearness Committee that had approved my parents' marriage.

Father was in his workshop and Patience in the yard when Hannah knocked. I unlatched the thick wood door, and she reached her bony arms to embrace me. My face pressed into the long bill of her bonnet until she pulled my head down with gnarled, powerful hands. She kissed my forehead, leaving behind a hint of moisture and a coolness.

"Dear Lilli," she said. "This is a dreadful shame. If Helen were alive, thee could have remained with us despite thy father's doings."

"Dear Hannah, these are trying times," I replied, unsure of her full meaning. "If Mother were alive, they would not have come to pass. But please, come in." I pointed to a chair before the hearth, where a fire burned hot. But she ventured only far enough to let me close the door against the unseasonable wind behind her.

"We lost thy mother," she said in her ringing voice, "a champion of the needy. Now we lose thee from our classrooms! Our most promising young instructor!" Her head shook side to side.

"What can thee mean?" My voice was quavering.

"The School Committee would like to offer thee a respite from thy duties. And we

31

can offer thee a Clearness Committee, if thee desires it." Hannah's glittering eyes peered past me.

A respite? I wanted nothing less. And why a Clearness Committee? Why was I being judged as out of harmony with Friends' ways, when all I'd done was be my father's daughter?

"Is thy father in?" Hannah asked, just as the door of his workshop opened.

"Who's come, Lilli?" Father stepped into the room, his work clothes stained and shabby. Seeing our visitor, he rubbed his callused hands together to clean them. "Come in, Hannah!" He reached toward her, his cheeks warming. "Won't thee join us for tea? I'll take thy cloak."

"No, Samuel," she replied. "I've come to express our sincere desire for thy recovery and restoration, and to deliver this." From the pocket of her plain gown she pulled an envelope of bone-white paper.

Father took it. On its face it read NOTICE OF DISOWNMENT. Unable to speak, he stared at his sawdust-covered boots.

In that quiet, Hannah and I beheld each other. Her wrinkled cheeks held no trace of gladness to uplift them; dark hairs poked forth above her upper lip. When I met her speckled eyes, I sensed her voice in me: *Help him repent. For thy whole family's sake, but especially for thine.*

A hard knot formed in my throat. She turned, opened the heavy door herself, and picked her way down our brick path. Father shut the door and fastened it with an iron latch that his great-grandfather had forged. Then he gave out a moan.

Perhaps the full weight of his disownment was falling on him. It fell on me then, for I knew I might never again be considered free enough of his pernicious influence to teach young Friends at the Meeting school. My life's ambitions had all been staged within that august building.

Holding the sealed envelope, Father paced the room, his lower teeth biting the lip above. His head was low, his black hair unkempt and falling over his eyes. He lowered himself into a wooden seat before the fire and stared without seeming to see. Then, with a flash of his wrist, he threw the envelope into the hearth. It smoked and burst into flame. I inhaled sharply.

"That's done," he said, "and I'm relieved. No one can make me feel badly for doing as I wish." He wiped his outsized hands over his face and looked at me. "It's deadly to be always aiming for perfection."

"Especially when one falls so short of it."

My voice was quiet, but he heard. I stared defiantly and trembled as he glared in reply.

But he let his feeling go. A tiredness took its place. "I tried for thy mother's sake," he said. "I never was suited to be a dutiful Friend."

Perhaps — neither was I.

When all else fell away, one shelter remained. I'll call it now the house of Johan. I entered it gladly in spring last year, on a Fifth Month evening.

The two of us were traveling a footpath along the Wissahickon Creek, bathed in air redolent with pollens and perfumes. We strolled slowly in our cocoon of silence. My hand was ensconced in his, a signal of our increased closeness since Mother's death. Children laughed and shoved and teased along the banks of the shallow creek. The sun was falling behind stands of thin trees on the opposite bank; as the air cooled, mosquitoes rose from the dirt, butting against our ankles in search of skin and blood. We came around a curve and saw a pair of lovers seated on a rock that stretched into the water. How earnestly they beheld one another. Perhaps it was this sight that spurred Johan to pull me to a stop beneath a blossoming magnolia. I stood wondering until he spoke.

"I have something to tell thee." He clasped my hands in his large, callused ones, and his face paled against his locks of red hair. "I've decided to leave for Pittsburgh soon. Peter's coming along."

His words stunned me. He and Peter had spoken in my presence of leaving to work in steel; they seemed drawn to that new industry like prospectors were to the California gold rush. But I hadn't been convinced they'd go. Johan had four years left on his commitment to Father's workshop, and Peter had never spent so much as a night away from Germantown.

I stared at Johan's broad-planed face. *But what of me?* I thought.

As if hearing this, he answered. "I want thee to be my wife."

His words relieved me, almost. I dropped his hands. "Why does thee *tell,*" I said, "instead of asking?"

He flushed with an abandon more to my liking, then reached for the tree and snapped off a pinkish-white magnolia blossom. For the duration of several breaths, he beheld its display of petals, as if gathering courage. And then: "Nothing speaks so boldly as a flower." He placed the effusive specimen in my hands, his brown eyes beseeching. "Will thee marry me?"

I wanted to say yes. Mother had thought us an ideal match; she'd bent my ear more than once to whisper hopes of a union. She'd seen the reddening of our cheeks at the family table, heard evidence of his fine mind, observed the growing sympathy between us. Several days before she died, she'd even received a leading that he should join our Meeting and we should marry. She'd reported it to me with radiant eyes, clasping my hand, much as he just had. Yet she'd had no chance to season the leading — to find if truly God had sent it, or if it was born merely of her wish to leave me settled.

I wanted to say yes to Johan, yet I hesitated; this was likely the most influential decision of my life. Any marriage would lead to both misery and joy. How could I know which might dominate ours in years to come? I examined the magnolia's veined petals, its many glistening and sticky pistils surrounded by stamens laden with pollen. Truly, a flower *is* a bold thing, exposing all its offerings to its insect lovers.

My answer burst from me. "I will." Warmth traveled outward from my heart till my body seemed to swell.

The pleased look on Johan's face grew

ever more daffy, until I craved to touch him. I stepped forward, and he opened his arms to me. With my head for the first time against his muscled chest, my ear pressed to his heartbeat, my body feeling his limbs through the linen of his shirt and pants, I came to understand the meaning of that strange word *swoon*. I leaned into the cave of his body, which emitted a compelling odor that I decided must be that of a man's desire. I pressed my nose forward and inhaled deeply at his chest. He let out an involuntary moan.

I stepped away to regain rational capacity, then said, "How are we going to make a marriage happen?" I'd stopped attending our family's Meeting out of shame over Father and hurt at my unwanted furlough from teaching. And Johan hadn't joined another Meeting after he'd left New Jersey and come to work for Father. This meant there'd be no committee to assess our readiness, no elders to approve or disapprove our union, no worshipping assembly to house it.

"We could marry with a justice of the peace," offered Johan.

I agreed, though that might require taking an oath; this was how Father and Patience had achieved their marriage. Yet I wanted

37

Father, at the least, to see the rightness in our union.

"Has my father approved?" I bruised a petal of the magnolia and inhaled its honeyed scent, perhaps more like a woman's desire.

Johan looked down and scuffed the dust with his boot. "He dislikes me."

This was true. Father was a less aesthetic man than Johan; he would consider anyone deficient who wrote poetry, as Johan did, and took time to marvel at a flower. I tried to keep the dismay from my tone. "Has thee asked?"

"The answer was no."

He watched for my response. And Father's refusal did cause the hot-air balloon of my happiness to sink a bit. But then I cut the ropes that were holding that buoyant balloon near the ground. I let it rise and float.

"I'll do it anyway!" I cried, elated. "In Pittsburgh!" Excitement swirled through me. I'd build my own life, away from the disgrace and gloom of Father's.

Johan stood to full height, radiating what I see now as impetuousness but saw then as an admirable power in a man several years my senior. "I'll do well for us," he said. "There's so much growth in steel! But I need time to find a position. I'll send money for the train as soon as I can."

What was this? He and Peter would leave me behind? I pulled his arm. "No! I'm coming, too! We can marry as soon as we get there, or even before we go."

He ran a hand over his stubbled chin. "I don't want us to start our life together in a rush. Give me a chance to find us a decent place to live and save up some money. I've barely got enough for my own fare and a few weeks' food and rent."

I had but little money myself. Regardless, I ought to have refused to stay. With the sharp voices of Father and Patience rising to my room each night, the old stone house held little comfort. And without my teaching work, no purpose filled my days. Standing beneath that flowering tree with Johan, I ought to have told him, "I'll borrow to pay my way. I don't care if we sleep in an alley. I want to leave as badly as thee does."

Instead, I agreed to meet the two of them in an undetermined span of weeks or months, dependent on their luck. I gave Johan and Peter the right of their sex to travel at will, and accepted the confines of mine.

All that remained was for Father to learn of the young men's plan.

Peter had long disliked our family's simple

ways. Our parents hadn't even brought gas lighting or water pipes into our house, and this separated us from the general crowd of forward-thinking Philadelphians; it even separated us from those many Friends who didn't hold the testimony of simplicity as near to their hearts. And Peter didn't intend to spend his life making furniture, as had our father and grandfather. But Peter had always been quiet, so Father had little inkling of his opinions until shortly before his departure, when the two of them were attempting to remove an oversized rolltop desk from our wagon.

They'd fetched it for repair from a Chestnut Hill household and needed to unload it. Our horse was restive; her hooves were caked in mud and most likely uncomfortable. The two men were struggling to remove the heavy desk amid her shifting — but it would have made extra work to unhitch our horse, then hitch her up again to get the wagon to the neighbors' barn. So Father yelled for help, and I left my sewing to hold the horse.

"There, there, Sarah, we'll clean your hooves soon." I scratched the hard place between her eyes, with its white diamond marking. Short hairs and dirt rose around my fingers and clung there. She banged her head into my belly, threatening to nip, huffing her frustrated breath onto me, and this kept her hooves still long enough for Father to pull the remainder of the desk from the wagon. Too much weight fell on Peter, however, and his footing faltered. He jerked Father's hold on the desk away, and it landed on the toe of Father's boot. Father fell back onto the street, with his foot trapped beneath the desk.

"Bloody hell!" he cried, the worst epithet I'd ever heard him utter. "Between this horse and thee!"

"I didn't expect that much weight." Peter flushed as he heaved the desk off Father.

"Thy attention has been poor all week." Father rose with a grimace. "Thee used the wrong sandpaper, and carved that letter backwards, and applied a second coat before the first had dried."

Peter muttered toward me. "He never forgets a fault." His hair hung in his eyes, and with the back of his hand he shoved it away.

I didn't feel compelled to defend my younger brother at that moment. I hitched our horse to the post and ran inside to gather the items needed to treat Father's foot. Peter helped Father walk inside and settle into a chair, removed his boot, washed

41

Father's bloodied toes, and bandaged them. Somehow this struck Peter as an opportune time for revealing his plan.

"Thee won't have to bother about me soon," he started. "I'm leaving for Pittsburgh in early Sixth Month with Johan."

Father shifted in the chair to turn his contorted face to Peter. "This is how thee informs me?"

My brother lowered his eyes to the wood planks, looking younger than his twenty years. "Without Mother here, I've got no reason to stay."

"No reason? How can I keep up with orders without thy help? Who'll do the carving? And Johan — scoundrel! Was this his idea? He said he'd work five years."

"I'm going. We both are. It was my idea." So I had my brother to thank for luring Johan away. Peter swished the bloody rag in the bucket of water and wrung it out. His demeanor remained bland; only the shaking of his hands showed his feeling.

"The two of you are going to ruin me! And thee will never have a better opportunity than taking on this business."

"I don't want to live exactly as thee has!" Peter turned to me. "Isn't this a miserable house to live in?"

I nodded. Father said nothing, but his

eyebrows drew together at that unexpected hurt. Then Peter added, "I won't always be a helper if I work in a steel mill. I can rise in the ranks."

Father snorted. His neck and face swelled red. "Rise in the ranks? Being the master is far better than falling in with any ranks. It won't be more than ten or twenty years till thee takes over here and has an assistant or two to do thy bidding!"

Ten or twenty years must have sounded to Peter like a lifetime. And Father's rage, no matter how reasonable its origins, could no longer affect my brother. Father pressed hard for several days, even offering to pay Peter and Johan five dollars more per month despite their having room and board supplied, but he couldn't halt their plan. It seems young men don't like to see sameness too far into their futures. This only increased Father's misery at his own unchanging future.

As it would have increased mine, if I hadn't known that soon I would, in secret, follow. Johan, Peter, Pittsburgh, and some sort of teaching work — these were to be the cornerstones of my reconstructed life. It was this belief, along with my own fleshly weakness and desire to be loved, that opened me to further seduction.

■ ■ ■ ■

We'd kissed before, but always standing up
— beneath the grape arbor, beside the
garden shed, against a kitchen wall when
Johan came in for a slice of bread or a cup
of water. Thus I failed to understand the
power of a full embrace. So on the night
before Johan and my brother left for Pittsburgh, I hardly hesitated at Johan's whispered request. I consented to wait till the
others were asleep, then to ascend to his attic aerie. And when I left my childhood bed
to climb that ladder, I didn't know how
readily our intimacy would arouse the craving animal in me. I didn't know it would
snap the chain that had always held that
animal to its stake.

Johan greeted me with warmth. I slid
beneath his feather quilt into his lean and
muscled arms. And with surprising speed
his suspenders came down, and his shirt
gave way to naked skin — skin that proved
startlingly and thoroughly inebriating. His
chest and arms seemed made of velvet; his
lips and tongue, of something finer. Swiftly
we moved to a place that had no time in it,
nor even physical existence. It was a place
comprised entirely of sensations, which

came in subsuming waves; a place I swam in, like a fish; a place in which no rational thought or worry could interfere.

"Thee is lovely," he said, mouth brushing my ear as he unbuttoned my bodice; on reaching the busk of my corset, "I'll just open this"; in a low and humming voice as he opened its clasps, "I never believed I'd find a woman who could make *sense* of me, and who makes sense *to* me"; untying the neck of my chemise and pulling it to my waist and gasping at my appearance, in a sort of exaltation: "Thee is that woman." Then, as my hand toyed with the red curls at the back of his neck, he nuzzled his way downward to my breasts, and the kisses and sucks he gave there took away my last remaining sense. I yielded to his requests for more, then more. I allowed him to do whatever he wanted — indeed, what I wanted. I floated and floated until the rules of land were but a memory farther than the stars.

I disliked his entering, however, and what came next felt highly peculiar. These parts of ours couldn't truly be meant to go together, it seemed — until mine widened to admit his. He moved his swelled part farther into me, smothering his face in my neck and hair, and his voice came from deep in his chest when he said, "I love thee."

I replied with equal ardor. Then all at once a pulse began to pass between our parts, and some radical force transfixed him, as though he held his hands on a bolt of lightning. When that force released him, his weight collapsed upon me.

My head was pressed into his neck, where I heard his pulse beating fast, then slower, then slow and steady. My eyes swarmed with tears, for we had claimed each other, and I believed I'd found my home inside his arms. He seemed to me as guileless as a newborn lamb. When he raised his torso to gaze into my face, his own face shone like a beacon. Then my fingers touched the wetness between my thighs and found bright blood, which frightened me and loosed my tears.

"That proves I was thy first," he whispered. "As thee was mine." His face was serious as he reached for a cloth to place beneath me. "We've sealed our marrying intentions." He wiped my tears with his hand, and we kissed some more, our former urgency replaced by a languor that was unfamiliar and precious.

"Thee is so lovely," he said in wonder, and I rejoiced as I returned the sentiment. "I'll write soon with our address and money," he vowed, as he'd been promising for weeks. "As soon as Peter and I have work and a place for us all to live."

I fastened my clothing while his fingers traced the outlines of what he'd so recently sucked and embraced. After a parting kiss, with our lips clinging and soft, I lowered myself down the ladder and returned to the small room I'd slept in for all my years of unknowing.

I lay awake awhile, feeling as if I'd been broken apart and waiting for my pieces to reassemble into a new whole. And as they did, I felt myself expanding into more than a young person who loved learning, an erstwhile teacher at the Meeting school, a daughter mourning her mother. In those moments I became a woman, with my curves finally knowing their fuller purpose, my mind understanding more of what draws and keeps the sexes together, my soul satisfied to know this man who would become my husband. There was sorrow in this passage, but also pride.

My time of shame began in glory.

The morning after I was thus transformed, at the first hint of light, Johan and Peter and I dressed and ate a hurried breakfast. Then we left for the depot several blocks away. We stood alongside the rails in near darkness, the two of them inflated with the hope brought on by any journey, me struggling not to spoil it all and weep. Peter's hazel eyes were bright and his cheekbones rose in a half smile as they talked excitedly. The horses came into view, hauling the yellow car behind them; my dear men hoisted sacks of belongings to their shoulders, gave hurried embraces to the one they were leaving, and stepped aboard for their six-mile journey downtown. Soon after, they would catch a train to start them toward the thriving city of Pittsburgh, some 350 miles of track away. I had written down the route they'd take on various railroad lines, knowing I'd soon be taking it myself, and had tucked those notes beneath my mattress.

In the days that followed, I walked about in a half stupor, dreaming of times to come. I had no unfamiliar sights to entice me, no unknown places to explore, such as Johan and Peter had at every moment in that far-off city. I imagined what they might be doing — working amid gleaming machines in a factory aglow with molten metal, settling temporarily into a boardinghouse, seeking out the cottage or the flat we would inhabit. And I bathed in memories of my hour's intimacy with Johan. I walked about the house and yard and did my marketing in a haze, as if lit from the inside by that awakening. It was a glorious Sixth Month, and my excitement blossomed along with the flowers. I relished the baby birds and animals bobbling about, the vegetables and fruits burgeoning in our back plot of green, the leafing of the trees. All around me lay proof of the gorgeousness that arises from the interplay of male and female parts.

Then my own body began to ripen and swell. My monthly flow was days late, then a week, then two. I feared these signs might indicate a state I'd never thought to face without a husband.

The blood remained obstinately absent each time I checked. Daily I grew plumper and more distraught. And Johan never sent the promised address and funds, nor even a word on his progress. Peter sent no letter, either, perhaps because he'd always been more easy with a chisel or a saw than with a pen. Nevertheless I felt betrayed by them both, when I wasn't worrying that they'd come to harm. It seemed that these two men, the keys to my rejuvenated life, had dissolved into the ether.

Loneliness became my intimate companion. It wrapped my body head to foot. As I lay in bed some nights, my heart beat tight and hard in the little space that loneliness had left me. On one hot night I threw off my quilt and shuffled down the stairs and escaped to the backyard, where I shook my limbs and torso, trying to get that trap of loneliness off. It clutched me like a too-tight skin and stifled my breath, as if feeding on the air I needed, taking what could have kept me well. And when the nausea of pregnancy came, it seemed as if my loneliness came forth into the porcelain bowl on my washstand.

I wasn't used to uproarious friendships. I expected no great gaiety from life. Mother's fierce adherence to plainness and our obedience to it had always kept us isolated, even among Friends, most of whom saw no harm in playing games of whist or euchre or in wearing current fashions. Few were as sober as our family, as hardworking or grim. Yet this loneliness that overtook me after Mother and then Johan and Peter were gone, it took away even the small pleasures I used to hoard, leaving nothing between me and a hard wall of sorrow. By the time autumn came, as I grew a baby with a horrid knowledge that the baby and I couldn't remain together except to our disgrace, I found no joy even in the blaze of leaves, the return of cool nights, or the scents and tastes of the vegetables and fruits that Patience and I spent weeks drying, canning, and otherwise preparing for the cold season ahead.

I found newness and pleasure in one place only. I went to bed with the dark and rose before first light, and every morning the sun and clouds conspired in a fresh performance that was unrepeatable and stunning.

I wanted to go to Pittsburgh and track Johan and Peter down. But I had no address, not even the name of a neighborhood in which they might be lodged. I hadn't the means to travel there and search, and even if I had, where could I have stayed, as a young woman in an indecent condition? Aside from all that, my vomiting would have made the train ride calamitous. I kept quiet, trying to keep my grief little enough to hide, praying a letter would come before my condition became obvious to others.

Meanwhile, Father grew more surly by the day. He tried out man after man to replace his son and apprentice and found them wanting. At meals he snapped at us; Patience snapped back. If she wanted a window open, he wanted it closed. If he thought the day had been fine, she cursed its early darkness. And as they grew further acquainted, the venom they exchanged over such minor matters became more poisonous. But I kept quiet, wanting to be unnoticed. I continued in my household work and attended to the postman's comings and goings assiduously.

I thought to call on my former classmates, or on the students and the kindly parents who'd doted on me for how well I'd served them, if only to relieve the tedium; but these Friends would have been dishonored merely by engaging in teatime with the disowned Samuel de Jong's daughter. If I'd confessed to my far worse dilemma, I would have compromised their consciences with my secret — and increased our family's disgrace by revealing that yet another of its members had a loose hold on virtue — and handed them the power to ruin me.

I waited for a letter from Johan through Sixth Month and Seventh, then Eighth, Ninth, Tenth, and Eleventh. To spend months in waiting may sound like a passive state, but in truth, it was quite strenuous. I prayed day and night for the address and train fare to arrive. Father's behavior worsened; he was sour to all whom he encountered, and most nights he drank and complained of minuscule injustices loudly enough for passersby to hear — until he finally made his way to bed, at Patience's insistence. At such times I couldn't help but pity her.

Demand for his cabinets had hardly slowed, due to his skill. But no neighbors or acquaintances would take me on for day jobs when I sought them. Thus I had no way to earn money. Perhaps my own unhappy and resentful manner was as much to blame as Father's was.

By Twelfth Month, Germantown was ensconced in snow. The postman did manage to get through most days, delivering mail by the opening in Father's workshop door. But I received no letter.

Soon after the new year began — a full year after Mother's death, when my pregnancy was more than six months along — Patience forced me from inertia.

Father had gone to get a saw blade replaced, and I was shoveling the most recent snow off the back porch so we could reach the outhouse. The sun was at its peak, making sweat run down my face as I shoveled. Patience came out the kitchen door, approaching me with some strong intention. The skin around her blue eyes wrinkled as she narrowed them against the brightness.

"Thee shouldn't be doing that." She crossed her arms over her chest.

"Doing what?" I stilled the shovel.

53

"Lifting that snow." A smile flitted across her mouth, revealing her small and even teeth. "Unless thee wants to bring on an abortion."

I was stunned at her understanding. I had in fact been half hoping to bring one on, not merely then, but in strenuous walks and hill climbing. I'd considered throwing myself down the stairs, but this frightened me too badly. I had nowhere near the funds that I imagined a surgical abortion would cost, and I feared a furtive visit to its hidden practitioners even more than I feared self-injury. It wasn't possible to come to womanhood without hearing of some desperate soul who'd perished afterward from bleeding or infection.

My pulse quickened as Patience brought her rough-skinned face to mine, filling my view. "I've been watching you. I've heard you retching in your room. I've seen you adding fabric to the waists of your skirts." She pulled me to her — easily, since she was stronger — and moved her coarse hands along my belly to confirm her knowledge. "You're a disgrace!" she hissed, shoving me away. "I'm going to tell your father and have you banished from this house!"

She appeared fierce and angry, but I'm certain she was pleased inside to have found a way to be rid of me. Her distaste for having her husband's daughter in the house had been ill disguised from the start. As soon as she'd married Father, she began asserting her discontent with my housekeeping. The way I washed the supper pots using Mother's method annoyed her no end, for instance, as she thought it was too frugal with water.

"Two grown women in a house," she told Father in my earshot, "is one too many. Tell her to follow my ways or find another house." Father replied with a grunt — no doubt pressing a tumbler of beer to his lips.

My pregnancy gave her a chance to swoop in like a raptor and dislodge me from my lifelong nest.

In panic I begged her not to tell Father of my circumstances. I said I'd leave in any case. But she had no intention of sparing me.

"What makes thee better?" I said. "Thee shared a bed with a man before marrying. Thee could have become pregnant then."

She glared in disgust. "Don't pretend the two of us have anything in common." Then she marched out to buy meat at the market.

I rushed to pack an old leather valise, aiming to leave before she or Father returned. What should I take, without knowing where

I was bound? Some items to sell should come along, I realized: the gold ring from Grandmother, the cashmere shawl from Great-Uncle Clarence's trip to India, the silver belt buckle that had come from a great-aunt to Mother, the silver candlesticks, three pewter thimbles. All of these Mother had bequeathed to me in her will. But though I roamed the house in wild pursuit, checking closets, trunks, and cabinets, I found not one of them.

On instinct, I entered my parents' bedroom and opened the trunk Patience had brought from Ohio. Beneath sundry effects I found a small cloth purse. I pulled open its strings. Inside it held a listing of these items from a Philadelphia pawnbroker's shop and twelve dollars remaining in bills and coins. Patience had pawned precious things that by rights were mine.

Her treachery ought to have been evident to me before; in her months with us, though she had no paying situation, she'd come home with a new gown, a hairbrush, a hat, hairpins, and a pair of shoes. She'd been gilding herself with my inheritance.

Quivering with outrage, I took every bit of the remaining money, added it to my cloth purse, and secreted the purse beneath the lining of my valise. I decided this was more a restitution than a theft.

Then I hid some of my remaining items — including my diaries, some leather-bound books, a few trinkets, the silver spoons from a box in the kitchen, and my wedding lace — between the blankets in the trunk at the foot of my bed. I hoped against evidence that respect would keep Patience from searching that trunk and pawning what she could. Many more items that rightfully belonged to me were arrayed throughout the house, but they'd have to wait till I had a home worthy of the name, if they remained by then.

I waited by the warm kitchen stove for Patience to return.

"I know what thee did," I said as she unloaded vegetables and meat from our wicker basket. With the confidence of the wronged, I pushed my face into her ruddy one. "Father doesn't look kindly upon thieving, and neither does the Commonwealth of Pennsylvania."

Her face blanched. In such an unfamiliar role I shook and sweated, but I managed to effect a trade: her secrecy for mine.

That evening I told Father I was taking a governess position downtown to save money for further education. I could get a position at a different school, I said, if I had more training. To my mixed relief and disappointment, Father neither spoke a word against the plan nor found reason to doubt it. The next morning, when I traveled downtown on the same railway car that Peter and Johan had taken, I was embarking on a very different journey.

At a newsstand, I obtained the morning's papers. I sat on a bench and scoured the advertisements for any place that might shelter me. There were many notices from midwives who offered housing and medical services, but I hadn't near enough money to pay the prices listed. I found one notice of a women's refuge run by the city, but its name included the word *Magdalen,* which gave away its nature as a place that served women of the night — and the description expressly excluded those who were with child. At last I found a discreet listing in the *Public Ledger* for the Philadelphia Haven for Women and Infants, which offered shelter to "friendless women" and listed visiting hours that very afternoon. I prayed that I was correctly perceiving the nature of the place.

On that bench I sat for several hours, my hands in the pockets of my cloak, my mind a whir of regrets and supplications to my Inner Guide. For months I had failed to consult it, much less to follow its edicts. Perhaps this is why it stayed silent as I sat and suffered.

At last, avoiding puddles of slush and animal waste as best I could, I walked to a stuccoed edifice on Tenth and Fitzwater Streets, arriving shortly after the opening time. Climbing its few marble steps, I entered an arched doorway into a foyer and joined a line of twenty or so creatures at least as miserable as me.

We didn't speak to one another. Each head and face was hidden by a hat or bonnet and a shawl. One after another of the applicants filed into the office and dragged herself out again, having been deemed insufficiently worthy by whatever person was judging them inside. On departing, some cried out threats of killing themselves or their babies, saying they'd prefer that to the almshouse or the street. My body was atremble by the time my turn came to sit upon the bench opposite the desk of the inquisitor.

Stern and long-faced, she introduced herself as Mrs. Anne Pierce, the superintendent of this establishment. She began her inquisition gently. "What brings you to this shelter?" "How far along do you judge yourself to be?" Then her questions grew more pointed, so that I thought her last name, Pierce, was apt. "Have you been with child before? Was this man your first lover? How many times did you lie with him? Did others think you good? Have you ever been taken before a magistrate? Have you broken any law? How often do you drink alcohol? Do you take patent medicines regularly?"

I blessed my upbringing, for I could truthfully reply *yes* and *never* and *no* in their proper places. She stood and paced the small area behind her desk, three steps one way, three steps the other. Her tall form was clad in a gown that was demure in color and design but made of costly wool, of the sort that only expert weavers can produce, in the old way, by hand. On such small observations I focused my thoughts, fearing the chasm that yawned behind them, into which I'd plunge if she would not take me in.

At last Anne Pierce sat and proclaimed her decision. Upon considering the virtue of my previous life, and impressed by my former employment as a schoolteacher, she considered me deserving of a bed at her charity.

"Our furnishings are spare," she informed me, "and our rations, meager. But we will protect you from the damages of publicity and offer you a chance for repentance and reformation."

I expressed my gratitude, saying that I asked no more.

She demanded to know my lover's name then, saying it was necessary for admission, so that her solicitor could try to procure damages and support. The money, she explained, would reduce my burden and help pay the Haven for my care. Spelling it out for her as she wrote — JOHANNES ERNST — and hearing him described as "the male offender" made the situation bitterly clear.

"The promise of marriage," said Anne, "is one of the oldest lies in the lustful man's book — often laced with exclamations over the woman's beauty."

How right she was.

As I sat in her office, then followed directions to the Haven's one empty bed, I considered my foolishness. I hadn't known Johan well enough to give him my trust. He'd left his parents and siblings in New Jersey to come to Philadelphia; as explanation he'd offered only that his youngest brother would inherit the farm, so he needed to find his own situation. Had there been other reasons underlying his departure? Had he left in disgrace? Or had he been taken by the same wanderlust that carried him next to Pittsburgh? For that matter, was his family an upright and responsible one, as I'd assumed, or were they a pack of wastrels?

How can one truly know a man, if one considers him as a singular being? The individuals in a family fit together like pieces in a puzzle, forming a larger picture, making clear the nature of the whole and its parts. But Johan came to me unmoored, careening, a piece set free.

Now I'm the same, a puzzle piece without its puzzle, careening among other unmatched remnants. My body shivering on a stone bench in the courtyard of an institution for the shamed and exiled. At last, confessing my story to a page.

If I strain my ears, I can hear poor Nancy's cries.

How ill prepared I am for my turn on the birthing table. I've only seen our horse give birth, and some sheep and cows in the neighbor's barn. They betrayed discomfort merely by the twitching of their legs and the pleading of their widened eyes.

Do the animals keep silent for fear of attracting predators? Nancy would have drawn a horde of predators by now, if she were in the wild.

Suppertime is near. I ought to go inside. The day's meager warmth is rushing up and dissipating with the light. Though the wool cape I brought from home does spread wide enough to cover my belly and keeps the bulk of me warm, my feet are numb inside their slippers, and my fingers are stiff from the cold.

Yet I fear the news inside.

Dear God, please hold Nancy and her baby in thy Light.

Will I scream as Nancy does?

At supper, a jubilant Delphinia made an announcement: Nancy and her baby boy are well! Whereupon we regained our appetites and gave thanks and enjoyed the cheese and hot bread and the cobbler made from a donation of last fall's apples.

Delphinia stood squarely in the doorway as we left the dining room, passing encouraging words to each resident, reaching an arthritic hand to pat one upon her shoulder, to push a lock of hair behind another's ear. I placed myself last in line. On reaching her, I requested permission to visit Nancy on First Day, the day after tomorrow, before chapel. She consented. Then I asked whether the Haven's solicitor had found any trace of my baby's father through his Pittsburgh colleague. That flame still flickers in me.

"No word from the Pittsburgh office," said the elderly matron. "But don't lay much hope in this, my dear. Our solicitor has gained support only a dozen times in over two hundred cases." He also has convinced a few dozen men to marry the women they wronged, she added, though most of the women were distrustful and married in despondency, only because they lacked another means to food and shelter. Yet the hardworking Ladies' Committee of this charity considered those cases a success — "which they were," noted Delphinia drily, "unless those people had wanted happy lives."

I joined the others in the parlor, agitated by fruitless thoughts of Johan. But the tiny stitches calmed me down.

This must be why we choose to embroider our evenings away. After stirring hot vats of laundry, wringing out the steaming cloths, and hanging them on lines; after scrubbing floors on our knees, helping Cook peel potatoes and knead heaps of dough, wiping away the grime that falls to every surface from the city air, and unpacking crates of donated supplies left at the back gate, we should want nothing more than rest. But without work to occupy us, our minds wander to places of uncertainty and dread. Better to sit in an upholstered chair, lean toward the orb of a gas lamp in the parlor, and draw a brightly threaded needle in and out of a dishtowel or an apron. Better to form lovely flowers than to consider that the promise of our youth has bloomed and died.

We also do this piecework because the goods are sold at a shop, through Anne's arrangement. The coins earned go directly to the Haven, to defray the costs of our keep. Each woman costs the Haven four dollars ninety cents a week, but most can't pay so much and won't earn it by embroidering, either. Most of us will leave with a debt. I'll be here longer than most, so I've given Anne some of the money I came with.

Now that I'm diary-keeping again, I can hardly bear to pause my pencil. I never realized it till now, but writing and Mother must be linked for me. For even as I balance this notebook on my abdomen and draw a hand across its page, the memories come flickering of my small slate and the hours I passed learning to form letters at her knee. Perhaps that's why I lost my urge to write when she died two winters ago, and why resuming the habit is so profoundly settling. For writing works upon me like her soft hand on my brow.

Mother was a God-loving woman with an independent mind, a beacon in our Meeting, a model of common sense and tenderness. She and I didn't always live in accord — I dashed out many lines that prove this, especially when she dismissed my thoughts without adequately considering them. And I feared her standards, for she brooked no infringements of the Discipline. But her fierce devotion and the control she exercised kept our family united. She had strength enough to fill in for our wavering and doubts. As soon as she was gone, Father, Peter, and I began to split apart — from one another and inside ourselves.

With her gone I've felt no Spirit anymore, not in my silence or in my talk. Yet in writing here, I begin to sense a glimmer of it.

Ah — a sharp jab inside. This baby kicks and turns day and night, and even seems to lean into my palm when I apply it to the orb of my belly. Steadily my little one comes more to life, while my feeling for its red-haired father shrinks.

One day that feeling will be no larger than a pea and will grow dry and wrinkled. One day I'll throw that shriveled pea to the dirt and crush it beneath my heel.

Third Month 18, First Day

I'm trembling from what I've just seen.

In my months here, I've come to dislike the superintendent. Yes, Anne means to help us; her devotion of time and funds to this hard cause is only admirable, and she does much good. She speaks regretfully of the "limits of our institution," wishing for the funds and space to keep women and babies together longer and to find families for all the infants. As she tells us, no other charity in the city protects and hides those who've taken but a single misstep or been shamefully abused.

Yet Anne's punishing nature hinders her kind intentions. She works us hard, save for one period a day, despite our increased need for rest. She restricts our every word and deed — we can't leave the premises, at threat of expulsion; we can't speak of our pasts and how we came to be here; we can't even laugh when rare levity strikes, for to her we laugh in the face of God, before whom we ought to be somber and repentant. We do speak in quiet voices of our histories when we can, to unburden ourselves and be known to one another, but the threat of discovery makes our hearts beat out of time. And now I've learned that she doesn't even allow us peace during the three weeks of motherhood we're allotted before we must leave to make room for another.

A short while ago I took breakfast with Gina and the others, then traveled a long hall to the recovery room where Nancy lay. Bars and shutters covered its windows. The door had extra locks on its hallway side to keep girls in at night, since several early occupants had fled without their infants, to escape the responsibility of keeping or placing them. I couldn't help but compare this barren room to the homely chambers I saw new mothers resting in when Mother and I brought meals to their families. Those women barely stirred for weeks, except to nurse, while others kept up the household.

Nancy greeted me warmly, though her skin was ashen and her brown eyes were ringed with darkness. "Sit," she said, pointing with her chin to a chair by the bed. I sat, and she moved her head to indicate the swathed package in her arms, giving it a winsome smile. "Here's my little lad."

The baby looked not unlike a newborn mouse, with minuscule hands and a pale, wrinkled face. The sides of his head bore cotton gauze, apparently covering damage from the forceps. His eyes were hooded by swollen, nearly translucent lids.

"Lovely," I murmured, attempting sincerity.

She sniffed his scalp and moved her lips over its coating of pale hair. "He's the sweetest thing." She leaned to kiss his nose. The baby gazed vaguely in her direction, his eyes swimming with devotion.

At first I felt startled at her fondness for him, since she'd spoken harshly of the servant who was his father. Then I looked at my bulging belly, where my own baby had begun to kick and wiggle, as if sending out a rhythmic message. A surge of nausea passed through me; a squeezing force took up my heart. And all at once I understood: Nancy can't help but adore her son. She grew him inside, and pushed him out in mighty suffering, and now this tiny creature needs her — belongs to her — as no other person ever will.

And I will feel the same. I won't merely love the baby inside me when it shows its face. I'll adore it with all the fierceness that ever bound one creature to another.

"He's beautiful," I told Nancy, sincerely now.

"Don't it seem a miracle?" She leaned into her pillows. "How they come from inside us. It don't seem possible."

She held up her small charge; I thought

69

she wanted me to hold him. My arms tingled, anticipating his weight, and I moved them forward for her to make the transfer. But she pulled the baby back to her chest. She'd meant only to give me a closer look.

"He's got all the parts he should have, in all their proper places." She reddened. "I had a mind he might . . ."

I nodded, recognizing the belief she held. Many of the inmates are afraid their babies will be malformed because they were conceived out of wedlock.

"I'm calling him William, after my dad." Nancy raised a hand to scratch her nose, and the baby's head lolled back at an alarming angle. "Oh! I forget how weak he is!" She propped up his neck and stroked his cheek, staring.

"May I hold him?" I asked, unable to resist.

She began moving him to me, but his distress grew with stunning quickness. His limbs pushed against the swathing cloths; his mouth opened into a bawl that revealed pink gums and a glistening interior. So she opened her dressing gown and guided his mouth to her. With his head in the palm of her hand, she lowered her thin face to gaze upon him. As he sucked, his face and body slackened into complete ease.

I cleared my throat, embarrassed to see her naked breast. Then I scolded myself for prudery. For what could be more natural than an infant taking nourishment from its mother?

"He needs thee," I said. Could I say nothing more useful? But Nancy locked her eyes with mine, and a flicker of joy passed between us. Then she dampened it.

"We mustn't rejoice in the offspring of our sin." She was quoting the young Reverend Williams, who often preaches here. He wants us to feel nothing but a gray desperation at the births of our children, followed by a grand relief at giving them away.

Just then an infant's cries erupted in the hall, and Nancy stiffened, appearing to dread their advance. Anne strode in, holding a baby as new as Nancy's but with a febrile hue.

"Feeding him again?" Anne demanded. Her tall body was as tensed as an archer's ready bow.

Nancy's excuse tumbled out. "He was crying, and I knew he'd stop if —"

"If nothing." Anne pointed toward a clock on a corner table. "You're to keep track on that clock and save half your milk for this baby, as we discussed. It's her turn now. At even hours you nurse this one, and at odd hours, you nurse your boy."

Nancy put her finger in William's mouth to dislodge him, then pulled her gown closed. Again he transformed in seconds, his face pursing tight, his limbs jerking. With unsteady hands Nancy laid him in the bassinet, where he continued his protest. On the front of her gown, wet blotches formed and grew.

"Take her." Anne reached with the other crying infant toward Nancy. "We're calling her Mabel."

A tremble passed through Nancy as the infant applied herself to a nipple with eagerness. Nancy turned her face toward the shuttered windows. Reaching to her, I brushed tendrils of brown hair from her forehead and wiped away the perspiration there.

So this was how Nancy would spend her three weeks before giving William to an adoption agent and finding her next domestic situation. Nursing every hour! I hadn't known we might be put to such a use. Of course a motherless babe does need a nurse, but must it be Nancy? Must her troubled, lonely soul be interrupted in this brief chance it has to love its own?

In his bassinet on the floor, William gave up his protest. His eyes closed; his chest began to rise evenly. As the unknown infant drank, Nancy dozed, too. She looked as if she'd fallen from a great height into the bed, so thoroughly was her weight surrendered. I stared at Mabel; if she carried syphilis from her mother, then Nancy would catch the disease through her nipples, and so would William. Anne was neatening up the room's effects, so I gave a cough to gain her attention.

She turned to where I sat, impatient.

"How did Mabel come to be here?" I asked — for someone had to think of Nancy.

Anne turned her palms up in a gesture of unknowing. "An old woman brought her. She claimed the mother handed the child over in the street, saying she'd return shortly. The mother never returned."

"Would that be untrue?"

Anne focused her gray-blue eyes on me. "We've heard that explanation a thousand times. It could as well be that an unscrupulous person had the mother pay a hefty fee to get the baby adopted — then kept the fee and passed the baby to that old woman, with no intent of returning." She walked to a corner and dropped herself to a wooden chair. "Or the old woman herself might have promised the mother, for a fee, to find the baby a family, then brought it here instead."

"Why is it that falsehoods and babies so often go together?" I asked.

Anne gave me a baleful look, as if to say she was too occupied with the resulting problems to answer such a question. Her foot tapped the wood floor like the tail of an overstimulated cat.

"I wonder how thee knows Mabel is free of disease," I said. "The women in our Meeting would nurse an infant only if they knew the mother's condition."

Anne flushed. "I examined the baby."

I said nothing.

"Doctor Stevens taught me her methods. Lilli, this baby would die without a mother's milk. Would you have me let her perish?"

I wouldn't, not at all; yet I prayed silently for Nancy's safety.

Anne stood. "Nancy," she called.

The girl opened her eyes.

"Miss Partridge will bring a second bassinet, since Mabel will stay in this room until you go."

Nancy nodded slightly.

Turning to me, Anne said, "I suggest you leave her to her work." Then she adjusted the folds of her skirt and left the room.

I rose to shut the squeaky door and pulled the chair closer to Nancy. I patted her leg through the blanket. "It isn't right," I whispered. "A new mother needs rest!"

"I don't know what's right." She stifled a sob. "I feel weak."

I took her large hand in my smaller one. "Was thy confinement very bad? We feared for thee."

Nancy's face crumpled; her tears dropped to Mabel's flannel wrap. "They cut me with the forceps when they pulled him out. I've been sewed, but I can't stand without passing blood. I can't sit, either. There's swelling down there. Doctor Stevens says it's normal, but . . ." Her words stopped; her mouth opened. As I stroked her leg and aimed to keep calm, she moved her hand to feel her own forehead. "I'm warm. Should I be warm?"

"I should think so, after such a struggle." In truth I had no idea.

"My milk has only started coming in." She sniffed. "That's what Doctor Stevens said this morning. And William is hungry. I haven't got enough for two!"

"If only I could help" — for once more I was unable.

She looked at my belly and gave a slight smile. "You'll have your own soon enough."

I shivered. "If only I didn't have to get it out first. How did thee manage for so many hours?"

Nancy's shadowed eyes regarded me gravely. "What choice did I have?"

A sensible answer to a fatuous query. The supper bell pealed in the hall, and Nancy frowned. "You have to go."

I leaned and kissed her cheek, then shuffled from the room. As I pulled the thick door shut behind me, I felt that I was sealing her into a vault. The metal hinges squeaked the entire way, so that by the time the door clicked shut, William was awake and wailing.

In the chilly hall, breathing in smoke from the parlor's fire and the earthy, yeasty odors of our next meal, I leaned my tired bulk against the cold plaster wall and tried to endure William's protest.

I couldn't endure it. I opened the door and stepped back into the room. As Nancy nursed Mabel, I lifted William. His lightness surprised me. With his bundled body warming my chest, I swayed side to side and started to sing. In my head I heard Mother's clear voice joining mine in the one hymn she'd allowed herself, despite the frivolity of singing, because it used Friend Whittier's words:

O brother man! fold to thy heart thy brother;

Where pity dwells the peace of God is
   there;
To worship rightly is to love each other,
Each smile a hymn, each kindly deed a
   prayer.

My chest ached like some gaping hole. William stopped his wails, softening against me. I lowered his tiny form into the bassinet, and he made no protest.

"Now sleep," I whispered to Nancy.

She looked up, bleak with fatigue, and nodded.

I'm too tired to write more — except to say that I'm still here, one person holding another inside.

■ ■ ■ ■

NOTEBOOK TWO

■ ■ ■ ■

The hour is late. All the others are asleep. I'm seated in the second-story bath, on frigid tiles beside a window, for between the cramps and the baby's kicking, I cannot sleep.

I asked Anne after supper if I might place a sealed letter in my folder here, in case my child should one day seek its origins. She warned me against caring too much for my offspring.

"It's best to consider the baby like a tooth that must be extracted," she advised. "An infected tooth you're better off without."

"I'd like there to be some words from me, if the child should ever come here," I said.

"You're headstrong," she scolded. "Don't be a fool. I'm certain no other girl here would even consider leaving a clue to her identity behind." She said my use of *thee* and *thy* alone would give away that I'm a Friend — and did I want my bastard, as she put it, "to roam from Meeting to Meeting in search of its mother"?

I reminded her of what I'd revealed at admittance — that my father had been disowned and I no longer attended our Meeting, which left me with no spiritual home save that inside myself. So my child wouldn't find me, if it did roam thusly.

Since I couldn't be dissuaded, Anne bid me to do as I wished.

In the hours between supper and bedtime, in lieu of embroidering, I wrote several versions. I crossed out more than I retained, then burned those tortured pages in the kitchen stove.

With my face and page bathed in milky moonlight, I'll try once more.

1883. 3rd mo. 18

My dear baby,
I'm writing most of all to say I'm sorry. Thee will be born soon, and in three more weeks we'll have to part.

Of course thee can never forgive me. No apology or reason can suffice. Yet I want to leave something I've touched, a page for thee to hold and read in my absence.

Will thee wish to know thy origins?

One day — at how old? — thee might trace thy way back to this charity and learn that being sent to strangers was not thy fault — and see that, without me, thee has gained a better life.

I loved thy father. He seemed sincere and true. We agreed to marry, and I allowed him an intimacy I shouldn't have. It came clear I'd been deceived, but the force of life in thee carried on, as it cared not how it was planted. So I alone will welcome thee.

Tonight, dearest, we live as one. I believe the moment we meet face to face will be my happiest, and my saddest.

Here is my love. Here are my wishes for good. Please know I'll send these toward thee, day and night, for as long as I shall live.

What hardships might attack thee — without me to repel them? How this grieves me to consider.

I wish my words could hold thee.

My baby, I honor thy soul.

Mother

Third Month 19

Anne came into the foyer this morning and stood over me while I held a dripping boar's-hair brush aloft, announcing that I should stop scrubbing the oak planks at once.

"You'll assist us in the office each morning but Sabbath," she said. "At least a year has passed since any serious filing has occurred. I was a fool not to enlist you sooner. An educated girl is a rarity here, and I'm certain you can be trusted."

So in lieu of continuing to squat and scrub away the remnants of animal droppings that come in on people's shoes, I returned the bucket and brush, then followed Anne to the office. The room was mostly taken up by a wide mahogany desk, and Delphinia sat hunched over it, her pen gliding across a piece of parchment, a gas chandelier with three bright globes hanging over her. Two tall oak cabinets stood to her side. The bench opposite the desk, where I'd had my entrance interview, completed the room's functional effects. I sat upon it.

Delphinia was greatly pleased that Anne had provided her with a helper. She indicated with her knobbed hands the piles on nearly every surface, including the floor. I told her I relished the chance to work with paper rather than with soap, and her smile grew. Then Anne pulled a thick folder from a cabinet and said she was off to visit a potential patron. Delphinia rose and added a stack of annual reports to Anne's satchel.

"Only ninety-three dollars have been donated in the two and a half months of this year," Delphinia told me. "The residents have paid a hundred more. But our expenses are over three hundred a month. The state supports most every other charity in the city, but they've refused — again — to give us even a dollar."

"How is the place still open?" I asked, alarmed.

Delphinia sent Anne a questioning look. Anne nodded consent, so Delphinia explained. "The cook and I have gone without salary for two months."

"I take no salary," Anne added hastily. "And we haven't paid the mortgage since December. Our banker agreed to wait till April. The people I'm off to visit — they must say yes."

The matron and superintendent exchanged a look of anxiousness that was tempered by mutual respect. Then Anne donned her hat and coat, stood erect before the open door, and directed her body outward with the force of an arrow.

Delphinia cleared her head of their fiscal emergency with surprising quickness — a necessary skill in this place, to be sure. She came to stand beside me, giving off a pleasing scent of bergamot and dust. She instructed me to begin with the piles upon the floor, sorting loose papers and folders into categories. Next I should find their places, in alphabetical order, in the unlocked oak cabinet.

"The cabinet beside that one is locked," she explained, "because it holds the folders of all the girls who've come through here." She showed me where its key hangs on the wall, hidden by a scarf, and said to put personal items about the residents inside.

After a few moments of sorting bills from letters, my hands held Nancy's folder. Someone must have gotten it out to make note of her delivery. I placed it to the side, meaning to wait till I had several pieces to file in the locked cabinet. Then the cook rushed in, her wide face sweating.

"I got nothin' but turnips and onions to fix for dinner," she told Delphinia. "These girls'll get sick if they eat that once more."

I nodded in hearty agreement. So Delphinia put on her cloak and left to go plead for a further extension of credit at the market. After examining me with her beady eyes, the cook returned to the kitchen.

I took up the folder, closed the office door, and sat on the bench. Nancy had whispered to Gina and me that her fall had come from trusting a fellow servant's vows. She'd revealed her condition to him and begged him to marry her immediately, she said, but he left the household that very night. Her tears appeared sincere as she told us, yet a hesitation in her manner had made me doubt.

I opened the folder and stared at a discharge paper from the city hospital. Raising my body with effort, I stood nearer to the gaslight, for the script was cramped and crabbed. The paper revealed that Nancy — "a housemaid of sixteen years and one month, of sound constitution" — had been violated with regularity by the master of the house and had become pregnant by this means. He beat her on discovering the fact. She took up potions that left her ill but failed at their purpose of feticide. Subsequently she threw herself down the stairs to end the pregnancy — not once, but twice in succession — and was injured. Another housemaid brought her to the city hospital, and the note I read was based on the housemaid's testimony.

One month later, Nancy was discharged to no one, still pregnant and owing a debt to the city for nourishment and care, having had no way to pay her costs and refusing to inform the city of her relatives' whereabouts.

The city would have placed her out to whoever would pay them for her work, to resolve her debt, but Nancy was spared by reason of "impending motherhood."

Anne's interview notes, put down in her spidery script, continued the story. Nancy had confined her bulging abdomen with a corset and served food at a restaurant to earn her keep, until the corset caused such agony that she could no longer wear it. No wonder she'd feared William might be malformed, with those laces constraining his growth — not to mention the potions she'd taken and her repeated falls. When she could no longer pay her rent, the landlady told Nancy of this refuge.

Last I read the notes of the Haven's solicitor in Philadelphia, William Stone. He'd met with Nancy's employer to request damages and support, and the beastly man claimed to have no knowledge of how Nancy had come to be with child; he called her account "the fantasies of a lonely housemaid," threatened a libel suit, and shooed the solicitor away.

I closed the folder and felt behind the scarf, reaching for the key to the oak cabinet so I could hide the folder away. How many horrid narratives must be locked within those deep drawers! Though I would not do so, I wanted to read them all, the way a child is compelled to pick at a scab until it bleeds. Then the Haven's front door whooshed open, and Delphinia's heels clicked across the foyer toward the office. I thrust Nancy's folder into a stack and kneeled to the floor with other papers in my hands. I forced my breathing to slow and my countenance to settle.

Delphinia entered, bursting with the satisfaction of having arranged an immediate delivery of ten pounds of mutton bones — some with meat! — and a peck of potatoes. She settled behind the desk again and resumed her correspondence.

It is some hours later, and I've come to understand Nancy's reasons for lying to Gina and me. Why would she have wanted to recount and thus to relive her defilement and degradation? But it appalls me that she and William are the ones who'll carry forward the shame of those events. Instead, disgrace and shame ought to torment — no, to destroy — the master of that house.

How is it that shame affixes itself to the violated, and not to the violator?

The meal bell rings. Even with such trouble in mind, I'm eager to taste that mutton.

Life at this charity never spares its occupants.

This afternoon I strolled the Haven's
courtyard, where the crocuses and daffodils
have opened their blooms completely. How
grateful I was for that square of green
tucked between two wings of the building
that confines us. I took small breaths of
humid air, because I have no room for filling breaths. Then all at once an inmate
named Mary — a small person in a constant
state of agitation, with muscles as taut as an
out-flung whip — opened the French doors
to the courtyard and ran past me.

She held a wooden chair before her and
yelled to someone behind, "I'll show you!"
This threat was garnished by indecent
expletives. Placing the chair before the high
fence that separates the courtyard from an
alley, she stepped up and — as best she
could — cleaved her body to the planks.
Despite the impediment of her round belly,
she clambered to the top and heaved herself
to the other side, to freedom. I heard a thud
and the pattering of boots on bricks. My
spirit trilled to picture Mary running free,
though reason tells me she was better off
confined.

Anne and Delphinia came rushing out,

followed by a crowd of girls with their heads craning forward. I doubt anyone was truly sorry to find Mary gone. She'd proved crude and unrepentant after admittance; she'd never ceased her railing against the doors being locked to prevent us from going anywhere except this courtyard and the clotheslines; she'd even brought in alcohol and partaken of it by evening, and her roommate Sally told us that intoxication had made Mary's language fouler. But Anne and Delphinia took a walk through nearby streets to try to find her while we inmates settled down to spoonbread and beans.

With our supervisors absent, Sally informed us of a note Mary had received from the father of her baby, entreating her to come back. Knowing of his wayward nature from Mary's testimony, Anne had refused to approve Mary's discharge.

A ways into our meal, Anne entered the dining room and took her place at the head of the table. Though her carriage was prim, the purple half-moons beneath her eyes revealed fatigue. She breathed in audibly and released a sigh. "I aim to take in only girls of good moral character," she said, "but my judgment can be flawed. I owe you an apology."

This admission of fault stunned me. My

mother would never admit a flaw. I hoped to tell Anne later that her error was nothing compared to the good she does.

"Did you find Mary?" Sally called.

"No." Anne's discouraged face showed that her heart extends even to the unrepentant. "I denied Mary her release," she continued, "because the man who'd offered to take her in was a scoundrel. But I do understand that it's wearying to be locked inside this house."

Then she told us a story. When she and a pair of concerned doctors opened this institution ten years ago, the inmates had been sent out to walk, under veils, from four to five each afternoon. But the nature of the humble group was soon recognized, and they were hounded by a growing crowd. The veiled girls returned with their souls beaten and began refusing to go out. So Anne turned the hour's walk into a rest.

"I should have expected the cruelty," Anne added. "My younger sister took her life when she faced such hatred within our family. That's when I gathered doctors and friends to create this charity."

There was no sound, no stirring, in the dining room then. Whoever had a forkful of food suspended in her hand retained it there. All eyes avoided the others. We filed out soon in silence, and all the evening, scarcely a word was spoken.

Third Month 21
It's not yet dawn. Gina is sleeping in the bed beside mine. The yellow flicker of my candle softens the whitewashed walls.

I want to report my conversation with Gina earlier this night. Beset by cramps and the crashes of a thunderstorm, we were unable to sleep. We took up our needlework and began to converse, whispering so as not to disturb those in the room beside ours. Gina unraveled a wool scarf she'd found in the donations closet and began to knit a hat for Nancy's son. I continued knitting socks for my baby, with feet perhaps three inches long; Gina said even this would be too big.

Gina's hands moved with startling quickness, for she used to produce children's goods for a fine shop in her native Italy, and she made fast progress on the hat. Then she put it aside and unfurled a square of white lawn, threaded a needle with green thread, and drew it through. I asked quietly what she was embellishing.

"A piece to cover my baby — what is the word?"

"A receiving blanket?"

She nodded.

"Has thee chosen a name?" I craned my head between our beds to read the initials at the bottom of the cloth. She had previously stitched them in blue and was surrounding them with green leaves and vines.

"Don't see." She covered the area with a hand already curled and stiffened from overwork. Then she rolled up the bottom of the cloth and began instead to add a vine at its top.

I was a little offended at her secrecy. "Why can't I see?"

Gina hesitated, then confessed. "I put a letter for the family name."

"Won't that name come from the family who adopts thy baby?"

She glanced at me as her needle flew. "My — husband's parents are taking us."

"Husband?" I asked. "Husband's parents?" How could this be true?

It isn't quite; it has become the *claimed* truth. The Haven's solicitor had good luck in his attempt to gain support for Gina. He wrote to her lover, Stefano, at the home of his parents, who'd known Gina during their courtship. It turned out Stefano had died while laying railroad track. When Stefano's mother opened the solicitor's letter, it served to alert her to the existence of a grandchild.

Even a bastard grandchild was too allur-
ing to reject. So this woman, Angela,
hatched a scheme and came to the Haven
to convince Gina to take part. Now Angela
is spreading the word that Stefano and Gina
had married in secret before he died. When
Gina and her baby leave this place, they'll
take up residence with Stefano's parents.

Though she'd done it by lies, Angela had
accomplished a splendid feat. I looked up
from my knitting needles, expecting to find
a glow on Gina's smooth cheeks. But her
face was wan against her profusion of dark
locks, and her lips quivered. She stabbed
her needle in and out of the cloth.

"Why is thee unhappy?"

She spoke as if each fact was a shred of
bone pulled from a mouthful of food. "I told
Stefano we made a baby. He said he didn't
love me. He wouldn't see me anymore. Now
I pretend I am his widow, only because they
want the child."

"What does thee want?" I asked. How
seldom one is asked this question, and how
clearly it portends one's happiness.

She spat her answer. "To go home to Italy.
But I have no money for the boat. And I
have to go back alone."

"Thee can sew beautiful things and sell
them," I offered. "In a year or two, thee can

95

leave the baby with its grandparents and go home."

Gina's countenance became still, like the wind before a storm. Then she erupted in sobs. "But how can I leave my baby?" She stopped sobbing abruptly and began embroidering at a fevered pace.

"Thee could marry here and make a new home," I tried. "Widows marry." With her full-featured loveliness, Gina would draw many suitors.

But she jerked her head side to side. "A real widow could marry. Not me." She pushed her needlework away and raised a hand to the silver cross on a chain at her neck. "God knows the truth."

I didn't understand, since she is a Catholic. "Couldn't thee confess and do penance and be absolved?"

Gina shook her head vigorously. She's already taking on that weight for one lie, she said — the lie that makes her baby not a bastard — partly because the baby will be better off. But if she undertook a marriage under false pretenses, she'd be lying in a church. "You don't know. That goes straight to God." She stared at me, shaking her head, and a tear fell to the blanket below. I reached between our beds to touch her shoulder, but she shrugged my hand away.

"Doesn't Angela go to church still?" I asked. "And isn't Angela lying?" As soon as I said these words, I berated myself for my idiocy.

She moaned. "Oh, what I did! I made her a sinner, too."

I said Angela chose this path on her own, but Gina remained dismal. She calmed herself by reminding us that dark thoughts are bad for our babies. We fell into silence, since we had no other sort of thoughts to offer.

Gina blew out the candle and fell to sleep, and a ferocious feeling constricted my throat. I asked myself, *What do I want?* And the answer made me queasy.

I still want Johan to love me. I want his unusual way of thinking to guide me in seeing common things afresh. I want to feel his silken skin against my own. I want his tender care extended to our baby. I want to do what we spoke of doing, our hands touching over the oak table one night after the others had gone to bed: explore a strange city, join in marriage with no encumbrances from Meeting or family, fill a house with furnishings he builds for us, bring children into our intimate world. He promised to make a canopy bed — a canopy bed! I'd make curtains to surround it. And tucked between them, we'd lie together. . . .

Instead of all that, I'll give our baby to an adoption agent and return to the small house in Germantown that the de Jongs have occupied for nearly two hundred years. I'll enter again the unpleasant realm of Father and Patience — a thought that brings dread and halts my breath.

Yet there will be good parts to returning. When I step into that house, my months of hiding will vanish like a dream. I'll be *me* again, returned to the place that formed me. I'll find comfort in Mother's kitchen, where each cast-iron pot and wooden bowl and stirring spoon is known to my hands. I'll treasure the things she chose or made, the signs of her attention that inhabit every cranny, the green shoots in our gardens that prove her influence endures. Within hours I'll have loaves of dough rising in the hollow beside the hearth, a ham blanching on the stove, a pot of spring greens boiling. I'll set the table and light our lamps as dusk descends.

I can breathe in now and feel a hint of the peace that used to gather in that hour before supper. When Peter and I were small, unless a crisis in some other family propelled her out, Mother would sit in the rocker beside the hearth and read Bible tales to us. Young

Peter rested upon her lap, I sat at her feet, and together we basked in the bubbling of pots, her clear-toned voice, her violet-water smell.

What a gap yawns between those days and now, with Mother in the ground and me seated on a hard mattress, heavy with child and grieving over our coming separation.

At six the waking bell will ring, and our usual round of chores and meals will begin.

Third Month 24

I'm close to delivery! Dr. Stevens has started me on her protocol: a bitter quinine tonic, a concoction for preventing constipation and headache, and chloral hydrate at bedtime to encourage rest. The medicines nauseate me and dull my senses, but they haven't lessened the only symptom I minded, apart from the cramps — which is nerves.

My nerves are growing ever more bothersome. I spend rest hours in the courtyard and can only stare into the air, dizzied and weak. I keep believing that the constant twinges and pulling pains mean that delivery is imminent.

I described my condition to the doctor this morning, lying flat on the cot in her examination room as she felt gently along my belly.

"You could have these symptoms for days," she replied. "Perhaps another week."

"Another week?" I protested. "That would be maddening!"

Amusement raised the corners of her lips. "Many find it so." And in a moment, nodding her small head: "Good. The baby's heartbeat is robust. Its body is head down, legs up." She reached her slender arm up past my protruding belly and patted my crown. "Simply wait, and stay as calm as you're able."

I mentioned that her medicines are making me feel ill.

"You should be grateful for them," she scolded. "Doctor Prestweiss developed this protocol for the married women at his retreat. They'll remove any blockages or weakness that otherwise might make you sick after delivery." I made no reply. "My use of this protocol has kept the death rate here extremely low, Lilli — four mothers in over four hundred births. And only one of those died from childbed fever."

Though these numbers were meant to be encouraging, I made a frightened face as I rose to my weary legs.

"You should be grateful," she repeated. "Last year at the city hospital, forty-two women per hundred died of childbed fever."

How appalling! I did express my gratitude before shuffling off to make way for her next patient.

Like her colleagues at the Woman's Medical College, some of whom I'd met in Germantown, Dr. Stevens is imbued with the fortitude of one who aims to improve the lot of her sex. The clothes on her slender form are wrinkled, and more of her hair escapes her bun and cap than remains tucked within them; to me these things are to her credit, for she focuses on what matters more.

But please, Dr. Stevens, don't let me become the fifth mother to die here! And don't let my baby die!

Each time the muscles of my belly tighten in a cramp, I wonder whether my time is nigh. I wonder what will become of me and my baby when we leave this place. I wonder what young woman will take my bed, and what happens to all the desperate girls whom Anne must turn away. At the window I stare out to the far-off stars and think, *What is the purpose of all this suffering?*

I know the Bible's answer, the one I heard at Meeting and from Mother's lips a hundred — no, five hundred times.

Do not despise the Lord's discipline,
nor lose courage when thee is punished.
For the Lord disciplines those whom he
  loves,
as a father the child in whom he delights.

What terrible love. Right now, I've half a mind to refuse it.

I've swallowed my drams of chloral hydrate. A stupor overtakes me. I hope to sleep till the morning bell.

Third Month 25, First Day

I'm confined to my room, spared even from attending chapel, because last night I rose from bed to take part in silliness despite my medicated condition — and I fell from a chair in the bath!

The folly began when three giggling girls from next door came to our room, guided by a candle's light, and presented the irresistible idea that we all view our bellies in the mirror by the tub. It's the only mirror in the house, vanity being against the rules, and was placed in that room only to ensure we don't go about with soap on our faces — judging from its high placement on the wall. But no doubt inmates before us have put it to this other use.

One by one, prodding each other forward,

we stood upon a chair in our nightgowns to peer at our enormous stomachs. There was much excitement, whispered at first, until we got to squealing over each belly whose rotund contours were revealed. When my chance came, I climbed onto the chair, pulled the cloth of my white gown close, and turned to see the full effect. An enormous ball of baby protruded at my front, and I wondered, *Who is in there?* and then, *How will I get such a large thing out?* When I turned again to step down, my foot slipped and twisted, and I fell to the floor

I needed help to stand, for my ankle couldn't bear weight. Then Delphinia burst in, having been roused by our noise. She demanded we return to our beds. She scolded me particularly — "I expect better of you" — and fixed me with a stern look. She stayed and helped me wrap my ankle all the same. To judge from the twitching of her lips, I'd say she found our exploits at least a tiny bit amusing.

However amusing it was, I'm stuck in bed today, lying at a slant because my belly is so tight and full that I can't lie flat. I'm as near to bursting as an overripe plum. In any position, my bulk impinges on my breath. How *will* this large human exit my small frame? Who *is* in there?

Stay calm, Dr. Stevens advised. I'm trying.

A little while ago, Delphinia brought me a breakfast of boiled eggs and toast. I told her of my occupation with book and pencil and how my supplies are running low. She agreed, upon my promising to reimburse her, to buy some inexpensive notebooks and pencils for me, the next time she goes out.

An hour or so has passed. I remain in bed. Delphinia has brought up a new roommate, Sophie, to take Nancy's place! She seems frightened and is very far along in her pregnancy. I meant to smile in welcome, but the drugs are causing peculiar effects (sweating and flushing, with my vision and hearing and reflexes strangely dulled). So when Sophie dashed a wary look at me, I felt uncertain whether I was offering back a pained or a pleased expression.

The unfortunate girl can't be more than fourteen. Her eyes are hooded by darkness, and there are long scabs on her bony back and legs. I observed them when she returned from her bath and was dressing in clothes from the donations closet.

I think she was whipped.

She rests now in the bed beside mine, and with eyes shut she has taken on the aspect of a deer, gentle and delicate. The rough smell of our lye soap and another odor, a strange one, rise from her. On the wall above her head hangs a square of linen that bears an embroidered motto of this place: "Through hard work we are redeemed."

I'd guess a lack of work was not the cause of her predicament.

It's a late hour; I've awakened again with pains, despite the dose of chloral hydrate at bedtime. Gina snores gently, her face as pretty as the drawing in a fashion advertisement, with its gentle expression and pale skin and the brown curls that fan across her pillowcase. Little Sophie is moaning in her sleep. My mind is heavy, for now I know what brought Sophie to her sorry state.

Anne called us to the parlor late in the day, demanding that we all attend. With painstaking slowness, Sophie and I descended a flight of stairs and walked to the parlor, where the chairs had been arranged to face the front, just as they are for chapel. Anne stood where the reverend would stand, but with her back to us. Her statuesque form was clad in muddy boots and a dampened cloak. I sat beside Nancy, my head hardly reaching to her shoulder, and I watched her dandle William in her lap, relishing her delight.

Then Anne turned to us. Several girls gasped to see her face, it was that angry.

"A cruel article concerning our institution appeared in *The Day* this morning," she told us. "The reporter admitted that he wasn't granted admission to the place — of course he wasn't! — but said he'd spoken with a woman 'intimately acquainted' with it, whose name he couldn't give."

She said the woman claimed this charity had turned her from a moral person who'd made but a single mistake to the one the reporter saw before him: an inebriate nursing her newborn in a brothel. The details of how this charitable institution had made her a drunkard and a prostitute in such short order were absent, but the reporter slandered our refuge nevertheless.

"And what was that reporter doing in a brothel?" Anne demanded, brandishing her arms. "Doesn't this cast doubt on his qualifications to write of virtue?"

However slight his qualifications, the man took it upon himself to describe Anne's establishment as providing nothing more than "the care and shelter of the deliberately vicious." The way of the transgressor is not made sufficiently difficult here, he claimed, for the inmates enjoy three meals a day, meals that often include apple pie and mutton.

The cook had made those special dishes only during Mary's brief stay; a few girls smirked with satisfaction at this strong hint that Mary was the turncoat. But Anne's concern lay with us, her remaining charges. She looked us each in the face directly; I shook inside when my turn came to brave the knifepoint of her stare. Then she spoke with cutting force: "I don't expect you to speak *well* of this place. No. I expect you never to speak of it at all. That is our gift to you: that you can leave this episode of your lives behind. But if you hold any malice in your heart against us, you may not have this gift." She pointed toward the front door. "I demand that you leave my institution at once. Leave us now, and never show your face here again."

When no one stood, she moved on to her next demand, requiring us to do what previously she'd forbidden. She told us to reveal how we came to be with child, so that no one might be mistaken for an unrepentant sinner. She prodded each along, demanding that she tell her truth, or Anne would tell it.

Nancy and most of the others flushed pink and said "rape" or "violation." When asked to name the male offender, several said he'd been a stranger. Nancy named the employer upon whom she had depended; at this, Gina turned in her seat to view our former roommate with a puzzled stare. Some of the girls identified a relative — one, a cousin; another, an elder brother; in Sophie's case, it was her father, and he had whipped her when he learned his seed had sprouted. The girl's voice was hushed when she spoke; her face was pinched and pained.

Gina and I were the only ones to claim breach of promise of marriage — the only ones whose condition could be explained by untempered passion and poor judgment. Gina spoke haltingly, her face expressing both mortification and a hint of gratitude that she didn't have a worse story to tell. Then I told of my own indulgence in the flesh and of trust given undeservedly. Sophie's eyes bored into me as if to say, "You know nothing of true degradation." With this I had no argument.

Then Anne read from the lengthy reply she'd sent to *The Day,* in which she bemoaned the prejudice heaped upon the Haven, the small numbers of women it is able to assist due to meager funds, and the many more who go without help. I recall eloquence along the lines of this: "It is a sad commentary on the community that a girl

— perhaps a mere child — is cut off from help and hope, and finds every door fast shut through which she would return to an honest life. Surely one opportunity for reformation may be allowed."

Not only did Anne draft her defense this morning, but then she rushed for hours through the city, from door to door, and through the force of her intentions has prevented all but one donor from withdrawing their pledges. A doctor even agreed to make the mortgage payments for the entire year.

Thus Anne has saved this institution from having to close and cast its occupants into the street.

Once she'd finished her recounting, we rose to our feet and clapped as one, and surely others felt as I did — that this woman has, by her courage and her sympathy, given me hope for the world's salvation.

Third Month 26
Sophie entered labor this morning, not long after starting on her chores. The birth was quick. With sorrow we passed the tidings ear to ear: her baby boy was stillborn. She rests now in the recovery room's second bed, alongside Nancy.

The infant being stillborn shouldn't surprise us, Delphinia said at midday, and it shouldn't scare us, either. Sophie arrived even more poorly nourished and roughly treated than most, and she was too young to have carried a baby well.

Later this afternoon, Dr. Stevens gave me an embarrassing and painful examination. With me lying on my side, she reached her hand in to measure the dilation of what she called my os uteri. "Opened to the size of a penny, nearly," she said. "Your labor will likely begin tonight."

I'm frightened. This diary is my one true friend; if only it had the power to pray with me.

Third Month 27, midday

Pains woke me in the dark and have occupied me since. Sally has taken temporary charge of the infant Mabel so Nancy can sit with me, as she wishes to help me through. She says it's fine to write while she sews beside me.

A strong one. The pain rolls over and flattens me, as if I were a sheet of paper beneath the roller of a press.

To think that every person I've laid eyes on had a mother who endured hours or even days of this!

Delphinia came in to report that the

delivery room is being aired and washed with carbolic acid and is almost ready for my arrival. Sophie left, she told us. An aunt took her in.

Another surge, so strong that I could barely breathe.

Each one assaults me slowly, rises to a vicious peak, and — at last — subsides.

Nancy's face is puffy from tears. She needs to replace the cloths at her breasts often. Though she's still nursing Mabel, her breasts are weeping out William's share of milk.

He's gone, her William. She couldn't pay ten dollars to the adoption agency that works with the Haven in order for them to find him a loving family, so he was sent to the foundling department at the city almshouse — the dreaded Blockley. Nancy believes he'll be placed out with a family soon.

She gave him up after eleven days, instead of the twenty-one days we're allowed. Anne advised against it, not only because she wished for William to get a solid start through Nancy's milk, but also because she believes that three weeks of motherhood will strengthen our spirits. Yet she had weakened Nancy's spirit by having her care for two.

Nancy said it wasn't the strain of nursing

two, however, that made her relinquish William early. She simply found it too heart-rending to adore him when she knew they had to part.

Another wave of agony takes over, then recedes. If only there was a way to be freed of my own flesh!

Nancy reminds me — the only way through is to endure.

She fetched my gold locket from my valise. Through each contraction I hold the slender oval between my fingers and imagine its picture of Mother inside, its strand of chestnut hair tied with a black ribbon.

I can write no more. I pray to have good news soon.

■ ■ ■ ■

NOTEBOOK THREE

■ ■ ■ ■

Third Month 31

My baby was born two nights ago. Seven pounds, five ounces in weight, and twenty inches long.

I lived the agony, yet somehow I marvel and disbelieve that she came from inside of me!

How is it that every mother discovers this miracle, yet doesn't proclaim it in the streets?

When the doctor said the head had crowned, I reached between my thighs, and my fingertips met a scalp. There was a hardness. On top of that was hair as soft as milkweed floss. I gave two more mighty pushes, and the whole body emerged.

A girl! A joy. Her breathing and color were deemed acceptable. Things were done to me and to her, as if at a shadowy distance, until she was placed upon my chest.

And there she thrummed, a singular human, giving off a vibration as familiar as my own.

I thought, *I already know thee.*

Of course! Because in me she came to life.

She squirmed to my nearest breast and opened her tiny mouth to claim its nipple. I saw then how her hair grows in a spiral beginning at the peak of her head, as if she rotated while forming. With her weight upon me, I let my fingers follow that path. I leaned my head forward to her scalp and inhaled, finding her smell — the intoxicating, slight smell of her scalp.

She seems so unformed and pliant, so thoroughly helpless, apart from her glossy eyes. These are fully opened and inquiring. Dr. Stevens has deemed her the most wakeful newborn she has ever seen. "Your baby stares," she noted, "as if she could eat the world with her eyes." She said most babies shut out the world by sleeping.

Already, dear Charlotte, thee distinguishes thyself.

I'm calling her Charlotte, but her new family will give its own name.

There are nineteen days until we part.

She'll never know: her father's hair is also red.

I never knew it was so draining to care for

an infant. From seeing others tend them, I understood nothing of how urgent each action feels. And I didn't know how such moments, stacked together, sap one's strength, or what great weight the word *tired* can carry. I haven't slept more than an hour continuously since — since: I can't remember when.

At least I've worked out a way to write while she nurses. A pillow on my lap, this book upon it, and her body by its side. What a thrill, to do something other than stare at the plaster wall and count the clock's ticking while she sucks!

She sucks and sucks. She sucks some more. My full milk hasn't yet come in, but she has to suck or else she frets, then cries. My body feels her cry as if it were a bell ringing to announce a fire.

"Wakeful and watchful," the doctor called her. To that I'll add, in constant need of soothing. My nipples are split and scabbed. She sucks away the scabs each time she applies her grip, and new ones begin to form as soon as she detaches.

Another small respite, with the baby drowsy at one breast and a notebook on my thigh.

I want to know: What is it that enables mothers to continue feeding, cleaning, holding, and pouring forth concern, throughout the days and nights, despite this drastic lack of sleep? I should be crippled by it — I *am* crippled by it — yet I go on.

It seems my every self-protecting limit has dissolved.

This baby has broken my will! The will that used to protect me above all, and some new one has grown in its place. This new will makes me serve her needs and has no mercy for me.

Bless Nancy. She strokes my forehead with her dry, wide palm when I grow discouraged.

We're in the recovery room together, Nancy and Mabel, Charlotte and me. We'll stay in this room until others require it. Anne considers it best to keep the mothers apart from the mothers-to-be, so our meals are brought to us. Mabel mostly sleeps, leaving Nancy with little to do, so she holds Charlotte now and then, and looks wistfully upon her, no doubt thinking of William.

Someone must hold Charlotte, or else she bawls and shakes her arms and legs; her face grows red and blotchy.

But I mustn't blame her for always needing to be held. How startling this world must be! A vast stretch of unbounded air. How can she be expected to lie alone in such hugeness, when she is used to living in a dark womb that supplied her everything?

My problem is how deeply she affects me.

The doctor cut the fleshly cord that connected us, but an invisible one has taken its place. I begin to suspect that this one can be neither cut nor broken.

Fourth Month 1, First Day

My full milk came in last night. Now Charlotte gulps, and milk trickles from the sides of her mouth. How marvelous: I am a mammal! Kin to the cats and cows that nursed in our neighbors' barn, and to all the furry mothers of field and forest.

And Charlotte? Like any newborn mammal, she nurses furiously, gulping and gulping. On completion she emits a belch, with her belly grown as rotund as my breasts.

She looks at me now, with glittering eyes and slackened jaw. I look back, gratified.

There are new sensations to get used to. The sharp pain that shoots across is the milk rushing into the ducts, Dr. Stevens said. Then comes a tingling and a burning as the milk flows out, which she explained is also typical.

Apparently my dishevelment is beyond the typical. When Delphinia brings meals to Nancy and me, we trade pleasantries and recite the mealtime prayer of this place: "Lead us this day in right action, Lord, that we may become living proofs of Thy grace." But this morning Delphinia could hardly speak for staring at me — at my hair unbrushed and falling from its combs, at the shoulders and front of my wrapper dotted with spit-up milk, at the clothing I've piled on willy-nilly to keep me warm.

"A mother should care for her appearance," she instructed. Her silver hair was pinned back neatly, and her clothing, though softened by wear, was orderly.

"As if I wouldn't care for my appearance," I replied, "if this baby gave me the chance." Though in truth I spend most of the precious minutes while Nancy holds Charlotte in writing, not primping.

Delphinia took pity. She brushed my hair, pinned it into a fresh bun, and refreshed my supply of clean clothing. Her ministrations brought on relieving sighs, and when Charlotte began to nurse again — her strong mouth pursing and pulling — my weariness had eased, and once more she seemed the dearest being on earth.

Her father was almost so dear to me.

I don't think of him when she nurses, or when her legs travel the air like an upsidedown chicken's as I clean her bottom, or when I rinse her diapers in a tub or fold her laundered clothing or stare at the clock as she sucks and the hours crawl by. The orbs of her cheeks are nothing like his big, broad-cheeked face; her pert lips and urgent sounds resemble not his wide mouth and well-spoken sentences. I don't think of him even when I stroke her red hair.

I think of him when she looks into my eyes and seems to say, *Thee is my only love.*

Her father loved me thusly. Or, I believed he did.

Fourth Month 3

The day is sunny and blustery. Wind whips pollen and tree blossoms into the window screens. Through the bars on the recovery-room windows, I see the other girls hanging damp laundry on the clotheslines that run along one side of the building.

Mabel left yesterday, taken by an adoption agent to a family with several other orphans, leaving Nancy free. She went soon after to an intelligence office to apply for housemaid positions. But before Nancy stepped out the door for the first time in months, she fretted, for she would have to lie. She couldn't tell honestly why she'd left her previous household or why she hadn't asked that household for a letter of reference. She practiced telling me she was new to Philadelphia and had labored in homes far from here — but the fabrications tangled on her tongue.

She did return to the Haven with a new position, as the maid in a rooming house for women. Then she passed her last afternoon and night on the bed beside mine. Sometime before dawn, I woke to stifled cries and saw her face buried in the flannel that had covered William. Perhaps she was seeking whatever scent of him remained.

When she woke early this morning, she converted that blanket to a scarf. We had our breakfast, brought in by Delphinia. Then, sighing with anxiousness, Nancy dressed in the maid's uniform she'd brought here, a black cotton gown with a white apron and cap rimmed in eyelet lace. She added cloths inside her corset and chemise to absorb the milk that would drip from her, since she'd no longer have a nursling to relieve her of it. Delphinia brought her a pretty hat and coat from the donations closet, which cheered Nancy.

In the foyer, we gathered to say goodbye — Delphinia, Gina, Charlotte, and me. Nancy flitted among us like an anxious bird, distributing her parting affections. We roommates shared no information that would allow us to find one another. As Anne has advised, we must pretend never to have been in this place. So the finality of our parting added to its sadness. With one last sigh, her green eyes flashing with wetness, Nancy moved her tall self out the door and down the marble steps and out of sight.

Her flannel scarf has set me thinking. I'd planned to feed my notebooks to the kitchen stove before departing. But perhaps I won't. In the privacy of night, in my narrow room in Germantown, I'll want to recall my months here and the baby I left behind. These pages can serve as my scarf of words.

Without Nancy and Mabel with me, I have more chance to think. I want to draft another letter to my baby.

1883. 4th mo. 3

Dearest Charlotte,
I find myself concerned as to thy proper upbringing.

Most of all, I want thee to be loved. After this, I want thee to honor the Light of God within thy mind and heart.

And then — dear one, before marrying, do guard against excessive passion — with the fierceness of a sheepdog

123

protecting its flock from wolves. Thee may inherit a weakness. Please! Be intent on resisting.

Where does thee live, Charlotte? Has thee grown up within a caring fold? If only one day I could see thee.

I won't even know thy name.

Never mind. I can't possibly copy this and leave it for her.

Fourth Month 6

What a morning! My milk was blocked. Delphinia dipped cloths in hot water and applied them to my chest. The heat relaxed me, but no liquid came when Charlotte sucked. It seemed my milk had turned to paste. My baby cried and kicked, which caused me grief, which used up my last remaining strength — whatever stores I had squirreled away in my bones.

I lay Charlotte in a bassinet, a place she hadn't tolerated before. At first she cried quietly, as though to assure herself that she wasn't being weak by consenting to rest outside my arms. Finally the two of us slept, and my milk came loose, and I woke soaked to the waist. She drank from me in ecstasy.

There is something fierce and wild in her. Her legs and arms appear spindly and frail, yet she kicks and fixes her grip on my clothing and sucks with the power of an animal.

Without Nancy, I have no one to talk with and no one to hold Charlotte a little. An animal panic begins to overtake me at being in this room around the clock. A woman after labor must stay as still as possible, said Dr. Stevens. But soon, she said, she'll let me take Charlotte outside.

Fourth Month 9

Charlotte is twelve days old. Delphinia wheeled us from the recovery room to the courtyard this morning, and I rose from the chair and walked a few circles around the stone path to invigorate my legs. Oh, how the outside air brightened and cleared my mind! As if I were a window wiped free of dirt. The tree branches were beginning to push out their dainty slips of green, and overhead, the early birds flitted about, carrying bits of dried plant matter for their nests. Then a breeze came on, and Charlotte smiled to feel the cool air move against her skin. This was her first time outside, her first smile! I told Delphinia, who claimed the smile was a sign of indigestion.

For warmth I'd wrapped Charlotte in a blanket, but she wriggled free and waved her limbs. Delphinia laughed. "I've never seen the like! An infant who doesn't like to be swaddled!"

But I understand. I, too, can't bear to be confined. Not long ago, I thought nothing of the actions I could do on my own — prepare a meal, hold a conversation, buy goods at a market, explore shelves of books in the library, plan a lesson. Now it's hard even to reach for my slippers or to raise a bite of food steadily to my mouth. For I must do every single thing with Charlotte in my arms.

How can one baby demand so much? To keep her resting and not wailing, I must lie fixed in place while she nurses or dozes, her mouth tight on me like a manacle — no matter if I'm hot or cold, at ease or pressed into an uncomfortable position, whether I have an urgent need to relieve myself or change clothes or function in some small way as I used to. Her weight makes my arms throb from the near-constant holding, day upon night upon day. My legs grow numb and begin to jerk, till at last I must move, let the numbness turn back to sensation, and all the while endure her cries.

And how those cries affect me! Until now, no matter how much I've cared for a person, with the exception of Mother in her dying hours, and despite how dreadful this sounds, I've found it easier to bear their suffering than my own. Not so with Charlotte. My shoulders, back, arms, and neck ache from holding her; my nipples are scabbed and sometimes bleeding; yet the most worn-out, painful part of me is my heart. It stretches so wide when she's contented that I believe its fibers are tearing. When she suffers, it shrinks and throbs and hardens into a knot.

Never before have I even thought of my heart as the muscle it is. Never has mine seemed to expand and contract in concert with my feelings. It hurts continually now from responding to the inconstant creature that is Charlotte.

Anne sees that I can't be asked to nurse a second infant.

I've written nothing yet of what happened after I was moved to the delivery room. I was shaved — which the doctor said prevents disease. She placed me on towels and bathed me with a cloth. Then she left to examine Sally, who was feeling faint, and all the others in the house.

After some time of worsening contractions, Delphinia brought a dinner tray. I ate one bite of chicken and vomited. She sat with me till the paroxysms ceased and watched me endure several onslaughts of pain, then told me I was doing very well, because I tried not to brace against them, which only makes them fiercer.

I passed a long night in this way, awake. In the morning, the doctor returned and washed her hands in chlorinated lime, then began to execute a process she said is used in the best maternity hospital in Philadelphia: a quick-acting cathartic, then a bath, then the rupture of the waters.

Next I spent some long time pushing in agony. I hardly knew where I was, or with whom. Periodically Dr. Stevens pushed her hand inside me to discern how open I'd become. A problem emerged: though my os was fully dilated, the baby couldn't pass beyond. Would I have to be brought to the hospital for surgery?

At last the doctor thought to give me a catheter and discovered that my bladder was profoundly full, blocking the passage. All the power of my pushing had only forced my poor baby's head against my bladder — which may help explain her alertness.

Merely two more pushes and the baby was out. Delphinia bathed her as the doctor gave me morphine and depressed my abdomen gently to expel the afterbirth, then dosed me with quinine until my ears were ringing

— the sign she'd given enough. She approached me next with a dropperful of some other draught and I protested, saying I wanted no further treatments. Already the morphine and the quinine were having peculiar effects. I had close in mind what a doctor's overzealous dosing had done to Mother.

"These unmarried girls lack the common sense of a lady," Dr. Stevens said to Delphinia, as though I wasn't in the room.

Delphinia gave a hard stare. "With all they've been through, they're anxious of being harmed." Then she laid my baby gently onto me.

My body trembles still from its long struggle. The doctor said I would soon forget the pain, but I haven't forgotten. I awaken from brief rests in a sweat, heart hammering, and recall the hours of fruitless pushing till the catheter cleared the way. I was mad with agony, yet the doctor only yelled to push harder, harder.

That struggle, it turns out, was the easier part. Now the dear person I must keep alive is outside my womb, and no need but air is filled without my effort.

Today was typical. She nursed or dozed with my nipple in her mouth for sixteen hours of the past twenty-four; I counted.

The other hours, she had to be in my arms, or she would scream.

A moment may come when I have nothing left to offer — when it will all have been sucked out.

My hand shakes as I write. Oh, for a few hours of sleep! Tiredness penetrates me — as if I were a rag doll, with tiredness as my stuffing.

Fourth Month 12

Charlotte is crying. I can hear her through two closed doors. Yet I'm determined not to respond because I'm furious, furious. I'm seated beside a claw-foot tub in the room across the hall, and Charlotte is in the bassinet, screaming for me, and I have reached the end of my patience.

Here is what has just occurred. The recovery room is on the first story. The furnace sits beneath it, in the basement. The coalman arrived with a delivery as I was reaching to put a dozing Charlotte in the bassinet, aiming to drop myself into bed right after. And do mark, please, that this was one of the few times in her fifteen days of life when she was unwary enough that I might attempt this.

But as I lowered her slowly through the air, the round iron cover on the side of the building slid open, and coal descended raucously through a chute into the basement.

At the first burst of falling coal, Charlotte's body startled from head to toe. Her face contorted into a mask of misery, and she began to wail. I pulled her to me again, and she affixed her cruel mouth to my nipple, from which she had barely dropped away. The pain shot into me as it does every time, but for once I didn't clench my jaw and wait for it to subside. I put my finger in her mouth and detached her. I placed her in the bassinet amid the noises from below and ran out of the room.

I'm shaking on the cold floor beside the tub, this notebook clutched to me, while she cries in our room, alone. Of course my flight brings no relief; my muscles clench to hear her. Yet I can't tolerate her insatiable need. She sucks beyond endurance. I want only to use my chamber pot, to brush my hair and put it up with combs, to bathe, to put food into my body — and most of all to escape the state of nervous vigilance she keeps me in.

Hear me, diary. I meant to keep her the full three weeks before the adoption agency took her. But I won't. I can't. Why endure nearly another week of this? I want to go home. I'll speak with Anne and let her know. I'm ready to give Charlotte away.

I continued my mutiny, covering my ears against her cries, and she actually ceased her protest. I tiptoed to our room and found her sleeping and lay in my bed alongside the bassinet! The two of us slept straight through till supper, when Delphinia brought in my tray.

Thanks to a generous food donation, the fare was ample. I devoured the roasted chicken, the bread with butter, the cobbler made with peaches from some steadfast canner's remaining stores. Delphinia beamed to see such an appetite. And for the first time since her birth, Charlotte looked about calmly and seemed at peace.

I suspect the poor baby has never had a decent rest till this, despite my endless trying. One might be tempted to think she's determined not to sleep for fear of losing me.

Yet our dearth of sleep has brought that very outcome closer. I've sent word to Anne and now must only last through one more night.

Delphinia told me few girls make it to the full three weeks. "The ones who do," she observed, "are saddest."

Can this be so? Am I protecting myself from the agony of losing her by parting early — as Nancy did?

Fourth Month 13
There is no protecting oneself from this.

We spent another night nursing and dozing, and the adoption agent arrived in our room early today. She was a tall, frowsy woman who introduced herself as Miss Emmeline Trout. As she spoke, gaps showed in her mouth where teeth had been; apparently her wages are too low for her to afford a dentist. This was sad and discouraging to see, as was her patched and worn clothing — for her sake, and also for Charlotte's. Because what sort of a family would adopt a child from an agency whose employee's condition spoke so plainly of hardship? I feared it would be an impoverished one. Would my baby go hungry?

I'd obliged myself to give Charlotte to this agency several months ago, having made an agreement through Anne. Looking at the vulnerable creature in my arms, however, I wanted better.

Emmeline encouraged me to hand Charlotte over. "We got a family what's eager and willing," she said, reaching.

But I couldn't move my arms forward. *Do*

it! my brain commanded, without having any effect.

"Yer a sentimental one," said Emmeline, baring her gap-toothed smile. "No harm in you carrying the baby to the office in place of me."

So I clutched my living bundle close and followed Emmeline down the hall and into the office.

On hearing of my hesitation, Anne stood from her chair and brandished the adoption papers she'd signed after I'd verbally affirmed the agreement. I'd been continuing in the way of Friends by not signing any vow of truthfulness — any contract — since claiming special truthfulness at one moment infers that our words are otherwise untrue. But as I watched Anne, the thought went through my mind that because I hadn't signed, perhaps they couldn't force me to comply. Anne, too, might have been thinking this.

"Now hand the baby to her, Lilli." Anne tightened her lips, keeping her blue eyes steady on me.

I remained unable.

Anne caught Emmeline's attention and gestured toward me, and Emmeline understood; in a wink she'd slid her skinny arms under Charlotte and scooped her away. A cold spot formed on my front.

"It's best you go quickly," Anne instructed her. And I'd thought Anne to be a kindred soul!

Emmeline stepped into the hall with her bounty and headed toward the front door. Charlotte began to bawl. Anne moved out from behind her desk, seized my upper arms, and tried to push me onto the bench so I couldn't follow.

"We must be brave and do what's best for the baby," she said. "Give her the chance to overcome the disgrace of her birth."

But I wrenched away and ran. "Come back!" I screamed at the retreating woman. "I'm not ready! I'm entitled to the full three weeks!"

And to think it was I who had initiated our early separation.

Emmeline halted and turned, her face pink with discomfort, her small gray eyes pinpointing me. She held Charlotte to her threadbare bodice, but my baby leaned her head toward me and emitted a wail. I rushed at Emmeline and reversed her trick. Instantly Charlotte gripped my wrapper with her inch-long fingers, pushed her head into my chest, and kicked her feet with excitement.

By then Anne had reached us. Her muscles

were tense with disapproval. "Lilli," she admonished. "More days won't make this easier."

I could only whisper, for my chest and throat were clenched. "What if they don't love her? What if they're cruel?"

At this, Anne's aspect softened. To Emmeline she said, "You can bring a letter from the family, can't you? Since this will put Miss de Jong at ease."

Emmeline's face went blank as thoughts transpired beneath its surface. She consulted a watch from her skirt pocket. "Our office is closing in two hours. The family expects a baby today."

"I'm entitled to keep her longer," I asserted. Charlotte began knocking her cheek against me, giving out her grunt-like sound that signals hunger.

"She *is* entitled," Anne told Emmeline. "But taking the full allotted time won't help. Today's Friday; why don't you come back Monday with that letter. We'll make sure she's ready."

I raced to the recovery room and pushed shut the heavy door, then curled with Charlotte beneath the blankets. I satisfied her thirst and breathed purposefully to calm the thumping in my chest. Then the door opened, and Anne walked in. She sat on the bed formerly occupied by Nancy. A weariness settled over her, and her back slumped.

"I don't know what I should do," I began, intending to apologize. "It may —"

Anne straightened. "I expect you to comply with our agreement when the agent returns on Monday. And despite your being in recovery, you must go to chapel with the others on Sunday, to be reminded of what's right. The cook can take the baby."

I agreed.

Meanwhile, I have Charlotte for a few more days.

I do hope to find assurance enough in the family's letter and at chapel to strengthen me, for she will surely find a better life without her mother's disgraced company.

Fourth Month 15, First Day

The hours at chapel have only worsened my dilemma.

I took a seat beside Gina in a foul state of mind, only slightly improved by an early bath and a change of dress. The sight of the other girls neatened and wearing clean clothes did cheer me, however. And fortunately it was the elder Reverend Williams's week to preach. He never smirks or jests at our expense or castigates us, as his son does.

"Ah, but you are bright and fresh today,"

he called over his lectern — though most would have viewed our group as stained and ruined. "It is well that I bring you a message of hope."

Hope? Every leaning head perked up to listen.

"For just as spring comes to the land," he intoned, "as insects and mammals awaken in the dirt, and plants begin their pilgrimage toward the sun, so each human life has its springtime. You must every one of you remember, whatever your misfortunes and missteps have been, that this is — yes, *this is the springtime of your lives.*"

Delivered in the crackling voice of a gray-haired man with a hunched back and a cane, this counsel was affecting. Certainly we do have youth on our side. In the bodies around me, I sensed an easing. Perhaps all the former freshness in our hearts is not decayed by sorrow. Perhaps something new and untainted might arise!

Reverend Williams moved his sparkling eyes from one to another of us, promising: "If you will live in service of God, then you will find happiness. Indeed, and this is my message for you today, you will find more happiness than the woman who has never strayed."

Breaths were taken in or released through

his small crowd of listeners. He raised his arms and lowered them, as if suppressing our potential errors. His voice acquired a singer's earnestness. "For when the sinner repents, her belief is far more fervent!" he called. "Her hunger for good has been fed by its absence. Do you think the truly repentant can sin again?" We awaited his answer. "The repentant sinner can bear only to pursue good. Only to pursue good! *And she will be redeemed.*"

He paused to push unruly curls from his angular face. Beside me, Gina gave out a sigh and straightened her spine as if relieved of a weight, despite being filled to bursting with her baby. Others shifted in their seats, loosening their limbs; some wiped moistness from their eyes.

I wished I could share in their relief. Though I had no desire to be disrespectful and even loved this man for his intentions, I found myself beset by irritation at his constructs, which struck me all at once as flawed beyond repair.

For one, most of the young women who pass through here are not sinners, but victims; what did Nancy and Sophie, for instance, do wrong? So why should they be told to seek redemption?

For another, what of the men who put us

139

into our condition? Shouldn't they be made to kneel before the Lord and spend their coming years in repentance? Who searches out their souls and makes them pay?

And what of the families who've let us bear our crosses alone, the families who've chosen appearances over love? Surely they too ought to consider their sins.

The reverend raised his half-bent arms and waved them about, continuing to illustrate his points. A younger man's vigor came to his face; his voice gained force and clarity. The faces around me grew flushed with gratitude and hope, just as he wished them to. But I couldn't join them. Instead, I mourned the weary, twisted nature of my heart. I marveled at the simplistic notions of well-meaning people that grow ever more tiresome. I wondered how Gina could accept his words, how her eyes could glow adoringly, when she'd so recently bemoaned the lies that will underpin her new life.

And I considered the lie that will underpin my own life. The lie that Charlotte never grew in me, was never born, that all this never happened. We each have our own version of that lie. It's the currency with which we buy our return ticket to society.

I wanted to call out to the reverend: How can anyone here truly live in service of God, or create an honest love with any human being, with this lie forming the rotten center of our selves?

Steeped in this alienated condition, and whether despite or because of it I didn't know, I felt an odd state overtake me. I began to float away from the scene at hand, as if I were a passenger on the deck of a boat that was leaving. Then it seemed as if an insistent wave pulled me overboard — and I was engulfed by a warm and luscious sea. I was insensible to the others. I breathed underwater, like a fish. A buzzing sound entered my head, and I felt this: unbounded happiness. As if occupying some antechamber of God's house, I floated alongside a pure and vibrating force. I began to shiver as waves of joy passed over me.

Was this the joy I'd heard other Friends describe? An ecstatic union with my Inner Light of God?

It must have been. Yet with that joy came a crystal-clear awareness of my failings. I saw laid out the whole of my upbringing, which had urged me to live honestly; my coming situation, where lying would be the rule; and the cowardice that had kept me from admitting this divergence.

In Meeting for Worship, at school, and at home, I'd been taught not to conform to the world as it is. My mother, grandparents, and teachers, our Meeting's elders, and the writings of weighty Friends had exhorted me to live instead as if the world were what it *ought* to be. Mother reminded me not to be ruled by convention or by shallow pleasure every time she forbade me to wear a ribbon in my hair, or when she chose plain cloth for our attire, or refused to let me see a concert or a play or read a fanciful book. "Our time and skills are meant for beneficial use," she'd say when she had me join her in sewing clothes and quilts for other families on First Day afternoons rather than roaming with the neighbor children. "We mustn't distract ourselves," she'd tell me. "We must keep our eyes and minds free of intoxicating influence, to perceive the wisdom that grows beneath the surface."

Year after year, she strove to scour away the vanity that might make me timid to stand out. I was meant to grow into a person who would dare, as she did, to act on the inspoken words of my heart, the messages of my Inner Witness to the Divine will.

Yet our circumscribed life had kept me faithful to the bounds it dictated. Had I ever needed, before her death, to put myself at odds with anything but my desire for frivolity in order to pursue right? Not once. The guidance at hand had never failed me. I was ruled entirely by convention.

And now that I faced an actual choice, I wasn't planning to distinguish myself. I would cast away the baby who sustained her life at my breast. I would refuse to bear my personal cross. Like so many others in my circumstance, I would let myself be turned into a fraud.

Amid this scouring of my soul, I heard dimly the needling voice of Reverend Williams: "Repent of thy sin, and accept the saving grace of thy heavenly Father."

But the moment I let go of Charlotte and pretend she never existed, my life of sin begins. Lies will color — no, suffuse — my most intimate relations. The pain at my center will stay closed in and festering, while lies spread like a layer of lard beneath my skin.

A message sounded in my brain: *Remember the courage of thy ancestors.*

Some early Friends suffered beatings and imprisonment and sacrificed their homes and livelihoods in order to uphold their right to draw close to God without a minister's interceding. My own elders were raised amid slavery and condemned it when doing so was hazardous. They forswore the luxuries created by slave labor, such as cane sugar and cotton. They gave goods and funds to help the enslaved escape; some even helped transport those who were escaping. These Friends risked much to behave rightly and retain their freedom of conscience, yet I planned to take the coward's way.

My throat grew clogged till I could barely breathe. I dropped my knees to the floor and lowered my head.

After some period, the vibrations in me quieted. The reverend's voice had ceased, and those around me were rising to their feet. Gina nudged my arm from above, her face questioning. I found myself able to stand. I walked unsteadily to the kitchen and reclaimed my bastard from the cook, who'd taken her for a stroll and was extolling, remarkably, upon the quiet contentment of this baby. Then Gina followed me to the recovery room, wanting company. Seated in a wooden chair, her belly resting on her thighs, she told me she couldn't wait to leave this institution behind and begin to regain her virtue. She settled into tatting lace for the sleeves of her baby's christening gown — since a christening is one of Angela's first plans.

It seems Gina and I are caught in opposing tides. She is eager to ride the incoming waters toward shore and to walk a jetty of lies into a more righteous life. But my body is trembling, despite my having slid beneath the covers and applied Charlotte to my breast, for a new awareness has pulled me so far out from solid ground into the wild ocean that I may never find my way back.

My baby sleeps in my arms, in blameless beauty.

Fourth Month 16

Sorrow ate into me last night like a rat chewing through a wall. For I was still planning to hand Charlotte over to the adoption agent, despite my chapel awakening, as I have nowhere near the courage of my ancestors.

I rose before seven and stepped with Charlotte to the kitchen to fill a breakfast plate, as Delphinia hadn't come. Then I returned to eat in the recovery room, hunched in bed with Charlotte at my breast. Soon after, the door opened. Emmeline entered, removed her wrap, and took the chair beside me. Avoiding my eyes, she proffered a shabby envelope, which I tore open.

There was a strangeness to the letter's language. It seemed to convey not a real family's sentiments but someone's idea of what I would wish to hear. *We're well sup-*

145

plied with money and a large house. We'll give your baby a happy life. Insipid platitudes, rushed together, and put far too bluntly.

So I questioned Emmeline — aiming to find out if only the letter was a fake, or if even the existence of a decent family should be doubted. She offered more of the same: "They'll treat her like their own, they will," and "None but the best families come to this agency, ye needn't trouble yerself." Her long face flushed with extra warmth, which happens to those unaccustomed to lying. Then I asked if anyone from the agency would visit Charlotte to be sure the family was caring for her properly, and if I could receive a periodic report.

She took a breath and held it. Leaning over my bed, she released her breath, giving me a hefty dose of spring onion. "If ye care that much," she said — and then she halted.

"Then what?" I shifted a restless Charlotte from lap to shoulder.

Emmeline shook her head and pressed her dry lips closed.

Where this urge came from I don't know, for I'd never bribed a soul — but I rose from bed with Charlotte clutched to my chest, and with my free hand I took a dollar from my purse. I proffered it to Emmeline. Her eyes grew large, but she snatched the bill and pushed it into her dress. Like a mouthful of oil, that dollar greased her tongue.

"I shouldn't tell ye," she said, "and ye mustn't tell Mrs. Pierce."

I gave a solemn nod of agreement. "I'll be grateful for any advice thee can share."

She moved closer to me and whispered. "I visit once a year till each child reaches the age of independence. Most of our families do their children justice. But the things I've seen with them bastards, miss, would give you chills. Oh, those families claim they'll treat 'em fair. But they haven't the money to feed their own flesh and blood. No, there's no charity in taking a bastard. They see the chance for free labor, which is the entire reason they'll take it."

"Free labor?" I said. "From a baby?" Charlotte gave an exhalation, and dampness seeped through her clothing to my forearms.

"Oh, they'll grow up right quick." She joined her hands, stretched out her knobby arms, and cracked her fingers. From the pocket of her skirt she removed a wad of tobacco. With this tucked in her cheek, she leaned her bony frame forward again. "I'm only saying this once and shouldn't say it at all. They'll feed the babe enough to keep it alive and give it clothes. But once it can push a broom or clean a stall or hold a needle, they'll make it work. No wages or schooling, and they'll beat it for any sign of gumption." She paused to suck at her tobacco, then added in a deeper tone, "Mind ye, we do get better families wanting a baby. But what can ye expect for a bastard?"

She stood and spit into the sink. The powdery smell of Charlotte's skin and the urine in her diaper mingled with the bittersweet reek of tobacco juice.

"Can't thee find a better family for her?" I begged. And then, "I have more money." I quelled the sob in my chest.

"There's no use in asking to be treated different from the rest." She indicated Charlotte with a jab of her chin. "Who'll take such a one as that, if they want to raise a lady or a gent?"

Such a one as that! About my Charlotte!

It had been one thing to consider keeping my baby in a surge of honesty, despite the promise of her rose-colored future with another family. It was quite another to discover that her life would be disgraced and impoverished without me. The lump in my throat descended to my gut, as if I'd swallowed a rock. My next words came out small and pinched. "Is it best that I *not* give her away?"

"Not if ye care that much, miss." Emmeline shook her head with vigor. "It'd make no sense to give the baby over, not a whit."

She waited for a reply. Receiving none, she bowed to me and left. Soon after, I received a visit from Anne, which I experienced as a fleeting dream.

Few people will have the strength to associate with you, Anne said.

Should I care more for being liked than for being true?

How can you hold on to your misfortune? she asked.

I leaned to kiss my baby's forehead and to inhale her elusive scent.

Thee is no misfortune, Charlotte. Thee is a blessing.

Fourth Month 17

Between changing, nursing, holding, and tidying up, it's a wonder I can write. But I need to decide where to go, because I can't go home.

Some naïve, good-hearted person might tell me to try. But my status would threaten Father's livelihood, not to mention that Patience despises me already; imagine how her cruelty would grow if I disgraced her house. And I couldn't bear to see Father's belief in my goodness vanish with his first sight of my baby. Besides, Patience would never let me stay.

No. With grief eating at my heart, I decided to ask Anne how I might obtain a sewing machine. I could easily make clothes, I figured — plain ones, at least — and support Charlotte and myself in this way.

Anne was out, but Delphinia obliged me with a consultation. I sat on the bench with Charlotte, who stared through the many-paned window at the falling rain.

"What can I do for you, dear?" The matron peered across the desk at me, giving off a hint of irritation. Her deeply lined face was surrounded in a halo of white hair. It occurred to me that she must be very tired from caring for the inmates here, and that my change of plans had strained her further. Quietly I told her I'd decided to become a sewing woman and asked whether she knew how I might obtain a machine.

"You can apply to a ladies' aid society for a grant," she said. "I'll give you an address. However, sewing work pays poorly. Many a widow has failed to feed her children through it."

"I could work in a garment factory," I offered. "Then I'd earn better."

Delphinia sighed. She rested her elbows

on the paper-piled desk, then propped her chin on her upraised fingers. "Would you, then? Do you have any idea what that entails?"

"I don't," I admitted.

"You'd work twelve-hour days, six or seven days a week. You'd be made to buy your own needles and thread from your employer. Docked pay or even beaten for speaking a word to another worker or for arriving a minute late. And paid barely enough to buy the meanest food and rent a corner of some dirty, shared room."

I stared in reply. Her face was warm with passion.

"Where would you keep your baby?" she asked, baiting me.

I was quiet.

"One young woman left this place determined to support herself and her baby through factory work. The wages were too low for her to place her baby with a wet nurse, so she tried day boarding. Do you know what that is?"

"No." My hold on Charlotte tightened.

"Her baby spent its days with an impoverished grandmother who sat on a stoop and watched hordes of children go at their mischief. The babies sucked on rags soaked in sugar water and laudanum, which makes

151

babies sleepy and takes away their appetite."
Her face grew stiff. "Without the milk it
needed in the day, that baby died within
weeks of leaving here."

"The poor thing!" My heart contracted.

"Not actually." Her voice lowered. "The
babies who live will learn to crawl. This
means, if there's no money to pay for day
boarding, their mothers have to tie their legs
to a table or some other heavy thing before
leaving them in their sordid lodging. Do
you know the reason?"

I shook my head.

"So they won't get burned on the stove or
climb out a window while their mothers are
at their factory shifts." Delphinia stood and
came around the desk to plant her sturdy
frame before me, perhaps to increase the effect of her words. "So if you worked at a
factory," she continued, "your baby would
spend most days without your milk, either
at day boarding or bound to a plank and
placed upon the highest shelf."

"Why?" I asked.

She took a breath and roared her answer.
"To try and keep away the rats that do eat
children."

This pronouncement finished her. She
collapsed onto the bench beside me and
seemed to pull her mind away, as if to

replenish herself.

I ought to have known that such horrors could bedevil even well-intentioned people. I should have known it from the evidence that life presented to my eyes and from the sad stories that Mother had brought home. But instead, I'd held on to a common prejudice. Regardless of my sympathy for the families she'd assisted and for the others I'd seen suffering, in some dim recess of my brain, I must have believed they'd wasted money, or failed to work hard, or otherwise exercised poor judgment and — I dread to say — brought on their plights.

I looked down to find Charlotte's head leaned back, her nostrils and lips moving with her breath like petals in a soft rain. She'd fallen asleep without me having to nurse her first!

I thought of rats eating her.

Delphinia stood suddenly and took a swallow from the cup of tea upon the desk. "Factory work is out of the question," she said. "And a sewing woman doesn't earn enough to live in anything but squalor."

"But haven't any others here been able to keep their babies and live decently?" I didn't want my hope extinguished.

"Certainly they have."

"How did they manage?"

"They had families or acquaintances who were not above taking them in." She found my eyes with hers. "In this way, Lilli, it can be a blessing to belong to the lower classes."

"In what way, exactly?"

"People who have suffered and known hard limits may have a more realistic understanding of mistakes and bad fortune."

My body felt heavy enough to fall through the floor. Every aspect of my former life, even its relative lack of suffering and limitation, now seemed a curse.

Then Delphinia's face lost expression, as if she didn't wish to influence me unduly. She told me of the one profession for which I was an ideal candidate at present: that of the wet nurse. "Families of means often hire wet nurses for their newborns," she explained. "They do so when a mother has perished in childbirth, or fallen ill, or finds herself unsuited to nursing."

I refreshed myself with a full breath. "I'd be glad to help such a family, so long as I could bring Charlotte."

Delphinia colored with pleasure, assuring me that a family would be glad enough to have me that they'd certainly allow Charlotte to come along. "Some girls are too rough for this work, but you'd be well suited for it," she opined. "You'd be given the finest food and treated gently, all to support the quality of your milk. And the wages are excellent, perhaps twice as much as what other female servants make." Her demeanor puffed with optimism. "In less than a year, you'd have the means to lease a sewing machine and set yourself up as a seamstress — with some money saved to make up for shortfalls." She lifted a stack of papers and bounced it on the desk to neaten it. "All with no sacrifice to yourself or your baby." She dropped the stack to the desk, which caused a loud report and startled Charlotte from her sleep.

"How can I find a family that needs a nurse?" I asked as my baby began to fuss.

"I'll tell Mrs. Pierce you'd like to apply. Doctors often write to see if we have any candidates for the families in their care. I'm sure she'll recommend you."

I sent a prayer of thanks into the ether.

This love for Charlotte is like a hardy plant that rises in me. If I had to chop it down, its roots would fester — and corrupt the soil of my being.

Not three hours after my talk with Delphinia, I was called to the office in a rush. I appeared before Anne with spit-up on my shoulders and Charlotte at my breast. "If I take her off," I explained, "we'll have no chance of hearing each other."

Anne nodded and closed the door, bidding me to sit. Lifting a fine parchment envelope, she said, "A doctor has written in urgent need of a wet nurse. The baby is his patient's first, only a week younger than yours. The mother is unable to nurse him."

Charlotte must have felt my heart quickening. She stirred and gave a cry.

"Will they find me suitable?" I asked.

"I believe so." She gave a parsimonious smile.

"And Charlotte will come along." I intended merely to confirm the point, but Anne raised her eyebrows.

"Dear girl," she said. "An honorable couple couldn't accept a bastard into their home."

"Delphinia Partridge assured me . . ."

My words trailed off as Anne wagged her head. "Miss Partridge means well, but her understanding of the circumstances —"

"I won't go." Tears slid down my cheeks. Their source must move closer to the eyes in mothers.

Anne bent across her desk to bring her stern face closer to me, so that I saw the crumbs at the edges of her lips. "Don't be foolish. A baby doesn't know the difference.

156

She'll go to a wet nurse in a more modest situation."

"What does thee mean?" A crawling sensation spread over my arms.

"Someone who's nursing a few babies at once, who'll charge a fee you can afford and do just as you would for her. With the money you save at this work, you can start anew, perhaps in another city. You'll reclaim your daughter before she's old enough even to know you from another."

Why would Charlotte cling to me so, if she didn't know me from another? I swallowed and pressed her close.

"This family will pay twenty-five dollars a month," said Anne, "and no expenses, aside from perhaps six dollars a month to place her out."

The salary astounded me. As a new teacher, I'd earned thirteen.

"Consider your savings after a year." Anne joined her slender, neatly tended hands before her on the desk. "You may never get such a chance at advancement again."

That statement gave me pause. Could my life's choices be so reduced that this would be my best chance at advancement?

The clear answer was yes. "Can I meet the family," I asked, "and then make my decision?"

Anne's mouth pursed, but with effort she spoke pleasantly. "Of course. And if they don't suit you, then you may find some other option in your few remaining days of lodging here, isn't that so?" She paused and stared. "You can't stay more than a day or two past three weeks. You know how many are desperate to fill our beds."

Panic snaked through my belly. She rose to signal my dismissal, patting down her skirt. I rose with Charlotte and started out the door.

"Neaten yourself and the baby," she called. "I'll send for the doctor and someone from the family."

Back in our room, I settled Charlotte in my lap, then wrote to the Philadelphia Ladies' Solace to ask for help obtaining a sewing machine. I want to set that alternative in motion, despite Delphinia's discouragement. It can't hurt to have another way to earn a living, however insufficient.

I left my letter in the box by the door and carried Charlotte into the courtyard, where I walked the slate path around and around. She made happy noises and rubbed her face into my shoulder. A longing for home arose in me as I took in the sharp perfume of the white narcissus that lined the path, the musty smell of dirt, the frilly daffodils. I thought of the hundreds of spring-blooming bulbs Mother and I planted in years past, which by now must be passing their heady fragrances through the windows of our old stone house. Might I walk there with Charlotte someday and point out to her these lasting effects of her grandmother's and her mother's hands?

I walked a few more times around the enclosure, slowly so as not to bring on the bleeding that I now know occurs after giving birth. Then Charlotte and I went inside, sprinkled with sun and softened by the air. Anne met us at the side door and bid me to neaten up and come to the office, for the doctor and the baby's father were due at any time.

For Charlotte I chose the white petticoat and gown that Gina had made for us. While pinning on a clean diaper, I pricked my finger accidentally and marked the gown with a spot of blood. I adjusted the pins and combs in my hair, changed the rag over my shoulder for a clean one, and headed down the hall with not a little nervousness.

Anne stood tapping her foot outside the office and waved me in. Opposite her desk stood two men. One was clean-shaven, with a large brow and keen, attentive eyes; the other, very tall, with a pinched face and a frivolous moustache. The first man proved to be the baby's father. The dour man who looked me up and down intently was his doctor and gatekeeper.

"I'm Doctor Snowe," said the dour one, bowing his thin frame slightly. A nervous odor enveloped him. He gave a smile that revealed several gold-capped teeth.

"Albert Burnham," said the other man, tipping his head. The fine lines and dark shading around his eyes suggested weariness and worry.

I greeted them, and a bit of awkwardness ensued as we sought a modest seating arrangement. Finally they stood with their backs to a wall and allowed me to occupy the wide bench. In my lap, Charlotte began to wiggle.

"Miss de Jong is the best you'll find in any place," said Anne from behind her desk.

"I'll decide that," said the doctor, sniffing. He turned to me, his pencil raised, ready to record my words in his notebook. "When did your family come to this country, and from where?"

"Of what interest is this to thee?" I had no intention of describing my family.

"Your nature is quite influenced by your heritage, Miss de Jong. The Irish girls are wont to drink. The Germans are industrious but tough. The Italians make tender mothers and have plenty of milk. The Scots are —"

I interrupted. "And every one has that of God within her."

A flash of amusement crossed Albert Burnham's face.

The doctor's pencil wagged as he wrote. "I take it you're a Quaker."

"I no longer attend Meeting."

He nodded. "Judging from the surname, of Dutch extraction. And might you know when your family came to the United States?"

"In the late seventeenth century." I suppose I have some pride in this — unwarranted, since it reflects no choice of mine and certainly no virtue.

Yet the doctor seemed to dislike the information. He turned to his client and whispered, seeming to mean for the other man to doubt my suitability.

"Continue the interview," ordered the baby's father. "My wife was unhappy with the coarseness of the other nurses you sent."

The doctor made a noise in his throat. "As you wish."

He instructed me to stand, which I did, and to move in a circle so he could examine my every side. I began to quiver as I received

161

praise for my physical attributes, which I've never gotten in such abundance nor wanted less. I was called fresh and rosy, suitably plump, possessed of an adequate musculature, well proportioned, and without a single facial defect that might suggest inferior character. Clear eyes, a well-formed and modest-sized nose, white teeth, medium lips rather than large. All was taken to reveal a strong constitution and an even disposition. But Dr. Snowe sought further proof.

"Are you given to temper, miss? Have you ever had a problem with excessive appetite or excessive passion?"

"Clearly she has principles," said Albert Burnham. He looked away and cleared his throat. "Or *once* had."

I found no words for speaking. I bent my head to Charlotte, who waved an arm and banged me in the face, giving out a hungry moan.

"Must she answer?" said Anne impatiently. "I tell you, she has a modest and an unassuming way."

I was surprised but grateful that she'd describe me thusly.

"A baby drinks in the sentiments along with the nutriments," said Dr. Snowe. "They form his body and his mind." He turned his thin torso toward Albert. "Your wife's esteemed father would expect a thorough evaluation of the temperament."

Albert nodded and looked at me. I had to speak.

"My students," I began, "found me patient and inspirational." The two men stared as though I'd grown a second head.

"You're a teacher?" Once more, Albert appeared amused, but the doctor didn't. He leaned to whisper something that made Albert color slightly.

Worry stabbed my heart. Might I be rejected? I softened my demeanor, so as to seem more pliant. Then Charlotte began to bawl outright.

"You ought to evaluate the infant while you can," Anne suggested. So I held out my unhappy baby. Her cries were subdued by interest as the doctor felt her arm, peeked under her gown to gauge her plumpness, examined her skin, looked into her eyes, touched the bottoms of her feet to judge her reactions, looked up her nose, and otherwise investigated her condition.

"She's how old?" he asked. She stared at him, neck upright, which Delphinia says is beyond her age.

"Just under three weeks," I replied quietly.

"And you verify that this is your baby?" With his forward-leaning head and bulging eyes, he looked like a frog about to shoot its tongue at an insect.

"Of course she is," said Anne. "Why else would Miss de Jong be in my institution?"

"Well then, you have a sound specimen," he affirmed. "Early signs of superior intelligence. Clearly your nurturance is more than adequate."

I felt pleased, despite the circumstances. But by this time Charlotte was rooting at my chest and kicking, bringing a tingling to my breasts. The milk was on its way, and my front would soon be wet if her crying continued.

Anne stood and walked to me. "Give her over."

As I did, Charlotte turned her round face in my direction and opened her mouth in a cry.

Anne spoke to the men. "I'll take the infant to Miss Partridge, our matron. She can distract her till you're through." She began to step out, then said over Charlotte's wails, "Miss de Jong is not above hard work, despite her level of education. We require it here."

With that she carried Charlotte away. The doctor shut the door and moved toward the bench where I sat.

"Just how much education do you have?

What subjects did you teach?" He formed his lips into a prune.

"Twelve years of schooling and two years' training for my work. I taught rhetoric and composition."

He pulled his head backward on his neck and complained into the ear of his client: "Too much learning agitates a woman's mind and brings unquietness to her milk." Then, to me: "One doesn't expect to find your type in such an institution."

I nodded, familiar with his fondness for types.

He peered at me. "Are you willing to work as a household servant and get no special treatment?"

"Yes." That was obviously the correct answer. It seemed I wouldn't be receiving the consideration and fine foods Delphinia had predicted.

"Well, you're of good stock," he summarized, looking over his notes. "Possessed of a fine pink complexion and a full head of hair. Evidently you're amply supplied with milk, as the infant has grown portly in a short time. The deposits of subcutaneous fat are impressive. And your milk is young." To his employer he said, "Since her baby is a mere week older, Henry will get the rich milk suited to his age. He needs that to increase his weight."

The other man grew somber at the mention of his son's condition.

"But we need to be certain of her milk's quality," the doctor said. "There's a life at stake. We'll need to examine her mammary glands and take a milk sample with a pump. I'll bring it to the hospital for a microscopic inspection."

To his credit, the father reddened — as did I. By this time I was holding my arms at a slight distance from my front, for my milk was wetting my underlayers, and I didn't want to push my bodice against them and make the wetness visible.

"Is that necessary? The baby gives us proof," said Albert.

Then we heard quick footsteps, and with a swish of skirts Anne entered. She asked the state of our proceedings with a prim demeanor, and the doctor desisted from his last pursuit. Instead, he cleared his throat. "May I have this young woman's medical records?"

Anne unlocked the cabinet with current records and handed him a slim folder. He perused the pages and looked at me.

"All's in order," he said. "Have you nursed any babies besides your own?"

"No," I replied.

"Why do you ask this?" said Anne, her dark eyebrows rising.

"Anyone engaged in charitable work with infants ought to know that babies can carry syphilis from their mothers." He raised a hand to twirl a tip of his moustache as he spoke. "With their wet little mouths on their nurse's nipples, they pass the disease along."

"I'm aware of that," Anne said. "But I know how to examine the infants."

"Oh, do you?" Dr. Snowe snorted. "Then you ought to teach the medical profession. We can't yet claim such certainty."

Anne fumed. I thanked Charlotte silently for her nursing rigor, since it had spared me from taking on a foundling.

"I presume, Doctor," Anne said, "*you* have ensured that your charge has no diseases to pass to Miss de Jong." She pressed her wide lips closed.

I heard his answer gratefully. "I've been his mother's doctor for many years, and through the pregnancy and delivery. There's no possibility of contagion."

Outside, a church bell rang four times. Drops of milk trickled to my stomach. The doctor's expression changed to one of sympathy.

"I have one more question," he said to me. "What brought you to this reduced

167

condition?"

Anne coughed once into her hand; I turned to the window. Two jet-black crows pecked among the roots of a tree. Crows can live a hundred years, some in devoted pairs.

"I was betrayed," I whispered.

"What? Speak up!" said Dr. Snowe.

My shout came fierce and guttural. "I was betrayed!"

The doctor blanched and pressed no further. Albert Burnham looked at the floor, his face abruptly stiff — as if he might have betrayed a girl or two himself. Then he leaned to the doctor and gave his consent.

"We'll hire her, then," the doctor told Anne. "Twenty-five dollars a month."

What a fortune! Anne looked to me. Speedily I consented. The doctor pulled from his jacket an agreement for Albert Burnham and me to sign in duplicate. I had no chance to read it, for Delphinia's quick footsteps and Charlotte's wails were coming near, but at my word, Anne signed in my place. Then the matron burst in with Charlotte, and I stayed behind while the men were escorted out.

To what exactly had I consented? As I nursed, I read the agreement. I was surprised to see that the family would pay the

Haven a placement fee of thirty dollars, which might help explain Anne's and Delphinia's eagerness to move me toward such work. Also I'm to have cleaning and cooking duties in the Burnham household. And the agreement lists two addresses: one downtown, on Pine Street, and the other in the Tulpehocken section of Germantown, to which we'll go for summer — less than half a mile from my home. I could be spied by someone I know! Worse yet is this: I can only visit Charlotte once a week — and not at all for the first two weeks.

Oh — and I'm to begin tomorrow.

I must be grateful and not afraid! So much is going smoothly. Delphinia even said she'll bring Charlotte to a wet nurse herself. She hopes it will be a young woman who gave birth here several months ago, who lives in an area of squat row-houses south of Rittenhouse Square, not a dozen blocks from the Burnhams. Her mother allowed her to come back home with her baby, and she's taking in others.

"She's not refined," Delphinia told me. "But she has a gentle way."

When tears escaped my eyes, Delphinia patted my shoulder and echoed Anne's earlier assurances. "Don't fret, Lilli. Anyone can care for them at this age. It makes no difference to the babies."

Charlotte has just gotten her last bath at her mother's hands. No, not her last — only for six months or so, until I've saved enough to lease a sewing machine and a room. She's nursing at my left side now, warming me with her still-damp flesh, which makes me think of rising dough.

I wish to remember our weeks here. To remember that a dishpan serves as her tub, a strip of cheesecloth as the washrag. To remember how she wriggles her limbs and looks into my eyes happily as I dip the cloth in warm water and draw it across her, avoiding the stump of her umbilical cord. To remember how washing her naked form brings back the moment when she was placed upon me, the moment when I recognized her as my own.

Yet early tomorrow I'll leave her with Delphinia, who won't bring her to the woman near Rittenhouse Square after all. That one had no place for another baby. She'll bring her instead to a woman named Gerda who resides in a part of the city I've never had cause to visit. It must be hard to find a wet nurse who's willing to take in a bastard; Anne had to canvass among their advisory board to get this recommendation.

The items I've gathered from the donations closet for Charlotte — diapers, pins, binders, shirts, and more — are wrapped in a wool blanket at the foot of my cot. For her travels tomorrow, I've laid out the gown that Gina made, along with a miniature cloak, a hood (in which is pinned a fortnight's payment), and a cap I knitted. Her nurse will be more apt to treat her caringly if she arrives well dressed.

Beside Charlotte's bundle sit my clothes — the plain ones, which are tight but befit the Friend I used to be, and the more worldly things selected by Delphinia for my new position. She brought them this morning in a tall pile. "Don't think I'm giving you so much for your own sake," she said. "You'll need to dress well for the Burnhams."

First she offered a green satin bodice with velvet at the sleeve ends, a matching skirt, and an overskirt trimmed in velvet. These gorgeous items, she said, I ought to reserve for my arrival at the place and for any social events I might have to attend with the baby. She also gave me two shirtwaists with shell buttons down their fronts, a long brown skirt and brown bodice trimmed with brown ribbon, two white caps, and ankle-high boots with French heels, which I hope won't lead me to fall in the street. Mother would have deemed this frivolous clothing a scandal. Ribbons! Velvet! Green satin! I was exultant.

"Try some on," urged Delphinia. I selected the green outfit and a cap and ducked behind the dressing screen. The moment I stepped back into view, Delphinia gasped and rushed from the room. She returned with a large hand mirror.

"Look!" She chuckled with glee as she held the mirror at various angles and distances. I gazed giddily into the mirror until she tucked it under the bed, whispering: "Don't tell Mrs. Pierce!"

Encouraging vanity is not Anne's way. But already Delphinia and her mirror had given me an insight — that if I had been differently born, I would have made a convincing lady. Even with my hair in disarray, and my complexion shadowed by a dearth of sleep and sunlight, I looked elegant, *important.*

If Mother could have seen me, and heard my thoughts, she might have said, "Anyone can be outwardly improved by fine fabrics and tailoring. Attend to thy soul, Lilli, and life's true riches will unfold."

Of course that's right. Yet I was thrilled to see myself made outwardly pleasing.

But how can I write of such matters? A

warm being has nursed to satisfaction and sleeps in surrender at my side, knowing nothing of our imminent separation. I stare at her tender face, her slackened lips, her nostrils that flare as she exhales. Tendrils of damp hair cling at her temples. Her puffed-up abdomen rises and falls beneath her gown. Her knees poke upward, and her tiny hands are curled at her chest. I watch her, and to my mind comes a verse of the Song of Songs: *Behold, thou art beautiful, my love; behold, thou art beautiful.*

She opens her indigo eyes to stare into mine, then nurses more. What pleasure, to feel the tug of her lips, to hear her gulp and see lines of white slide down her chin.

The house and street are silent around us. It seems only she and I are awake, though some young woman upstairs may be troubled by discomfort and wondering if her labor has begun.

I must put this pencil down so I can cradle my Lotte in both arms and kiss her silken forehead and croon to her.

I am my beloved's and my beloved is mine.

Come morning, to secure our future good, I'll leave my beloved behind.

■ ■ ■ ■

NOTEBOOK FOUR

■ ■ ■ ■

Fourth Month 18

This morning I dressed my darling and myself in traveling clothes. I nursed that bundle of softness once more. And as she fell into slumber, head and body going limp against me, I slipped my nipple from her mouth and gave her to Delphinia.

Her limbs jerked; she began to wail. I lifted my valise. As though stepping off a cliff, I stepped out the front door and down the steps and into the Burnhams' shiny carriage.

The driver urged the horse into motion. The carriage bumped over rutted streets. And the feeling that came over me was terror. With each turn of the wheels pulling me farther from my baby, I sat on my hands and panted, my mind like an enormous bell, clanging: *What will become of her? What will become of me, without her near? What have I done?*

Soon we pulled in front of a narrow three-story brownstone, only a few blocks from elegant Rittenhouse Square. The driver deposited me and my valise before its door, then left to care for the horse. I wiped away my tears and slowed my heart with willful breathing.

I climbed the marble stoop, and before I'd even knocked, a young maid swung open the door and curtsied. She was a picture of formality in her starched black gown, white cap, and lace-trimmed apron. After introducing herself as Margaret and thanking me for accepting their wet-nurse position, she brought me through a hall into the kitchen, which was large and homely. Then we went up one flight of thin, curving servants' stairs, down a short length of hall, and up another narrow stair to the servants' story. She pointed my way into a slope-ceilinged garret — a cramped room holding a bed that met three walls, a chest of drawers, a washbasin and pitcher, a chamber pot, and an empty trunk. An oval window at the foot of the bed brought in light and air.

Margaret seemed responsible and thoughtful, though she can't be more than fourteen. She'd taken pains to clean my room in advance and to set me up with a fat feather bed atop the mattress. The home's gas lighting doesn't extend to the servants' story, so she ran to fetch me paraffin candles from the cellar. I'll be glad for them. Their light and smell will link me to evenings at home when we sat together around the oak table, Mother and I doing our own work while Father and his helpers kept their books.

In her melodious voice, Margaret told me of the feeding arrangements till now for the infant, Henry. The mistress fired two wet nurses in quick succession, so for several days the cook's daughter nursed him during the day, as she'd recently weaned her own son. At night, Margaret hand-fed the baby with a bottle of boiled cow's milk, water, and sugar. The artificial food upset his stomach, so he bent his legs in pain even as he drank, then spit up substantially after. Margaret had to perform her household labor in the day as well.

"We need the help badly. Thank you again," she told me, leaning on the door frame.

"I need the position badly, and I'm grateful for it," I replied.

She said she'd return to let me know when the mistress was ready to meet me. She stood a moment longer in a near-trance of fatigue, her blue eyes half closed and staring into space, before clicking back to alertness and running to whatever task I'd interrupted.

During her short absence, questions spun through my head. Was Charlotte being delivered to her nurse at that moment? What sense could she possibly make of my arms and breasts, my familiar smells and sounds, being so suddenly gone?

Soon Margaret summoned me down a flight of stairs to the doorway of a sitting room. She curtsied to the lady inside, who motioned from her desk for me to enter.

The room was lovely, with a gold velvet settee and matching chairs, tapestry-like drapes over its tall windows, and an Oriental carpet that cushioned my steps. The person behind the cherrywood desk looked lovely, too — with refined features and a pile of light brown curls upon her head. Her clear green eyes spoke of intelligence. Yet instantly she was unpleasant toward me. She appeared no more than a few years past me in age, and she held herself erect, as any woman in a tight corset must.

"My husband says our doctor chose better this time," she began. "So I needn't examine you." She observed me a moment. "You're well dressed for household help."

I flushed. "These clothes were donated to

the — the place where I was living."

"And where *were* you living?" She raised her well-shaped eyebrows.

"A lying-in hospital."

She ought to have known this from her husband. But she raised her hands in a questioning gesture. "A hospital? Are you ill? Doctor Snowe can't have overlooked this."

I decided to be as blunt as she. "It was a charity for unwed mothers."

"Ah." She nodded. "So you're no improvement over the other nurses. In fact, you're worse. Two of them were widows. Our cook's daughter is married." She emitted an odd sound, half laugh, half snort. "Our doctor must have determined that at least your *milk* is pure."

I reminded myself that I should expect no better, since I was no longer within Anne's sheltering walls. "Yes," I replied, nodding slightly.

The lady shrugged. "You'll be gone before my son can even speak. I'm sure you'll have little influence."

I was stunned. She was dismissing the effects of my work before I'd even begun it. But I kept nodding. "Yes, madam."

"Call me Clementina," she said. "When someone calls me *madam,* I think they

181

mean my mother."

It was easy to perceive that vanity, not egalitarianism, motivated this request. Yet her preference served me well, since I was raised to call people by their names, not by titles.

"What's *your* name?" she finally asked.

"Lillian de Jong. Usually I'm called Lilli."

She gestured with her head toward the door. "The nursery is down the hall to the left, Lilli. Once you've fed the baby, go to the kitchen and ask our cook to assign your other duties." She turned her head down to the papers spread before her, then raised it once more. "Do you wish to keep this position, Lilli?"

"Yes, Clementina," I replied.

"Then never let my son's cries rise to a level that disturbs me. I have a newspaper column to write nearly every day. And do as our cook tells you; don't seek *me* out. If I need you, I'll send Margaret." Down went her head. I was dismissed.

It must pain Clementina to squeeze into a corset little more than a week after delivery, not to mention that she must be binding her breasts to stop her milk. These things might help explain her dourness. I made such excuses readily while walking down the hall — until I saw her son.

A baby's whole body being visible at once, one can form an instant sense of its condition. And already this boy gave off an air of anxiousness and privation. He lay on his back in a finely wrought metal crib with dulled eyes and a pinched expression. The elegant petticoat and slip of white nainsook covering him couldn't disguise his misery and lack of vigor. I leaned over the rails, and he emitted a whimper that made me lift him immediately.

I sat in the rocker and opened my clothing. A shudder passed through me as I guided his lips and mouth to my nipple. After a few seconds of fumbling, he latched on and fed.

I was as put off by the neediness of his suck as by the large size of his head, with its dark eyebrows and its nose that was far broader than Charlotte's. He nursed more quickly than my darling and sank into oblivion. When I placed him in the crib, he didn't startle or awaken.

I waited a moment, marveling at this simplicity, and grateful, and hoping my milk would improve his condition. Then I went off to find the cook.

Unfortunately I set her against me by descending the wide front stairs and walking through the foyer and hall to the kitchen at the back of the house. When I entered her domain, she turned an angry face my way. A stout woman of middling height, she had a ruddy complexion and thinning hair held back severely with pins and combs.

"You *must,*" she reprimanded — stepping back from her cast-iron pots — "use the back stairs into the kitchen. Don't make the Burnhams see a servant unless they call for one." She removed her thick-lensed glasses to wipe away the fog brought on by the steaming pots. She told me her name was Frau Varschen — "and that's the only name you ought to go a'bothering."

I focused on her stocky black shoes, my eyes stinging with tears, as I apologized for having taken the wrong stairs. "My family didn't have servants," I explained, "and most people we knew didn't either."

This made her laugh, a harsh sound that set my skin to prickling. "D'you think I learned to be a cook by having one?"

I was a fool. "What I ought to say," I corrected with embarrassment, "is that I'm not as knowledgeable as thee about the right ways of behaving. I promise to learn quickly and to do as thee directs."

Her irritation eased slightly. "Come find me in the kitchen or the garden when Henry sleeps. I'm here six-thirty in the morning to eight at night, every day but the Lord's. I'll find you a task."

"But when can I make up for the sleep I'll lose at night?" I asked. She wanted me to work around the clock! To mute my forwardness, I looked down at the floor's pine planks.

"I hear you'll be the best paid in the house," she retorted, "and that comes with hard labor."

She turned back to the polished stove, took up a wooden spoon in each hand, and stirred whatever filled her pots. Then she turned again to examine me, apparently perceiving my depleted condition. Exhaling through her nose and losing some of her fierceness, she pointed with an elbow toward the back stairs.

"You go settle in," she directed. "I'll make the soup today."

So her heart can soften, which is a lucky thing. And I do enjoy getting my hands dirty in the kitchen and the garden, which may help bring her view of me around.

I should have unpacked and rested, but I gain a sense of company when I confide my doings here. Without Charlotte, I have no other true companion — apart from the sun, which is the most faithful friend of every creature and growing thing. Now it

185

sets, filling the window at the foot of my bed, pouring its glow over these words, bringing a measure of ease to a worried mother's heart.

Henry woke me, calling out in hunger. My heart thumped wildly and my throat narrowed, for I thought his cry was Charlotte's, and she'd been stolen from my side. I shot up in bed and banged my head on the sloped ceiling — a rough way to come to one's senses. Out the window the moon was visible, hot and yellow, staring in like a single eyeball.

Henry's calls were rising in pitch. Clementina had said never to let them disturb her. I pushed the covers back, turned sideways, and planted my feet on the cold planks. Shivering, I lit a candle and scuttled to the second story. I nursed and changed him, startled at his thinness, then laid him back in his crib. From his big feet and hands, I guessed that one day he'd tower over me. I paused to watch his rib cage rise and fall beneath his clothes, marveling at the ease with which he sank into sleep and pleased by the slight improvement in his pallor.

Yet back in my room, I'm ridden with guilt. I give my care to a stranger while Charlotte has been stripped of the love she needs and rightfully owns. She may even be wailing for me, unheeded, at this moment.

Who is this Gerda? I won't know for thirteen days.

Dear Lord, please give my baby a kind face that peers down at her, a lilting voice that soothes her cries, rich milk that fills her belly. . . .

In the darkness of this slant-roofed room, miles from the one who needs me most, I'm unable to find a reassuring thought.

I recall the counsel Paul gave to the Corinthians: "Be watchful, stand firm in thy faith, be courageous, be strong."

"And go to sleep while thee can," my mother whispers inside me.

Charlotte's dear countenance comes into my mind, first with its features pressed together by the rigors of birth, then growing smoother and more distinct, then showing the glinting eyes and smile she gave at feeling her first breeze. . . .

Fourth Month 19

I'll be in need of much humility in this household.

Two of Clementina's friends were coming to tea. In preparation, she had me dress Henry in his best lace shirt, petticoat, and slip, and told me not to swaddle him. When the ladies rang the bell and were announced by Margaret, he was nursing avidly. But his mother had me detach him and carry him down the back stairs while he burrowed against me, seeking darkness.

I joined the women in the foyer, where Clementina kissed her friends — "Letitia! Marie!"

Exclaiming with gladness, they shed their feather-laden hats and light cloaks into Margaret's arms.

"Let me see the little fellow!" said Letitia. She was the tall and dark-haired one. Her cheekbones were raised high and her mouth was open with pleased anticipation.

"Do let us look," echoed the shorter and plumper Marie.

Clementina gestured for me to lift him. I did so. Their smiles fell; they must have been startled by his anxious, big-featured face. Then Henry scowled and emitted some half-digested milk that landed on Marie's silk-covered shoe.

"Oh, it's nothing," said Marie, observing her shoe in dismay.

"Margaret!" Clementina called. She glared at me as if I'd done the spitting up until Margaret ran in. "Clean this for Mrs. Forman."

Marie handed the shoe to Margaret,

doubtful.

"Let's have some tea," called Clementina, aiming to restore the festive atmosphere, and the ladies moved into the parlor, with Marie hobbling unevenly behind. They sat at a small round table to one side of the room. I found a settee nearby, where Henry began to root into my chest, leaving wet spots on my gray bodice. I've managed to fit into some of my plain clothes, and I'm combining them with the finer pieces Delphinia selected so as to be less of a spectacle.

Not that anyone would notice my clothing in a parlor such as theirs. The walls contain portraits of relatives who look out with fixed expressions, fierce or stern; the wallpaper behind them is riotous with stripes and flowers. Carved lintels adorn the window frames, and wide, ornate moldings follow the ceiling's perimeter. A mirror half the height of the room reflects the large parlor dome on a stand before it. Inside the clear glass dome, stuffed tropical birds cavort on branches, trapped in false joy.

The women settled into their seats, arranging skirts and bodices. I sensed a pall caused by Henry's unwell condition, but perhaps I misperceived, for the visitors made no mention of it.

"What a lovely table!" said Letitia. Before

them sat the two fruit tarts and the pile of sweet buns that Frau Varschen and I had prepared.

"Scrumptious," concurred Marie. To my amusement, she blew a kiss at the confections.

Clementina was unimpressed. "Margaret!"

The girl came in flustered, her freckled cheeks pink against the bounteous brown curls peeking from her cap. "If you'll forgive me, I've treated the stain, but the silk —"

"Never mind." Clementina waved her hand to the side. "We'll find another pair tomorrow. Serve our tea."

Margaret's face was impassive as she poured and served. She must be used to such roughness. But I'm not, and I feared becoming its next target. For Henry had begun to moan, wanting into my clothing. Then he began to cry outright.

"Have you been to the new Frank Harvey play at the Olympic Theater?" Letitia asked Marie, overriding Henry. "*The Wages of Sin.* It's splendid! The costumes! And the story, *bien sûr,* pure heartbreak." She put one hand over her chest and lifted her tea with the other to take a delicate sip. "A young woman should have married a good man who loved her, but she distrusted him and sank into vice by marrying a cad."

"I wish I could go," Marie said. "With my husband sick, I've cut back on outings. But there's nothing like a good production to bring one's feelings to the fore." She bit into a tart and gave its shiny fruits an appreciative look as she chewed.

"Have you been, Clementina?" Letitia said.

Clementina brought her attention to the table briefly. "I'm reviewing it for *The Herald*. I found it trifling. The same story of a foolish woman who steps outside the bounds allowed her, only to be ruined by a man. I'd prefer it if she'd triumphed."

Inwardly, I couldn't help but agree.

"Of course," said Letitia tightly. "It's the opposite of what you did in marrying Albert. You wanted to marry a cad but ended up with a good, educated man who loves you."

Clementina stiffened; Marie's face darkened.

"He wasn't a cad," said Clementina, "he was an actor. He loved me."

Marie brightened with kind intention. "When will your review appear? I love your clever words."

Henry gave out a loud squall.

"Ah!" groaned Clementina, gesturing at me. "This nurse can't quiet him!"

191

Letitia raised her head — piled with elaborate curls like Clementina's — and swallowed her bite of tart. "He must prefer his mother," she said sweetly. "I know my Lizzy does."

Marie concurred. "I don't take on the menial parts — the feeding and the changing. But when my boy needs comfort . . ." She made it plainer. "Well, no one's as good as Mother."

Clementina blanched, but Letitia pressed further. "We won't mind if you hold him, will we, Marie?" She looked at her friend.

"Oh, no." Marie shook her petite head side to side.

Clementina stood and thrust her arms toward me. I passed Henry over and laid the rag that catches his spit-up across the beaded shoulder of her bodice. She sat with Henry and fixed a sympathetic look on her face, but she kept his body at a distance, as though he were a muddy boot. He wailed louder and twisted his head toward me as Clementina struggled to contain him. She pushed his bottom down onto her lap. Her guests watched closely, raising forks to mouths.

"What's gotten into him?" said Clementina. "Nurse, fetch what you need to swaddle him. I don't know why you insist on keeping him free."

I flinched at her dishonesty as Letitia whispered loudly, "These nurses never do as we ask. You'd think, for as much as we pay . . ."

I was rising from the settee to do as Clementina had commanded when she screeched. On her lap, beneath Henry, a stain spread across her lavender skirt.

Placing Henry on the floor, she grabbed the rag from her shoulder and dabbed at the urine. Her friends looked on with widened eyes, then applied themselves to their tea, faces tight in disciplined composure. Henry raised the pitch of his wail and thrashed his legs. Clementina lifted him and thrust him into my arms, where he mouthed me frantically. Turning to her guests, Clementina brightened her demeanor and bared her teeth. "Please excuse me a moment."

"Of course," said Letitia, a smile starting at one corner of her mouth. "We'll have a chance to catch up, won't we, Marie?"

"Very good," Marie said airily, looking at nothing with studied innocence above the rim of her raised teacup.

Clementina rushed out — nearly colliding with Margaret, who was en route from cellar to kitchen and who backed against the wall with a bucket of coal to each side. The lady raced upstairs, and I followed — assuming that, in her company, I may use those stairs. She entered her bedroom and slammed the door.

I walked into the nursery and peeled off Henry's clothes. After cleaning and diapering him, I settled in the rocker to nurse. From down the hall I heard Clementina's angry movements. Soon, in a different gown, she stood at the opened nursery door. The sound of laughter rose from the parlor.

"You humiliated me," she hissed.

Hardly! I took a long breath in and out, knowing I'd best not speak. No wonder two nurses had already failed to please her. Perhaps they'd even left by choice.

She stormed down to her purported friends. I rose with Henry to shut the nursery door and sat again. Soon he was nodding off, yet I didn't dare leave, in case he awoke in distress and cried, and she found this humiliating as well, with her friends to witness once more that she would not — could not — comfort him.

It's deep in the night. The house and street are silent, save the ticking of the grandfather clock in the foyer two stories down. I've just nursed Henry and returned to my room, and again I'm ridden with guilt. Because even as I find Henry's intimacy with my body jarring, my heart must incline toward this baby. He responds with eagerness when I enter his room, and the very act of nursing unites us in a deepening calm.

Yet there is a difference between this sympathy and what I feel for Charlotte. When Henry's in distress, my response is tolerable. I can finish folding a blanket, or slice an apple, or write a few more words. Whereas I used to feel Charlotte's very breathing in my body, and when she cried, a knife's tip scored my heart.

Thus, with Henry, I can rest.

So even as I worry over Charlotte, a secret part of me is glad to be more free.

Fourth Month 20

I sent a note by post to the wet nurse Gerda this morning, inquiring in simple language how Charlotte is faring. If she can't read, I hope she'll find someone who can. I asked her to answer with a letter or a messenger and promised to repay any costs — though I have but a few dollars remaining, till I'm paid on the first of next month.

Then, with Henry fed and sleeping, I started down the back stairs to get my instructions from Frau Varschen. I stopped on hearing her loud words.

"She's mixing up the household! Talking alone with Mr. Burnham!"

My skin shrank. The man had entered the nursery before leaving for his office, while I was dressing Henry; he was pleased to see an increase in the baby's vigor. The visit had taken no more than a minute.

"I don't mean to be contrary," tried Margaret, "but Mr. Burnham only wanted —"

"Shush!" said the cook. "There could be trouble, I'm telling you."

They fell to silence. I waited briefly, then descended the stairs and opened the door into the kitchen. Margaret sat at the table, her head bent over a plate of beans. Frau V. kneaded dough on the lid of her trough, picking up the heavy heap and slamming it down repeatedly. The stove burned hot, and the cook's face was pink and sweaty.

"Shall I start on the soup?" I asked, the pulse quick at my throat.

Frau V. nodded. "We need beef juice for my bean soup, and the bones are boiling." She gestured toward a pail. "Take some beans and sort out the dirt and rocks."

I filled a plate and sat beside Margaret. As we searched for debris, I felt much unrest and sensed the same in Margaret's quick breaths. The cook broke the quiet.

"How do you like this house?"

"It's well built," I said, "with good materials." I looked up at the exposed beams of the kitchen ceiling, which are incredibly thick, then at the stone hearth, where a rack of lamb roasted over a pan. The aroma made my mouth water.

"But it's far from the finest house on the block. Are you used to finer?" The cook gave a laugh, then applied the back of her wrist to wipe sweat from her temples.

"Oh, no. I'm used to a small stone house with nothing fine about it, except my family."

Margaret piped in. "Where is this house? How many sisters and brothers?" She dumped her beans into a pot on the stove and got another plateful from the pail.

"The house is in Germantown," I said. "I have a brother. He's twenty-one, which is two years younger than me." In my mind I added, *and I don't know where he is anymore.*

"Is he handsome?" Margaret covered her smile with a hand. I pictured Peter pushing his golden-brown hair from his broad forehead, saw his hazel eyes and sturdy shoulders.

"I suppose so. The girls at school found him handsome." To me, gentleness had been his more salient quality.

"Germantown's not far off," observed the

cook. "Will you be having visitors?" She divided her dough into four parts and began forming one into a loaf. "Margaret's family came in from the country once. We ate in the kitchen, and Mrs. Burnham had nothing bad to say about it."

Margaret smiled without covering her mouth this time, allowing me to see the dimples at its corners. "Frau Varschen loves to lay out tea."

"I won't have visitors," I said. "My mother died more than a year ago — my brother left for work in Pittsburgh. My — my father, he —"

Frau V. stared. "Why are you here? Can't you find work that lets you live at home? Your father needs you!"

The two looked at me expectantly, but I couldn't speak. I was basking in an unfamiliar pleasure. They didn't yet know of my disgraced status, and this gave me a sensation as refreshing as a swim in a stream on a bright, hot day. Perhaps they took me for a mother who'd just weaned her child.

They gave up waiting for my response. Margaret and I dumped our beans again into the pot and scooped up more. Frau V. left her braided loaves to let them rise, then shook down ashes and loaded coal into the stove.

"That was two years ago," Margaret said, "when my family visited. My sister writes, and Frau Varschen reads the letters to me."

"Thee hasn't gone to school?" I asked.

She shook her head. "My oldest sister went three years, but then my father got his leg crushed at the lumber mill. She left school to work at the cotton mill, and when each of us turned five, we joined her there."

A stunted childhood, and then a life of serving others without cease.

"I'll teach thee," I told her. "I am — I used to be — a teacher."

Frau V. turned from the stove, face glistening. "A schoolmarm! I knew there was something grand about you. If it's not money makes a person grand, it's book learning."

Margaret clapped her hands excitedly and stood up. "I'm going to learn my letters!" She reached her arms about me.

I couldn't recall the last time someone had clasped me tight, and I relished it. Too quickly she withdrew her arms and sighed. "I have to ask the Burnhams first. I can't take my time or yours without permission."

"You ask Mr. B. tonight," said the cook, nodding.

"I'll do that." Margaret's mouth formed a frown; her blue eyes gathered moisture. She expected disappointment.

"And if he says no," Frau V. added, "I'll put too much pepper on his eggs tomorrow and give him a fit of sneezes." She threw her head back and guffawed, and Margaret gave a smile. Then the cook cried out, "This calls for my spring tonic!"

Margaret brought three earthenware cups, and Frau V. ladled her tea from a pot on the back burner. My mother had made a tonic each spring, too, using roots and greens from the woods. The three of us drank the dark liquid, our faces bright and pleased despite its bitterness. The hot tea traced a path of relaxation through me, until Henry's cries penetrated the calm.

As I nursed him, I considered the cook's concern at Albert speaking with me. Why did this arouse her ire? Why wasn't she upset instead by Clementina's disinterest in her son? She's gotten strangers with breasts full of milk to provide his nutriment, but why withhold her love?

Henry may always feel homeless, for he was exiled at birth from his native land.

Just listen to this hypocrite! The baby who gained her form amid the beats of my heart and the sounds of my voice is farther from her native land, and even more an exile.

■ ■ ■ ■

There's trouble here, more than I knew. Frau Varschen was right.

After supper I fed Henry, then began rocking him to sleep. The Burnhams were in Clementina's bedroom and had failed to close the door.

"Can't you stay in?" I heard him say.

Her voice was harsh. "I have a ticket to the orchestra. Letitia's expecting me."

"But you went to the orchestra last night."

A drawer banged shut. "Tonight a new cellist begins."

"But I left the office early. I hoped to see you for supper." Footsteps moved across the floor.

"Albert, I need to keep up. My column will suffer if I don't."

"Well, I need a wife. I suffer without one."

"You have a wife!"

"But you shun me. And our son — have you laid eyes on him today?"

"Yes. We visited with friends."

"Has he gained any weight?"

"I haven't had a moment to put him on the scale."

"Doctor Snowe said weighing was essential."

201

"I'll ask the nurse to do it tomorrow. Albert, I don't like babies. You knew that."

"I thought you'd change."

"I don't intend to be anyone's cow. You got your son; now let me be." At that, she strode through the hall — I glimpsed a light blue gown with an enormous bustle — and down the stairs. The front door opened and slammed.

In a moment, Albert stood at the nursery door. He was clad in what must have been a smoking jacket, a frivolous satin affair with ribbon at its lapels. Though his face was ruddy, he spoke with deliberate calm. "My wife has gone out. I need a quiet night after a tiring week."

"Ah." I nodded, wondering why he needed to tell me this. Henry lay heavy against my chest; his eyes fluttered as he moved toward slumber.

Albert cleared his throat. "Would you bring Henry to my study? I'd like to see him."

"Where is thy study?" I asked, uneasy. Margaret was clanging pans in the kitchen, washing up; Frau Varschen had gone and thus could neither condemn me nor protect me.

Albert turned toward the front stairs. With a wave he bid me to follow.

I didn't see as I had a choice, so I walked behind, carrying my sleepy package. We turned in the foyer and passed the parlor; Albert opened a carved oak door to a room smelling of leather and tobacco. A wood fire crackled on the grate.

He gestured for me to sit on a large stuffed chair, near to the hearth, and he sat on the facing one. He looked handsome, with his prominent cheekbones and the unblemished skin of a man in good health. His lips are large, like Henry's, but a large forehead offsets them, giving him an intelligent appearance.

Observing all this made me even less at ease. He didn't look at ease, either. But he gave me a thin smile.

I turned away, intrigued by the hundreds of leather-bound volumes lining one wall. Here was the real wealth of the house. Titillation rose in me; this collection wasn't censored by Friends' prohibitions. One day when no one else was about, I might return and explore. I might even try to read a novel or a play. Johan had loved to read the works of poets he called the Romantics, though this had caused friction with his parents and their Meeting. I remembered the name Wordsworth.

Albert pulled a cord to call for Margaret.

She arrived in seconds, whisking stray bangs from her forehead.

"Brandy, please," he said. "Bring the one that just arrived, the cognac, for myself and the nurse."

"Oh, I don't drink brandy," I corrected — as if, in any case, I would drink it with him.

"Wine, then?" His face was stripped of expression.

"No alcohol." I turned to Margaret. "Nothing, please." She nodded and left, then returned with a decanter and one glass. Her manner was tight and awkward, and she kept her eyes from me. Did she suppose I was intentionally making myself her better by sitting with Albert? She poked at the fire, added a log, and left.

Albert drank, his mouth pursing around each sip of the liquid before he swallowed it. Henry gazed, nearly asleep, in his father's direction. Albert made an abrupt, laugh-like sound, giving Henry a start.

"So you don't indulge in alcohol." He gave another laugh that galled me, then delivered his clever formulation: "A woman of principle, recruited from a charity for whores."

Mother had warned me that indulgent folk will disparage those who are less so. Nevertheless, his crudeness pained me. And how melancholy he looked, despite his sarcastic attempt at cheer. Unhappiness had slackened the muscles of his face and dulled his eyes.

"Let me have a turn with the boy," he said, reaching across the space between us. I passed Henry over, and he settled his son in the crook of one arm and watched him. Henry made no protest at the switch. When I commented on Albert's apparent comfort with holding a baby, he said he'd helped raise a younger brother after his mother died.

So we had a mother's death and a younger brother in common. Henry closed his eyes and sank against his father. I stared into the fire. After a silence — a state that Friends tolerate more easily than others — Albert spoke.

"How are you finding your time here?"

"I'm grateful for the work." I smoothed the fabric on my lap and felt a thrill at having no baby on it. If I could have risen and examined the books, that feeling would have grown to elation.

"The food and accommodations are acceptable?"

"Completely."

"And your little girl, she's provided for?"

Worry cut into me. "I know almost nothing of her situation."

"She's been sent to a nurse, of course." Albert's eyes narrowed.

"Yes," I said. "But I don't know how she's faring. I wrote her nurse this morning for news."

He nodded. "It's novel for us to have a nurse who can write well enough to send a letter." Reaching his free arm over Henry's sleeping body, he grabbed his glass and raised it to his mouth.

"Thee might consider it an obligation to educate thy servants," I told him. He swallowed abruptly. "Margaret has lived here several years, and she can't read or write a letter."

He eyed me, taking my measure. "You're feisty, Miss de Jong. But I suppose I forgive you. Quakers feel an obligation to educate everyone, don't they?"

"Everyone has the right to better themselves."

"So what is the Quaker attitude to fallen women?" he said. "Can you better yourself?" He took another sip, amused at his thought. "Say, do they even allow you in the meeting-house?"

"I no longer attend."

"But if you tried to enter, would you be admitted?"

"I don't know of any religion that welcomes a woman in my position into its place of worship." I stared, daring him to press further.

"Ah, then what's the good of this virtue you so heartily aim to maintain?" he asked. "Why bother with your *thee* and *thy*? Why not enjoy a glass of brandy?"

I wanted to protest, but my voice shut down. My face grew hot. Indeed! Why not speak as most others do, and enjoy a glass of brandy, if everyone considers me a sinner without a second thought?

Because habits live on. Because plain speech is a salute to the Inner Light in everyone. Because I cling to the ways of Friends. Because alcohol emboldens the passions and closes the eyes of the spirit.

Margaret returned at Albert's call, a picture of sweet refinement in her black dress, white apron, and cap. She refilled Albert's glass, put the decanter down, and inquired as to whether she could bring anything else.

Albert cocked his head. "Tell me, Margaret. Would you like to learn to read and write?"

Margaret stopped in place, head and shoulders shrinking toward one another, as if afraid of being mocked or punished.

"I'd be glad to teach thee," I reiterated.

"Then yes." Her carriage straightened. "That is, if it's all right with you, Mr. Burnham."

"I've got no grounds to deny it, as long as it doesn't interfere with your work. I'll inform my wife."

"Oh, thank you, sir!" She curtsied, and a grin spread across her freckled face.

He smiled slightly in return. "You're a good girl, Margaret."

When she left, he began to chuckle. "What are you doing to this household? Before long, you'll all be quoting that communist Karl Marx in the kitchen and plotting to take my place."

I resolved to search Albert's bookshelves for something by that man. I'd seen the name but didn't know his philosophy.

Albert took a large gulp of brandy and breathed out its fumes. "Do you suppose your example will do Margaret good?"

"Yes, it's good for her to know an educated servant."

"I mean your — situation," he said. "I shouldn't think you'd consider yourself a beneficial example."

His arrow hit its mark and spread its poison. Margaret might be appalled to learn my full circumstances, and even badly influenced.

In the quiet that followed, Henry began to stir in his father's lap. He opened and closed his lips in a fishlike way, then gave out his early hunger sounds that would lead to crying. I stood.

"May I be excused? Henry needs to nurse."

Albert put on a crooked smile. "I'd like to watch my son take sustenance from a fallen woman, since he can't take it from my virtuous wife." He took a full gulp from his glass.

Panic limited my breathing, as if a body had fallen on my chest. Alcohol certainly deserves its reputation for emboldening the lower appetites.

"But of course that wouldn't be appropriate." Albert put down the glass and raised Henry toward me as the boy's noises grew plangent.

"Of course not." With relief I stepped forward and took Henry.

"Miss de Jong, you interest me." His head swayed slightly as he watched me settle his son in my arms. Red spots colored his cheeks. He moved his hand toward the door, suggesting that I make my way out, then gave me a peculiar grin before shifting to a dreamlike state.

I left in haste with Henry and turned the key in the nursery door once I stood inside that room.

It's been an hour since, judging by the clock's tolling. I'm in my own room now, in bed, and the door has no lock. If Albert comes up here, I'll run to Margaret's room and refuse to be alone with him again.

Fourth Month 21

This morning, Frau V. and I were chopping onions for soup, and the kitchen air was dense with their pungent irritant. As tears wet our cheeks, she returned to the question I'd avoided answering the other day.

"Why aren't you with your father? He must need you, with your mother gone."

I gathered courage and told her of my clandestine pregnancy and my secretive departure. To my relief, her first reactions were sympathetic. But soon she became agitated.

"You didn't try to find the baby's father?"

"I had no address. He sent no letter, and my brother — he's not the letter-writing sort. He's rather shy." I took up a rag and cleared my eyes.

Leaving the board of onions, Frau V. reached into a package for a fish to scale. "So you did nothing?"

"I didn't have the money to travel to Pittsburgh. Even if I had, where would I have stayed, as a woman alone in my condition, and how would I have found them?"

She didn't answer.

"Besides," I tried, "I was weak. I could hardly hold down a bite of food."

These reasons had seemed insurmountable at the time. But in the face of this determined mountain of a woman, they shriveled.

She let out a huff. "And your family gave no help." She threw a scaled, beheaded fish into the bucket of ice at her feet.

I hesitated to agree with so final and condemning a statement. If Mother had lived, she would have helped. No — if Mother had lived, we would have continued to attend Meeting, and I'd have married Johan there. With her gone and Father derailed by grief, however, I had no one to count on. I told the cook all this. "I did give my baby's father's name to a solicitor," I concluded. "He might be found and convinced to give support."

"All right." She nodded. "Maybe that solicitor can get you some funds." Wearing a doubtful scowl, she rinsed her hands at the faucet in the iron sink, lifted the big soup pot to the stovetop, and added a dollop of fat. I pushed the onions off the board into the pot.

"But thee needn't worry," I told her. "I intend to become a sewing woman and raise my baby beside me."

She clamped her hands to her thighs and turned her substantial body toward me. "You intend to keep your baby? Without a husband?"

"Yes." I stirred the onions and dared to look at her. "She's with a wet nurse now."

A strained noise came from Frau V.'s throat. "I didn't know you were mad!" She gestured with her head toward the windows, indicating the outer world that would treat us terribly. "Your lives will be a torment!"

Her reaction flooded me with dread. But I reminded myself that the harder way is often the truer. Almost twenty years ago, my father and two others from our Meeting were conscripted in the War of the Rebellion. They opposed slavery, of course, but they opposed killing, too. So they stood among rifle fire unarmed and were much abused by the other men for their refusal to carry guns. They held firm, drew the attention of commanders, gained their release, and took part in tending the wounded instead.

"Why didn't you write to the baby's

father?" the cook demanded.

"I told thee, I had no address." What did she expect, that I would write to every domicile in Pittsburgh?

She stopped her labor to examine me. "But you can write to anyone care of the post office. You can write your young man that way." She walked to the table and sat on a bench, shaking her head. "Such a smart girl, didn't know that."

It's true; I hadn't known. I'd never had cause to know. "But even so," I objected, "why would he seek mail from me at the post office, if he has no need for me anymore?"

"Sit down," she directed, patting the bench. I picked up a load of potatoes and heaped them on the table. Her wide body took up much of the seating, so I stood to keep my elbow from jabbing her as I peeled. With a heavy exhalation, she reached an arm for the peeler.

"Give me," she said. "I can't stay still. You get a knife and start to cut them." As she peeled and I sliced, she continued. "Young men, they're ignorant. They don't know the value of a woman's love. But if you told him about the baby, maybe he'd come back. If you begged him, he might marry you."

I shook my head side to side.

She admonished me: "Don't be so stubborn."

I stood and walked to the stove to shake down ashes. When I lifted the top and poured in more coal, a wave of red heat rushed out. *My fury is that hot,* I thought. Turning to her, I asked, "Was thee ever deceived and abandoned by a man thee loved — the father of thy child?"

"My Joseph is a good man!" she exclaimed. "We've been married thirty-two years." She nodded and lifted her shoulders proudly. "We have seven children."

Just as I'd expected. "Then thee has no idea of the loathing I feel. To grovel before Johan for help or marriage? I'd rather live on the street! And don't call me stubborn."

"I see you won't be easy to convince." Her wry tone irked me further, and I replied with more than a little warmth.

"That's correct. If thee wants to help me, consider my poor baby's situation. I've never met her nurse, haven't heard from that woman despite sending a letter, and can't visit to see my baby's condition for nine more days. To be of use, join thy prayers to mine."

I ran out and up to my room, where I'll remain till Henry calls.

Could I have made Johan come back, if

I'd sent a letter? I must put this pencil down, so I can lower my head to my hands and weep.

Fourth Month 23
Still no word from Gerda. I pulled two pages from this book, one to write on and one to fold into an envelope and post with my last stamp.

I intended to bring this letter directly to the kitchen to see if anyone was stepping out and could mail it. I walked from my room to the second story, and in the hall I paused to rest on a chair, feeling light-headed. Clementina must have heard my movements, for she called me to her office. Her original purpose was cast from her mind when she saw my envelope.

"To whom can a servant need to write — her mother?" She toyed with a red pendant at her neck.

The woman has an astringent effect on me, and I didn't want to answer.

"No," I said. "My mother passed away." I fingered my locket, its metal as smooth to my fingertips as Mother's cheek.

"From what did she die?"

I spoke the truth that rose to my head. "From the bleeding and prescriptions of an allopathic doctor."

"My father is an allopath," she said. "A noted one."

"Pardon me," I replied. "This one killed my mother, so I didn't much like his methods."

"You might learn some diplomacy," she admonished — correctly, of course, given my dependence on her. And then, "Are you writing to your baby's father? You're using time while in my employ, so I must know."

With her wasp waist from her tight-laced corset and the expanded shoulders and high collar of her yellow gown, she looked more like a puppet than a woman, and her haughty expression only added to her theatricality.

"Oh, no," I said. "I have no way to reach him."

Her lips moved into a slight smile. She picked up an Oriental fan and opened it, then fanned herself. "What sort of a man was he?"

"He was kind, and more intelligent than average."

"Ah." She seemed disappointed. "Why didn't you marry him?"

"He went away and didn't send for me as promised."

Clementina looked out the window and pushed her lips together. "There are worse fates than never marrying. At any rate, I called you here to find out how often you feed Henry."

"When he requests it." I sank onto a gold velvet chair, for I was light-headed again.

She widened her eyes. "Make it every four hours. My father has just written to say that frequent feedings make their stomachs weak."

"If I can't feed him when he calls, he'll disturb thee."

"You may take him to the cellar if that happens. But don't light the stove down there, or the roots will rot." She stroked her cheek and turned toward the door, suggesting that I exit.

"He's only just getting up his weight," I dared to say. "He shows no signs of a weak stomach."

Clementina looked skyward and sighed. "Are you a doctor?"

"No."

"Then you don't know what's best for my baby. I'm following a doctor's instructions."

Lord save us from the doctors and their faddish ideas. Reason cannot compete.

Then Henry began to wail from the nursery down the hall. His mother and I examined each other across her broad desk as my breasts began to tingle and fill. She picked up a pen to begin some new task, and a bold question raced through my head and leaped over the barriers I threw up hastily to confine it.

"May I ask why thee doesn't care for Henry?"

She lifted her head, pausing her pen. "I was raised by a wet nurse. Are you saying this does a child harm?"

"I have no experience with the effects," I said.

She widened her eyes.

"Forgive me," I added.

"I won't forgive you. You've no right to ask such a question. But I'll tell you exactly why. I see no point in being enslaved by his bodily needs when you can fulfill them in my stead." A glimmer of some feeling passed behind her eyes, like a fish seen through dark waters.

I made no reply but looked at the ornately flowered wallpaper behind her, keeping my face unaffected. I thought I might understand her behavior, just a little. In sealing her heart against her son, she can retain a modicum of liberty.

"I have a column to write," she said, pointing her pen toward the door. "And by the way, don't sit in my presence unless invited."

I hurried off to the nursery to answer her

baby's calls. As he drank, I thought how Mother often said I was too fiery, and I promised myself I'd be more deferent. I've always detested apologetic simpering, yet I must learn to do it. I can't afford not to.

I finished with Henry. There was no one in the kitchen, so I put on my cloak and walked my letter to the collection box on the corner lamppost. This was my first venture outside in nearly a week, since I'd arrived at the Burnhams'! How strange it felt to step down the front stoop into a rush of strangers pursuing their business in all directions, with the urgency of that business tightening their faces. Or perhaps it was the unpleasantness of their surroundings that made them look so peeved. Carriages and wagons barreled past, their iron-rimmed wheels grating on the cobblestones. Coal and wood smoke thickened the air, and all about in heaps lay the dung of livestock driven earlier to market. The garments of many of these people were finer than what some wear in Germantown, but it appeared that their enjoyment of each moment was less. Many in Germantown can open their doors in spring to the scents of grasses and flowers and to air kept fresh by towering trees.

One might presume that I was homesick.

I mailed my second letter to Gerda.

Margaret is stopping today at the stationer's for a pile of notebooks and some pencils, some for me and some for herself. There are but a few coins remaining in my purse.

Fourth Month 24

Day six away from Charlotte, and no word from her nurse. I did receive a letter from Anne — a record of my lying-in costs, with some of the balance forgiven, and the amount due represented by a line of zeroes, because she'd been so extraordinarily generous as to apply much of the Burnhams' fee to my debt. So in three or four months I may have enough saved for a month's rental on a room and a first installment on a sewing machine.

Delphinia and Frau V. have cast doubt on this way of earning our keep — but I have no better. No school would hire a teacher with a bastard. And I might get a grant to buy a machine from that ladies' aid society; Delphinia promised to send on any correspondence.

Last night I began to put Clementina's new feeding schedule into action. I commenced my absurd strolling around the bins of beets, cabbages, carrots, and horseradish in the cellar, dodging the braided onions and garlic suspended on nails, while Henry squalled. All was not bleak; the stone walls gave off a pleasant, earthy smell; a blanket draped over us kept the chill at bay. And I did wait for the first four-hour interval to pass, wearing a path into the dirt floor and turning my old slippers dark. But before the next appointed hour, Henry fussed so that my aching breasts sprayed out their milk, and I put him to me. He curled his minuscule hand around my forearm and kneaded my flesh as he gulped.

Earlier in the night, Margaret and I had our first lesson. She's intelligent and will make quick progress if she practices. The bits she'd learned from her sister will help her make a strong start. In a month or two, she may be ready to write a simple note to her family.

And who knows what other good may come from her pen. Perhaps the Lord has put me here for Margaret, and her for me, with some larger purpose.

Frau V. had me turn the soil in the small kitchen garden behind the house. Though they don't strictly need a garden downtown, where markets are abundant, she prefers the freshest possible herbs and greens in the spring, and roots in autumn.

I was glad to have time in the open air, which was soft on my skin and enlivened me. But being in a garden put me in mind of how I've changed. At home I'd loved pushing a shovel into the ground, turning the dirt over, smelling its musty dankness. Today, however, as I shoveled row upon row of good soil, with many worms and a grand brown richness, I felt an aching hardness in my breasts, and an ache in my arms from so many hours spent holding a baby, and a dizzying ache in my mind from thoughts of Johan. Because he abandoned me, I'm committed not only to our infant but to another, and must serve his peculiar parents besides. On my life's loom, the warp and woof are so disarrayed that I can no longer weave its cloth. Yet Johan, the agent of my disgrace, strolls merrily along his chosen way, with no alteration in his prospects, no lessening of freedom, no suffering on account of our hour of intimacy.

I pictured his long face coming close to mine, seeking a furtive kiss, as he had often done after we'd agreed to marry. I pictured throwing my whole body into him and knocking him to the ground. Liar, thief of my innocence, scoundrel of the lowest order! I wish I *could* go to Pittsburgh and tell him what his hollow promises have wrought. Yet I see no way to make this happen in my obligated state.

So little is permissible for a woman — yet on her back every human climbs to adulthood.

Fourth Month 25

The morning's post brought no word from Gerda. My ever-growing anxiousness may explain this peculiar vision that came to me.

I'd fallen asleep in the rocker with Henry in my lap. Not long afterward I awakened, or so it seemed. I felt the cool air from the partly opened window, and the damp of Henry's diaper. Then, with just as much seeming realness, I saw the lanky figure of Johan stoop to enter the nursery door. He held a worn felt hat to his chest. His eyes were downcast, and he'd grown a scraggly beard. He looked up and stared at me, his look so intense that I felt its heat.

Then the vision vanished, leaving only questions. Is he in trouble? Or is this merely another of the many fearful visions I've had since leaving Charlotte, whether sleeping or awake I can't be sure?

All the rest have featured Charlotte being taken from me — so that madmen can subject her to disfiguring experiments, or because she's been stricken with some hideous contagion, or thrown in a river. Or sometimes I have simply lost her, having turned my head to follow the flight of a bird and turned back to find her gone, which sends me running about the muddy streets of some village or tripping along the cobbles of a city street, anguished, calling her name.

Now this vision of sad Johan. What can it mean?

I'm becoming like some early Friend, beset by messages and urgings, though mine may come merely from my own fears.

My worry over Charlotte grows.

The doctor came to examine Henry at midday, and Clementina sent me to the kitchen. I sat with Margaret, Frau V., and a day jobber named Flo. Flo had come to help Margaret shake the winter's grime from the rugs, wash curtains, wipe the baseboards, and much else for the house's spring cleaning.

We ate beef stew together at a table on the back porch, despite the chill and the rain falling beyond the roof. Flo was tall, and her carriage was straight. She wore long braids and had brass bracelets up her arms. The quilted pouch about her neck gave off a penetrating scent. We all spoke of pleasant things, until she learned that my baby is with a wet nurse.

"I hope she isn't with a baby farmer." Her voice was smooth and low. "My second baby died that way."

She'd worked in a cannery at that time and had to put her baby in day boarding, she said. While the mothers worked, the caretaker subdued the infants with rags soaked in sugar water and laudanum — just what Delphinia had described! Within two weeks, her son was down to skin and bones.

"I left the cannery to nurse him," Flo said, eyes brimming. "I didn't know how I would pay rent. But he was too weak. He couldn't hold the milk I gave him." Within days he was dead of starvation.

Drug dosing! Starvation! I looked at my plate, at the gravy pooled to one side, the threads of stewed meat too small to lift with a fork. I wanted to comfort Flo, but I couldn't. I stood and sought privacy in the kitchen, where my mind flapped and flew into the walls like a wild bird that couldn't get out.

I washed dishes in great distress, flushing as if I had a fever, then went to check on Henry. And there was Clementina, sleeping on the braided rug beside his crib. The remains of tears had dried in salty courses down her face. This was a fresh mystery! Had the doctor brought bad tidings? Or did Clementina feel a modicum of tenderness for the one who'd grown in her? Did she suddenly regret her alienation from his care?

She might have merely needed to be alone, for Albert had been at home, bothering her for company.

I stepped out and climbed to my room. When Henry woke and called, I listened for her movements. She rose and left. I found no sign of her apart from a flattening of the rug.

I'd just placed Henry back in his crib, where he'd rolled into a merry ball and was trying to reach his foot, when the front bell rang. Margaret called out that she was covered in coal dust in the basement, sweeping up after a delivery. Clementina must have been nearby, for she answered the door. Her sharp voice told someone to go around the back, and a young boy's voice replied, "I need to see Miss de Jong, ma'am. My aunt sent me."

"You must go to the back," Clementina repeated. "Take a right at the end of the block, turn into the alley, and it's the fourth gate on the right."

My heart tumbled as I raced down the kitchen stairs and through the hall to the foyer. The boy stood in the open doorway. He wore a high-collared blue coat with brass buttons — an old military coat, much too big — that hung open atop baggy pants tied with a rope. He had a pasty, pock-marked complexion and was very thin.

"It's all right," I said. "He's my visitor."

"He must go around the back," Clementina insisted. Her nose was wrinkled, for he gave off a pungent scent.

I turned to her and tried to catch her eye. "Please let me speak with him outside. He's here about my baby."

She ignored me and yelled at the boy: "Leave my doorstep!"

He started running down the street, and in my slippers I followed.

"Stop, please," I called. "I am Miss de Jong."

Fortunately he pulled his legs to a halt. We stood against a brick building and caught our breath as traffic barreled past. The boy said in a trembling voice that his aunt Gerda had sent him to say the red-haired baby is fine.

I thanked him very much for making the trip, then asked whether conditions were good in the house, if it was clean and airy. He emitted a mildly affirmative but unconvincing sound and wouldn't meet my eye.

The reason may only have been shyness, or fright at Clementina's treatment. But he was not a good emissary for Gerda's cause.

Then I asked how many babies she cared for.

"Three or four," he said. "It changes by the day."

I stood openmouthed as a streetcar bounced by, jammed with riders. This situation sounded like what Flo and Delphinia had warned me about.

"Please, miss," the boy said, peering up at me. "I was promised my fare."

I had to get my purse, so we walked rapidly down the block, into the alley behind the row of attached houses, and through the backyard gate. He stood outside while I ran past Frau V. and up to my room and down again. I gave him two dimes to pay his streetcar fare and to reward his efforts. He smiled, revealing several blackened teeth, then stepped off as I entered the back door to the kitchen.

At that moment Clementina stormed into the kitchen to upbraid me for the low quality of visitor I'd received. "The neighbors will think ill of us if we draw paupers to our door," she said, "and speak with them in full view of everyone."

I forced myself not to reply, though inwardly I fumed. Does she expect that I can lodge Charlotte with a queen, who'll send her courtier in a gilt carriage to report on my baby's status? Isn't it enough that my daughter sucks from a woman who feeds many at once, while Henry feasts alone?

After Clementina left, I made an effort to explain what I'd found out to Frau V., for she looked curiously at me, but I could barely speak. She moved toward me and put a fleshy hand to my forehead.

"You're hot," she said. "Get to bed. I'll send up yarrow tea."

I thanked her. After stopping in the nursery — where Henry was asleep — I ascended to my room.

But I didn't intend to rest. I had a plan. I resumed sewing some light sacks for Charlotte, since the air has been unseasonably warm, and her wool and flannel clothes must be stifling. I was using the scraps of muslin and cotton that Margaret had given me from the rag basket, saying no one else needed them.

When Clementina returned before supper and stomped up toward her sitting room, I met her there. I begged her forgiveness for coming without being called and asked if I might go tomorrow first thing to see my Charlotte at her wet nurse's house. "With the warmer weather," I said, "she needs the items I'm making her."

"It's good that you were honest and told me you wanted to go a week early rather than doing so behind my back," Clementina replied. But she didn't give permission. She wanted to know why I haven't given Charlotte up, as the baby causes me such concern and expense. I explained that Charlotte matters more to me than anyone alive. Clementina's face remained unmoved, and her green eyes scrutinized me, as if to find my true motive.

I began to shed worried tears, which I hated to do in her company. I had to figure out some way to convince her. My mind cast about for something she might understand. Guessing that she loved music, since she'd gone to hear it many nights, I said that I needed to hold my baby, to hear her particular sounds, because otherwise my spirit was tuneless, like an instrument with no player.

Clementina's face fell. She touched her cheek; a sheen came to her eyes. "I've known that sensation," she replied. "How eerie that you'd mention it."

I cleared my throat in the quiet that followed. She snapped her attention back to me with a new regard. "Of course you should go in the morning. You'll take my carriage."

I expressed my gratitude and took my leave.

I suspect I am feverish. It must be due to fevered emotions. The milk that builds up in the four hours between Henry's feedings does make my breasts ache, but that wouldn't cause this heat.

I must wait one night only — several thousand more breaths — and then can see and hold and kiss my plump-cheeked darling, the most accomplished player of that instrument called my heart.

■ ■ ■ ■

NOTEBOOK FIVE

■ ■ ■ ■

Fourth Month 26

The household is in a crisis and I've become too ill to travel, for my milk is blocked entirely.

Henry screamed in my lap and shook his legs when he tried to nurse last night, and all the others were awakened. The Burnhams watched through the doorway, clad in dressing gowns. Margaret set off to the kitchen and readied her supplies, then set to hand-feeding Henry again. As she tried to get him to take the bottle, he craned his head toward me and cried, his mouth as wide as a baby bird's. But once I'd left, he sucked cow's milk and sugar from the rubber nipple.

Margaret said he's suffering at his return to the bottle, spitting up and contracting his legs into his belly. Hearing his distress from my room above makes my breasts throb, but no milk comes forth. Hot cloths and massage have proved useless. Clementina sent for Dr. Snowe, the man who had evaluated my worthiness, and he replied by post that he'll call tomorrow.

Perhaps I've got influenza, with this fever and the nausea and the dizzy spells. I wouldn't be surprised, as the windows in this house stay mostly closed to keep out noise and dirt, and the gaslights and stove put out poisonous vapors continually — not to mention the chamber pots and the ever-filling pail of diapers. From now on I'll keep my window raised.

It's evening. I've pulled myself to the end of my bed to look out, seeking solace in the world beyond my own tiny realm. On the street three stories down, the lamplighter is kindling lamps in a line, creating a string of radiant beads. The sidewalks are swelled with people in fine attire. Hansoms led by powerful horses rush by, bringing their passengers to the theater or some other enchanting place. They all pass onward.

Now I see two young boys in matching caps and vests; they face wearily in opposite directions, each with a bag of papers around his neck, offering the news to passersby. They look no more than seven and ought to be asleep by this hour. Is their mother right now looking out a window for a glimpse of them approaching, or listening for their staccato steps on the building's stairs? Or does she work late, too, pasting flower petals together or cracking nuts or performing other piecework? What would she do if they didn't come back? Someone could kidnap them, like the poor Ross brothers were kidnapped in Germantown, one of whom was never found. That story frightened Peter and me awfully when we were small.

High up in this slant-ceilinged room, warmed only by a candle and the fetid air rising from below, I'm unable to find a reassuring thought. I send a message into the ether for a passing angel to carry to my baby: *Stay well, my darling. Mother will come soon.*

Fourth Month 27

The doctor arrived this morning in a sweat, having traveled here on horseback. "Today's my surgery day," he told Clementina loudly in the hall. "I've got two hours till my next operation."

Clementina called me to the parlor and stood to his side as he felt my forehead and neck, shot questions at me, looked down my throat and in my ears, and prodded at my chest through my clothing with his sharp

237

fingers. Then, though this was already decided by physical impediment, he pronounced me unfit for nursing. He diagnosed not influenza but something else entirely.

"She has a breast infection as well as blocked ducts, and her milk is no longer safe," he told Clementina. "If the blockages don't open soon, pus will gather and form abscesses, and I'll have to cut them open."

I flinched.

"What's the cause?" asked Clementina.

"It comes of having too much milk. She'll need to release it more often — if she becomes able to nurse again."

If? Clementina glanced at me with a grimace. It seemed she recognized the damage done by her father's feeding schedule. The doctor took her expression as a sign of concern for Henry, which perhaps it also was.

"The boy continues to gain weight?" he asked.

"Several ounces a day," I replied. I'd been charged with weighing him each morning on a calibrated scale.

"Excellent." Dr. Snowe restored his instruments to a leather bag. "A few days of artificial feeding won't harm such a hearty fellow."

This gave me hope that Charlotte — who

was hearty when I left her — won't have declined much in our nine days apart.

Dr. Snowe ordered me to take a series of hot baths to bring my fevered blood to the surface and cool it. He left a glass pump so I could try to get the milk moving after each bath. Dismissed, I started toward the back stairs.

"While you're here, doctor," Clementina said, "I'd like an ointment —" Just as my ears perked up, the door to the parlor closed.

This afternoon I took three baths in the kitchen, and what a strain this put on Margaret! For hours, she did little but heat water and pour it in the tub, then haul cooled water out of the tub and heat more water on the stove and pour it in the tub, then bottle-feed and change Henry.

At the end of it, I'd never been so clean. If I were beef, I'd have been stewed. But my vomiting and weakness persisted, and my breasts were so taut as to be growing shiny. I pumped three times to no avail.

When the doctor returned at evening, I was unable to walk, so he ascended to my room. In my left breast he found a solid area and declared it an abscess. After putting me in a chair and laying old newspapers around us, he sliced it with a lancet. Blood, curdled milk, and pus ran into his collecting bowl. He pressed on the abscess to release more fluid, and a roaring began in my head from the pain. When the last trickle ceased, he applied strips of linen to my front and had me lie down. Already the pain and swelling were reduced; with what voice I had, I thanked him.

He went to pull the kitchen bell on the second story and returned to my side. Frau V. stomped upward, audibly disgruntled. But when she reached the servants' story, apron dusted in flour, she laid her eyes on me and began to stammer. "I had — I had no idea you were so bad off."

I tried to reply but wasn't able, for such a show of sympathy brought my suffering clearer, and I was overcome.

"You must feed this young woman only cooked vegetables and fruits until I give further instruction," the doctor told her. "Tend to her wound. And put hot compresses on the other breast, or we'll have another abscess."

Frau V. looked at him peevishly. She isn't fond of this sour-smelling, imperious man with his twirled moustache. She promised to comply but let out a groan about the extra work as she made her way down the stairs. My debts to her and Margaret grow by the hour.

Then Dr. Snowe applied cotton and gauze to the wound and offered me ten drops of laudanum in water, promising easy sleep and a pleasant mood. I'd never taken laudanum, for its opium and alcohol are addicting. But I drank the liquid down, and it did put me in a far more comfortable state. He said I can nurse again once the incision has healed enough not to reopen — if the fever is gone and I still have milk. My eyes closed; my head was impelled toward the pillow. He left.

The rest I had under the influence of laudanum was a peculiar one. Noisy voices rose with unusual clarity from the kitchen, along with the clatterings and clinkings of kitchen work. The sounds felt sharp and irritating inside my ears. Frau V. seemed to have a visitor downstairs, perhaps a servant who'd accompanied a friend of Clementina's. I'd drift until some sound awakened me, then drift some more. Sometime in the night I heard the outraged voice of Clementina: "As if I'd accept such treatment. Thinking I would be such a woman as that." And then, "*I'm sorry,* you say — as if that could fix it."

My fever broke in the night. When I surfaced to another day, the house was

241

briefly quiet.

Fortunately Frau V. is an experienced caretaker of the sick. She changes the cotton and gauze hourly and cleans the wound with a calendula wash. The compresses she brings for the other breast are calling forth enough milk to lessen the swelling.

Mother's hands were cool; Frau V.'s are warm and fleshy. Mother's voice was sedating; Frau V.'s is harsh. But as the cook leans over me, she smells pleasantly of roses.

Fourth Month 28

This is my twenty-fourth birthday, and Charlotte is a day shy of one month old! I want no gifts but to touch her tendrils of hair, as soft as the hair at a goat's throat, and to kiss her cheeks and belly.

Those gifts won't be mine today, but I've had some lovely surprises. Margaret had asked my birth date at a writing lesson, and she hadn't forgotten. When she brought my breakfast of cooked fruit, she gave me a pair of sheepskin slippers, saying they'll warm my feet when I rise in the dark for Henry. And she must have told Clementina, for the lady called me to her bedroom. She sat before her dressing table, surrounded by pots of rouge and powder, an engraved silver tray filled with cut-glass perfume

242

bottles, and an iron curling rod heating over the wick on its stand. She stopped brushing her long hair to hand me a woven shawl of golden-yellow wool. "To cover you while you nurse," she said, "when you can nurse again."

I was moved by her kindness and her optimism. I wrapped the shawl around me, proclaiming it heavenly soft, and thanked her.

For her part, Frau V. refilled my supply of tinctures and teas and applied a hot linseed poultice. She said my cut is healing fast. Then she brought up, from her own garden, a salad of the first tender and delicate lettuces of the season.

"Don't tell," she whispered, "because the doctor said cooked, not fresh. But these first shoots have extra force. To help you recover. I raised seven children on roots and herbs. They all have children of their own now." She insisted that I nurse Henry soon, whether or not the doctor allows it. "No milk, no job. You'll be off to the poor-house, and your baby, too."

I intend to heed her counsel.

This is my second birthday without Mother. The locket with her hair and picture nestles at my neck. The warmth of its shining metal makes it seem alive — though that warmth comes from my own body.

Which makes me think how, in my very body, my mother does live.

Perhaps our bodies are like patchwork quilts, made up of kin from decades and even centuries past. Charlotte contains all these patches and offers her own as the next in line — one more reason to cherish her.

Margaret has gotten the afternoon off and is right now rushing to Gerda's to visit Charlotte. She perceived my worry and decided to take action, since I'm too weak to travel. What a caring girl! I gave her my last coins for her streetcar fare.

Godspeed, dear Margaret. I hope thee finds my baby well.

Margaret has returned, and my life has shifted on its axis.

"I don't like to tell you," she said upon entering my garret. "But that place is not right for babies. And your Charlotte — her condition isn't good." Her blue eyes were intent; her freckled face was drawn.

"How did thee know which was Charlotte?" I asked.

"She wore the white gown you said you sent her in, which is filthy now — and she was the only one with red hair. There were three babies, and all looked bad."

"Was thee allowed to hold her? Was she thin?"

"I asked to get close, but the woman said she couldn't allow that for anyone but the mother. Your baby did look thin. The place is terrible, no more than a shack. The smell was awful. I doubt there's clean water."

"Bless thee for finding this out." I rose from bed with her hand to steady me.

She shook her head, distraught. "Don't bless me. I should have taken her away."

I descended to the second story in my bedclothes. In the hallway mirror outside Clementina's bedroom, I saw my disheveled state — the swollen, red skin around my eyes from crying, the many hairs straying from my bun like torn filaments of spiderwebs. I burst in on Clementina, who appeared to be arranging her clothes into outfits for the season.

"Please forgive me," I said. "I have to fetch my daughter at her wet nurse's and bring her here. She's been in an unsafe situation for ten days."

Clementina gave a sigh. "I'm concerned about your milk," she replied. "We need to build it up again. Strong emotions will injure it." She pulled more skirts and bodices from her wardrobe, considering how well they went together; her leisure increased my agitation.

"I'll be much happier when my baby's faring well," I said, trying to keep my voice soft. "Besides, she might unblock my milk and increase my supply for Henry."

Clementina removed a satin-trimmed polonaise from her massive wardrobe and laid it atop a skirt and overskirt of brown satin. At last she nodded yes, and I took a full breath in and out. "But only," she said, her face stern, "until your milk is re-established and pure enough. For Henry."

I thanked her and started from the room.

"Wait," Clementina said. "How far is this place?"

"A few miles north."

"I doubt you're strong enough to walk, or even to take a streetcar or a train."

"Oh." I turned to her. I hadn't one coin remaining for my fare.

"Take our carriage and driver." She looked me up and down. "As long as you neaten your hair and change to suitable dress."

She returned to her task, and I didn't dare ask another question. So I went to the kitchen to find out how to get the carriage. Since the cook was only waiting for her dough to rise, she offered to walk the several blocks to the stable while I changed my clothes. I wanted to embrace her, but she brushed my arms away.

"I only do what's right," she said.

The carriage is here!

Fourth Month 29, First Day

My darling has taken her fill many times since yesterday and slipped into a happy stupor. But I can never get my fill of her. I stare and stare, as in her rightful place she breathes and rests, milk clinging to her tiny lips. I feel giddy and uncoordinated, like a bee covered in pollen, unbalanced and heavy from touring flower after flower.

The stuck milk of recent days is bursting out, and it's more than my little one can hold. Periodically I lean over a bowl on the washstand and squeeze my breasts, and milk sprays in all directions. I tasted a drop from my finger; it was sweet and light and left a powdery texture on my tongue, perhaps from the sugar in it.

Margaret's description was too restrained to have prepared me for Gerda's street. The carriage driver referred to it as Drunkards' Alley and said even the street cleaners avoid it, to its inhabitants' detriment. The air stank from heaps of manure that were circled by hordes of insects. Piles of rags, bones, and rotting rubbish littered the dirt.

247

The front doors of many of its two-story shacks hung off their hinges; most windows were covered in boards or newspaper. And naturally the Burnhams' shiny green carriage drew attention there. As the horse brought it to a halt, barefooted children in ragged clothes ran up, holding out their hands and calling, "A penny! A penny for food!" I rose from the padded bench, stepped out, and walked to the house, feeling heartless for not giving them coins but having none.

Gerda's shack had a functioning door. I knocked on it as children whispered behind me: "Who is that? Why is she here?" No answer came from within, so I called, "Gerda! Please open the door!" In quick response came a baby's cry.

I knew that cry! The flimsy door easily gave way. I pushed into an unlit, smoky space that appeared unoccupied. I walked around a table of rough boards to see, along the back wall, three crates. I stepped closer; each crate contained a baby, tied down by strips of cloth fastened to the lattice of the crate. One was my Lotte, bawling by then and clumsily craning her head toward me. I praised her with every cell in my body for holding on to life.

I untied the stays and picked up her thin

and trembling form, then knelt to collect the blanket and clothes piled by her crate. I felt I had to leave immediately — as if I were a thief. The other babies looked desperate, worse than mine, with bulging eyes, and limbs that lacked the will to move. But I only said a prayer for them, sick at heart and sorry, then rushed out to the street.

I stood on the packed dirt, my stunned baby blinking against me. From his perch behind the horse, the carriage driver stared. An old man was resting on a log before the next shack over, smoking a pipe and stroking his whitish-yellow beard. He spit to the ground, then called to me.

"That yer baby?"

I nodded. "Can thee tell Gerda I've taken the baby named Charlotte away?" By then Charlotte was rooting at my shirt, causing my clogged breasts to ache. I opened the carriage door and raised my foot to a step.

"Gerda might not notice yer baby's gone," the old man called, "and she won't know the name." He took the pipe from his lips and gave a dry laugh, more like coughing. "Don't know why a lady like you would hire a baby farmer. Undertaker's here least once a month." He shook his head side to side, then took a puff from his pipe, concluding, "Public Health oughta shut 'er down."

Indeed. Charlotte writhed against me, seeking milk. I felt my breasts responding. "Report her to Public Health," I urged the man, "for the sake of the babies."

He puffed and said nothing.

Children were touching their palms to the carriage, to its green sides warmed by the sun. Several had tied shreds of cloth to its tall wheels, which would give them some amusement when the wheels began to turn. The driver shooed them off as I shut the door and dropped to the cushioned bench.

As we began to move away, I pulled the curtains closed. In the filtered light I held my baby to me and kissed her, my tears wetting her grimy face. Her body shook, and she gave a terrible wail.

If hearts could break, mine would have then. For I had my answer as to how she'd fared: she'd suffered our time apart with all the force of her little being.

Her clothes smelled of smoke and dampness, her diaper stank, and her breath bore the odor of alcohol, betraying Gerda's medicinal method of quieting babies. But her scalp held a hint of her real smell, slight and sweet. As I kept my nose to her head and inhaled, my breasts began to release their milk! She attached eagerly to my unwounded side and choked at the volume but kept sucking until her belly grew taut. Then she fell to sleep, like a baby kitten.

On arriving back to my room, I undressed her. Her ribs were visible, and her arms and legs were far thinner. Beneath her sodden, stinking diaper was an aggravated rash, red in front and worse in back. She vomited onto her chest and gave out unhappy cries as I washed her with a cloth and cool water from a pitcher, then patted her dry. I used Frau V.'s calendula and comfrey salve to dress the rash.

When I finished, as if applying a salve to me, she stared lovingly upward, made whole by our reunion. But I despised myself for putting her in the care of a woman I'd never met. If Margaret hadn't gone to Gerda's — I cringed to think. If my darling had died . . .

She wears no diaper now, since her rash will heal better in the air. Frau V. told me this when she came upstairs to examine Charlotte. Based on the lack of fever and the keenness remaining in her eyes, the cook predicted that she'll gain her weight back quickly.

I believe she will recover. It must be so.

I find myself intoxicated by her face at rest — the flawless skin and its faint flush of pink, the delicate dusting of red-blond hairs at her temples, the nostrils that puff slightly

251

with each breath, the bud-like lips so softly parted. Upon my lap, this treasure sleeps a leaden sleep.

Fifth Month 3

Payday was two days ago, the first of the month, and Clementina had nothing for me. To start, for the time I was sick, she considers me not to have been in her employ. "Surely you understand," she said, hardly giving me a glance as I stood before her desk, the last in line. Worse still is that she docked all my remaining pay for the doctor's visit and medicine, *and* I owe her fifty cents more. Frau V. and Margaret got their money, and of course I don't begrudge them. Yet it was awfully hard of Clementina to give me not one cent for all my efforts since I've arrived here. And even though Dr. Snowe examined me and pronounced my milk safe for Henry, and I've begun feeding both babies, the mistress says she'll pay but half my wage until my bastard is accommodated elsewhere. I haven't dared to put Charlotte in her sight, but I did protest that she's still thin. The lady was unmoved.

"Inside this house," she said, "your care belongs to Henry." She said to obtain newspapers and find a place for Charlotte right away.

She fails to understand any position but her own. What to her are defensible shifts in our financial arrangement have the effect of leaving me penniless. She feels no obligation to consider others apart from how they serve her.

And how am I to pay a wet nurse to take my Charlotte?

Clementina and her doctor forbade me meat and sweets; I relished a chunk of ham and a slice of pecan pie in the kitchen.

Today Henry's umbilical cord stump fell off — a little late, observed Frau V. while she poured warm water into a kitchen basin. We gave the slippery fellow his first bath, which startled and pleased him.

There's more to tell. Frau V. called for me before supper, and I went to the kitchen by the back stairs, carrying Charlotte. The cook washed her hands and dried them, then sat at the table. Charlotte watched with some of her former alertness but elicited only a fleeting smile from the cook, who had something else occupying her mind.

"Sit down," she said, gesturing. "I know what I'm talking about." Her face pushed out, daring me to defy her.

"Yes?" I sat as directed.

"I spoke with the mistress about your situation. You must contact your baby's father to demand support, as a condition of your employment. Either that, or you must begin a civil suit against him."

Why would Clementina care? She certainly doesn't care a whit about Charlotte. I said this, and here is Frau V's interpretation. The lady may not understand why I keep my child, but she does value my services and character. When Frau V. suggested to her that my life following this employment would likely be disastrous, a spark kindled in her heart.

With Charlotte in my arms and her eyes moving from the cook to me, I had the courage to speak honestly. I said I appreciated their concern but was not prepared to reveal the existence of our baby in a letter to Johan — which might only increase his wish to stay away. Nor would I seek restitution in a court proceeding that would be published in the newspapers. I offered instead to write my brother through the post office, as she'd earlier told me was possible. If he sent news, then I'd decide whether to write Johan with a request for support.

We wrestled with our differences. Finally she relented as to my writing Peter, saying she would explain my points to our mistress.

But she wanted me to tell Peter about Charlotte and to have him urge Johan to make reparations.

I assured her that Charlotte and I will get by on our own after my time here, for surely others will see our virtue and not block our progress toward a decent life.

"Get by on your own?" Frau Varschen said. "Be seen as virtuous?" Behind her thick glasses, her eyes lifted to the ceiling and back to me. "I doubt it."

"Why?" I asked. "I'm young, I have skills, I have principles —"

"Principles? Bah! If only everyone had them. How can you make it alone with a bastard? Do you want to end up a strumpet?"

"Of course not." I stared at her, aghast. "That won't happen to me."

She rolled her eyes skyward again. "So why does it happen to so many like you — because they love to be poked by drunken strangers?"

I blushed. "I'd guess not."

"Something bad happened," she said, "and no one gave them a second chance."

A bad feeling took up residence in my stomach then.

Be that as it may, I wrote to Peter in the manner I'd described. I used Clementina's fine parchment, which Frau V. procured with permission. I struggled over what to write and decided on this.

1883. 5th mo. 3
Peter de Jong
General Delivery
Pittsburgh, Penna.

Dear Peter,
No letter has come from thee or Johan. How is thee faring? How is Johan? I am not well. Please consider returning, or at least write me immediately, care of the Burnhams, 18xx Pine Street, Philadelphia, Penna.

       With love and concern, thy sister,
               Lillian de Jong

Frau V. may have pulled this mule onto a path unwillingly, but now I'm trotting down it, and my spirit is aflutter with the possibilities. Perhaps Peter will return, or offer us shelter in Pittsburgh. Perhaps the hole that has threatened to swallow us will fill with solid earth instead!

Fifth Month 5
I've just nursed and changed Charlotte, then Henry, then Charlotte, then Henry. I

run from one to the other, up and down the stairs, day and night. Apart from strict necessity, what keeps me rising to my tired feet? It must be the delight these babies bring.

Henry reveals deep dimples when he smiles. His brown eyes open wide. He gurgles when I place him on the changing table. Charlotte, by one week his elder, stares upward and grins while I clean her, making a percussive sound that seems to be a laugh. Within seconds she can go from smiling openmouthed to pursing her brow to pressing her lips in discomfort to belching and sending curdled milk to the folds of her neck to grinning toothlessly again.

I carry her around and around in our limited realm of garret and third-story hall, showing her things. I point out my window at the birds perched on the roof across the street, amuse her with silly facial expressions, let her try to trace a crack in the wall's plaster. I sit before my trunk and help her touch my clothing and shoes, a brush, a hair comb. She grabs my clothing in her clenched-up fingers. Her grip is so powerful that a stocking tore when I tried to make her release it.

Her growing plumpness soothes my conscience.

I brought her to the kitchen today, and Frau V. showed me how to place her on her stomach. For a few seconds at a time, Charlotte held her arms and head up, as if flying.

"Our baby learns quick," said Frau V., patting my daughter's diapered bottom.

Of course Clementina is correct; I reserve my finest care for my own baby.

Frau V. has me drinking nettle tea to rebuild my strength. Soon, she said, nothing will remain of my wound but a bluish scar.

Fifth Month 7
With never sleeping more than two hours straight because of a suckling at my breast, I can barely follow a simple train of thought, much less form a plan for Charlotte. But Clementina grows ever more stone-faced toward me, and I need to earn full pay. Albert has forgotten to bring the papers. Frau V. promises she'll bring one tomorrow.

There's trouble here. The Burnhams often argue in the dining room. And lately, while I nurse one or the other of my charges in the night, bitter tones pierce the darkness. Worst was last night, when from Clementina's bedroom came yelling and the sounds of objects and bodies shifting, and then a bout of sobbing from her. She hasn't emerged today. Margaret has said nothing of it but brings meals to her mistress's room. Albert skulked out early.

This afternoon I brought the infants behind the house to the narrow yard and settled us on a blanket. Simply breathing the air born of such rampant blooming and sprouting did us good. Henry lay on his back, cooing at passing clouds. When a breeze blew over and the leaves flitted about, Charlotte dashed her head side to side, openmouthed.

The newness of such things as clouds and leaves to them is marvelous.

Yet something has me bothered. I've been shown today two instances of desperation among the flying creatures. At early light I woke to squawking from the tree below, and out our window I spied a father swallow, greatly agitated, defending his nest of babies from a hawk. A parcel of will he was, flinging himself before the hawk every which way it traveled, poking his beak into its side, until finally it desisted. And later, on the blanket out back, while Henry drank at me and Charlotte moved her limbs, a mother robin flew at a hawk, flapping her wings into its head and screeching, then aiming all her force like an arrow into its side. She attacked until the harried giant left her nest alone.

These parents must risk their lives continually to win their babes another day.

My Lotte nearly died by being too far from my protection. Frau Varschen was right: I hadn't understood the danger.

Fifth Month 9

The cook brought in the *Public Ledger* this morning. Among the many advertisements for wet nurses was one placed by a woman describing herself as a healthy Irish Catholic mother seeking a baby to nurse because she had lost her own baby at birth. She claimed to offer a clean home and asked one dollar fifty cents a week, which was higher than some. Margaret said the address was ten blocks southwest of here, in a section known as Shantytown.

I sent a note asking to come right away, and the woman sent back a rough but legible note saying yes. Clementina granted me freedom to go and gave me a dollar-fifty advance on pay. So now I owe two dollars to her, which she noted in a leather-bound account book on her desk.

With dread I packed the light cotton clothes and blankets and other things I'd sewed for Charlotte, dressed her, and plunged us down the alley and into the street. Every noise fascinated her — the clacking of horses' feet on cobbles, the carriages and wagons bouncing past. As we drew nearer to the nurse's address, vendors called vigorously from their carts, offering oysters or pepper pot, asking to grind scissors or fix an umbrella or buy a household's rags. A woman stepped out her door to pour a bucket of filth into the street, and I had to jump aside to keep my boots from being flooded. We passed a factory emitting smoke and an awful grinding sound. Yet Charlotte's eyes never stopped roving with joyous vigor. Holding her neck high, she graced the area with her gleeful smile. I began to suspect that there's a kind of ecstacy to be found in giving oneself over to a clamor.

At the nurse's address sat a brick rowhouse — far better than Gerda's shack, and on a block of solid buildings. I raised the knocker and dropped it. Charlotte gave a start as the door swung open. A weary face peered upward at us, the woman being even smaller than me.

"Ye must be Miss Freid," she said. Black eyebrows formed a thick line above her squinting eyes. Her straggly hair was pulled loosely back, and her clothing sagged on her narrow frame.

"No, I'm Miss de Jong," I said, "and this is Charlotte." I tried to incline Charlotte's face outward, but she pushed firmly into me and drew her head down, tightening her little fists on her blanket wrap. "I was sorry to read of thy baby's passing," I said, expecting to hear of a recent loss and meaning to investigate its cause.

The woman nodded, pushing her mouth into a frown. "Three years ago next month." When I said nothing, she continued, "Ya don't forget."

"No," I said, and we stood there. Three years? Could she even have much milk to offer? If she did, it wouldn't have the right composition for a newborn. Dr. Snowe had indicated the importance of this.

"I feeds 'em plenty, as if they was my own," she said. "I'd be as a mother to your baby. Yes, I would."

My heart stepped up its pace, bringing on a flush.

"Such full hair the baby has." As she reached an arm, the sleeve of her dress pushed upward, revealing a suppurating sore on the wrist. "Ye don't have ta be skittish! Let me hold her."

I reached Charlotte halfway, my throat so clamped it let out an involuntary squeak. What if this woman had some contagious disease, such as syphilis? An unclean scent arose from her. I pulled my darling close again, turned around, and plunged us into the dusty street.

"Come back, miss," the woman yelled, but I didn't turn. I ran for as long as I could, the sack of Charlotte's clothing banging my leg, until she began to cry. I sat on a stoop and held her body to my pounding chest, aiming not to succumb to hysteria. My uneven pulse sounded in my ears. I swallowed, trying to moisten my mouth. Sweat came to my skin and cooled me slightly.

Charlotte wanted to feed. I walked between two houses into an alley, sat on an overturned barrel, and opened my clothing beneath my shawl. While she took comfort, my muscles began to loosen. I became aware of my own hunger and chewed a hunk of bread from my pocket. She finished quickly. Opening her blanket across my lap, I changed her diaper and clothes in the warm, humid air.

Where was I to go?

The Haven was at least two miles away. But it was the only friendly place I knew.

I disliked being viewed by strangers as I traveled the residential streets. The women seated together on their stoops grew quieter when I passed, and I heard some whispering after. What secrets might they have seen written upon me? My appearance was no doubt peculiar, for I'd combined rich women's hand-me-downs with my plain attire. I probably had spit-up milk down my back, as I've often found it there when I undress. And when was the last time I'd combed out my hair? Even the features on my face might have been in disarray — for how could they look right, when powerful feelings were coursing and tumbling through me like leaves and sticks in a swollen stream?

At last we reached the Haven's door. I rang the bell. Delphinia pulled back the curtain at the nearest window; on recognizing me, her look moved from suspicion to pleasure. She undid the several locks from a circlet of keys at her waist.

"What joy!" she said. "We hardly get to see a girl after she leaves. You both look well!" She reached through the doorway to stroke Charlotte's head.

For a moment my heart unclenched at seeing her pink face framed by wisps of white. Then all at once I grew righteous. If she'd seen Charlotte when I'd first rescued her from Gerda's . . .

"Thee sent her to a baby farmer," I said. "She nearly died."

Delphinia's face blanched. "She went to a

fine place." She straightened her back and lifted her head. "Three dollars for two weeks, it turned out, and you'd left only two, so I put in my own dollar, which was a hardship."

"I'm very sorry. But if thee calls that a fine place, then I'm the queen of England. That woman was a baby farmer, with two other infants who won't live out the month." I paused to choke back a sob. "She robbed us both of every penny."

Delphinia scrutinized me, apparently deciding I was too upset to reason with. "Don't stand in the doorway," she scolded. "Come this way." She wrested the sack from my sweating fingers and ushered me through the hall to the office.

Anne sat at her desk, neat and serious, and beheld me with curiosity.

"Lilli says her baby went to a baby farmer," said Delphinia, eyebrows raised.

"Sit, my dear." Anne indicated the bench where — full of naïve hope — I'd sat but three weeks earlier to be interviewed by Albert Burnham and Dr. Snowe. "We can't be held responsible for what happens to the babies," Anne told me. "A servant of one of our benefactors brought your girl to his sister and vouched for her."

"Well, thee was sorely misled." I explained

what I'd found.

"Surely it wasn't that bad," said Delphinia, reaching her arm to pat my shoulder.

I pulled away. "In ten days, Charlotte became nearly a skeleton."

Anne sighed and addressed the matron. "We'll have to tell the Hollingers. Apparently their man's judgment can't be trusted."

That was all — no apology, no regret. Anne returned to her papers, and Delphinia brought me to the recovery room to see Gina — who has had her baby! We were thrilled to see each other. Delphinia fetched us tea and oat biscuits from her private stores. As we relished them, I got a good look at Lucia, who has her mother's dark hair and paleness — and, fortunately for her mother, a peaceful disposition.

When the matron left to supervise the inmates at their chores, Gina asked why I'd come. I described our plight, and here is the amazing consequence: Gina is going to nurse Charlotte along with Lucia! She'll start soon, probably this coming Seventh Day, after she takes up occupancy with her dead lover's parents. I offered one dollar fifty cents a week, which she said was ample. When she held Charlotte a moment, the change brought only pleasure to my baby

266

— a promising sign.

Of course Clementina is dissatisfied and annoyed with the delay. Yet I'm certain this will be a safe situation, as Gina is healthy and good, unlike those who merely claim to be.

Fifth Month 12

Clementina called me down a short time ago and handed me a letter. I almost couldn't bear to look, so badly do I crave news from Peter. But look I did. It was from Delphinia on behalf of Gina, who can't read or write. Gina left yesterday for her new home and expects me and Charlotte this very afternoon! Delphinia supplied an address on Centre Street in Germantown that's not more than a half-mile from Father and Patience.

Clementina said I can go, and of course I must. But I dread putting Charlotte outside my protection again. She's not yet six weeks old, and delicate. A Holland bulb's nascent flower, half-formed within its sheath. A damselfly only half-emerged from its casing, not yet able to stand or walk or find food, for whom the careless brush of a human finger could mean a lifetime of disfigurement.

If Henry were cast out so expeditiously,

267

would his parents notice? It might take a day or two.

This parting from Charlotte is harder, now that I've seen her harmed. But there's a world of difference between Gina and Gerda.

I hear Isaac Penington's words of long ago, which as a child I'd recited when teachers bade us to:

Give over thine own willing,
give over thine own running,
give over thine own desiring to know or be
   anything,
and sink down to that seed
which God sows in thy heart
and let that be in thee, and grow in thee,
and breathe in thee, and act in thee. . . .

I pray my seed can grow and breathe and act in me, and bring me toward a home where I can live with my own child.

The hour came when I could delay no longer. For speed, using coins that Frau Varschen pressed upon me, I took a train to Germantown, keeping my head hidden beneath my old gray shawl and Charlotte hidden beneath my yellow one. Perhaps due to the bouncing of the car, she fell to sleep.

The other passengers, mostly workingmen, were reading papers or staring out the sides. No one but me stepped from the train near Chelten Avenue, which was relieving. I knew this section but a little; people called it the Yards.

I followed the tracks to the coal yard, which was rambunctious with noise. I asked a man with a coal-blackened face to help me find the correct block of Centre Street. He pointed behind me, so I doubled back toward a dirt road. I moved down a slight hill, past a wide-open area, and toward a stretch of recently built row-houses in good repair. I pulled the shawl off my perspiring head and undraped Charlotte, who shot up her head and looked about as if helping me to find the house.

The front doors of all the homes were propped open to let in the slight breeze. The buildings bore no numbers, so I walked toward one to ask for assistance. By luck, Gina herself sat in the foyer, dandling her baby!

We embraced, laughing at the awkwardness of doing so with babies in our arms, then examined one another's darlings; she commented on Charlotte's cheerful vitality, and I noted Lucia's delicate features, which gave her the look of a living doll.

I pulled a chair from the foyer wall and sat beside Gina, who said she was tired but confident she'd have milk for two. She'd already been feasting on meals prepared by Angela, who works most days at the hosiery mill but cooks and helps with the baby at night. The house held the fragrances of garden herbs and the syrup of long-simmered tomatoes.

"Angela's glad to have us," Gina said. "She sings all the time." She bent closer, whispering: "Everyone believes. They say, 'Stefano and Gina married in secret before he died.' Even Victor, her husband, believes." Then she had me lean out the door and look to the border of the coal yard, to an area she called the piazza. A dozen men sat at tables, playing cards, smoking, and drinking from squat glasses. Now and then a man yelled out in Italian, and others shouted back. "Victor is there," she said. "He is a stonemason, like my father. He is finished for this day."

I asked where she would keep Charlotte, so she directed me to follow her into the room off the foyer. Two cradles stood against a wall, one of them reserved for Charlotte; a bed for Gina lay alongside. I marveled at the luck of having two cradles.

"People help us," Gina said. "It's good

here." Her eyes linked with mine, and we grew teary, knowing how unlikely such an outcome had appeared while we'd lived side by side.

"I'm glad for thee." I looked down at Charlotte. "And for her!" Our eyes caught and we embraced once more, babies clutched to our chests.

The house was modest and clean; the air was fresh; its occupants, it seemed, were loving. All signs pointed to an excellent situation. I hated to hand Charlotte over, but hand her over I did. Gina stood on the front porch, a baby in each arm, to watch me go. My Lotte craned her head toward me, and I turned away. A sharp pang shot through my chest as I began walking alone up the dusty road toward the train. And then I heard her wail.

I closed my eyes and asked inwardly to be informed if I was making a mistake. I waited to hear words in my mind that might come from a deeper authority than my own worries.

"Turn back!" I expected to hear, or "Don't leave her again!"

No warning came.

Fifth Month 13, First Day
Last night's thunderstorm brought a spar-

kling morning. I spent it in the kitchen garden, where the seedlings of chards and lettuces, parsley, squash, and so much else were crowded close. With the wet soil loosening their roots, it was easy to thin them, to give the remaining plants more space and light. And what a pleasure to find so much that has overwintered! We can make several soups from the parsnips, carrots, potatoes, and onions that were missed at harvest, with nothing needed from the market except bones. Frau V. said she'll spend the savings on finer meats and poultry for the Burnhams and keep slivers for me and Margaret. I found tender leaves of spinach and chickweed, too, and new sprouts on the surviving stalks of thyme and sage. Henry balked at my milk afterward, probably because of the radishes and bitter greens I ate as I thinned.

When I gardened at home, I often considered how the growth of plants resembles the gradual growth of the spirit. And seeing life make its way from seed to plant does bring one a glorious hope. All through the plant's movement toward maturity, it is beautiful: adorable in its seedling state, full of promise as it sends its stalks up and out, then gorgeously fulfilled as it offers its yearly profit.

Yet this no longer seems to me to describe the trajectory of the human spirit, which can easily be thwarted by circumstance and become warped and bitter.

Are we so much less fortunate than plants? Or am I the warped and bitter one, who fails to see the profit in my struggles?

Regardless, I loved much about this morning. When my hands are immersed in dirt, my mind drifts away, and my body is left to take part in the buzz of aliveness where the so-called lower creatures dwell. Today the plants and trees and dirt and rocks vibrated with that power. I felt the sap flowing in the trees, delivering its timeless message: renewal comes.

Margaret returned from church in late afternoon, and we resumed her lessons after supper. We sat on the hooked rug in her room a dozen steps from mine. She pulled her lesson book from beneath her mattress and showed me page after page of carefully formed letters. No wonder I've seen light beneath her door when I rise at night. She can write all the uppercase letters now!

When I praised her progress, she shared her intention to write not only to her oldest sister but also to Rosa — a friend in Germantown. She wants to make a sampler for her mother, too, to show how well she makes use of her time. I'll help her choose a verse of Scripture for the bottom of it.

We practiced the lowercase. She sounded out each letter after me, and next I had her trace each one on the page with her finger. She felt a good deal of excitement, sometimes exclaiming "Oh!" or "I wondered how that sounds!"

Advanced composition was my forte at the Meeting school; my students, by Margaret's age, knew their letters forward and backward and upside down. I guided them in crafting arguments, not in learning the alphabet. But teaching Margaret her letters this afternoon was equally rewarding. There was such a sweetness in guiding her hand with mine.

Soon her hand grew tired. It's strong and rough from hauling and scrubbing, but holding a pencil is a new kind of work. I got up to leave and noticed a drawing upon her nightstand, with "Meghan Tooley" written in neat script at its bottom.

"My oldest sister drew that," she told me. "She's the one that went to school."

"What's that building?" I asked.

"The cottage where my family lives. See the stream?"

I nodded. "How far from here?"

"Some forty miles."

"Does thee miss it?"

Her somber nod told me she did. "But I don't miss the cotton mill." She told me that her entire family besides her father gets up before dawn for black coffee and biscuits, then walks to the mill for eleven-hour shifts, six days a week. She did this with them from age five to eleven, which is why sometimes she coughs. "Everyone coughs," she said, "from the fibers and dust in the air."

Because their combined wages had been hardly enough to feed and house them, Margaret came by train to the city, being the one among her siblings who spoke well and had the best manners by nature. She found her job with the Burnhams through an intelligence office. She sends back twelve dollars a month — most of her earnings, and more than she made at the mill — and spares her family the cost of keeping her, besides.

Our conversation ended abruptly, for Henry called out. My time is marked in segments sized by a baby's stomach.

As I nursed him, I felt glad to be in this house. Today was First Day, and I found no moments for silent waiting. But teaching Margaret was my worship.

NOTEBOOK SIX

Fifth Month 15

Today we closed the windows against a heavy rain, making it an ideal time for removing the grime that wafts in from the street and covers everything. Since Margaret was already serving Clementina and two lady visitors in the parlor, in addition to her usual round of tasks, I began to do this job rather than cooking through Henry's morning nap.

I fetched rags, a bucket, the lamb's-wool duster, and a feather brush and began in the dining room, making fast progress. I wiped the cherry table, the chairs, the dishes, and the sideboard. I cleaned the glass cabinet doors while peering in at charming items of painted porcelain and silver. Then I stepped into Albert's study and lost my focus. For the basic features of the world seemed encapsulated in that room — in its collections of shells and rocks and feathers, its stuffed pheasant under a dome, its array of insects pinned to velvet trays, its foreign stamps under glass. The walls held botanical drawings, a painting of people in baggy pants hunting tigers amid odd-shaped trees and hills, and a wall hanging embroidered with an unfamiliar alphabet and roughly rendered people and animals.

Whether these items gave evidence of an active mind and wide-ranging adventures or had merely been purchased to give such an impression, I couldn't say. But I was enthralled. What drew me most were the things I'd spied while sitting before the hearth with Albert and Henry: the books that crammed the many shelves.

I read the titles on their spines as I drew the fluffy duster across them. Some works of geography and natural sciences I recognized, and an encyclopedia. Yet I felt slight in the face of the many titles and authors I didn't know. A Friend's guarded education aims at depth in useful subjects and in those that develop one's inner compass; the more fanciful works are roped off as unwise influences. At a duster's length from a feast of uncensored ideas, I longed to grab hold.

I remembered the name Albert had said while teasing me — Marx. I found the *M*s among the alphabetized rows. Then to my eyes leapt not Marx's work but a small book bearing a grand gold-lettered title on its thin spine: *On Liberty.*

I slid the volume from its place and abandoned the duster. The book was published not long ago in London; on its dedication page, a John Stuart Mill credited his wife as part author and offered their work as humbly and earnestly as a spiritual seeker. And though I opened to pages at random, messages of penetrating importance beamed out from every page.

I came to perceive his chief message: that we are oppressed and caged by notions of what's proper, imprisoned by what it's thought suitable to want and do. Certainly we need rules to protect us from human beastliness, but society's conventions do more than that; they strangle thought and innovation in too wide an arena. Why can't we choose more for ourselves? When public opinion controls us "in things with which it ought not to meddle, it practices a social tyranny more formidable than many kinds of political oppression . . . penetrating much more deeply into the details of life, and enslaving the soul itself."

What astonishing words. I stood with book in hand, amid the ladies' laughter from the parlor. Through the guidance of my own modest measure of Inner Light, I've chosen to remain Charlotte's mother and to carry the burden of disgrace that this requires. But *why should* it require disgrace? In the world that Mill envisions, perhaps it wouldn't.

"Who can compute what the world loses," he asks, "in the multitude of promising intellects combined with timid characters, who dare not follow out any bold, vigorous, independent train of thought, lest it should land them in something which would admit of being considered irreligious or immoral?"

Which is precisely where I've landed.

If I could only meet this writer and speak with him about my case. Could he help me find a place where prejudice wouldn't block me from teaching, even marrying?

I felt such a longing for this imagined place that my legs grew weak. Despite my duties of the moment, I dropped to the floor with book in hand, settled my skirts about me, and turned the pages to see what else this Mill believes. Already he had given me a precious awareness — for while reading his words, the crushing weight of my entrapment fell away ever so briefly — and in that glimmer of relief from it, I perceived its heaviness.

The front door slammed, and quick footsteps came through the hall. Into his study walked Albert Burnham.

"Miss de Jong?" He stood drenched in his mackintosh and hat, face dripping with rain. I stood hastily and grabbed the duster from the shelf, book still in hand. He gave a small cough. "Have you found good reading, then?" he inquired, bending to see it. "J. S. Mill! An excellent choice." He wiped the wetness from his face and began to remove his coat. "The man rather inspires one to live a braver life, doesn't he? The end justifies the means! Damn the consequences!"

I hadn't seen those words, nor sensed that Mill meant them. But if Albert believed in unpopular behavior, perhaps this was why he wasn't affronted by my existence.

"Come," he said, gesturing to the upholstered chairs. "I'm here to get some papers, but there's no hurry to it. I may as well dry off before starting back." He draped his mackintosh and hat over pegs on the door.

I took a step toward a chair, then stopped.

"Sit," he said, though he remained standing. "Let's compare our thoughts on liberty."

"I'm dusting for Frau Varschen," I said. "I shouldn't have opened this." I lifted the slender book.

"Are you a follower of Utilitarianism?" he

asked, undeterred. "Or perhaps its sister, Consequentialism? Or its progenitor, Machiavelli, in all his unbound glory?"

"No," I said. "Or, yes. I don't know." In haste I searched my mind for anything I might have learned on these subjects; I found only anxiousness.

"Perhaps you haven't read widely in philosophy," he said — certainly true, but not the reason I wasn't yet seated across from him, expounding on the published minds of the Continent. I had work to do, and our conversation would raise suspicion. It occurred to me that his freedom to expound on whatever he likes relies partly on his ample means, which enable him to eat regardless of others' opinions of him.

He drew his fingers across his forehead and through his damp hair, looking at me with keen hazel eyes. Then he reached to a box on his desk, withdrew a cigar, and began to whittle its end.

"I don't know what philosophers they have women reading these days," he muttered.

"It's not that," I said. Yet no neat summary came to mind. "Please sit and get dry," I said. "I'll return to finish the dusting later." I stepped to a shelf to file away his book.

"Don't." He gestured with his head. "I have no use for it. Not much philosophy in imports!" He emitted a bark-like chortle. "Take it to your garret. Old Mill should make stimulating company." He smiled as he sat down and reached for a match to light his cigar.

"But," I said, moving the book toward the shelf, "I shouldn't have —"

"Ridiculous." He struck the match and inhaled, then emitted a line of smoke. "I haven't opened that since university. Keep it! It's yours. We can talk more once you've read it."

I was going to take my leave, clutching the book and the duster, when the raucous sound of a piano burst through the wall separating us from the parlor. I shrank instinctively against the shelves, not wanting to be found with Albert. Shouts of laughter joined the music, and Clementina's voice erupted in the hall.

"We need a fourth!" she yelled back to her friends in the parlor. "I won't have either of you playing wallflower!" Her staccato footsteps came toward us, aimed at the kitchen beyond. "Margaret! We've got the player piano going! Come dance!" Hearing no reply, she called, "Where is that girl?"

285

Albert stepped quickly into the hall. "Will I do?"

She gave a start. "What are you doing here?" Then she muted her tone. "Supper isn't for hours, darling."

"Came back to get some documents," he said. "But I'm always ready for a dance with my beautiful wife."

She did look beautiful, from what I could see around the doorway's edge — her face flushed with happiness brought on by music and company, her eyes gleaming, tendrils of hair straying charmingly from the curls pinned beneath her cap. A lace collar accentuated her slender neck, and lace-trimmed cuffs lent gracefulness to her supple wrists and fingers. She didn't see me, pressed as I was against the shelves, and I was glad. Her demeanor would have soured forthwith and set my stomach cramping.

"Will I do?" her husband asked again. He looked lovely, too, his eyes opened wide and his large features softening as he gazed at her. The smell of his cigar wafted backward, a not-unpleasant, barnlike scent.

"Certainly you'll do. Why, you'll do wonderfully!" She moved her head toward the parlor and raised her voice. "A surprise, ladies! Albert is here, and he's willing to dance!" The couple joined arms on the hallway carpet and strode toward the parlor.

My talk with Albert had ended so abruptly as to leave my response to his gift still on my lips. "Thank you," I whispered. I brought the book to my cheek, as if greeting a friend, and slid it into my apron pocket. Then with greater speed I moved about the room and into the foyer and upstairs, wiping and dusting, all the while listening to the dancers stomp and laugh to the rambunctious music.

In my previous life, loud music and dancing had seemed no more than incitements to impulsive behavior. Yet that celebratory stepping and the piano's torrent of tones brought cheer even to this erstwhile Friend.

Fifth Month 18, near midnight

I ought not to read so late — but I've opened *On Liberty* and come upon an idea that seems to turn Mill's other ideas on their heads.

We can pursue our true wants, Mill writes, only when doing so harms no one to whom we are obliged.

Of course this must be so. To behave otherwise would be immoral. Yet how it changes everything!

I am obliged to Charlotte.

The freedom I seek is to remain her

mother, in word and deed.

I have harmed her in seeking this. Only because of prejudice, though — only because of prejudice.

Mill wishes to do away with such limiting judgments. Yet with it present, infecting our world, the promise of his idea of liberty belongs only to those whose survival is unaffected by narrow minds. That is, it belongs to those who have little need of earning money, and not only that; it belongs to those of that group who are essential to the survival of none.

How many are there of these persons — uncommonly removed from their fellows — who may press against the walls of common morality? The most of us are saddled with near-constant obligations: raising the young and sheltering the crippled, doing farming and manufacturing, tending the sick, lowering the dead to their graves. Does Mill realize just how few can take this liberty he trumpets?

There may be cruelty in such a philosophy. It posits a world we cannot occupy — and makes us feel doubly trapped for knowing it.

But I won't blame Mill for this. He must have known the sting of prejudice and had his own life narrowed, or else how has he understood its hazards and its costs?

In the philosophy of Friends, one seeks comfort in the Lord when humans fail to understand one's revolutionary aims.

If only my aims were considered revolutionary.

If only I could speak with Mill and arrive with him at a more practical form of liberty. For we take our steps through this world linked arm to arm, affecting one another. Mustn't we all accept a partial freedom, a limited but not obscured horizon?

Another idea begins to tickle my mind. It starts with this: I can be considered free only if I can choose.

And what do my choices matter, if they're of no consequence to someone else?

Then only because my choices affect others can I be called free!

There is no such thing as liberty, then, if I am not obligated.

Yet if I'm obligated, then I am not free.

I've wound my thinking into knots. I need to sleep.

Rain is dashing into the oval window at the foot of my bed. Down the street, in the moonlight, a patchwork of blooming trees and bushes glows. A splendid scene. Yet as I watch, the wind and rain are liberating flower after flower from their stems and hurtling them to piles of rotting petals.

Does all beauty end in rot?

Late night is the playground of despair.

Fifth Month 23

We've moved to the Burnhams' estate in Germantown!

The heat was coming on fast, so Clementina decided we should move sooner than planned. Margaret and I spent days packing essentials at the Pine Street house — amid the scoldings of Frau Varschen, who despises disorder. She never comes here for summers, since her home in Moyamensing is too far, but she had strong ideas of what remedies and staples we should bring for the summer cook. In all the rush I had to forgo my visit to Charlotte — but I took comfort in knowing I'd live much closer soon.

Finally we departed. Margaret and Henry and I bumped along in a rented carriage behind the Burnhams' gleaming green one. Following us were three wagons burdened by barrels, crates, and trunks, with broad-backed horses pulling their weight.

When we reached the main street of Germantown, I looked through the dust raised by our cavalcade to familiar sights: churches, banks, and other grand buildings of stone and brick, before which elegant citizens gestured in conversation; small homes and stores where rougher-looking people stood or crouched about, gulping from cups and spitting. Small children spun tops and chased each other; older folks hawked items from barrels or crates. Aiming to recognize no one, I moved my eyes quickly over them all.

We passed the road that led to the old grist mill, now torn down, where Peter and I had explored and built forts from scraps of wood. We passed the road to the ice-skating pond where Johan and I had courted. We passed the lane to Sterne's meadow, and how I longed to leap from the suffocating carriage and gallop to that place where gigantic trees hold court, casting patterns of shade and light on ferns and bluebells. We passed the market square, where it's said Africans were auctioned long ago, and the home of abolitionist Friends who'd sheltered people escaping from slavery. We passed Coulter Street, down which I glimpsed our peak-roofed, stuccoed meetinghouse, wide and long, with no decoration to distract one from its sober purpose, and I sent a greeting to Mother, who lies in the burying ground beside it. We passed the school where I'd been a student and then a teacher, acknowledged for my intellect and virtue, the qualities upon which I'd built all visions of my future life.

A small herd of goats was crossing at Centre Street, so our cavalcade halted, mere blocks from Gina's home. I took the chance to send my tenderest intentions toward Charlotte; perhaps she felt a flutter of air at her cheek as she nursed or dozed.

Then we passed a certain street that leads to a certain lane with but a handful of small houses along it, built of wood or stone, one of which contains Father and Patience, and my own little room, and — in the attic — the mattress where an hour's indulgence set my path askew.

I sighed.

"Are you all right?" asked Margaret.

I kept my face still and nodded.

A group of schoolchildren stopped to stare at the Burnhams' bright carriage. I drew back from the window so as not to be seen — and barely in time. A cluster of Friends clad in grays and browns poured from a building and turned our way. At their lead was the beloved headmaster of the Meeting school, a man so long and lean that his head seemed to pierce the clouds and his feet barely to trod the earth. Once he told me that a letter I'd written to my colleagues —

which recommended that our students write and deliver more speeches on subjects of vital interest to them — was worthy of being carved in stone. How worthy would he find my occupations now?

Then I spied my cleverest student, Louella Lynes. How confident she looked, her head raised in its chaste bonnet, her carriage upright; how untrammeled by the world, with her arms swinging wide, her clear-skinned cheeks raised in a smile, her mouth opened to emit a pronouncement. She'd taken me as her model. I flattened my body against the seat and covered my head and face with a shawl.

I released myself from the shawl's steamy tunnel only after the carriage turned left onto Walnut Lane. My family and I rarely visited this stately district. Its inhabitants seemed to occupy a separate world of cricket clubs, churches with hired priests, fashionable clothing, and parties meant to bring on gaiety and inebriation. Grocers and other vendors delivered goods directly to their doors, so that even their servants had little cause to take part in village life. The farther we traveled into this realm of estates, fields, and woods, the safer I felt from discovery.

Margaret began to chatter about the

house, which belongs to Clementina's parents, and about the summer cook, Miss Baker — extolling her delectable food, especially her cakes and pies, and her thorough preparation of the place. Margaret said we could expect everything to be spotless and lemon-scented. She caught her breath and fairly shivered as our carriages and wagons careened onto a curving driveway and toward a stone mansion that was as frivolous as a stone house can be, festooned with painted woodwork and garnished with turrets and gables.

The horses halted, lathered with sweat. A coachman ran up to tend them. We disembarked, and then began a time of puzzlement.

The mansion's windows were shuttered, and its ornate double doors were locked. A sputtering Clementina located a key in her bag and used it. First the Burnhams, then Margaret and I stepped onto the foyer's thick carpet, encountering musty air and darkness.

"What's happened here?" Clementina fanned her sweating face. Her pin curls lay wet against her forehead.

Albert stepped to her side and placed his hand on her forearm. "I'm sure there's an explanation."

She shook his hand off. "I don't want an *explanation*. I want a meal and a clean house. But whatever the explanation, it needn't concern you, need it? The tedious work to remedy it won't be yours."

Her husband flushed. The comment was true enough — and I took her statement to mean that *she* would put herself to work upon the remedy, alongside her servants. But Margaret gave me a baleful look that dissuaded me from this notion. Then a deep voice called through the opened doorway.

"Hallo there!" A gray-haired, brown-skinned man bobbed across the grass, poking his cane into the ground ahead and pulling himself forward by it.

Margaret whispered, "It's Mr. Pemberton. He's the caretaker of this house and the neighbor's."

The tall man climbed the stoop and crossed into the foyer, pausing to recover his breath. Removing his hat, he nodded in greeting.

"How are you, sir?" asked Albert, bowing his head.

Mr. Pemberton replied in a rumbling baritone. "I'm right as rain, but Miss Baker took ill last week. Her fever's high. Doctor says it's ague. Ordered five days' more of rest at least."

"Five days?" Clementina said.

Even Albert looked put out. Margaret sagged visibly. Clementina huffed. "She could have arranged for others to come."

Mr. Pemberton nodded, acknowledging the point. "She's been too sick to see to that," he said. "She sends sincere regrets, madam."

Clementina winced at his use of the title that she said makes her feel like her mother. Then the elderly man spied Henry in my arms and gave a broad smile, showing teeth yellowed by tobacco. "The newest family member! Let Mr. Pemberton have a look."

I moved the sleepy boy forward. The caretaker patted Henry's scalp and radiated goodwill toward the baby and me. I basked in his kindness.

"That's enough," snapped Clementina. "We'll be needing to begin the work Miss Baker hasn't done."

I flinched, but Mr. Pemberton didn't. He let her attitude roll off him like water from a duck's feathers. He turned toward Margaret and I, giving a wink that recognized us as his compatriots in service to this challenging woman. Then he used his cane to propel himself out the door.

Albert sighed. "Well, it can't be helped." He removed his straw hat and hung it on the elaborate wood and cast-iron hat stand. Leaning toward its oblong mirror, he gave his hair a few strokes with a comb.

His wife snatched the ivory comb and banged it down on the stand. "Yes it *can* be helped. You get our drivers busy unloading. You'll have to join in, Albert."

Albert pulled his head back on his neck and stared, about to speak. Then he looked to Margaret and me, sighed once more, and stepped out toward the wagons.

Clementina turned to us, her slender form vibrating with irritation. "Already we had nowhere near the help my parents had to keep this place in order. Now this! You'll have to set up the kitchen and prepare our meal, girls. Next you'll make this house habitable, which will take no slight effort, I tell you." She ran a finger along the mahogany banister that curves up the stairs to the second story, examined the depth of dust on her fingertip, and shuddered.

For several days, we did little but vanquish dust and unpleasant odors while Clementina lay on a divan in the parlor, complaining of a toothache. To any who came near, she bemoaned the absence of the kitchen helper, butler, and two more chambermaids that her parents had employed when she'd been a child in this very house, not to mention the inconvenience of Miss Baker's absence. She fretted over the inadequacy of our work as we shook out and aired feather beds and pillows, curtains, rugs, and mats; scrubbed floors and polished them; wiped and dusted every surface; kept the kitchen stove fueled; cooked and washed up after meals; brought water in and waste out; unloaded deliveries from the grocer's buggy; hauled ice from the ice wagon; and on and on and on — with me stepping away to care for Henry.

Eventually Clementina moved to a stuffed chair in her bedroom and pored over every theater and musical review in every paper she'd had delivered, opining on the shortcomings of this reviewer and that. Then she turned to the *Ladies' Home Journal and Practical Housekeeper,* a new publication she'd subscribed to under pressure from a visitor. She addressed herself as ferociously to those pages as she did to us. Later she critiqued the publication to Albert in the dining room, telling him she didn't care what substances worked better at removing grease stains from the collars of men's shirts or vomit from a child's bedclothes. (Luckily, Margaret and I mostly needn't concern ourselves with stain removal either, for the laundry is sent out.)

"You need something else to occupy you," Albert observed in reply. "Why not see a performance and write up a review?"

She exhaled loudly. "I've told you. My column has been discontinued for the summer. I can't keep current at this distance."

"Then you're consigned to a summer of rest and sociable activities. Sounds enviable to me."

She scoffed. "Overseeing our servants is hardly leisure. You're the one with true leisure when at home, since you do none of the management."

It *is* odd that Albert takes no responsibilities within the property. And neither of them pays much heed to Henry, except on a whim. But it's Clementina who makes our work bitter. She seems convinced that her distance from necessary labor makes her more important than we are.

Yet keeping still only feeds her irritability and unhappiness! I suppose that's justice.

Through all this, Margaret retains an admirable cheer. Her cough — a remnant of the cotton mill — has been activated by the dust. But she moves with purpose and gleams with vitality.

"Aren't thy muscles sore?" I asked as we beat yet another rug outside. Mine were aching.

"Nah. I've always worked this hard." She released the rug to the ground, pushed her sleeve to her shoulder, and flexed her substantial muscles, then laughed, surrendering her whole body to the sensation. "I love coming here." She breathed in the vital air and gestured toward the gardens that began at the edge of the work yard. "You'll love it, too, once we're done with the spring cleaning."

"Indeed," I told her. Because I do love Germantown.

Yet how strange to know that while Clementina was growing up amid this splendor, I lived close by in a far simpler house and found especial satisfaction in Friend John Woolman's writings on the importance of living modestly. Doing so has many benefits, especially these two: it spares us all from needless work, and it gives us time to advance the human lot more meaningfully.

I do find meaning in my work here, though — especially in Henry's gabled nursery. It's cheery, with striped paper on the walls and large windows that offer views of leafy trees. When I lift him from his crib, feel his feather-soft skin and solid weight upon me, and relax into the steady squeezing of his suck, he brings me to a place beyond worry, beyond the passage of time. Then I place him on his back and wave my fingers above, smiling as he tries to reach. He grunts, churning his thighs and feet in the air. I lower a finger; he grabs hold and pinches tight and crows over his great accomplishment.

Where does it come from, this urge to master the skills of one's species?

Some force moves all living things to excel. Surely this proves we are endowed with bits of our Creator.

On the floors, while cleaning, I found a total of twelve pennies and tucked them in my apron pocket. This is all the money I have till the First of Sixth Month, over a week away, when at last I will be paid.

Fifth Month 25

I'm pleased to report that even Margaret's patience has its limit.

The Burnhams still have no cook. After I fixed Clementina's tea this afternoon and Margaret served it, Clementina walked into the kitchen and stood watching us at our cleaning. Her hands were on her hips; her face was dour.

"You must work faster," she said. "The kitchen is not fully outfitted. Our spare bedrooms haven't been touched. My parents are on a boat from the Continent, and the entire house must bear no sign of neglect by the time they arrive. Margaret, remember to change to a clean uniform before our mealtimes. It's bad enough we have to be served by a maid. Lilli, I'll expect your clothing to be free of milk or infant" — here she waved her hands, seeking the word — "spit-up. Everything must be perfect during their entire fortnight's visit, or your pay will be docked." She exhaled audibly. "Do you understand me, girls?"

Margaret bowed in reply. I nodded. Clementina stormed out, and Margaret pressed her lips into a prune and narrowed her eyes. "Do you understand me, girls?" she whispered. "Your pay will be docked, docked, docked, if you don't work faster! Everything must be perfect! Perfect, perfect!"

She grabbed the hearth-broom and ran back and forth across the wood floor, wielding the broom crazily in the air. Then we began to work at double speed, racing to wipe dishes into a bucket, scrubbing them with haphazard motions that sprayed water about, whispering "Faster! Faster!" to each other, and generally behaving in such a ridiculous manner that our aprons came untied, and soap bits hung from our garments, and we were laughing too hard to continue doing anything but hold our cramping stomachs. Tears trickled down our faces as we gasped for breath. I half wished Clementina would come in and find us in this state, though her rage might have scared the feathers off a chicken.

Then Margaret and I stepped out back to satisfy our thirst and splash one another at the pump, which spurts water of the most heavenly freshness.

Our clothes were wrinkled and damp and darkened by dust, our hair flew free of our buns and stuck to our necks and foreheads, and any pretense our boots once had of decency had long been abandoned to the swish of mop water and the showers of dirt from the rugs. As if we had nothing to lose, we laughed uproariously and doused each other with cold water, renewing our bodies and our spirits.

Fifth Month 27

It's First Day morning. The Burnhams have gone to St. Luke's Episcopal on Main Street — a cathedral in the European style, lavish with arches and marble and stained glass. At breakfast, Clementina spoke animatedly of the friends she'd see there and the outings they'd plan, while Albert hoped to arrange a game of cricket. They went upstairs to dress, the lady with Margaret's help, then donned their hats in the foyer. Clementina called to me, so I ran down the back stairs and came forward. Though she had on a most fanciful hat, bestowed with several birds' worth of feathers, and a pink dress that made her look mild, she addressed me with her usual disdain.

"Eat nothing you shouldn't. This is a workday for you, so don't shirk. There's a chore list on the kitchen table, and I expect everything done by our return at midday."

I gave a curtsy, hoping fruitlessly to enter her better graces. She stepped out to their carriage, and her husband turned from the doorway, looking summery and cool in a beige linen suit and straw hat. He gave me a wink and a cheerful nod that lifted my mood, then alighted into the carriage. At the driver's crop, the horses pulled them away.

Then Margaret left on foot to attend a Catholic church, Our Lady of Solace, where she favors the priest. As she has the whole day for her own, she'll be staying through the social afterward.

Once they'd left, I walked through the mansion's rooms and gazed on its shining floors, its wallpapers of dizzying patterns, its ornate upholstery and furnishings. Though pleased to have had a hand in its beautification, I felt as out of place in the splendor as a robin might feel among peacocks.

I took refuge in the list of chores. I emptied ashes from the kitchen stove, fueled it, filled the woodbox, prepared ingredients for the midday meal, swept and mopped the kitchen floor, and scrubbed the pots from last night's supper. I avoided seditious behavior — not a crumb of cake did I eat, nor a drop of tea imbibe. I nursed Henry till his belly protruded and he slept. Yet I found no ease, even with him. He seemed a stranger to me, a stranger who lives off my body while my Lotte sucks at another's.

I rose to my room, a cavernous, slant-roofed attic space with beams above and unpolished planks below. It smells of camphor and dust, but I adore it. In the day, the sun enters in a dappled pattern, its force muted by high trees at the back of the property. In the night, moonlight penetrates its corners and cools my thoughts. But I'm the first to use it as a servant's room, and it hadn't yet been cleaned.

I fetched rags and soapy water and began to weave a damp rag among the heaps of forgotten items — the old spinning wheel and loom, the hat racks and clothes dummies, the trunks and crates and barrels.

They fairly glowed with hidden meanings, as if they could have spoken of who had used them and what they'd done, if only my rag would find and free their tongues.

My eye was drawn to a stack of papers piled upon the floor. The top item was a musical score inscribed "Clementina Appleton." Tucked inside were four parchment awards naming Clementina for best violin performance, four years in a row. I opened a school copybook next and saw page after page of the exquisite handwriting that young Clementina had cultivated. The topic she wrote upon obsessively? Music. Playing it, listening to it, studying it — adoring it.

Beside the papers lay a china doll. It had a pale face, painted green eyes, and light brown curls, not unlike Clementina's, and it held in its arms a tiny violin. Though lifeless, unmoving, fixed in place, it spoke to me of Clementina's early passion — which struck me as bittersweet. Then it spoke to me of something more. I felt myself a castaway, just like the doll — a relic whose purpose has passed, now hidden out of sight, serving only to remind the accidental viewer of a potential that has vanished.

I took up this notebook.

I'm in close walking distance to the Meeting I attended twice weekly for nearly all my years. And for the first time since leaving, I feel not defiance, or hurt, but a frank and open longing. I miss the buoyant silence of our Meeting for Worship. I want to join my mind with the stream of awareness flowing through the meetinghouse. With eyes closed, I used to hear it in my mind as if it were an actual stream, flowing at the level of our heads, growing fuller and more solace-giving as one mind after another calmed and entered.

What if I did join in on some First Day, while the others in this household were out? What if I walked there during Henry's long morning nap, which can now be counted on, and took a seat in the women's section? Perhaps someone who'd disapproved most heartily of Father — probably the flat-faced Edgar Dinkles — would lean to my ear and whisper, "It's best for thee to go." I'd rise, stiff as a dressmaker's dummy. His hand pressing at my back would speed my progress toward the door.

Someone else might follow me out and comfort me — perhaps a friend from school who hadn't married and moved away. But I could never tell her my predicament.

The Burnhams have come home. I hear them in the foyer. It's time to ready their food.

Tomorrow afternoon, after too many days without seeing her, I'll visit my baby.

Fifth Month 28

My steps were rapid as I traveled the mile or so to the eastmost block of Centre Street. Gina welcomed me, holding Lucia to her, and led me to the doorway of their room. My Lotte lay on her back in a cradle, sucking at her fist, until I called the sweet melody of her name. Then she turned her gaze to me; her breath became a pant, and she opened her mouth into a grin.

Oh, my love! I took her in my arms and exulted, as if a lost piece of me was fitted back in place. She had neither forgotten nor forsaken me.

She mouthed at my breast, insisting on being fed, as if to confirm that I still belong to her. As she nursed, she paused to rub her cheek against me, the edges of her mouth turning up. With her inch-long fingers she pulled and patted at my chest.

Then Gina and I sat at the kitchen table, babies in our laps, eating bread and cheese and salty pickles. I even got to enjoy a sugary cup of tea without fearing Clementina's censure, though Lucia's round eyes were fierce as they roved about, and I pretended she was discovering my treachery, to amuse myself and Gina.

Lucia can raise her head now. It's covered in black curls, like her mother's. But my attention was mainly fixed to Charlotte. Her facial features have gained more shape. At nearly two months old, she shows less fussiness and more lively interest. She reached for my bread and cheese, and banged her fist against my hand in trying to grab my teacup, causing me to spill lukewarm tea on her — which seemed to interest more than to upset her.

As Gina and I talked, I observed her new family through the kitchen windows. Victor, dark-haired and slim, was feeding a pig in a pen and two goats on tethers. Angela, light-haired and plump, pounded and shaped dough on a wooden slab, then fed the loaves into a brick oven that had a fire burning underneath. Their small yard held a grape arbor, fig and apple trees, berry bushes and vines, a kitchen garden, and a small fish pond with painted tiles at its perimeter. Indeed, I was much impressed with their industriousness. But when Angela came up the back stoop into the kitchen, her tone was harsh.

"Every noise wakes your baby." She faced my way as she washed her hands over a tub. "Lucia sleeps the night. But your baby wakes and screams." She pointed at Charlotte, who lay contented in my lap. "She wants to nurse always!" Angela opened her wet palms, exasperated. "I rock her so Gina can try and sleep. But your baby, she cries and cries."

"Has thee tried a bottle —" I attempted.

Angela shook her head, drying her hands on a cloth. "She don't take it."

Gina looked at me sideways with a sympathetic expression that seemed to say, *It's all true, but I'm sorry for how harshly it's coming out.*

My reactions tangled in my chest and ached there. I must be grateful to these women, for Charlotte is undoubtedly a challenge. But I would put up with this difficulty willingly, and wouldn't let her scream through the night, if I could care for her myself. Not to mention that I would never let my own charge, Henry, suffer so. I hoped the nights of crying wouldn't damage Charlotte's temperament.

"You should pay more," Angela said, "two dollars a week, not one fifty."

I was dismayed. This would delay my plans to set us up independently. But I understood her reason — and I had no choice. Contritely I said, "I'll start next week."

This calmed Angela. After taking off her apron and changing from dirty boots to clean ones, she patted my head and Charlotte's with a forceful hand. She told Gina something in Italian. Then she excused herself, explaining that she was due at a neighbor's to make decorations for an upcoming religious festival.

I handed Gina three dollars for the previous two weeks, which I'd borrowed from Clementina and Margaret, and reiterated my promise to pay two dollars starting next week — by which time I'll have been paid for my own work.

Gina patted my leg and tucked the bills into her skirt pocket. "It is good Charlotte stays here. I need money." Her body leaned closer, bringing me the scent of lavender soap. "Angela says I don't. But I have my plan. I take Lucia to Italy, after I save." She kissed Lucia on the scalp, then looked across the room, her plump face absent with homesickness.

Victor entered the kitchen from the yard and washed his hands. He was clean-shaven, with glossy hair and well-proportioned features. His son — Gina's purported husband — must have been handsome. Victor dried his hands on a towel, then reached to shake my hand. His hand was warm and reassuring, but his words were not.

"Where's your husband?" he asked. "How long will this baby stay? How do you know our Gina?"

I stuttered as I tried to frame replies, and Gina jumped in to rescue me. "We met at Fessler's Market. Her husband works in Pittsburgh." She turned to me, her look matter-of-fact. "And you go to him soon, Lilli. With Charlotte."

"That's correct." I nodded. "A few months longer, no more than that." I gulped back all the incriminating words I might have offered. A church bell tolled and saved me from further questions.

"Three o'clock! I got a rehearsal at Angelo's." Victor strode through an archway into the next room and grabbed what I took to be a case for a horn. The front door banged after him.

Gina placed Lucia in a bassinet, then led me and Charlotte outside, where she checked the bread and fed the fire. Charlotte grabbed my pointer finger and sucked it. I stroked her red hair, so much like her father's.

For him, she is not a whisper of a thought. I prayed again for a letter from Peter.

When a church bell struck five, I placed

Charlotte not in the cradle but in Gina's arms, hoping to soften my departure. I covered my head with a shawl, stepped into the afternoon's oblique sun, and walked to the Burnhams'. I took back ways through meadows and woods, my sadness soothed by air that was redolent with life expanding. My soul exulted at this good world, where everything is made purposeful by God's animating force.

Fifth Month 29

Clementina's temper has burst forth like a flame all day. She began to assert it early this morning, when I was making breakfast. Henry called from his crib; since Margaret was emptying a bucket of kitchen waste in the back, I had to leave my work to get him. When I returned, with him mouthing my apron, the toast was burned. So I tried again, with Henry in one arm (which proved no easy way to slice bread). I placed the toast rack before the hearth, then sat to nurse. But I didn't turn the rack soon enough, and once more the bread turned black. Clementina came in, yelling.

"What's that wretched smell? Where's my breakfast?" She gave but a second's glance to her son. Before I could answer, Margaret entered and instantly saw that I was serving too many needs at once.

"I'll look for something in the attic for Henry to lie in," she said. I met her words with a grateful look.

"You have five more minutes to prepare our meal," said Clementina. "My husband has to get downtown." She grabbed a strawberry from the table and devoured it. Also on the table sat a cup of tea and a small pile of shelled peanuts.

"Are these yours?" she asked, pointing, for both those items are forbidden to me. They were indeed mine, but I feared the increase of her rage too much to answer. My stomach clenched as she spilled my tea into a bucket. "I'm taking note of this violation of your terms." With a slight blush, she swept the peanuts into a cupped hand and tossed them into her mouth. Raising up her nose and balling her fists in indignance, she marched out.

Margaret returned carrying a padded wicker basket, perfect for Henry's size, and a wheeled frame for it to rest on. She said this might have been the very basket Clementina had lain in, an observation that failed to make me sentimental. I laid a dishtowel on its musty padding and placed Henry down. Then we raced to prepare omelets and toast and broiled ham while the Burnhams engaged in a heated discussion in the dining room.

"A fellow in *Harper's Magazine* says a girl's education should fit her for *a woman's life*," Clementina said.

"Sounds sensible," replied Albert.

"A woman's life? He means doing all the filthy, boring, never-ending labors of the home — while constantly pretending to be contented and sweet. Oh, and doing these things while amusing others with modestly informed conversation and musical performances of fitting mediocrity."

"But my dear, you *are* sweet. Others do your filthy labor. And your conversation is informed — though you refuse to entertain with music. And you're free to learn whatever you please, regardless of what this writer claims. Everyone's got an opinion about the proper education of girls. Find one that suits you better!"

"Albert!" Her cry was dismal.

"All right, you tell me what's the matter."

"That man's view is typical, and you know it. But a woman doesn't exist merely to make life pleasant and convenient for others. Has she no right to a livable existence herself? To say a girl's education must prepare her to be a wife and mother only — and to say, as he does, that this education should take place entirely in the home — why, it's a bit like saying a colored man's education ought to occur only in fields and to make him fit only for planting and picking cotton. Don't you see? It's a virtual prison women are kept in — a cage decorated with words like *moral* and *pure*!"

"Surely you can't think your life a prison," protested Albert. "It may be a cage, but it's a gilded one. Dearest, why are you so unhappy?"

"Aaaarh!" yelled Clementina.

A chair scraped the floor. Footsteps pattered up the stairs. A door slammed shut and a bed creaked, revealing her new location.

By that point we'd finished assembling their meal. Margaret's face was pallid. She whispered, "Should I serve Mr. Burnham?"

I nodded. "Fill a plate for her, too," I whispered, "and bring it upstairs. She was awfully hungry."

Margaret nodded and carried the tray into the dining room. Amid the clatter of serving, I sat a moment to eat my cracked wheat and cream, staring at the wild daisies that Margaret had put in a vase. Amid its flimsy white petals, each flower had a fiery orange sun at its center.

Clementina has just such a fiery center, I mused.

As do I.

Instantly I grew panicked at my virtual imprisonment in this unhappy house. My heart rose to my throat, beating irregularly and making me breathless. I grabbed my shawl from the kitchen bench and rushed to the back porch, which overlooks the work yard and, beyond that, a stretch of gardens. A fog descended in a wall of soupy mist. Someone clambered onto the porch behind me, and I turned, expecting Margaret. A hot-faced Albert stood there, dressed for the office in a summer suit and bow tie.

He cleared his throat; awkward seconds ensued. Agitation emanated from him, and the strain of standing still in such a state. I felt no differently myself.

"Shall we take a turn about the property?" he asked. "I don't mind the fog. Do you?"

"Not much," I said, wondering again why he doesn't revile me as his wife does. He also seemed immune to the fear that she might grow suspicious if she saw us walking together. I wasn't immune. Each step on the brick path seemed one step closer to bursting the balloon of her temper and threatening my employment. Yet I wouldn't let her cage me.

We stepped side by side without speaking as beads of water settled like a chilling blanket on my skin and hair. He made fretting sounds, and I sought solace in the garden and its flowering trees. The dogwoods were impressive specimens, far larger than the one I'd viewed each spring from my bedroom window. When I was a girl, during its annual week of glory, I'd gaze at its spread of white petals veined with pink and the clusters of tiny yellow flowers at their centers. I'd wish to lie upon that flowering dome as one might wish to be held aloft by a cloud. But my older self was not so dreamy. I noted the hard branches beneath the blossoms. I knew a cloud was but a gathering of chilly vapors.

Albert thrust his body forward along the path and mumbled to himself. Finally he burst into speech. "Why is my wife unhappy? She stormed away because I asked her this. I don't understand. She has two houses, abundant help, a healthy son, and" — he reddened — "a husband who adores her."

"Perhaps she feels she was meant for a freer life, without a child and a household to run," I offered.

"I believe you've got it." Albert turned to assess me anew. "Did you know she gave up a career in music? Actually, her parents forbade her to pursue it."

A career in music! Her parents forbade it! So that was what the doll and musical scores and copybooks indicated. My words came out before I could think: "She's haunted by that."

"Yes, she's haunted." He spoke slowly, as if first realizing. "If only I'd understood the extent of this before I yoked my life to hers."

The mist turned cold on my arms and face and at the back of my neck. We turned onto a brick path toward a grape arbor. By Eighth Month, the arbors behind my home would droop with clusters. The scent they wafted was so delectable and elusive that I would breathe and breathe and never breathe enough. My lips tingled, anticipating that scent.

"I met Clementina at a dance," said Albert. "She holds her own as a partner, I assure you. Maybe I shouldn't have married such an independent woman."

"May I speak frankly?" I asked.

"I'll tolerate nothing less, Miss de Jong." The set of his mouth was equal parts serious and jesting.

"She wants to escape from others' control," I blurted. "To decide for herself. She wants what women rarely can have — the chance to determine her own way."

"Ah," he said. "You'll be needing to take another work from my Pine Street library. J. S. Mill has written a treatise on that subject called *The Subjection of Women.*"

I wondered if this work might address my troubles with his other treatise.

"Soundly trounced for it, he was," continued Albert. "And no wonder. A degree of subjection can be awfully convenient." He chortled.

I had no ready answer.

"Miss de Jong, have you ever fancied yourself a free thinker? A rebel?"

"I'm not versed in those terms," I said. "But the Society of Friends has valued the spiritual equality of male and female for over two centuries. All flesh is equal in the eyes of the Lord."

"Interesting." He pulled a handkerchief from his jacket and wiped the accumulating wetness from his face. "But what of equality in areas besides the spiritual?"

"Ah." I broke off into quiet to consider this.

"This may well be what Clementina is on about," he mumbled.

Indeed. And Mill seemed once more to be my dearest ally. Might he have even considered a woman such as me while decrying women's subjection? I might have dared to ask Albert to bring that screed to Germantown, if he were to stop in at Pine Street, but his brow was creased, and his lips moved with some preoccupation.

In silence we traveled past the flowering honeysuckle, the sage plants that reached already to my waist, the feathery stalks of yarrow bursting upward into lace. We passed the stable, where the coachman in trousers and a livery coat — their summer regular — was harnessing a horse to the carriage. I peered into the dusty space. At back was a closet, and nearby, a staircase, perhaps leading to a second-story room where a coachman or a groomsman might have slept, when the Appletons had one around the clock.

The stocky fellow inclined his head of red curls toward us and nodded. "G'morning, Mr. Burnham."

"Good morning, Randall. About ready with that carriage?"

"Of course, sir."

"Thank you, Randall."

The coachman gave me a suspicious glance with his small brown eyes as we passed.

"How do you like our summer place?" said Albert.

"It's quite comfortable." I pulled my shawl over my head, for the mist had cohered into insistent drops. "But . . ."

"What?" he asked. "Has Henry been difficult to manage?" He leaned to take a sprig of lavender, pinched it, and brought it to his nose as rain dripped down his face. I hadn't noticed till then that he wore no hat. His nostrils widened as he inhaled, and his lips curved upward. Pleasure drives him, I saw then. We resumed our walking.

"Oh, no," I answered. "Thy son isn't difficult. The opposite, really. I — I merely find it odd to be — so close to home."

"Where is your home?"

"I spent my life in Germantown, until last fall."

His face lit with surprise. "Why don't you visit?" A furry form streaked by, nearly tripping him. His attention followed the cat, who was no doubt pursuing a small rodent.

I tried to reply. "I'm — surely thee can imagine — well, I can't disgrace my family by showing up as a — as someone considered — ungodly."

"Ah, I'd forgotten your situation," he said.

Yet I devote my every hour to his. I swallowed that bitter pill.

"So do you believe yourself ungodly, Miss de Jong?"

It was a large question. Answering such sizable questions always involves me in falsehoods created by the need to simplify. But I tried to speak truly and briefly. "I trusted the word of the man I loved. I put too much at risk in doing so."

"Yes." He nodded. "This fellow betrayed you, as you told the doctor and me at that charity. Do you believe, then, that society shouldn't judge you for your part?"

"Society *does* judge me a sinner," I said, "so what I think is irrelevant."

"But what *is* a sin, in your view?"

I glanced sideways to see his face, which looked earnest and not prurient, as I'd feared. "I'd say it's a sin to behave with hate, to be untruthful, to betray the messages that come by the Divine Light. It's a sin not to remain open to perceiving those revelations."

"Your language is fascinating. You seem to believe that God troubles to send us individualized instructions. Isn't there a list of sins already written in the Bible for all to see?"

I sighed. It isn't easy for some to accept that God may speak to anyone. And I wasn't prepared to convince him that sin was more than a list of acts. I wanted to return to the kitchen. My hair and clothes were thoroughly wet, and I doubted he'd be going off to work in that sopping jacket. But he was undeterred.

"So in being intimate with your — man," he asked, "were you following God's guidance?"

I flushed. Certainly I've fallen short of the precepts of my religion. But I didn't feel I was doing so when giving my body over to Johan. Loving him felt godly. Do the senses trick us? Or do the senses tell us truly, and the world's restrictions only fail to let us follow them?

"I believed so," I said. "I certainly believed I was doing right."

Albert laughed in surprise. "Most people would consider you a worse sinner for that."

My throat grew thick. I rushed ahead, then took a turn toward the back door of the house.

"Miss de Jong," he called. "Forgive me."

He strode closer, and I took a sideways look. His pale face bore signs of true regret — widened eyes, mouth low at the edges. He pulled out his pocket watch. "Seven-forty-five. I'll need to change this jacket before I go. I beg your leave and thank you for the worthwhile conversation." He bowed slightly, then raised his head and gave me a crooked smile. "Unrepentant sinners make the best company." He ran sideways across

324

the grass toward the front door.

In a moment I stood dripping in the hot kitchen, where Margaret was drying the breakfast dishes. She gave me an inquiring look, but I didn't explain. I picked up a towel and began working beside her, with Albert's parting comment spreading like a bee sting in my heart.

"May I speak honestly?" Margaret asked.

"Of course," I said. This was a morning of honesty.

"I doubt any good can come of talking with Mr. Burnham." Margaret dried her hands, kneeled before the stove, and began refueling it with wood. "It's lucky Clementina retired for a nap."

"I'm sure thee is correct." I sighed. This girl who lacks even the earliest signs of puberty is more sensible than I am — perhaps for that very reason. Just then Henry's wails reached us, and footsteps clattered on the front stairway.

"Nurse! Where is that damned Lilli." Clementina rushed in from the hall holding her son, who twisted about in the blanket she'd lifted him with. She strutted to me and pushed him into my arms. "You didn't come when he woke. Feed him now, and change him. I couldn't rest with this boy wailing."

I sat immediately at the table and opened my clothes, then affixed her son to me. Margaret looked on with worried eyes.

"I'm terribly sorry," I told Clementina. "I stepped out —"

"I'm aware that you were walking with my husband," she replied coldly. "I expect no better of him. But of you I demand better, despite your blemished history."

I flushed once more. After she left I promised myself — not for the first time — that I'd keep to my duties and do nothing more against her wishes. For she holds the keys to my independence. Until I can get a sewing machine and a room and reclaim Charlotte, Clementina Appleton Burnham is my guide and judge.

Fifth Month 31

Miss Baker arrived yesterday! Fully recovered, and eager to make up for our days of bland fare and overwork. She's a tiny woman, perhaps fifty years old, with few wrinkles on her face but some silver in her dark, wavy hair. Her dress is modest and well mended. And, true to her name, she loves — indeed, she *lives* — to bake. So rather than making soup, I'm helping with sweets and breads during Henry's long morning nap — and enjoying her company.

Yesterday I made a rum cake while Miss Baker mixed a fruit-bread batter with a giant spoon. She called out my next steps with no recourse to instructions, for she knows the proportions of rising agents to dry and wet, and she improvises the rest. When she had me stir a cup of rum into the batter, I sneezed four times in quick succession. The fumes stung delicate places in my nose and eyes.

"You not used to liquor?" she asked from close beside me. At the edges of her narrow face, the gentle hairs were curled and white.

"I've never been so near to rum before," I told her. Even Father had indulged only in beer.

"I hope you ain't against all liquor." She huffed. "There's a piece I saw in Mrs. Burnham's *Ladies' Home Journal* claiming that folks who drink too much should blame their childhood cooks. Now fancy that. And the writer is begging cooks to stop using alcohol in cakes and gravies so as not to make folks like the taste and damage society. I declare, if taking liquor from the kitchen is the price of temperance, then temperance is overrated." She guffawed.

I replied that although I do support temperance, I'd never blame a cook for someone's drunkenness. This pleased her. "But I

327

won't be allowed to enjoy these sweets anyway," I said. "Clementina limits my diet, for Henry's sake."

"Soon she'll be wanting to take charge of how often you breathe and how many steps you take," she said. "Ain't that so?"

"It certainly is so." I nodded. "Has she taken charge of thee?"

"Yessum. Tried to cut my budget close for a while, after her mother left for Austria and made Clementina my mistress. But I said, 'Your mother trusted me to spend what I needed, just as long as the food was to her liking. I suggest you stop all this fussing and leave the kitchen to me.'" Miss Baker poured batter into a buttered pan. "Don't worry your head, Miss Lilli. You'll get your share of sweets."

Miss Baker is a woman of her word. Yesterday, after she provided for Margaret and me in the kitchen as richly as she supplied the Burnhams — with roast pork loin, potatoes, candied carrots, and greens — she tucked a piece of walnut pie wrapped in a napkin into my hand and another into Margaret's.

"Mind you don't leave crumbs for the mice," she said as she pushed us toward the door to the back stairs. She refused to let us help her clean the kitchen. "Plenty of chances in days to come. Go get some rest."

After almost two days' worth of her rich meals and desserts, my milk seems more plentiful, and Henry shows no signs of suffering. Thank goodness for an opinionated cook.

I see by looking back that my letter to Peter went out twenty-nine days ago. Since then, each time the letter carrier's bundle has fallen through the front-door slot and Clementina has collected it, my pulse has grown as insistent as a woodpecker's beak at a tree — to no avail. But this afternoon, Clementina called for me.

My hands were deep in a basket of peas in need of shelling; I wiped them and rushed to the parlor. Clementina sat on a padded chair with letters in her lap, scrutinizing an envelope. Her face was pink and sweaty from the heat.

"This has gone to three addresses," she observed. "First to a post-office box downtown. Then our Pine Street house. Then here."

As far as I could recall, only Father and Patience had the post-office box for the Haven. But when Clementina gave the envelope over, I didn't recognize the hand.

"If thee will excuse me," I said, starting

from the room.

"You'll let me know if it affects your employment."

I nodded, then raced to the kitchen to sit. Margaret and Miss Baker looked on curiously. On the back of the envelope was this: PHILADELPHIA LADIES' SOLACE.

A reply to my request! I ripped open the seal. Inside, on fine parchment and in an elegant and curlicued hand, was a florid rejection.

"Our aid goes only to the deserving," the writer explained, "who through no defect of character face hard limitations. The evils of indiscriminate almsgiving, and the dreaded prospect of giving encouragement to those who dwell in sin, are kept at bay by this principle."

This is precisely what Anne warned us about. This is why the Haven is so crucial *and* so hard-pressed for funds. I must have looked crestfallen, for Margaret came beside me and quietly asked, "Have you gotten bad news?"

"Yes," I whispered. "I'll tell thee tonight."

Miss Baker had the grace not to inquire.

Later, in the cool of evening, Margaret and I met for a lesson. Her private efforts had done much good: she could read a page of simple sentences. We worked on a new sentence, "My cat loves to eat fish," which led her to bubble over with anecdotes of her family's several pusses. When her fount ran dry, she told me more about her friend at church, Rosa, with whom she became acquainted last summer. Rosa was so pleased to see Margaret again at church service last week that she walked her to the driveway of this house after the social. Rosa works at a cigar factory — "but she doesn't smoke or chew," Margaret hastened to explain. She withdrew from her skirt pocket a note Rosa had given her, softened at its corners from frequent fingering. She asked me to read its contents, since she'd tried but wasn't confident she had it all.

"Won't you join in a celebration of spring at Valley Green this coming Sunday, 1 p.m. onward? Bring a blanket and a picnic. Reply to Rosa Jones, care of xx Herrick Street."

It was not a personal invitation but one that all invited would receive. Yet Margaret took it much to heart. We composed her exuberant acceptance, and after a fitting pause, I told her of my rejected request for aid.

"That's because you were honest," she said, appalled at my naiveté. "You ought to claim you're a widow."

I told her I won't make false claims.

"I know you wouldn't freely choose to," she replied. "But for Charlotte's sake, you should."

She said she'd start off lying for me, with my permission. She'd ask at church if anyone could help a widow set herself up. Someone might have an old machine to loan or give me.

I wanted to say yes, but I asked her to hold back. Though lying had been her idea, I wouldn't encourage it. This was just the sort of influence I mustn't have on Margaret.

I wondered, however: Might J. S. Mill support the use of falsehoods to help one cross a landscape littered with foul prejudice? At least until the world's a fairer place?

If only someone older and more experienced than Margaret could advise me.

If only I could speak with Mother. She's so close by — in the burying ground beside the meetinghouse.

Yes, I know the body after death retains no remnant of the soul; nevertheless I want to be near her, to have only dirt and coffin separating me from the body that carried and nourished me, my solid ground, my mast, my lodestar.

Sixth Month 1
I've been paid! What a relief it was when

money reached my hand. Twenty-five dollars minus fifty cents for Dr. Snowe's care and four dollars fifty cents to Margaret and Clementina for what I gave Gina. Remarkably, Clementina decided not to deduct for the days Charlotte was here this month. So I have twenty dollars and twelve pennies.

I whistled a tune as I moved Henry's carriage along the back porch, soothing him to sleep. Miss Baker had suggested that I let him nap outdoors, saying fresh air is good for babies. When Albert returned from playing cricket, after putting his bat into the stable, he walked to the back porch to observe me.

"I'd never have expected to hear you whistling," he said, withdrawing a handkerchief to wipe away a layer of perspiration from his face. "It doesn't seem the sort of thing a Quaker does."

I pointed to indicate his son, so that he would speak more quietly. "I was paid today," I whispered.

"Is it that easy to brighten your mood?" he whispered back. His jovial face came near to mine, and I caught the scent of liquor. "Why, I'd pay you ten cents a day just to see you smile."

I might have agreed, if he'd meant it as more than a jest. That ten cents a day would more than make up for the increased fee at Gina's, and another cause to smile would do me good.

Henry calls. It's time to become his nurse again. When I write, I forget that I don't belong to myself.

The Burnhams have gone to stay downtown overnight, and Miss Baker departed with permission to attend her neighbor's funeral, leaving me no duties beyond Henry. So despite my dread of being seen by familiar people, I hatched a daring plan: to visit Mother at her grave.

I believed I'd be unrecognizable if I wheeled Henry before me and disguised myself; Margaret agreed, helping to make it so by loaning me her violet cloak and straw hat, which I wore over the green satin dress from the Haven. I wheeled Henry's carriage toward Main Street and the burying ground, certain that I looked like an elegant mother out for a stroll — perhaps a South Carolinian transplanted north for the more bearable summer season.

I avoided bumps and mudholes as best I could, grateful for Henry's acceptance of the jostling. When the road grew smoother, he fell to sleep. I turned onto Main Street, then Coulter Street, and then the flat ground dotted with rough-hewn grave markers that protruded but slightly above the grass. To my far left, a wheelbarrow stood balanced on its haunches. I held still, observing: no signs of people. So I halted the carriage and walked to Mother's low stone. Along its rectangular top was etched the barest outline of her life: HELEN BROMER DE JONG, 1834–1881.

My hand went to the warm locket at my neck. I kneeled, staring at the ground that held her. "Mother," I called plaintively, without meaning to.

Then nothing more. My head began to throb. The muscles in my shoulders ached.

I'd come, oddly enough, to ask Mother's permission to lie. I wanted to claim to be a widow, since others might be willing to help me then. I hoped that Mother's nearness might let me see how to place a boundary around such dishonesty. Yet at that moment, I understood two things: She would have had nothing but disapproval to offer on the subject, and I would lie, regardless.

If Mother could have but laid a calming hand upon me, I might have broken down and told her everything. I might have found relief in unburdening myself, perhaps even changed my plans. But if her spirit could have perceived me there, I would have been cruel to awaken it, for my situation would only cause her pain.

She had reached her rest after enduring far more suffering than I. Shortly after I was born, Mother's father and brother died of typhoid fever. When I was four and Peter, two, she birthed twins prematurely; they didn't live. Then her mother died of consumption. And at forty-seven she faced her own death.

Yet until bedridden in her final days, she never flagged in providing practical and moral assistance. People of all sorts came to our house, seeking her guidance as often as they sought the articles of clothing and food we gathered for them. It seemed she grew stronger, not weaker, until the very end.

"Mother," I blurted, "where did thee find the strength?"

A ringing voice shot across the graves. "Is that Lillian de Jong?"

I raised my head, appalled. Old Hannah Purdes, the woman who'd delivered Father's Notice of Disownment, stepped from behind the wheelbarrow. I hadn't seen her since that day, when she'd said I would no longer teach at the Meeting school.

"Thee looks as if thee sees a ghost, child. I'm visiting my loved ones, same as thee!" Hannah hobbled over, having apparently declined in recent months. She clutched my arm, staring me up and down and back again. "No longer dressing plain, I see! Whose baby is that? Where has thee been? Thy neighbor said thee was a governess."

"I was — I am. We've moved to the family's summer house, not far from here."

Hannah pressed for details — the number of children, the name of the family, the reason I was responsible for the baby that day — and I stayed quiet, struggling over what to tell her.

"Dear Hannah," I said at last, "I'm near to fainting from the heat, and the baby needs changing. Please let me be on my way."

"Has thee visited home recently?" Her speckled eyes narrowed.

I answered no. Henry gave a moan and a snort, then sank back into measured breathing.

"Go soon. Thy father needs thee."

I couldn't ask if he was deathly ill, or if orders for his cabinets were slowing, or if something ailed his wife, without showing the full extent of my estrangement. But Hannah knew.

"Thee seems a human soul cast out by itself," she said to me, clasping my arm more tightly. "I see it, child. May I visit thee?"

How moved I was! Yet I couldn't allow this. Begging her pardon, and knowing my quick departure would do no good to her impression of me, I wheeled Henry's carriage away, leaving with more questions than I'd brought.

As if in counterpoint to that thought, Hannah yelled an answer to what I'd voiced at Mother's grave: "Helen de Jong found her strength in silent worship."

Looking back I saw Hannah's face poking from its gray bonnet, querulous and imposing.

As I walked toward the Burnhams', Henry woke and called out in hunger. I took a detour through a break in a fence into an unused pasture, and behind a wide tree I soothed him and was soothed. In that deeper state brought on by nursing, a bit of knowing came to me.

Hannah was incorrect. Mother's *calm* had come by waiting silently in Meeting, but not her *strength*. That came by extending wisdom and assistance to those whose welfare concerned her, whether family, neighbor, or stranger. Our needs made her brave and persistent. Our improvements sustained her. When exhausted, she rested and regained her force by reading the works of weighty Friends. Often she returned to the diary of Caroline Fox, an English Quaker, and spoke aloud the words Caroline had once heard articulated in her spirit: "Live up to the light thou hast; and more will be granted thee."

Through most everything Mother did — though outwardly it might have seemed to benefit only others — she gathered light and knowledge and stored it up within herself. Amidst that brightness, she could always find a bridge across her troubles, until her very end.

As must I, following in her way. I will be grateful for my work with little Henry, and for my service to unhappy Clementina and puzzled Albert, and for dear Margaret, who needs companionship as much as she needs learning — and most of all for Charlotte. These people are my lamps, who bring more light to me, however much that light may sometimes prick my eyes, and who thereby will help me see a way through trials to come.

Sixth Month 2
I came in from the garden this morning with fresh greens to find Miss Baker angling to hear my circumstances — though it grew

clear that she already knew from Margaret.

I answered sparely, trying to confine my attention to an examination of each lettuce leaf I rinsed and dried. No doubt sensing my discomfort, Miss Baker gave me to know that I'd find no ill opinion in her quarter.

"I've come down some myself, being a cook in service," she said, sorting good strawberries from bad. "My daddy ran a factory behind our house. My mama — she and two brothers and their mama came here from Tennessee. She played piano and sang at the Mother Bethel AME. When Daddy died, we lost the factory and all the money that came with it. But even when I was living high, I didn't think I was better than nobody. The good Lord made us all."

"I certainly agree," I replied.

Moving to the hearth, she tilted a hanging pot of water to fill a teapot. She was making burdock tea for Margaret, who'd taken to bed with a fierce headache. When I asked what I should do next, she gestured to a barrel in the corner. "Peel and chop them old apples. They're too sorry for eating plain."

She set the teapot on a warm spot on the stove and plunked a ball of dough onto a floured board. I peeled apples and sliced off rotted spots into a bucket, letting the occasional worm fall. Miss Baker saw my mincing expression.

"If you want to eat apples, you're bound to meet some worms." She smiled. "You liking your work here?"

I nodded. "Fairly well. I'm grateful for the position. And thee?"

"It suits me." She got out pans and buttered them. "Here and at home, I try to make folks happy with my cooking."

"Thy cooking makes *me* happy," I offered.

Miss Baker smiled, revealing buck teeth. "I'm glad." She lifted rolled dough into the pans. "You can better the world from anywhere you find yourself." She pressed a fork along the outsides of the crusts. "How is Mrs. Burnham? It's hard for her in this big old house, with her parents overseas and not half as many servants as they had. Course *they* used to entertain."

"Thee has been here a long time." A worm dropped into the bucket.

"Seventeen years. Since the mistress was nine. She was agreeable then, cute as a button, with none of the sourness you see now. That's on account of her blunted ambition, I reckon."

"The violin?"

"The violin. Played it like the devil. Girl of her upbringing is supposed to keep quiet and pretty, not be full of passion. Her parents doused her hopes of attending music school like ten fire brigades at a fire."

I pondered this as I inhaled the clarifying scent of apples.

"You need a sewing machine?" she asked.

"How does thee know?"

"Margaret told me. That girl thinks right well of you. Today's your afternoon off? You going to see your baby?"

I nodded.

"Well, instead of that, there's a rich lady downtown you oughta visit." She explained that the woman is a sewing-machine inventor with a factory and a shop and is known for her kindness to mothers in need. "After my daddy died, Mama bought one of that lady's machines on a time plan, with no payments due till we started scraping by." She slid her pie crusts into the hot oven. "Then it turned out I was half good at cooking, so I got sent out. Bless your heart, Miss Lilli, Miss Bancroft is doing well with that shop, and I wager she might even *give* you some old machine."

"She wouldn't give one to an unwed mother, would she?"

Miss Baker didn't answer. With a fork she mixed warmed vinegar and sugar in a bowl.

"Where is the shop?"

She told me the street and cross street downtown. Just then Margaret entered, having woken much improved, and poured herself some burdock tea. She heard my plan as I tossed the apples and strawberries in the sugar and vinegar and Miss Baker sprinkled cinnamon on top. Margaret assured me between sips of tea that she felt well enough to care for Henry. So I removed my apron and washed up, then gave Henry a nursing so he'd stay contented. As I sat with him, I came up with an idea.

With Henry in his crib, I raced upstairs and dug into a drawer to reach my plain poke bonnet. I hadn't worn it since leaving home, and as I put it on, I felt how pleasantly it shields the head and hides one's thoughts. I walked one story down to use the hallway glass, expecting to look like an imposter, someone only pretending to be respectable. Yet there was no visible difference between the young woman in the mirror and an upright Friend.

I decided not to wear the bonnet on the streetcar. That seemed too bold. I tucked it in my brown bodice, covered my head with my gray shawl, and left the house.

The streetcar let me out downtown. Soon the plate-glass windows of the store came into view. BANCROFT OVER-SEAM COMPANY

OF PHILADELPHIA was painted in gold-and-brown lettering on the glass. After donning my bonnet, I stepped up and rang the bell. The gleaming machines in the windows were lovely; the prettiest was painted black and decorated with gold filigree. A light-haired matron in a plum-colored dress opened the door, and I asked to see Miss Bancroft.

"She's not in. May I show you our machines? We have the most alternatives of any manufacturer in Philadelphia. We even have the new zigzag. Miss Bancroft invented it." She pointed to a framed newspaper article on the wall. I nodded, though I couldn't make out its words.

"I'd like very much to see the machines," I said. "But first I need to speak with Miss Bancroft."

"May I ask the nature of your business?"

As she waited for my answer, I grew more nervous to speak. But the store's odor of metal and linseed oil brought to mind our garden shed at home, which reassured me. "I'm told she cares about unfortunate women, and if only I had a sewing machine . . ."

"Goodness." The woman gestured into the shop. "Come in!"

I followed her to a counter and stood

before it. She put on a pair of eyeglasses and inclined her slim face toward me.

"What's your situation, dear?"

At the doorway to a changed self, I held my breath, then stepped through. Her mind was a blank slate for my tale to be written upon.

I released my breath. "My husband died — in a mining accident — in Easton. I was with child when he died. I have so little money left, and I'd like to sew."

Her face flushed with compassion. "How old is the baby?"

"Just two months." I saw Charlotte's grinning face, her feisty fist clutching an apple blossom in Gina's yard. I choked back a sob — a real one, but knowing it would help my case.

"Oh, my," she replied, shaking her head. "We do like to help widows when we can. If we get an old machine in partial trade for a new one, Miss Bancroft gives it to a widow on installment. No money down, and a payment due whenever you can make it." The woman opened a drawer and pulled out a ledger. "Mind you, sewing doesn't usually bring much of a living. But you could earn enough to keep yourself and one baby." She located a certain page, examined it, and shook her head. "No machines at present.

But I'll add you to our list. Will that suit you?"

Hope banged in my chest. "Yes, very well."

"Name? Address?"

In my haste to answer, I gave the address of my former home. If the shop does send a letter, Father will have to forward it to the post-office address I left behind — the Haven's box — and it will follow the same circuitous path as that letter from the Philadelphia Ladies' Solace.

So be it. I thanked the woman, my eyes warmed by tears brought on by shame as much as gratitude.

I traveled back to the Burnhams', knowing I would share my tale with Margaret and Miss Baker and feeling mixed relief and horror. People are so easy to fool. It's not at all difficult to take convenient detours around the impediment of truth.

Sixth Month 3, First Day

I must have fallen asleep last night in the rocker, for I woke with Henry on my lap and dawn creeping up behind the trees. I put him in his crib, where he slept on, and tiptoed to my room to record my nightmare.

I dreamed that Father — only forty-nine, in truth — had grown white-haired and weary. His tall frame was stooped as he walked with effort across the wide planks of our main room. Then he stopped short; his eyes became fixed, as if made of glass; his face went blank, and his big hands hung from slackened arms. Though his body remained upright, life had abandoned him.

Grief smacked me like some giant hand.

Then all at once, the animating principle rejoined his body. New vigor flowed through his veins. His shuffling walk resumed, and his face presented again the look of one alive, as if that peculiar death had never happened.

This sudden alternation between life and death occurred three more times, plunging me into grief and rescuing me from it, until the final time, when he sat in a mahogany chair — one that he'd carved and turned and joined himself — and, like a wind-up toy that has wound down for good, he ceased to be. His body took on the immense heaviness of death. It slumped forward, chest to thighs, head and neck dangling past the knees.

With a choking sob I crouched before him, my knees touching the toes of his worn leather boots. I threw my arms about his slumped head and calves, clinging, as if once more a child.

"Papa!" I called. If he could have but patted my crown and said, "Yes, dear Lilli," or "What new thing has my daughter seen today?" — but he was dead for good.

I woke with a crushing in my chest. What if something has happened to him? What was Hannah referring to? To be so close, yet unable to go . . . Should I go? I'd have to reveal my situation. Then he would exile me, as Patience did.

Perhaps this dream was a punishment for my dishonesty at Miss Bancroft's shop.

I've opened my locket to touch Mother's hair. It retains the faintest trace of her violet water.

This fragment of Mother's actual body, chestnut brown and silken, is my most precious possession. I hold it and hear that fragment of philosophy she held dear: "Live up to the light thou hast; and more will be granted thee."

What of the one who covers her light with the dirt of deception — can she ever reclaim it?

Tomorrow the Burnhams leave for New York City to meet Clementina's parents, who have arrived by boat, and Miss Baker and Margaret will listen for Henry while I visit Charlotte at Gina's, for I'm desperate to hold my baby. I missed our visit by going to the sewing-machine shop.

Darling Charlotte! Mother will soon be nigh!

■ ■ ■ ■

NOTEBOOK SEVEN

■ ■ ■ ■

Sixth Month 4, late

Our situation has taken an appalling turn for the worse.

I set off to see Charlotte today with a buoyant step. But as I neared Gina's neighborhood, traces of a noxious smoke began to reach me. I sped along the road, sweating under my concealing shawls, sliding on muddy places but managing not to fall. I came to a halt to recover my breath only when I reached that enclave — but I still haven't recovered my breath.

Mounds of rubble lay where several of the wood row-houses had stood. A sickening smell was rising from their half-charred, smoldering hulks.

I ran closer, hardly aware of my feet on the dirt road. The front door to Angela and Victor's had been red; no row-house standing had such a door. I searched among the threads of smoke, the expanses of charred beams and planks, the dampened heaps of plaster and possessions. At last I saw a rocking chair's curved base protruding. Near it were burnt spindles that could have been from a cradle; beside them lay a door-shaped rectangle, mostly charcoal, its unburnt edge still red.

In terror I called my baby's name.

"Gone!" said a voice. Turning, I saw a crooked woman on a cane approaching, her face a map of wrinkles. I moved toward her, intending to speak, but nausea bent me double. As I gagged over the ground, she spoke kindly in the rolling syllables of her native tongue.

I raised myself and croaked. "My baby! Gina! Lucia! Where are they?"

Through halting words and gestures, she informed me that they and others affected by the fire had been transported by ambulance to Germantown Hospital.

"When?" I asked.

Two days ago, she communicated, some with burns and breathing trouble. She pantomimed a person riding a horse and asked, "You want?"

Certainly I did. I raced the way she pointed and soon reached a low-roofed livery stable. I hired a hackney carriage for my very first time, counting on the ten-dollar bill in the cloth purse that hung at my neck.

"To Germantown Hospital," I told the driver as I stepped up to the bench. As we rolled along, I tried to understand the fare card that hung before me, but in my harried state, its many terms and stipulations were too confounding.

The driver stopped at the hospital's brick compound and agreed to wait. I rushed in and asked a woman seated in the main hall to direct me to Charlotte and the others. Consulting a list, she claimed to find no patients by their names, and she refused to let me tour the floors to find them.

I ran to the nearest door, opened it, and stepped into a smaller room. By the time the woman had caught up with me, I'd explained the situation to another worker. He banished my pursuer with a sour look, then examined the columns of his discharge ledger and found evidence of Gina, Victor, Angela, and two babies. Gina and her baby had left yesterday, both in adequate health; the ledger didn't say where they'd gone to. Victor and Angela must have taken longer to get from the house, for they'd been transferred to Pennsylvania Hospital, which could better treat their burns.

"What of my baby?" I asked. My future

happiness hung on his reply.

"She was also transferred." He ran his finger down the page and stopped. "No evident damage besides a cough caused by inhaling smoke."

I dared to breathe. "Where was she sent, then?"

"To the Children's Asylum at Old Blockley."

At first I couldn't comprehend. All my efforts since leaving home have been aimed at keeping us from the city almshouse — a massive stretch of human misery located beside a disease-breeding swamp. Even I, who barely saw a newspaper due to Mother's horror of them, knew that its supervisor and treasurer were recently convicted of fraud and thievery, and that not even its cadavers are safe from plunder: some of the newly buried are dug up and ferried across the river at night to be sold for medical uses. There are always fresh corpses, for between its substandard food and insufficient hygiene, Blockley is a veritable slaughterhouse.

I moaned, but the man behind the desk had no sympathy to spare. "We send all children there who lack a caretaker," he said, his cold eyes boring into me. Clearly he was certain that I was a defective mother. He had no way to know how it has anguished me to live apart from Charlotte.

And why hadn't Gina told the hospital where to find me? I'd trusted her!

"Did thee discharge them?" I asked.

He nodded.

"Why didn't Gina take my baby along, or find me?"

Again his eyes judged me. "She had no home herself. She was distressed to have no way to reach you."

No way to reach me? How could this be true? I realized and cursed myself. Since she couldn't read, I'd never thought to write out the Burnhams' name and address. I hadn't even told that information to her.

Of course she'd had to leave Charlotte; merely carrying two babies out the door would have been difficult. And the man didn't know where she'd gone. Not back to the same neighborhood, certainly, or the kind old woman there would have told me.

No, I couldn't blame Gina. I simply had to go immediately to Blockley and remedy the effects of my grievous error.

Thank goodness the Burnhams were en route to New York City to meet Clementina's parents. Miss Baker and Margaret might worry at my continued absence, and Henry would awaken hungry, but so it had to be.

I left the hospital and raced toward the waiting carriage. To the driver I called, "Blockley Almshouse, quickly, please." He gave his signal and the horse dashed off, with us bouncing behind.

Soon I'll hold and kiss my darling, I assured myself. *Soon she'll smile and gurgle. She'll tense her little limbs and wave them with the thrill of being in my arms.*

Yet my breathing came in fits and pauses. I thought of the diseases that must run quickly through the almshouse. A fine layer of sweat covered me. Inside my abdomen, the muscles clenched and twisted.

At last we crossed the Schuylkill River, which was high and frothy from a night of rain, and drew near to Blockley.

To call the almshouse imposing would be an understatement. Its many-acre compound is surrounded by high stone walls, which the carriage skirted at length to locate the gate at Thirty-sixth Street and Darby Road. On entering, we had to trace an arc around a group of well-dressed people tromping through, as apparently the place draws gawkers. Ahead stood a gathering of three-story stucco buildings, each perhaps five hundred feet long. These were surrounded by stretches of dirt, the monotony of which was relieved only by an occasional shrub or a tree.

The driver halted his horse before a building fronted by enormous columns that bore the word ADMINISTRATION. But I bid him to continue, until I saw a plaque on another edifice that listed the Children's Asylum among its holdings. The driver promised to wait, explaining the cost at 75 cents per half hour.

I hurried to a massive door and banged its knocker. The door was opened by an oily-bearded man in an ill-fitting suit. Fetid air eased out around him. I summarized my baby's situation and told him I needed to remove her immediately.

"Applicants are allowed only at certain hours," he said. "The Visitor of Children takes applications from one to four on Tuesdays, Wednesdays, and Thursdays from them that wants to board a child out."

"Surely a mother seeking her own child can enter at other times," I asserted.

"Not as far as I've seen." He shrugged. "And that baby's been a cost to the city. You'll need to pay the charges before you take 'er."

"Charges? Even if I never put her here and don't want her to stay?"

He nodded, raising a hand to stroke his beard.

"May I speak with someone else?" I had to get inside and find her.

Without protest he nodded and closed the door. Apparently he was accustomed to such a request. I waited on the wide steps and stared at the brass knocker of a lion's head, its mouth gaping and toothy. Soon a pink-faced nurse stood in the doorway, pulling at the hem of her apron and adjusting her muslin cap. Upon gaining a sense of my dilemma, she concurred with the man about the hopelessness of my endeavor.

"Yer in a right fix, ma'am," she told me.

"But this is my own baby," I explained. "Surely these rules don't apply." Her stubbornness was putting me in a panic; I felt short of air.

"We must follow procedure. A child can be taken only after yer situation has been *thoroughly examined.* So say the rules of the Department of Charities and Correction."

I felt the force of her indignation bearing down on me as she stood in the doorway above. No doubt the watery mucus in her eyes gave a clue to one of the diseases inside.

"Can I speak with someone else, to get an exception made?" I asked. "Or can I at least come in and view my baby?"

"Oh, no," she said gravely, plumping out her lips. "The managers would have our heads. But I'll tell ye what. Have ye got any friends that can write?"

"Yes." That lovely assertion buoyed my hopes.

"Ye'll need a letter attesting to yer character. Have ye a home of yer own?"

"Well, no. Yes. Sort of." I would ask Clementina if I could bring Charlotte there — except she was away. The nurse looked me top to bottom, perhaps noticing my haphazard attire.

"Ye must have a home," she said. "We don't let the children go just anywhere."

I filled my lungs and shouted, "My baby is just two months old and needs her mother's milk. No matter where we live, I'll keep her alive better than thee can!"

The nurse blushed to her ears. "Be that as it may, I can't go giving out babies willy-nilly to folks at the door. Go get proofs of employment, good character, and a place to live. Bring the baby's certificate of birth to prove yer the mother. Then apply to the Visitor of Children tomorrow between one and four."

How could the fundamentals of our city be so absurd? I stormed back to the carriage, determined to get what papers I could from Anne and return forthwith to find someone with common sense.

The driver said I'd owe a dollar twenty-five more, for we were switching back to a miles-based rate rather than a time-based one, which befuddled me. But I had him take us over the rutted streets toward the charity that had been my refuge. He wove us cannily among the wagons, buggies, carts, mules, goats, dogs, and people until finally we arrived.

I brushed the dust off myself as best I could, then rang the bell. Anne answered and invited me in. She led me to her office and sat behind her desk; I took the bench.

"Are you still employed with the Burnhams?" she asked. She must have doubted it from my condition. I told her yes but explained my baby's whereabouts and the obstacles to my claiming her. I asked if she could give me the birth certificate and a letter describing my character, lodgings, and employment.

Her face twisted, whether with concern or annoyance I was unsure. "You'll need to return tomorrow. Delphinia rushed off to a funeral and took the cabinet key. The birth certificate is in your folder."

I implored her to look for a spare key, which surely she must have about, and to write the letter for me.

She exhaled through her nose. "We don't

usually help a girl after she leaves. Our resources are severely strained already." She turned her head to the window, then faced me again. "You should let the baby go, Lilli."

"Let her go?" I blurted. "Thee would have her killed and buried in that horrid place?"

Anne cleared her throat and rose from her chair, elegant and unyielding. "I understand the hazard. The situation is truly sad. But some infants at Blockley *do* survive. And you must face the world you live in. You could start anew, were it not for this impediment." She began walking around the desk, indicating my dismissal.

"Impediment?" I stood. "I'm begging thee. Have the documents ready by tomorrow morning."

Anne nodded, her cheekbones made more prominent by her tight expression. "As you wish."

She escorted me out.

Even with no papers from Anne, I wanted to try to enter Blockley once more. So I had the hack driver return — along the same chaotic roads, through the same gate, past the same imposing buildings. This time the windows to the Insane Department were opened, releasing to the outdoors the expulsive yells and groans of the lunatics confined within. I recalled a photograph, circulated at Meeting during Blockley's recent scandals, showing inmates with grotesque expressions, their bodies held by stakes and chains. Some had blocks of ice strapped to their heads, ostensibly to cool their thoughts. I shivered as the driver swerved to avoid a line of curiosity seekers that stretched across the dirt toward that department's door. The well-dressed visitors craning their heads were awaiting their turns to gain a glimpse of the mad.

At the Children's Asylum, I stepped into the glare of the white-hot sun. Along the front of the building I tried the doors; all were locked. But at the back, a high row of windows ran for thirty feet or so, and a modest tree protruded from the dirt. It offered a chance I couldn't decline. I hiked up my gown, took hold of the dun trunk, and hauled myself to its lowest branch, then to the one above.

If I could erase what I saw next from my mind, I would do so rather than suffer my hand to write it down. But the hollow cheeks and feeble cries of those hundred friendless persons will never leave me. It might be less cruel of the nurses to give the infants arsenic when they're taken in, so as to let them be done sooner with their lot. Except that Charlotte is likely among them

— and a few others, as Anne noted, might somehow live.

I leaned to the windows and saw a single enormous hall with cribs in rows, holding perhaps a hundred babies, with only the littlest ones crying or moving. The rest lay silent and immobile, while their stick-like limbs and bony faces spoke volumes. Malnourished or dehydrated or diseased or all three, they looked as though they could exhale their souls with their very next breaths. Their swathing cloths were stained with spit-up, the only sign of their having been fed.

And who was caring for these frail beings? Two debilitated women were slouched in rocking chairs at each of the hall's four corners, and two more were seated halfway down each of the four walls. That came to sixteen — one per six or so children. A pap boat sat beside each chair, used for feeding the babies no doubt, along with a pitcher of grayish milk and a glass — probably for the women's nutriment. The women looked into the air ahead, each with a failing baby at her breast, perhaps thinking of the men who had violated them, run off, or died, or of their own misdeeds, or of the families who were unable to help.

My view of the large room was unimpeded, but the farthest rows of cribs were hard to make out. And with the infants swathed in coarse cloths and wearing identical brown caps, I couldn't discern if one was Charlotte. I scanned the rows again. Was that her? No, its mouth was larger. Was that? No, its chin was pointy. Nowhere did I see her fat cheeks, her lively eyes, her red curls that shine out when light hits them. But her hair would be covered by a cap, and her fat cheeks would have at least begun to melt away. Or her body might already have been ferried across the river and sold to dissectionists.

Dear Lord, I prayed, *preserve my Charlotte.*

I felt no relief, no reassurance from these words. But I must have spoken them aloud and been heard through a window, for a nurse returning an infant to a crib looked up and spotted me.

"What're you doing up there?" she yelled. "Get away!" The other nurses stared with alarm in my direction.

I scurried down the tree, catching and tearing the hem of my skirt on its trunk. My chest was so tight that I couldn't get air. Somehow I reached the carriage. I asked the driver to bring us quickly from the premises, which he did. He stopped outside the gate for further instruction.

Feeling as if a rock was lodged in my throat, I asked him to bring me back to the stable where I'd hired him.

He leaned his head of dark hair toward me and tilted it in a sympathetic look. "I gather yer in a kind a trouble, ma'am. If ye'll pay me nine dollars for all, that'll be enough."

Nine dollars? On seeing my stunned face, he said he'd shaved more than a dollar from the fee to make it nine, and I had to consent. Of course I'd spend every penny and beg for more to regain Charlotte — if she remains among the living.

I passed the ride back to Germantown in a stupor. At the stable I paid the man. As I walked away, cracks of lightning began to breach the sky, and booms of thunder answered. It was lucky that the storm kept other folks indoors, for I stumbled and keened and grew ever more despondent as I made my way toward Henry.

When I entered the kitchen door, Margaret rushed over with Henry in her arms, saying that he wouldn't take a bottle or stop screaming and fussing. The poor fellow grabbed me with his fists and scratched me with his fingernails while sucking at my swollen breasts. But soon he settled into a well-fed daze and slept.

I cannot sleep. Out the oval window at the foot of my bed I see the cold moon hanging, pitted with scars from untold battles. Bathed in its glow, I send up a prayer.

Charlotte, Charlotte, wherever thee is, please wait for me. Please live through the night. Please give me another chance to hold and kiss thee whose smells and sounds and sweetest flesh I adore, my baby.

Sixth Month 5

I wanted to leave for Anne's and Blockley immediately this morning. But Miss Baker wasn't coming in, for she had many errands in the Burnhams' absence. And she'd given the day's leave to Margaret, who had an invitation from her friend to a boat ride on the Delaware River. Since she'd already stayed up late to do what she'd neglected on my account yesterday, I could hardly blame her when she declined to take care of Henry again. When she left, apologetic but blushing with anticipation of her first boat ride, I said I would keep the kitchen fire going, make beef stew for our supper, and prepare two bedrooms for Clementina's parents, who will arrive with her and Albert in coming days — we don't know when.

I started on these things, then cleaned and fed Henry and let him lie on a blanket and make his strong efforts to advance. But as he grunted and rocked side to side, trying to use his stomach strength to roll over, I was as impatient as I'd ever been. When he grew fussy, I laid him in his crib. Then I walked about the house like a caged beast. In room after room I shivered, unable to eat or perform more duties, trying to find something to take my mind off my dire preoccupation. Books contained indecipherable letters; even my hand stirring the stew looked foreign, like a hook or a claw. Soon I was gagging with hard sobs. Having no one in hearing distance gave free rein to my distress.

Henry woke and cried again to eat. His call functioned as an alarm that set me into motion. I couldn't keep hiring hacks, with only ten dollars and change remaining. So I consulted the grandfather clock in the foyer, then a printed schedule, finding that a train going to Ninth and Green was arriving soon at the Germantown depot. I counted out five dollars. That ought to pay my round-trip fare downtown, my fares on streetcars, and the almshouse charge for three days' care — which couldn't be more than a dollar or two.

I tucked the money into my small purse, pulled its string to close it, and hung it about my neck. Then I did something that sickened me at heart, something I never would have done if my baby's life wasn't hanging in the balance: I painted laudanum, which the doctor had given me during my illness, onto my nipples, and I fed Henry from them. This way he wouldn't know of his aloneness.

In my anxious arms he fell into a deep and imperturbable sleep. I placed him in his crib and rushed out the door of that otherwise empty house and toward the Germantown depot.

I realized as I ran that I'd left the stewpot on the wood stove; the fire would burn out eventually, but nevertheless the stew might turn to mush and burn before Margaret or I returned. And I was frightened by what I'd done to Henry. I'd never given anyone laudanum before, not even myself. How long would he stay asleep? Had I given him too little, leaving him to wake and cry alone? Had I given him too much? Might one dose of laudanum — it was terribly unlikely — but please, dear God . . .

I reached the depot, the one near to my house, where I'd said goodbye to Johan and Peter. I barely looked about and kept shawls wrapped over my head and face, and fortunately I recognized no one among the others waiting. As I waited, the nearness of my childhood home brought on prickling sensations, perhaps not unlike what amputees feel in the areas of their missing limbs.

On the train, after paying my fare, I checked three times that the remaining money was still in my purse. Then I focused on suppressing my panic. When at last I arrived at Anne's, I found much to bolster me: the women had prepared Charlotte's birth certificate and a letter attesting to my character and my being the baby's mother, even telling of the fire and of Charlotte being sent without my knowledge to Blockley.

"I don't know what good a letter from me can do," Anne said as she handed over the envelope. "It hardly gives you the best provenance."

I said the letter and the birth certificate would do plenty of good — for how could the almshouse turn away a nursing mother, even an unwed one? I hugged Anne despite her stiffness. Then Delphinia saw me to the door. Unbidden, she gave me coins from her apron pocket, pressing them into my hand — 27 cents — along with a buttered roll.

"You'd best stop trying for the day," she counseled. "Return to your work, if you intend to keep it."

I sighed.

"Your little one was plump and strong when she left Gina's?"

I nodded.

"She'll stay that way a while longer."

"I have to try today," I insisted. "No baby there was plump or strong."

Delphinia squeezed me close and nudged me through the doorway. "Godspeed to you, then."

I rushed toward Market Street to travel across the river, my mouth pasty from the city soot. The women's help had lessened my fear, to the point that when I reached Market Street and stepped into a streetcar, it was with an almost jubilant air. The driver raised his reins and the horses were off, bells raucous at their necks. Then I took another streetcar to the almshouse stop and walked through the gate.

About forty small children were running about in rough-hewn garments on a patch of ground. Their bodies looked stunted, and every face I saw had deep pockmarks, perhaps from smallpox. These were the lucky ones who had survived. With a wave I saluted their hardiness.

I'd come to the Children's Asylum during receiving hours and called myself an applicant, so the robust woman who answered the door let me past. In the dim foyer, I was assaulted by a distinctive smell that mixed the aromas of excrement, old shoes, sweat, boiling soup bones, rancid grease, herbal tinctures, and mentholated unguent. Breathing shallowly, I followed the woman to an antechamber where a thin young man sat at a desk. A closed door behind him bore the words VISITOR OF CHILDREN on its square of opaque glass. The fellow at the desk told me that this official was occupied but that we could start on my application. I said I sought my own baby, two months old, named Charlotte.

He raised his chin, with its short whiskers, and appraised me as someone more income-supplying than expected. "Your own baby?" he replied. "So you left her on a doorstep with a note, and now you regret it?"

I informed him that I'd never surrendered my baby but that she'd been sent by Germantown Hospital because they had no way to reach me. He pulled out a leather book whose cover was embossed with the words ADMISSIONS AND DISCHARGES.

"Three days ago?" the young man asked.

I nodded.

"Two babies were admitted. One estimated to be two months old, the other, six months." He cleared his throat and ran his ink-stained index finger along the columns. "The younger, number 23259, was given the name Mary Foundling." He shut the book. "Perhaps that's yours. But if she remains among us, I cannot say. There's always a disease running through the nursery. Dysentery. Typhoid. Measles kills the most." He sighed. "The coroner gives us a list on Fridays."

Dizzied by his litany, I held to the side of his desk.

"You know about the charge for support?" He stared at me, then stood and fetched a chair from a wall and placed it beneath me. I sank onto it. "You know about the charge?"

"I know about the charge," I replied feebly.

The door behind him opened, and from the inner office stepped a short and fleshy man. He wore a striped suit and held a gold pocket watch. "Anyone to see me?" He looked about, widening his eyes and furrowing his brow.

I stood and followed him into his office. Its tall, opened windows let in the mooing of distant cows. The man shut the door behind us and introduced himself as Mr. Lambert.

"Lillian de Jong." I gave a slight bow before sitting. "All I want is my daughter, who is probably the one called Mary Foundling." I began to pull an envelope from my pocket and saw that my hand was trembling. "I have papers showing she's my daughter. She's here because her wet nurse's house —"

"So you want special treatment." He waved a plump-fingered hand at me.

"No," I said. "I only —"

"It's the duty of my position to see that our children are given only to respectable families or institutions. What would I tell the Board of Guardians if I didn't give you the same treatment as others, and your character ended up being unstable, or you failed to provide Mary with the proper surroundings?"

He gave me a vexed expression. I returned the same, observing the broken blood vessels in his nose and the glints of yellow in his eyes. He broke our stare, then shrugged. "I'm sure you're not a bad sort. You say you're the mother?"

"Yes." I handed him Charlotte's birth certificate.

He read a moment, then clucked as he handed it back. "There's a father listed, but his name isn't de Jong. Are you married?"

I kept quiet and decided not to show Anne's letter.

He picked up a cigar from his desk and took it into his mouth. "Unless you have a husband, I can't place a baby with you."

My hope sank with my stomach.

"That is," he continued, "until you're married. Then there'd be a trial period with the child." He lit his cigar, sucked at it, and released smoke in my direction. "You'd be visited, and reported to *me* for unfair treatment." He patted his chest, then leaned forward, reducing his voice to a whisper. "Some folks'll take foundlings and work them like slaves. We try to protect them from the worst sorts."

The worst sorts? As if I was one of them? I was near to screaming. I might never get through such a thicket of fools.

"My husband died last summer in a mine accident in Easton," I said. "All I have left is our baby." I held back a real sob that expanded painfully in my chest. "Thee must please release her to me."

"So you're a widow!" He grimaced, showing the gold in his teeth. "I'm a widower myself. And you're a Quaker! You people have unusual ways. Is that why you didn't take your husband's name?"

"Oh, yes," I said, emboldened. "We often keep our father's surnames."

All of this softened his approach. "If you

can pay for her keep, that's the first thing to do. It's two dollars for every day she's been here."

I gasped.

"Been here three days, you say. Six dollars, then, and you can take her. Providing you have a letter from your employer and can show proof of a safe habitation. Have you got that letter and that proof?"

"Well . . ." I had a letter that confirmed my unwed status and no "proof of a safe habitation."

He consulted his gold watch. "I'll be leaving shortly. You gather those things and return tomorrow."

"But tomorrow I'd owe eight dollars."

"That's correct." He showed his gold caps in a self-regarding smile, then put the cigar back in his mouth and puffed.

"By then my baby might be dead. I have nearly five dollars in my purse. Please let me take her."

"She's not yours yet." He held the cigar between his teeth and spoke around it. "She's the responsibility of the city. Once we've got your full fee and the letters, we'll see about you taking over her care."

Despite the urgency of Charlotte's plight, I saw no way around this blockade of a man. I had to return to Henry and — assuming he could be roused — to remedy his neglected condition before anyone saw that I'd left him.

I stood, wishing I was taller. "I'll see thee tomorrow," I said, as if it were a threat, "and take my baby from this awful place." Somehow I would make this true. I had to. I turned and left.

At the almshouse gate I considered ways of traveling the seven miles or so to the Burnhams' house. Walking would be too slow. The streetcars across the river would move quickly, but I'd have to wait for each to come, and after that, I'd be waiting for another streetcar or a train to Germantown — and all the while, Henry might be suffering. Trickles of milk traced paths down my abdomen. A laborer walked past and eyed my chest, then smirked. I looked down: my bodice was marked with two round blotches.

I hailed a passing hack. The man drove us well and fast, and I relieved my hunger with the buttered roll from Delphinia.

When I stepped out at the Burnhams' driveway, a challenge ensued: the driver demanded that I pay round trip, since I'd brought him far from downtown and he'd likely have no rider on his return. He spouted rates: this much for the first two miles, that much for each added mile through four, then a different rate per mile, which came to four dollars seventy cents one way — which meant, round trip, I owed him nine dollars forty cents. He bent his wiry body toward me from his seat, the reins in his lap, counting on his begrimed fingers.

Meanwhile, inside the house, for all I knew, Henry might have been choking on his spit-up or even passing into a comatose state.

I raised my hand to stop the driver's tabulations and said that he'd no doubt find a rider at the Germantown depot, as well as a watering trough for his horse. From the purse at my neck I took all the money inside — four dollars and coins. I had but five dollars remaining in my trunk. I handed the money over and began running toward the back of the mansion. He shouted after me but didn't abandon his horse to take chase.

I entered the dim kitchen and heard no sounds. The stew had turned to a charred mush in the cast-iron pot. I hid the pot out back, then raced up the servants' stairs to inspect my little charge. I picked up his body, finding his bedsheet and clothing thoroughly soiled. As I cleaned him, he opened his eyes — with effort, as though the lids were heavy. When he registered my presence, hungry cries seized his frame. I sat and opened my layers, and he drank. I kissed his forehead with a hard mix of regrets: sorry to have drugged him, and sorrier still not to be holding my Lotte.

Soon Margaret returned, thrilled by her outing with Rosa, who'd brought a picnic and read to her from a book of aphorisms. I was cleaned up by then and had readied a fresh supper. As we ate, I asked Margaret to care for Henry tomorrow, to which she consented. Then I asked to borrow money, which she had to deny. She'd sent most of last month's pay to her family already, and the rest had gone to stamps, pencils, and stationery. In fact, she intended to write to her sister about her rekindled friendship with Rosa, my arrival in the household, and other developments in her young life. And could I help her to do so, she asked, on this very night?

I couldn't very well deny her, despite my panicked state. We took down our hair and got in our clean, starched bedclothes, then sat on the hooked rug in Margaret's room. It was all cruelly pleasant compared to Charlotte's situation. The windows were opened to the darkness and let in a beguiling breeze as we began Margaret's first written message to the world.

"Dear Meghan," she began, with me

dictating the spellings. "I am writing this myself." She paused, pencil in the air, breathing rapidly. Then she stood. "I have bubbles inside! Is this joy? I can't keep still!" She lifted her legs high, tossing her curls shoulder to shoulder as she danced, then leaned to kiss my cheek. For precious seconds, my troubles were replaced by her exhilaration.

Upon finishing the letter, she retired, and I crept downstairs and took a piece of stationery from Clementina's desk. I wrote a note with her fine pen and ink, attesting to my husband's recent demise and my reliable employment and lodgings in her household. "I welcome the chance to house Mrs. de Jong's baby," I wrote, "because this will allow Mrs. de Jong to stay longer in our service." With many flourishes and not a little satisfaction, I signed "Mrs. Clementina Burnham."

I tucked that letter and the birth certificate into the pocket of a plain dress from home, which I'll wear tomorrow when I leave to do what I've realized I must do to get the needed money.

If Clementina were in, I'd ask for an advance on pay; if Miss Baker were here, she might have loaned me something. But as things stand, the only method in my control is to take a page from the book of Patience. I'll gather some valuables from my room at Father's and pawn them. I'll gain entry to the house by telling them I've completed my governess assignment, then take what I can and depart.

I will lie to my own family.

I've fallen into bed, with failing courage, and trembling.

Sixth Month 6

Miss Baker was angry at our mistress for banishing me but could do nothing. Margaret whispered that she was so sorry, and I replied that it wasn't her fault, she had to tell the truth. She said please come to the kitchen door and wait behind the bushes, so I did. I crouched there, sweating in the dusk and sending mental messages to Charlotte — *Stay alive another night! I'm coming! Breathe, my darling!* It seemed a long time till Margaret brought a candle, a blanket, a cup of water, bread and cheese, and an orange, and set me up where I am now, in a closet in the Burnhams' stable that is thick with spiderwebs and the stench of mouse droppings and leather harness pieces left to molder. Margaret warned me not to use the candle until late, for otherwise the Burnhams might see.

It's been several hours since. I've lit the candle. With the water being gone, and my bosom painfully full, I pressed my milk out to the cup and drank it along with the remaining bread. It seemed nearly cannibalistic to drink from my own body, but I couldn't pump water from the well, and what else could I have done with the milk, which had to be let out and would attract vermin if it dripped to the floor? The liquid brought a touch of sweetness to my misery.

Oh, diary, how grateful I am for thy page, which will hold my terrible story.

Before dawn this morning — how was it only this morning! — I woke in the dark in my attic room and waited for the grandfather clock to chime the hour. The Burnhams were away, with no indication yet of their return. At four I arose and woke Henry to change and nurse him, knowing I'd be gone many hours. As the sky lightened to gray, I laid his sleeping body back in his crib, hoping this would be the last day I'd leave him. I would get the money I needed, and at Blockley I'd either find out that Charlotte was dead or pay to release her.

I dressed as plainly as I could; to do otherwise would have startled those at home. I ate bread and milk at the kitchen table as the clock struck five. Then, leaving a sleepy-eyed Margaret charged with Henry, I entered the gloom, with a shawl covering my head, money in a purse at my neck, and various papers tucked into my skirt. I aimed to get the full eight dollars and to be at Blockley by one o'clock, when Mr. Lambert would return.

Despite the urgency of my mission, I relished the cool and vitalizing air. It seemed every bird and other creature was poised in stillness, waiting for the day to enliven it. I moved rapidly down Walnut Street, wondering whether Patience had already taken the valuables from the trunk at the foot of my bed. I stepped along the cobblestones of Main Street, then turned and turned again, until I reached our brick-laid street, not much wider than a pathway.

In the corner barn, a cow mooed. Hooves scraped the wooden floor. I slipped in to stand before the rope that kept our horse, Sarah, in her stall; she huffed her excited greeting. I accepted the push of her head into me and ran my hands along the sides of her neck, relishing its velvety feel and her recognition of me. This was the horse who had pulled our loaded wagon across a spread of rocks, knocking Mother off and piling furnishings on top of her. But of course the horse was innocent. Father had decided to keep her.

Father. Was he all right? Might I find out otherwise?

A rooster crowed; another answered. I kissed Sarah's tender, twitching nose and left the barn. With my hand on the cold latch of the low iron gate, I paused to behold our two-story domicile, with its peaked roof and its mortar crumbling between the stones. My stomach fluttered, and my mouth grew dry. I picked up a pebble and sucked it, as I had done in childhood, to taste its minerals and bring up moisture. Peonies that Mother and I had planted along the iron fence were bobbing their flower-heads toward the flare of early sun. Along one side of the house, rosebushes stretched budding limbs in all directions.

To the left of the front door, the windows to Father's workshop were dark. But the windows to the right showed lamplight, and smoke came from the chimney. Someone was awake and had rekindled the hearth.

I dropped the pebble from my mouth and unlatched the gate. The sound of splashing liquid made me look up, and there stood Patience, emptying kitchen waste from a bucket into a gully between our house and the next. Her abdomen extruded; she was with child, and far along. I opened the

385

creaking gate and stepped toward her.

"What might be your business?" she demanded, not recognizing me.

I undraped the shawl from my head. "It's Lilli."

She put down the bucket and placed her hands on her belly. Her fair hair was pulled tight in a bun, and her face looked bare and swollen.

"I want to come in," I told her. "I need to collect a few things from my room."

I'd started out all wrong. The sight of her unnerved me.

She paused, her eyebrows low over suspicious eyes. "Aren't you coming back for good?"

"I'd rather not say."

She shook her head in refusal. "I won't let you past unless you tell me what you'd rather not say."

She lifted the empty bucket and began to walk fast toward the open door of our house. A horse's hooves sounded in the street behind us. She stood in the door frame like a log blocking the way of a stream.

I pulled the shawl back over my head to keep the approaching person from recognizing me, then took a few steps closer. "I need to get some of my possessions." I spoke softly, so as not to be overheard. "I only want what belongs to me."

Her tone was harsh. "That won't happen till you tell me."

"What's going on, Mrs. de Jong? Someone botherin' ya?" I recognized the deep voice of a local busybody whose visits had been dreaded by Mother. Patience looked up to address the man on horseback.

"Fine morning, isn't it?" She inclined her head to indicate me and added, "We're talking over private business."

"Good day, then." His horse's hooves rang on the bricks as it moved away.

I decided to tell Patience a sort of truth. "My baby is gravely ill. I need money for her treatment."

Her blue eyes narrowed. "You didn't keep the child."

"I did give her up, but —" I stopped. I'd have to reveal my situation to get into the house.

What is a reputation, really? A pile of platitudes, so often inaccurate.

Patience cut in to my thoughts. "You surrendered the baby, and now you want her back?"

"I kept her," I said. "I kept her, but now she's in the almshouse." My voice grew tight and strained. "I must get her out or she'll die."

Patience spoke in a whisper, but her face beamed with ugliness. "With a bastard in arms, you'll have no place with us. And while I'm in this house, not a single thing will leave in your hands."

"I have a right to my belongings, and what my mother left me in her will," I replied — "at least the items thee didn't steal!"

She seethed with dislike. "You'd best be off, or your father will wake and your secret will be out."

At the mention of Father, I lost strength. "Does he ask after me?" How I longed for his care, which had been seldom in coming. And how I hated myself for revealing this weakness.

"No."

"Thee has kept my secret, then?"

"You're a governess so far as he knows, and he's pleased with that." She adjusted the bucket at her front. "He has plenty to worry about, with his workers having abandoned him and our baby on the way."

My throat clenched with the force of tears unshed. "Thee won't tell him what I've done, will thee?"

So all my posturing came down to this.

She smiled, relishing my abject state. "No,

I won't tell him, on one condition." The smile disappeared. "That you go away and never come back."

How dare she speak so cruelly to me? "This is my home, and thee can't keep me out." I took steps forward. "I'm going in to tell Father what thee pawned of mine."

"He's already at the mill, buying lumber," she said, altering her earlier claim.

"Then I'll go in and take my things." I tried to dodge her body and step into the main room of our house, first to one side of her, then to the other. She and her bucket blocked whichever way I went. Her body had the fixed strength of a mountain. Over her shoulder I caught a glimpse of the long oak table we'd used for meals and studying, and our pie cabinet with its cut tin front. Beside the kitchen hearth, I knew, hung many of the items Mother had meant for me to inherit — the copper and iron pots, the wrought-iron utensils passed from daughter to daughter, the carved spoon rack. Those I would never get. I raised my arms, determined to move this imposter aside and run up to my bedroom to claim what was mine. But she was quicker. She raised the bucket and used it to shove me backward.

I reeled away, struggling to keep from falling on the peonies and the fence, and then that woman picked up a sharp stone and threw it at me.

It hit its mark. My fingers flew to my neck and came away with blood. I clasped my locket to see if it had been struck — it hadn't. But look what a tyrant Father had chosen in Mother's stead!

"Thee is evil," I yelled.

"My children will be respectable," she hissed. She stepped into the house and began to shut the thick wood door, speaking her last words through a narrow space: "Your name will not be spoken! My family will know nothing of you and your bastard!" At that, she pushed the door into its tight-fitting frame.

I stared at the old door a moment, then scurried away — like a stray dog.

I'd always been glad that our stone house had passed from generation to generation in my father's family. But at that moment I wished its insides would burn to the ground and its stones would be knocked into piles for farmers to cart away. They would become walls for pastures, and sheep and cows would rub their itching hides on the gray roughness and leave tufts of fur behind, and the memories of centuries would float into the ether.

I headed toward the Burnhams' mansion, not knowing what I'd do once I arrived. The trip took longer than it ought to have, for I was forced to stop and collect myself several times, sitting with my back to the road on whatever tree or large rock would support me.

I had in some hideaway of my spirit harbored the belief that my family, even Patience, would offer aid if I were otherwise without hope. But in those moments, hidden from the road, I scraped that belief out of me with a crude and rusty knife.

Finally I turned onto the driveway to the Burnhams' house. Perhaps I'd find a stash of bills inside and become an outright thief for Charlotte. A large carriage led by two sweating horses was just departing from the front door, its driver directing it toward the stable.

In terror, I rushed around to the kitchen door and entered, with milk dripping down my front and blood at my neck. A startled Miss Baker told me that the Burnhams had returned a moment earlier — with Clementina's parents.

I took the back stairs to the door of the nursery and found Clementina and her mother already in the room. Mrs. Appleton was tall and imperious in her French heels

and elaborate gown; Clementina held her
mother's arm for support as the two of them
beheld the nursery in a shared state of alarm
and disgust. They'd just discovered Henry
weeping and wet, since Margaret had been
unable to attend to his every need; even
worse, the brown medicine bottle sat on the
floor beside his crib, open, with the dropper
beside it. For in my near madness the day
before, I'd left them there. Thus the women
understood that Henry had been drugged.
Adding further to their revulsion were the
soiled bedsheet and clothing from yesterday,
which I'd heaped in a corner and neglected.

Mrs. Appleton stood by in frigid silence,
but Clementina's fury was hot — and well
deserved by me. She grabbed my shoulders
with hard hands to arrest my progress when
I tried to enter the room.

"Margaret!" she yelled over my shoulder.
Margaret rushed up the servants' stairs and
down the hall, wearing her best black dress
and starched apron and cap. At Clementina's probing, Margaret confessed unhap-
pily that I had indeed been gone for several
hours on this day and for all of the previous
one (managing to leave out confessing that
I'd also been gone the day before) — "to
try and find her daughter, a cause of great
concern to her."

Despite my tender care of Henry to date, my heartfelt pleas, my vow to make this up to her and Henry, Clementina dismissed me on the spot, giving me a half hour to pack and be gone. Her mother looked on, face as stiff as china. Not one hair of her bun stirred as she nodded her approval. Only Henry wanted me to remain; he aimed his head my way and screamed for me.

"Can't I please nurse him once more," I begged, "rather than leaving him hungry?" I couldn't bear his distress, and my bodily discomfort was growing in response.

Clementina put her powdered face close to mine. "Your milk is unsuitable. My son would do better to live on artificial food."

My words tripped over one another as I tried to explain again why I'd had to leave him.

"I've had enough of you and your endless problems," my mistress intoned, leaning so close I saw the tiny red vessels in her eyes. "Be gone from this house, and good riddance!"

I asked meekly for my money from the first of the month till today. Clementina reached into the beaded bag at her waist and threw a quarter at me, which I picked up from the floor. It was far less than she would have owed if I'd done my work, but I was lucky to get it.

I stumbled to my attic room. My body flooded with urgency as I thrust clothes and other effects into my valise. The attic was musty from dampness, and its odor suddenly revolted me. My head spun and my mouth watered with nausea. I lay back on the mattress, hoping not to be sick.

The sensations subsided as I listened to the household's noises. I heard Clementina tell Margaret to feed Henry with a bottle. Then she called that she was going to the doctor's to request another wet nurse. The front door slammed shut; a bit later, the pattering of hooves and rolling of wheels indicated her departure by carriage. Someone climbed the stairs to the attic story, and Albert entered my room, hot and dusty in his traveling clothes.

"If you have no place to go," he said, holding out a card to where I lay, his face awkward.

I accepted it. "Burnham Imports, Incorporated, 8xx Chestnut Street, Philadelphia, Penna.," it read.

"Best to call before ten or after four." He gave a tight-lipped smile. "I'll have more time to attend to you."

I thanked him and sat up, putting the card into my skirt pocket; he gave a slight bow and returned down the stairs. *At least I have a last resort,* I thought. *Perhaps even a friend.*

I finished packing and left that spacious attic room, descending with my valise to the nursery, where Henry lay drowsy in his crib. He began to make sucking motions when I entered, but I dared not nurse him. Leaning close, I whispered that I was sorry to have drugged him and kissed his plump cheeks repeatedly. He opened his brown eyes wide, startled at my passion. I picked up the bottle of laudanum from the floor and tucked it into my valise — since I'd paid dearly for it. Then I descended to the kitchen, expecting a final parting with Margaret and Miss Baker.

Instead, they gave me one more sheltered night.

Which brings me to this moment. The sky is dark. I'll use the outhouse, and pump some water at the well to drink and wash in. I'll dry off with the blanket Margaret gave me, assemble my hair, put on clean clothes, and sleep on my valise rather than getting mussed by filth from the floor — so that, in my efforts to reclaim my Lotte tomorrow, my appearance won't be so unkempt as to bar me from succor.

Before sunrise this morning, Margaret knocked at the door of the stable closet. I was assembling my belongings for departure, having slept little and done it propped against the wall so mice wouldn't crawl through my hair. She handed me bread and a boiled egg, which I ate rapidly, standing up. Then she gave me an entire pound cake from Miss Baker.

"She said she hopes you'll get Charlotte back and have that sewing machine soon," she told me.

I gave heartfelt thanks, tucked the cake into my valise, and buckled the straps.

"I wish you could stay longer — I'd bring meals out." Margaret's blue eyes went wet.

Moved, I said I couldn't let her risk dismissal for me, and besides, I had an urgent task ahead. I wiped hay and dust from my skirt and hugged her. We fit nicely, with her head at the height of my shoulder. I pushed my face into her thick waves of hair and smelled the freshness of her youth.

"I'll write to let thee know my address when I'm settled," I promised. "Rosa can read the letter and help with thy reply."

"I plan to get a primer, so I may be reading your letter and writing back myself!" she said. As we regarded one another, an earnest look came to her freckled face. She reached into the pocket of her apron and drew out a small carving.

"I want you to take this." She handed me a wooden horse with touches of brown paint on its eyes, mane, and tail. "My father made it before I left. To carry me safely on my journey."

A lump formed in my throat. "Thee is too kind!" I tried to hand it back.

"No," she said, arms clamped at her sides. "It'll protect you and your baby."

"I'll give thee something, then." I opened my valise and laid the horse inside, then found a tortoise-shell comb from Mother. I held it out, but Margaret refused.

"I had no friend in the house before you came. And you taught me —" She heaved a sob. Again we embraced.

"We can't leave the stable together," I said, pulling back.

She didn't move.

"I'll go first." I picked up my valise, covered my head with the yellow shawl from Clementina, and ran past the horses shifting in their stalls to the garden, then the road — leaving behind the kindest, most sincere girl I've ever known.

The chant in my mind was *Charlotte, Charlotte,* set to a rhythm called by my feet. As I covered mile upon mile, the sun moved above the horizon, heating the air, and my valise grew more difficult to carry. I stopped in an orchard and ate a sour apple from the ground. By then all the coolness that rises from the earth each night had burned away. A passing farmer offered me a seat in his wagon among sacks of radishes, and I accepted gladly. Soon we reached downtown and halted near a market where he would sell his goods. I asked if he knew of a pawnbroker. He recollected a shop not far from there.

I stepped into a shaded alley that smelled of urine and opened my valise to examine its contents. I had to keep, of course, the plain dress and the collar and sleeves that I was wearing; I decided also to retain the other set like it, the Mother Hubbard dress and sash I'd sewed at the Haven, the brown wool skirt and bodice, my pencils and notebooks, of course, and my toilet items and underthings. I would pawn the most valuable items — the lace-trimmed shirtwaists, the green satin dress with velvet trimming, the boots with French heels, the sheepskin slippers from Margaret, and the leather-bound book by Mill. Adding that last precious item to the pile, I held it close a moment and thanked its author for his understanding, even if the world isn't yet ready to give up damaging those outside its tiny spheres of propriety. I prayed that the unwed mother might someday gain her liberty.

The pawnbroker was a tired, pale man. His eyes twitched as he reviewed my offerings and explained our arrangement. He would determine the value of my items and loan me that amount; if I wished to reclaim my possessions within four months, I could repay the loan, along with monthly interest and a storage fee. In his ledger he listed each piece with a price beside it.

On telling me the total — three dollars twenty cents — he avoided my gaze, which made me suspect unfairness. But he rejected my appeal for more. Most likely I'd never reclaim the items, he said, and many of them wouldn't sell, and some needed laundering, "and if you had any idea how much more I give than I should . . ."

So I assented. He gave me the cash and a written duplicate of his accounting. Lifting my lightened case, I exited the shop, the string of bells on the door tinkling behind me.

I had but eight dollars and change. Another day had passed, so I'd need ten to get Charlotte out. Where to go? I took Albert's card from my pocket. His office was at Eighth and Chestnut Streets; I was only a few blocks away. By then the hour was ten — the many clocks and church bells downtown keep one well apprised — and he'd said to come earlier or later, but that couldn't be helped.

In a corner park across the street from the pawn shop, I took my hair down, combed it, pinned it up, and rinsed my face in a fountain intended to water horses, having no choice but to ignore the passing vehicles and people. It appeared that many others had used this water source for similar purposes, as fragments of soap and discarded rags were strewn about. I dried my face with the edge of my sleeve, lifted my valise, and moved my weary legs toward Albert's address.

A guard in a military-style jacket stood at the doors of the building — a tall, marble edifice that bore brass signs for many businesses. "What brings you here, lass?" he inquired.

I showed Albert's card and said he was expecting me. The guard bowed and let me pass into a commodious, high-ceilinged foyer with mahogany walls. The stone floor brought a welcome coolness to my feet. When I presented myself to a woman standing at a high desk, she picked up a flexible speaking tube and shouted into it, asking the assistant at the other end whether Mr. Burnham would accept a visitor. An affirming shout came, so she pointed to a set of wide stairs and said, "No need for the elevator. It's one flight up."

An elevator! I was relieved not to have to step inside one of those unsafe boxes and be looked up and down by its operator.

Albert stood in the doorway of his office, his manner pleasant and welcoming. He ushered me in. Then he slid the bolt lock on the door, which seemed unnecessary.

"Please take a seat," he said, pointing to a stuffed chair in front of the unlit hearth. He sat beside me in another chair rather than behind the huge desk. The room's many shelves showed an array of foreign objects, from ivory carvings and embroidered shawls to swords of antique workmanship. It smelled like a spice stall at an indoor market. Interior shutters covered the lower portions of its many tall windows, so that the light was dimmed and soothing.

"I'm pleased you came." He grinned. "This is my uncle's business, if you didn't know, and he's arranging contracts in England. So I'm quite at ease today." His eyes skimmed my form. "Are you hoping

I'll buy you a new dress, since clearly you're in need of one?"

Why did he seek to knock me off balance by referring to my looks? "I've come about a life-and-death matter," I told him.

"You've angered my wife, that's certain." He pushed his hair back from his forehead. "Drugging Henry was not among your duties. But I don't believe she'll kill you."

"No," I said.

"What are your employment prospects?"

"I haven't begun to look," I said. "My urgent need right now is —"

He stood, put on his reading glasses, and chose a sheet of paper from the desk. Handing it to me, he said, "Read this."

I began deciphering the scrawl. "Without further assurances of your intention to pay, Burnham Imports, Incorporated, must cease to —"

"Excellent." He took the page back. "That's as crooked as my penmanship ever gets. I'm guessing yours is neat and accurate?" He removed his glasses and cleaned them with a monogrammed handkerchief from his vest pocket.

"It had to be. Penmanship was a special consideration at my school."

"Then you can work here. I don't like typewriters, and I think handwriting presents a better impression overseas. I'll give you an advance on your pay so you can buy suitable clothing for our offices." He leveled his eyes with mine. "I'm pleased. We'll spend more time together."

"But —" I blurted.

He waved a hand to quiet me, then dropped into a chair, pushing his hands outward on his thighs to smooth his linen trousers.

"No need to object," he said. "The typewriter is a miserable invention. Until it can produce more than a sentence without the keys jamming, we'll need someone who can make my notes into presentable correspondence. Your skills will be better than the others here, I imagine, since you were a teacher."

"I appreciate thy offer," I finally said. "I'll be very pleased to accept it soon. But my baby's in danger."

Before he could respond, a knock came at the door, and a man's voice informed him of a telegram.

"I'm occupied," Albert yelled out. "Come back in half an hour." To me he said, "What's happened to the baby?"

"She was put in the almshouse after a fire destroyed her wet nurse's home. I need ten dollars to get her out, and I have only eight."

"Ah, so you've come to me for money." His face retained its pleasant look but lost some of its luster.

"I'll be glad to repay thee with work," I said. "Once I've regained my baby."

"But if you had a baby with you, dear Miss de Jong, how could you work in this establishment?" He gestured to the expanse of his elegant office. Leaning closer, he chuckled. "It wouldn't do."

"Of course not." My shoulders shrank inward. His eyes perused my form from shoes to head.

"I'm not as clean as I might be." My face grew hot. "I have nowhere to live."

He relaxed his posture in the chair, raised a hand to his chin, and smoothed his lips with his pointer finger. "Well, why not. I may as well offer you another sort of work."

In my chest I felt hope unfurling — the hope that some single act would lift me.

"I've been thinking this awhile, Miss de Jong." He brought his hands together in his lap; the gold of his wedding ring glinted in the aura of the standing lamp beside him. "The best a woman in your circumstances can hope for" — he cleared his throat and continued — "is to be kept by a good man. Don't you think so?"

Taken aback, I answered, "I pray that *isn't* so."

"Oh it is, believe me." He patted his thighs. "And I could be that man."

I noted how Johan's behavior had cleared the way for another man to consider me an instrument of pleasure.

Then he told me the terms. Ten dollars now and twenty every month, and I'd live in his small apartment by the Delaware. "It's a busy neighborhood," he allowed. "A short walk from here, but less — fussy. All sorts of people."

"And what would be my duties?" I asked, hungry for that ten dollars.

"You'd entertain me when I come by." He grinned and waved a hand sideways. "Particularly in the summer, when Clementina stays in Germantown." His manner enlivened as the idea grew. "And why not at the middle of the day, and some evenings the rest of the year, when my wife has plans? I'd give you a small allowance, too, so you could prepare my meals occasionally. Miss de Jong — Lilli, if I may. Your companionship" — and here he lowered his tone — "your *close* companionship would suit me."

I said nothing, but in my face he seemed to read my dismay. He stood and smoothed his cream-colored jacket. "A mere charitable gift would do you no lasting good. A lack of money is not what makes a pauper, but a lack of employment."

Apparently he was ignorant of those whose employment pays too little to end their poverty. And his notion of good employment was preposterously self-serving in this case. But I couldn't dwell on that. "I could keep my baby at this apartment," I said, confirming.

"If you must. Would that enable you to accept?"

"Perhaps. I need to think." How else could I get money for Blockley and find out if Charlotte lives? I rose from my chair, feeling I had too little air to call upon. My bosoms ached, for I hadn't released any milk since before dawn, and my hands sought to adjust the corset beneath my bodice. Albert's eyes followed my efforts.

"Overfilled?"

I nodded, embarrassed. "Is there a private room I might use before getting on my way?"

Rapidly he covered the several steps between us. "I'd like to help you myself." He lowered his head to stare at my chest and brought his hands to the buttons of my bodice.

I grabbed his wrists and pulled them back.

Evil spoke from within me when I asked, "How much will thee pay?"

"Two dollars, on the spot."

That would give me ten dollars, and my remaining change would pay for the street-car.

Without waiting for my answer, he kneeled on the thick Oriental carpet, inclined his head toward my bosom, and gazed upward in a pitifully desirous way.

Of course I needed to accept. But I was also moved by the lean of his handsome face toward me, his straight-cut hair slanting across his brow, his lips already loose and his tongue showing between them; I was half-enchanted by the complex fragrances the room exuded and the scent rising from his body. All this made me want to touch his head, to feel his warm mouth upon me. I unbuttoned my bodice, unclasped the busk of my corset, and pulled at the bow of my chemise to loosen its neck.

"All right, but thee must tell no one," I said. My voice felt thick in my throat.

"Who would I tell?" His hands pushed mine aside to move the chemise below one swollen breast.

His big head near my bosom shocked me; I thought of Johan, the only man who'd ever been so close. Something palpable was

407

breaking, as if a stick was snapping in me, or a pact was being torn to pieces and thrown away. Tears sprang to my eyes as I worked to take a breath.

Then Albert nudged my breast into his mouth. Milk rushed through the ducts and buzzed at my nipples, and both sides began to release their liquid. His lips covered my nipple and the smooth circle around it; his mouth pulled my delicate flesh; the tight muscles all through my body grew easier as he sucked. The milk on the side he wasn't sucking was wetting my chemise, so I looked about for something to catch it. He didn't notice, so rapt was he, when I plucked the handkerchief from his vest pocket. The white cloth read *ASB* in a neatly embroidered script. Clementina had certainly not embroidered those letters; even so, as I used the white muslin to catch my milk, the sound of her angry voice came to mind — "Albert!"

And there her husband crouched, gulping away at my breast. Though I like nothing about his wife, revulsion swept through me. I pushed his head off, which hurt as his teeth withdrew. He leaned back, licking white from his lips. His eyes stayed closed, his lips half smiling. With clumsy fingers I tied my chemise, fastened my corset, and buttoned my bodice. I ran toward the office door, then remembered my valise.

As I stepped back to the chairs and reached for it, Albert intercepted my hand gently with his. I felt the damp pillow of his touch. He tucked a dollar between my fingers.

"For one side," he said. "Your milk is very fine." He leaned his head down and forward, aiming to kiss me with his easy lips.

I wanted to kiss him. Yes, I wanted to abandon my body to his, to feel his fine clothes against me, the press of his suspenders on my ribs, the linen of his suit, the rising of his snake-like part, his capable arms pulling me in and down. I wanted to cleave my mouth to his and dive into those sensations, the very ones that had made me adore Johan. I wanted to let go of my terror over Charlotte, to drink forgetfulness from the river Lethe. As an option for a ruined life, I told myself, being this man's kept woman would be far from the worst.

Yet Charlotte was trapped at Blockley, most likely on the brink of death or dead! And I couldn't accept that consenting to whoredom was the only way to reach her.

I moved my head to evade his lips. I shoved the dollar into the purse at my neck, grabbed my valise, and slid the bolt open on his office door.

He didn't call after me as I tried my best not to run down the stairs. Traveling the high-ceilinged foyer, I kept my eyes to my feet. I rushed by the guard and burst onto the scorching sidewalk.

Which takes me to this moment. In the shelter of an alley hung with clotheslines, I'm seated on my valise, holding Albert's handkerchief at my nose. It smells of my milk and his musk.

Church bells are tolling noon. Mr. Lambert arrives at Blockley at one and leaves at four, and this is the last day of the week when he takes applications. I'm a dollar short, but that won't stop me. I'll go find out if Charlotte lives.

NOTEBOOK EIGHT

Sixth Month 8

Swirls of traffic and noise perplex my brain. My eyes droop with exhaustion. Yet I wish to write of how I found my Charlotte — Charlotte! — whose dear diminished weight is propped against me!

I set off yesterday with determination building in my chest like the heat of a slow coal fire. I crossed the bridge over the Schuylkill River by streetcar, reached and passed through the almshouse gate, and knocked hard at the Children's Asylum door.

On entering, I told the young man at the desk that I would tour the foundling department, and if Mary Foundling was my Charlotte, I'd give him nine dollars and change — every cent I had — and take her. He didn't answer my proposal but merely consulted his ledger.

"You owe the city ten dollars for Mary's

care and must pay in full." His flat eyes regarded me. "This isn't a market where you can bargain, miss."

When I retorted that the city would be better off with nine dollars than a failing infant, he gave out a guffaw. I steadied my feet on the floor and yelled. "I've spent four days gathering the items you require. Thee will take me to the foundling department. If my baby's there, she will leave with me today."

A man in a doctor's robe appeared at the doorway. He poked his head in the room, then crossed to the desk. "Is she the mother of one of our charges?"

The young man raised a hand and ran it along his chin whiskers, suddenly anxious. "She claims so, Doctor."

"Does she have proof?"

I pulled the birth certificate and forged letter from my skirt and handed them over. The doctor raised the round spectacles from a string at his neck, set them on his nose, and examined the pages. He fixed me with a keen look. "How did your baby come to be admitted here?"

"The Germantown Hospital sent her after a fire. They couldn't reach me. This man said that if I got certain documents, and two dollars per day — but every time I return, there's a new requirement, and more money due." Pressure came to my eyes. "I will take my daughter today if she still lives!"

The physician raised a sturdy arm and pointed at my adversary. "You again! Who told you to charge a daily fee to a parent taking back a child? You know this no longer applies."

I was dumbfounded. The young fellow paled. "Mr. Malos requires us to collect the costs of support," he stammered. "He — he'll have my job if —"

"Mr. Malos! That scoundrel. He shouldn't be allowed on the Board of Guardians. Yesterday he carted out of here at least sixty pounds of mutton and ten of tea, all belonging to the city. As if our patients don't need to eat!"

The young man appeared to have deflated. His shoulders sagged beneath his suit; his head dropped forward. The doctor put a warm hand on my shoulder.

"You owe nothing. I'll take you to the foundling department. I work in surgery, but I did a rotation there in my student days." He turned to the young man, whose gaze stayed downward. "If Mr. Malos gives you trouble," he advised, "say the chief surgeon forbade you to follow his orders in this case."

415

I thanked the universe for sending a reformer my way as I traveled beside the doctor down a stifling hall. We passed an open door that revealed a room of dining tables in rows; upon one table sat several dozen blocks of bread. Apparently they'd failed to rise. A worker with a long knife was struggling to cut slices from a loaf.

"Bakery rejects," my companion explained. "The guardians pocket the price difference."

We stopped on reaching the nursery. The stink of waste accosted us through the open door. How could any baby survive in such a thick miasma? The surgeon stepped past and nodded to a nurse standing by.

"We're looking for this young woman's baby," he explained.

She nodded and pointed to the cribs. The other nurses sat in rockers, observing us with heavy-lidded eyes, each with a swaddled baby at her breast. Behind the doctor I traversed the rows of infants — some with rashes showing at their necks, some with eyes encrusted, all silent in the small metal cribs bearing numbers and hastily assigned names: Stephen Infant, Anna Market. The doctor muttered oaths until at last we found the crib labeled "Mary Foundling."

The baby's gaze was fixed on the ceiling;

its limbs were immobilized by swaddling. But red wisps poked from beneath its cap. From the face poked a pert nose, a pair of dry, familiar lips.

"Praise God!" I called. I lifted her; she was far lighter. The tight brown wrap felt sodden at her bottom, and her tiny face was pursed with discomfort. But when I caught her red-rimmed eyes, a glint of recognition sparked there.

She summoned a high, short cry, and her cracked lips pursed into a suck. With no regard for the physician at my side or for what diseases she might have fallen prey to, I opened my clothing. She latched on hard enough to bring me pain, and for the first time I was glad for that.

It proved she had the power to want.

"You'll need to feed her often," the doctor instructed, "but not much at once. You've got to go slow when rehabilitating a baby." He let me nurse a moment longer, then asked, "May I examine her?"

With reluctance I removed her, and she began to cry with a high, brittle sound. The doctor held her gently in his articulate hands and moved away. I assembled my clothes and rushed after him to an examination table against a wall. Setting her down, he removed the cloths, the binder, the diaper — and revealed her visible ribs. Diarrhea soaked her diaper, and her bottom had a red-rimmed, oozing sore.

What a rule-following excuse for a mother I'd been. I should have forced my way in on my first visit and refused to leave without her. I understood then why someone might tear out her own hair.

"She's been here five days?" he asked.

I counted but lost track, my mind too panicked. "I believe so."

The doctor moved his agile fingers above her face; she made no effort to follow. "She's already marantic. She has little strength apart from what it takes for basic functions." He pointed to the wrinkled skin on her arms. "And she's dehydrated. See the pap boats by the nurses' chairs?"

I nodded.

"The grains in the pap cause diarrhea — and perhaps she's caught infectious diarrhea as well." He sighed. "We simply don't have enough willing mothers here to nurse so many babies."

There had been pap boats in Gerda's hovel, too, and three infants sharing one woman's milk; how had Charlotte survived ten days there? Gerda must have given the babies other liquids. Charlotte was far weaker this time. And the red sore frightened me. I pointed.

"That comes from diapers left on too long." The doctor squeezed the borders of the sore gingerly; Charlotte made a puling sound. "The liquid being clear is reassuring," he said, "but I'll give you lanolin to help it heal." He placed a hand on her forehead and behind her neck. "No fever." He felt the sides of her groin and neck. "No swelling. She's suffered neglect and a bad diet, probably nothing more. But if she develops a rash or a fever, or if your milk doesn't resolve the diarrhea and dehydration within two days, you must have a physician treat her."

Clinics for the poor had been one of our Meeting's causes. I'd find one, if need be.

"You'll want to keep her in the dark," the doctor continued. "Don't hold her often; it's too stimulating. Feed her small amounts at first, then one complete side, then a full feeding every two hours. Wash her bottom and dry it well at every diaper change, and bathe her daily." He took the cap from her head and searched her scalp. "No lice. That's lucky. In any case, let's get her cleaned before you go."

The nurse he'd spoken to at the door brought us a pan of water, a cloth, and soap. I slid Charlotte in, and her pinched features eased slightly at the touch of water. As I bathed her limbs and frame, wincing at the sight of her, I thought how difficult it would be to follow the doctor's instructions without a place to live. My distress must have shown, for the doctor brought his oval face nearer to mine, so that I could smell the bitter coffee on his breath.

"What she needs most," he said, "are your milk and love."

His words relieved me as I dressed Charlotte in a clean binder and diaper that the nurse supplied. The doctor recommended against swathing in tight cloths — "It's barbaric" — and gave me a blanket to wrap her in, along with a tiny jar of lanolin, two diaper pins, and four diapers from a heap of them. As he handed me these precious things, I looked at his face, noting the nicks on his cheeks from hurried shaving, the tired eyes.

"You've saved my daughter," I said.

He sighed, shaking his head. "*You've* saved her, with your persistence. But she'll need weeks to recover. Any longer here and she might have — there's no use to say. That's why we're closing this nursery next month and putting the foundlings into private homes. The staff here tries to help more than to harm, but when it comes to foundlings . . ." He patted my arm. "It's lucky your baby has you."

He escorted us to the door and bowed goodbye, his manner more dejected than glad.

I understood. Even as I rejoiced at holding Lotte to me, and committed myself to her recovery, I grieved for the many infants we'd left behind.

With Lotte as quiet as a stone at my chest, I caught streetcars downtown. On a bench I ate from Miss Baker's pound cake and suffered to watch my baby's dulled face. Then I fashioned a sling from my shawl and placed Charlotte inside, partly to help her rest, partly to keep her from public inspection.

I searched for somewhere quiet as I walked the downtown streets. Whenever I peeked inside the sling, Charlotte's expression looked pained — which was no wonder, given the mayhem. Drivers cracked whips and yelled commands; police tried with shrill whistles to prevent collisions; street vendors announced their services and wares; and farm animals made their way, two by two, with farmers prodding them home from market. As I walked, moving toward the river, the day's heat yielded to a cooler evening. I welcomed the cool but dreaded the onset of darkness, having never spent a night without shelter.

A stream at the far edge of a coal yard appeared to offer refuge. I crossed the empty yard, then sat on a rock and watched the stream meander into the Schuylkill River a short way off. I woke Charlotte with kisses and put her to me for a few moments' sucking. Then I undressed her and washed urine from her buttocks with splashes from the clear stream — glad for her strength when she protested at the water's chill. I dried her, applied lanolin, clothed her, and placed her in the sling. She went to sleep. We'd spend our night beside the stream, I decided.

As the bruised-orange sunset poured over the darkening river, I poured the coins and bills from my purse to count them. A scrambling noise emerged from a short distance away, where a tin roof leaned across coal heaps. I stayed put, expecting nothing larger than a skunk or a raccoon to emerge. But a squat man ducked out, his wide hand rubbing his eyes; under one arm he gripped a crutch, which took the place of his missing leg. He turned his meaty body and came pounding toward us, letting out peculiar utterances.

I gathered everything and ran. I outpaced him by so much that he gave up pursuing. But I dreaded to risk another such encounter. So I listened for the bells of streetcar horses and pursued their clanging to a more populated area. I took up a steady, pointless marching, this time finding reassurance in the press of other people and conveyances. Charlotte slept, regardless.

Darkness grew. I nursed Charlotte in little amounts when privacy was possible. In a prosperous section, lamplighters began to walk from orb to orb, creating gaseous haloes against the darkness. Fancy folk traipsed down the well-scrubbed stoops of their homes; they stepped into carriages, and muscular horses moved them toward their night's adventures. I continued moving my feet in succession. The monotony might have put me into a sort of trance, were it not for the spasms traveling my arms and neck from the unrelenting weight of Charlotte and the valise.

She wasn't vomiting, thank goodness. But her diarrhea and the sore required frequent changes, and already I had no more clean diapers and no dry blanket. A rag-seller with a burdened cart sold me fabric that I cut up with my penknife. At a public fountain I gulped cool water. Once, faint with hunger and weariness, I sat on a stoop to rest and ate the last of the cake from Miss Baker. Asked by a housemaid to move along, I walked some more. The stillness of the baby against my chest was like a knife pricking me. From its little cuts oozed my sorrow and my guilt.

Midnight neared. Out of the taverns and saloons came swaggering the men of high and low society, lewd and careless. Many turned their heads about as if seeking something. Women who'd previously seemed stranded against the buildings began to respond like marionettes whom the night's crude music brought to life. Some were dressed no differently than average factory girls, and perhaps were such; these ones stepped slowly forward, as if reluctant to succeed in drawing their quarry. Others wore festive hats and gowns and had paste jewelry at their necks and ears; these went boldly on display, approaching men with waggling gaits.

"Won't ya have a drink with me?" one called.

"Lonely, Johnny?" asked another.

Within seconds, these calls were met by eager bargaining.

I'd seen it in abusive homes while visiting with Mother, and now I saw it on the street:

how our far-lower wages force women to become the chattel of men. Yet what makes a man take part? Only a sickened soul could enjoy the caresses of a person chained by circumstance. Might some of these opportunists consider me for sale, as Albert had? I shrank against a brownstone wall, out of reach of the gaslights, and willed myself invisible.

An ill-matched couple aimed their unsteady bodies past me, heading toward a saloon. The man was short and swarthy; his muscles strained the seams of a faded suit; his fresh-shaved cheeks and chin shone pinker than the rest of his face. The woman, much taller, struggled along in high French heels, her bosom swelling at the neckline of her purple dress. Her eyes were ringed by black paint, her lips smudged with red. The man pinched her buttock, and she opened her mouth in a fraudulent laugh.

The last time I'd seen that face, a firm line defined the lips, and the eyes were swelled from mourning a baby's departure. I called out, "Nancy!"

She stopped and looked about the crowded street. I stepped from the shadows, called again, and waved. She stared, comprehending, and held up a finger as if to say, "One moment." She entered the saloon with her companion but soon burst onto the sidewalk and approached me in a puff of perfume and alcohol. I reached an arm toward her, craving a friend's embrace. She drew back.

"Please don't judge me," she begged, looking as if I were her accuser.

"Goodness! Who am I to judge? What happened to thee?"

Her words came in a rush. "The maid position was a trick. The woman runs a brothel and locked me up. She sent in men to ruin me."

"I'll help thee escape!" I exclaimed, my spirit rising. "Let's go right away!"

Nancy lowered her head and shook it. "There's no use. The manager would find me and beat me. And she'd take you, too!" Her eyes brimmed with tears as I considered these points. "You *can* do one thing for me," she said — "find out what family took my William, and where they live." She bent to bring her head to mine, showing me her bloodshot eyes, her pores clogged by paint, her unclean teeth. "I want to see him, even from across the street. Do you think he's well?" A tear drew a line of flesh through the rouge on her cheek.

That's when I remembered: Nancy had given William to the almshouse. The chance of his having been adopted from that nursery was slim. Most likely he'd been among the babies I'd left behind, if he wasn't already dead.

I held back my dismay. I couldn't possibly tell this to Nancy and increase her burdens. Already she'd been sent out to service and raped by her employer, had given up her son and then been made into a woman of the night.

Charlotte began making bird-like sounds beneath my shawl — her first joyful noises since I'd reclaimed her. She must have recognized Nancy's voice! And Nancy knew hers. My friend's sorrow parted like the Red Sea.

"You have her! Let me look!"

I pulled back the fabric. Charlotte tried to make another sound but coughed. Her eyes poked forth too prominently against her flattened cheeks, and her thinness was evident even through the blanket that wrapped her.

"She's ill!" Nancy stiffened.

"But she's improving." Already her complexion was less sallow, and her lips were moist.

"At least you've got her." Nancy eyed the saloon. "I have to go in. Where are you living?"

I told her our situation as rapidly as I could. She pulled a dime from her pocket. "I'm not supposed to keep money, but I have this. Take it." When I hesitated, she forced it into my pocket and kissed my cheek with her painted lips. "The lamps stay on all night at Broad Street Station," she advised. "Go there." She reached to squeeze my hand; hers was unnaturally warm. Perhaps she'd caught a disease — from her new profession or from Mabel.

"Thee can get away," I urged. "There are asylums downtown that help" — what should I call her? — "degraded women. Please go to one."

Her aspect sharpened with her thought. "There is one girl going to escape to the Magdalen Asylum."

I pushed. "Go with her. Please don't accept this as thy life."

In a choked voice she replied, "I'm not worth saving." Then she rushed into the saloon. A cloud of tobacco smoke wafted out in her wake — a fragment of the debauched soul of that place.

As it stung my throat, I prayed for strength. I had to make my way through this trial. I had to undo the damage I'd done to Charlotte. Then one day I'd seek out Nancy and prove her worth to her.

I set off toward Broad Street Station. The streets grew empty, save for an occasional inebriated man who wove about, gesturing and shouting into the silence. I'd heard that gangs of young bloods roamed the streets at night, but I met none. Then the street cleaners began their work, urging their horses from house to house, debarking to overturn full ash barrels into their wagons, and sweating as they shoveled up the grease and kitchen scraps, the manure, the occasional dead animal piled at the curb. When a policeman passed, tossing a stick hand to hand and eyeing me too eagerly for comfort, I veered onto a path between two buildings and began traversing the alleyway behind, where open drains overflowed with sewage. I tried to avoid stepping in their effluence and breathed shallowly. Over low backyard fences I saw gardens, clotheslines, sheds, privies, tethered goats — and these mundane sights of normal life soothed my fear.

Finally I arrived at an area of splendid edifices, with the four-story, granite-and-brick building of Broad Street Station ahead. Across from it lay a huge structure of stone blocks and bricks, surrounded by monstrous heaps of materials and machinery: our new city hall in process. The workers were gone till morning, but dust still floated.

I entered the train station. Throughout its long, low-ceilinged lobby, flames burned in wall fixtures and chandeliers. Rows of people slept on the floor or whispered together against the walls. Some showed the jerky movements and off-kilter expressions of the insane; some sat with opened, unseeing eyes; some lay in puddles of urine. Many had feet in poor condition, with their filthy shoes cast to the side, sodden socks removed, the skin blistered and bloated and scabbed. Nancy had directed me to a place where the neglected and the desperate cast their anchors before hobbling through the streets again in search of coins and food.

I took a spot along the wall and sat upon my valise. The man to my right coughed in his sleep; the cough and the large scrofula on his neck showed he was consumptive. A skinny, buck-toothed, hot-faced woman called for water; someone brought it. Charlotte drank and slept. Despite my fear, I managed to doze — but I woke soon to fingers groping and scratching at my neck, then pulling on the string of my purse.

I slapped away the wily hand in terror. The body slithered into the darkness beneath a set of stairs, and I didn't dare

430

pursue it. Then Charlotte began to kick. When I peered into the shawl, she flashed her tongue-revealing smile! My heart opened like an oyster, baring its tender part.

I fed and changed her and dozed again. But the cries of the thirsty woman woke me. Again she begged for water. A fountain bubbled close by, so I filled the chipped cup from Margaret and brought it to the woman. There was an ashen dryness to her skin. When she took the cup, the heat of fever touched my hand.

Fearing whatever disease she carried, which Charlotte would be especially vulnerable to, I had a nightmare-ridden sleep. At dawn I opened my eyes to the legs of a railroad policeman whose foot was nudging me awake.

"Move on out," he said. "The decent folk are coming."

Already passengers were entering with trunks and crates, and clustering at ticket counters. The sick woman appeared deep in slumber when the policeman reached her spot. But his efforts to wake her brought no response. While I changed Charlotte and applied lanolin to her sore, the woman's small, death-heavy body was loaded onto a baggage cart and pushed toward the carriage area. No doubt she'd be dumped in a hole in a pauper's field.

I pulled my body to the street, with Charlotte and the valise. I was afraid to pass another night at the station, so at gathering points I asked vagrants to tell me of inexpensive lodging houses. The ones who answered knew of places for men only; others were too impaired by drink or infirmity to help. I asked after a room at several decent-appearing taverns and was informed by gruff barkeeps that a woman on her own, even a widow with a baby as I'd claimed to be, would likely draw unsavory interest and danger there.

I kept marching and reached a peaceful block of brick row-houses on Clinton Street. Before one house, a carved wooden sign read THE WHISPERING PINES, WOMEN'S LODGING. My hope refreshed, I climbed a narrow stoop and rang the bell.

A crisp-mannered maid welcomed me into the foyer, which was clean and airy. Then the middle-aged proprietress arrived, puffing as she descended the carpeted stairs, struggling for breath against her tight-laced corset. I identified myself as a widow, and she asked to see my baby. Pulling back the shawl, I kissed my baby's forehead, aiming but failing to bring on her liveliness.

The startled proprietress inquired as to

my husband's name, the date and place of his death, whether I could produce a death certificate, how I planned to pay the lodging cost, whether I had steady work, why my family hadn't taken us in — and I stumbled in my answers. She pursed her lips and sniffed, as if detecting my lies by scent — or, more likely, confirming my lack of a place to bathe. Then she dismissed me.

"I'm sorry," she said. "We're unable to shelter those without work and upstanding reputations."

I was foolish to have dreamed of any other response at such a clean, pleasant location.

I returned to Broad Street Station, where I sit now, shielded from public view by a baggage cart, scribbling fast while Charlotte rests.

To my eyes, Charlotte and I are still cleaner than the other vagrants. But a string of sobering facts is evident. The longer one is homeless, the dirtier one becomes. The dirtier one becomes, the less charity one attracts. The less charity one attracts, the more likely one is never to rise from the street.

Yet how can I stop us from becoming unsalvageable, when I can only move in circles: changing Charlotte's diaper and blanket, discarding the used ones because I have

433

nowhere to clean them, buying old bed-sheets and rags from a cart and ripping them into squares for diapers and blankets with the aid of my penknife, finding an alley in which to relieve myself, nursing Charlotte, finding water to drink, changing Charlotte and applying lanolin, finding water in which to wash her bottom and my hands, nursing her, buying rags, tearing them into diapers and blankets, buying something of poor quality to eat. These tasks alone could keep me occupied today, tomorrow, and for weeks to come, without our making any progress.

How can I even think of making progress? Each time I nurse, I float into a state of depletion such that I can hardly form a thought, much less a plan. In fact, without a pencil in hand, I can't think at all.

What keeps me from complete despair is Charlotte. Her diarrhea is less frequent; her appetite increases; her look grows keener. Each improvement is a drop of water for the parched seedling that is my heart.

Sixth Month 9

To be the gainer of charity, one loses more than I knew.

This morning I set out to learn how to survive on the street. I sat in one place and then another, watching, with Charlotte quiet against me. And one thing that shocked me was the many children who spend their days begging and roaming. They are tough and persistent, following quick-moving targets with a repeated "Change for food?" or "Black your boots, sir?" (These ones have boot-blacking kits banging against their short legs.) Many persons drop coins into their hands. Some even sit upon the proffered stool for a boot blacking, despite an unclean rag and poor-quality polish.

These children sweep steps, unbidden, and demand a coin when someone leaves or enters. They sell oranges, newspapers, or pencils. Only the rare ones wear shoes: old boots with flapping soles, or slippers ill suited for the streets. Some wrap their feet in newspaper or rags. It affects me most to see their faces — anxious, cunning, and preternaturally alert, except when they withdraw from the press of traffic to count their coins; then the softness of their youth overtakes them.

Despite their chant of "Change for food?" I haven't seen them buying victuals. Rather, they pick up packets of cart food that others drop after taking their fill. In my great hunger, I've begun following their lead.

The first time I reached to the ground, I

was ashamed. But in the paper packet lay two warm chestnuts, whose buttery richness spread over my tongue. I reached eagerly for the next packet; in it sat a bit of salted pretzel, slightly damp — I tried not to think from what.

I might still find a room to let, if I had the money. To get it, I'd need to beg. So I looked for a place and chose a stately market house on Sixteenth Street. Perhaps a dozen others sat on squares of cloth before it, some holding paper signs attesting to the events that had rendered them homeless. When I'd walked through Germantown with Mother, we'd sometimes encountered such persons displaying their troubles; she'd complain of the city's lax rules against vagrancy and begging, which excepted from arrest anyone who was blind, deaf, dumb, maimed, or crippled, along with women and minor children. Because of this leniency, she said, a stroll in the streets could be heartrending, and such persons were not motivated to seek a better solution to their poverty. Mother preferred to help through institutions or with direct assistance to people in their homes — for people who *had* homes.

But what of those who didn't?

I drew closer to the outer wall of the

market building, grief and defiance mingling in my heart. As I reached to open my valise, Charlotte startled in the sling of my shawl, then sank back. I tore a page from this notebook and wrote, "Please help a widow and her infant." Then I claimed a spot among our new tribe, nodding in greeting to the others and drawing stares. I anchored the sign on the ground with the chipped cup from Margaret, which thus became our begging cup. And behind it I sat, my valise beneath me, becoming one more still point of neediness on a street thick with vehicles, any one of which might have careened onto the sidewalk and crushed us.

My whole being was aflutter at the strangeness, yet Charlotte barely stirred against me.

Children in rags sat nearby. One boy wore a tattered shirt and trousers; his bare calves were covered in burns. A girl with one foot bent sideways carried the remains of braids in her hair, perhaps put there by some caring hand. She sat upon a crate, holding to her flat chest a boy too young to walk.

My mother and her charitable friends had spoken of some parents maiming their children in order to live off the pity they inspired. Could these children have been harmed by intent, to loosen purses?

A sob escaped my throat. How could Helen de Jong's own daughter and granddaughter have become figures in this tableau of tragedy? If Mother could have passed by and observed our abjectness, and if she'd known the source of our predicament, I wondered if she might have laid it all upon my sinful appetite and withheld her coin.

To the right of my spot lay a man on a wool blanket, his crutches beside him, drinking from a metal flask. He was missing a foot; his scrawled sign revealed he'd lost it in the war. He stank of liquor and unwashed flesh. It seemed he hadn't noticed me until his arm shot out in my direction, proffering the flask. I declined, shuddering to think of placing my mouth over that dark hole and sucking down its enfeebling poison.

"Think yer too good for rotgut?" snarled the man. He adjusted the wad of chewing tobacco in his cheek and spit its juice into the street, fixing his half-closed eyes upon me.

In fact, I did think I was too good for it. I stared downward until he released me from his gaze. Yet who am I to say that the bottle wouldn't make a fine companion, after a prolonged time of despair and neglect? My father chose it, in far less dire conditions.

All through this, well-dressed servants

were stepping past with empty baskets. They walked into the market doors, then emerged laden with foodstuffs and small coins. Beggars nearest to the doors did the best at collecting, but some market goers were not moved by pity until they reached my cup. They tossed in pennies that clanked and settled. I didn't like to meet their glances, ashamed at how low I'd fallen, but I quietly called my thanks. When a plump-armed maid held out a fresh bun to me, however, I could see the deftly embroidered flowers upon her dress, and I was drawn to look up. Her pink face showed a mix of distaste and pity.

No doubt I'd looked at many vagrants in that way. The chewed bits of bun scraped and dragged as they fell to my stomach.

Then a street boy ran by, yelling "Coppers!" Beggars rose or were helped to rise. An old woman croaked to me, "Shove off!" So I thrust the cup and sign into my pocket and stepped away with Charlotte and my valise, flowing like water into the passing crowd. I followed the old woman; on coming close, I tapped her shoulder. She turned with a hard look.

"Why did we need to leave?" I asked. "Aren't most of us excepted from the vagrancy laws?"

"Excepted?" She opened her mouth to gape, revealing several holes where teeth had been. "You hain't been carted in yet? Every one of us that has two legs, even the blind, gets charged with vagrancy and three months' labor if we're hauled before the magistrate."

"But that isn't the law!" I said. "My mother told me it isn't!"

"I don't care what law they *write*. This is what they *do*." She spit. "Yer mother put you up ta begging?"

"Oh, no." I blushed.

"Well, best get back to Mother and tell her this: the laws and magistrates don't hardly meet no more." She gave a vicious laugh that ended with a fit of coughing.

The law may be more fair in Germantown, or else we hadn't bothered noticing how the beggars' numbers rose and fell.

I gained thirteen cents for my humiliation. Hardly the way to get money for a room. But I will buy myself an apple.

Sixth Month 11

Today was better, though it began strangely.

With Charlotte in my lap, I sat among others in a corner of the train station, seeking to escape the throngs of travelers, when our group was accosted by a tall preacher with

440

a stoop. He was clad in a faded suit that had half-moon stains beneath the armpits. Without any form of greeting, he raised his bent neck and began to shout lines I recognized from the Book of Job: "God has torn me in his wrath, and hated me. . . . He broke me in two; he seized me by the neck and dashed me to pieces; he set me up as his target." The preacher's face, shiny with perspiration, beseeched his unwilling audience of paupers. "Have you known the wrath of God?"

The curious and hostile eyes of young and old, sane and insane stared at him. Did he truly intend to set us up as miniature Jobs? Some vagrants nodded their heads grudgingly.

The man wiped perspiration from his face and neck. "Job claimed he did nothing to deserve his punishment," he shouted. "But he railed against God! He failed to accept his suffering as proof that he had sinned!" His visage sharpened; his nasal voice grew more penetrating. "For the innocent do not suffer! God only torments the wicked!"

Around me, angry sighs were passed. Perhaps others felt, as I did, that this man had done a simpleton's work on an unsolveable dilemma. Why do some suffer and some not? If only we *could* find reason in

441

the distribution of agony and ease. Not to mention that it was not God, but God's son Satan who'd sent Job's torments down. He'd made a wager with God — a wager that he could turn God's devoted servant Job against him.

Job's story hardly makes the case that suffering is sent down with an intended moral purpose.

"Ah, shut yer mouth," said a woman with yellow-white hair to the preacher. She spit on the ground and pressed her mouth tight. Two ragged young men rose from the floor, faced off with the man, then walked away, their muscled arms swinging at their sides. I trembled with the wish to challenge the simpleton — but this would have brought unwanted attention, not to mention that I'd never done such a thing publicly in my life. I rose, too, and left the station.

For the afternoon, the world seemed pleasing. Perhaps from gladness at escaping that harangue and at remembering how everyone is vulnerable to hardship, a tenderness welled up in me toward all the living. I found a stillness within our transitory state, relishing the passing folk intent on business or recreation, and loving the familiar clip-clop of horses, freshly curried and brushed, as they pulled grocery wagons house to house, stopping to deliver milk or ice or bread. The odors of meals escaped through windows, and hunger cut into me. When a bakery wagon stopped, I lingered to stare, and a small boy seated between burlap sacks held up a hefty loaf.

"Fifteen cents," he called. I gave him a dime and a nickel and tucked the bread into the shawl, at Charlotte's feet; she gazed down with curiosity. In a square crossed by footpaths and newly planted with trees, I sat and nursed her surreptitiously beneath my shawl, then ate piece after piece of bread.

The day was steaming hot. A trio of baby robins hopped about, flapping stubby wings; their parents flitted near, nervous and attentive. I watched a nurse on a bench read a newspaper and watched her young charges kick a ball. The date on her paper was Sixth Month, Day 11. Charlotte would be three months old in eighteen days! She lay against me, observing those who crossed the park or sat there — the men in suits; the women in form-fitting polonaises, with bustles enlarging their backsides; the servants in uniform, intent on errands. And how improved she was already! She smiled at a woman's jaunty parasol raised toward the sun and gurgled toward a pushcart vendor offering lemonade and peanuts. Her enthusiasic sounds caught the attention of a passing matron, who smiled into my baby's eager face, and this recognition cheered me, beaming as it did across a vast divide of circumstances. When I returned us to the train station this evening, there was a hint of the relief one feels at arriving home.

The station does offer more safety than any other place I know — apart from when a man ran through to warn that the police were making an obligatory sweep, and everyone evacuated for a short while. Usually the policemen look the other way, he said, since they depend on several among us who stay alert to goings-on and even report crimes.

Sixth Month 12

After another night of worried sleep, I took us from the train station this morning. I passed hours begging before the same market. I found packets to eat from the ground and drank heavily at a watering place for horses. Then I trod the sidewalks with a heavy gait, Charlotte in my shawl sling.

In time, exhausted and seeking quiet, I followed a path between buildings and settled beside a brick building that appeared abandoned. Its windows were heavily shaded, and no sounds or odors came from within. On the side stoop I sat, with the valise beside me, and took the chance to admire the returning pink of Charlotte's cheeks.

A large man turned down the path and ambled toward us. My body bristled when his bleary eyes lit on me.

"A harlot with a baby, eh?" He sneered, showing broken teeth.

"No," I replied, "an innocent mother who seeks only peace with thee."

"Then why're ya sittin' on the steps of a brothel?"

Was he correct? The brick building showed no sign of that purpose. He stared at Charlotte, who was staring back. I raised my hand to cover her eyes, inadvertently drawing his attention to the gold locket at my throat.

"Nice necklace," he said. "That from your best john?"

In a wink he stood before me. He brought his meaty fingers to my neck and ripped the chain away. Breathing through his thick, half-opened lips, he located the locket's clasp and flipped it open. My mother's slip of hair in its black ribbon fell to the path. When he stepped away, his boot ground it into the slimy bricks.

445

Pain burned in my chest as if he'd plunged in a knife. He raised the locket to his nearsighted eyes. "This oughta fetch enough at the pawn shop to get me soaked," he said, chortling through his phlegm.

I placed Charlotte on the stoop and stood, tears streaming down my face, emotion firing my every muscle. I took up a sturdy branch from the dirt and raised it.

"Give that back right now," I threatened, "or I'll smash thy head!"

The coward began retreating the way he'd come, and I despaired of ever seeing my locket again. So I pursued him and did something I'd never meant to do in all my days: I struck him. Yes, I smashed that stick with all my might into his back.

He stumbled and fell to the brick path, arms slapping down above his head. My locket went skittering into the dirt. I grabbed it and thrust it in my pocket, then collected Charlotte and my valise and rushed toward the alleyway that ran behind the building. Clutched to one side, my baby made no movement and no sound.

The beast followed, yelling obscenities, his boots slapping the bricks some thirty feet behind. I turned onto a cobblestone street and found myself in front of a narrow chapel beside a large church. Its door was ajar. I slipped in and closed the door. Charlotte whimpered as the man's footsteps clattered by.

What a contrast to my thudding heart was the total quiet and dimness of that sanctuary. High above, its windows of stained glass let through radiant beams of sun. I released my valise and fell to the cool floor, holding Lotte to me. I withdrew my necklace and examined it; the chain was broken, but from inside the locket the tintype of Mother looked out, her pressed lips and gleaming eyes showing her perpetual concern for the human condition. Not one strand of the hair I'd clipped upon her death remained, however. Never again would I hold a fragment of her.

Crouched in the clear air of that chapel, I smelled the stench of our bodies, thick and intimate. My clothes were dirtier than I'd realized; the golden yellow of my shawl was dulled by soot and dust. Charlotte was grimy on her exposed skin and hair. My boots were caked with manure, ashes, and urine-soaked dirt. Inside them, my damp stockings had rubbed soft places raw, and the keen pain of my feet overcame me.

Thus did my illusion of being less desperate than the other vagrants die, quick as a spark. Then, perhaps sensing we'd reached

447

a safer place, Charlotte began to squall.

I took us to a pew in the darkest corner, where she shook her limbs and cried.

"Sweet girl," I whispered, leaning over her, my body hot and shivery. "Mother is sorry. Mother is so very sorry."

While at the Haven, I'd believed I could live as my conscience dictated, without inviting suffering and endangering my daughter's life and mine. Why had I believed this?

If only I could turn our world to one that welcomed us.

I kissed her wet cheeks repeatedly, shushing her, hoping a church caretaker wouldn't be drawn by our noise. Her fingernails dug into my flesh like talons. But suddenly she stopped and slept, as if a lever had been lifted that silenced her.

A calm fell over me. And in this calm, I looked about the splendid place that humans had built to honor God. Its pews were oak, and finely carved; its walls were painted with lilies of gold and green; its brass sconces were decorated with vines. Halfway to its arched ceiling, red and green and golden light streamed through stained-glass windows, which showed the disciples and Jesus seated at the Last Supper.

The poet Whittier called such finery a

distraction from the holy presence. But I let that beauty cast its spell; it soothed my roughened spirit.

Weak, thirsty, dizzied by exhaustion and hunger, I lowered my eyes. A row of Bibles sat on the back of the next pew. I took one and turned its pages to the Book of Job, wanting to remember how it resolved.

When studying the Bible at school, I'd always considered Job's dilemma an interesting one — and difficult, yes, but theoretically. This time, though, when I read Job's cries — "He has walled up my way, so that I cannot pass, and he has set darkness upon my paths. . . . He breaks me down on every side" — I felt my own pain recognized. And when God replied by roaring about his unmatched powers and magnificence, asking, "Hast thou an arm like God, and canst thou thunder with a voice like his?" I was appalled by his bullying. Yet Job wasn't. Despite receiving not one word of apology from God, who'd allowed Satan to toy with him disastrously, Job surrendered his complaints. He claimed to detest himself and repented "in dust and ashes" for having protested his withering hardships. For God was all-powerful and magnificent, he echoed, and Job, nothing but limited and weak.

Was there something gorgeously profound in this? A beautiful bowing down before the force that gives life and extinguishes it? A relinquishing of our need for a sensible existence in the face of this force that can, on a whim, destroy us?

Or does Job's response show that the human relationship with God is merely the equivalent of a fistfight or an arm wrestle — a contest that humans always lose?

Perhaps Job surrendered merely because to do otherwise would have afforded no benefit. Was Job like a child with a tyrant father who recognized the need for outward compliance?

Or — and suddenly this seemed the truest — he may have understood that the only way to recover was to accept what had afflicted him. Blame was not the part that mattered. Job surrendered not with weakness but with courage, and thereby gained the ability to go on.

A chill set the hairs on my arms to prickling. I stared up at the stained-glass windows, no longer craving my own shouting match with God.

If my spirit is pressed even harder, I wondered, *will it yield something marvelous — the spirit's equivalent to olive oil or the juice of grapes?*

All at once I felt the shaking I'd felt once before, in the Haven's makeshift chapel. The vivid stained-glass scene came to life; the colorful figures seated at the Last Supper began to move and speak together. And one of the disciples was the thirsty pauper who'd died in the train station. She turned her head outward, transforming from a flat figure to a round. She rose from her stool, every bit as feverish and desperate as she'd been that night. She reached her bony, crooked arms toward me, gaping with an undisguised, enormous need I couldn't fill.

I knew not how long I sat, unmoving, captured by the buzzing strangeness of that altered state and seeing all my failures in her pleading. I hadn't loved my mother well, for I had stood by while she was poisoned. I'd meant to love Charlotte; look what I'd done. Why had I failed, when all my aims were good? In time it seemed I held not Charlotte in my arms, but Mother as she died. I heard words coming through her trembling body: *To love is to risk. To risk is to suffer.*

Finally I became sensible of Charlotte waking, shifting. On a cloth I changed her and stared into her dark blue eyes. She stared back, withholding nothing.

A rattling of keys through the wall told of

someone coming our way. Gathering Charlotte and my valise, I ran out and continued
moving till I reached Broad Street Station,
where I've given my remaining strength to
this recounting.

My nerves are raw. My body trembles. I'm
too tired to stand and beg — too tired to
compete for food packets from the ground
or even to chew — tired to the marrow of
my bones.

Some days have passed — two? Four? How
empty I feel. My locket with its broken
chain lies nestled in the purse beneath the
hollow of my throat. My baby, held upright
against my left side, moves her eyes about,
taking in the detritus of our homeless life.
I'm still affected by the doses of laudanum
I've been taking from the bottle in my valise.
The drug brings ease. My hunger fades; my
breathing slows; my suffering gives way to a
welcome euphoria. But Charlotte has gotten some through my milk, and thus has
been subdued and less inclined to motion.

To drug a baby is despicable — and I've
drugged two.

Confessing makes me crave to harm myself in retaliation, which brings on more
despair, which could lead me to take another dose, another.

Except that, just now, I've stood with Charlotte and poured the laudanum into the drain at the base of a fountain.

Who is thee, my ready friend, whom I entrust with all my secrets? Why do I sense an understanding heart, when thee is no more than paper?

There is perhaps some logic to it. I find hope and courage through this unburdening. In fixing events to a page, I can step beyond them, into the future — where I dread to go.

For my own honor is no longer a thing that I can cherish.

Was it a day ago, or three, when I changed my clothing to a cleaner set and retrieved Albert's card from my stained and dirty valise? With Charlotte at my front, I walked through a haze of heat and dust to the building on Chestnut Street — but this time the guard wouldn't let me past. Most likely because I held a baby and was not clean, he disbelieved that I had legitimate business with Mr. Burnham.

So I waited in the sun, against the wall of a building across the street, as the guard kept his eyes on me. My body ached from lack of sleep and the strain of holding Charlotte and the valise. When at last a clock struck noon, Albert emerged.

Not daring to speak with him in sight of the guard, I followed him several blocks to a tavern and approached him inside. After a moment's disorientation, he invited me to sit on the next barstool.

I whispered that I was ready to take the opportunity for work and lodging that he'd offered.

"Splendid," he said with less enthusiasm than he might have. "You've got sense after all. And you've retrieved your baby, I see." He gave a measured smile. "I'll bring you to the apartment. But wet your whistle first."

I was thirsty, so very thirsty. I accepted the drink he ordered from the stern-faced barkeep. It was a beer, my first. It tasted like the smell of urine. With the valise at my feet and Charlotte in my shawl, I took several sips, not minding how the effervescence rose to my brain. I took another sip, but Albert disapproved of my timid method. Grabbing the mug, he quaffed the frothy liquid, then banged the mug onto the bar and slid it back my way.

"Don't be dainty, Miss de Jong," he admonished. "It isn't a cup of tea."

The barkeep snickered, his body half turned to us as he dried a glass with a cloth.

"All right." I took gulps of the bitter stuff, relieving my dry throat. Albert finished his own drink. At my final gulp, I noted a wobbliness in my mind.

"Let's get you settled," he said, petting my shoulder with a new forwardness. "And you can clean yourself up."

I leaned to his ear and whispered. "It'll be ten dollars today and twenty dollars on the first of each month?" It relieved me to be making these arrangements.

He nodded. "As I said." Getting to his feet with some care, he added, "You'll like the apartment. Very private."

After having not even a square of floor to call my own, much less a wall or a door to shield me and Charlotte, I told him that privacy would be quite welcome.

He took the valise from me, and we walked to a neighborhood thick with taverns, markets, and boardinghouses. His apartment was in a new brick building near the Delaware River. Slowed by the heat, we ascended five flights of stairs. He unlocked the door and we stepped directly into the kitchen — very small, but the most modern such place I'd ever seen. Against its paste-white walls sat a new stove, cupboards, and an icebox. It had an indoor sink with a faucet, so water wouldn't need to be hauled up and down, and a long metal tub for bathing. After we huffed a moment from the steep ascent, Albert excused himself and stepped into what might have been a water closet — since a sound of urination emerged.

I stood by the tub, embarrassed, holding Charlotte and my valise, aware of the stickiness of my skin and wishing for a thorough washing. The apartment was stifling hot, but it had a dry and pleasant smell. Charlotte stared into the air, perhaps watching the dust motes that hung in the sunlight. I kissed her moist forehead. Then I looked through the doorway to the second room.

It held a middling-sized bed in a wooden frame. On its walls were an assortment of photographs, each perhaps eight inches high, that I quickly perceived to be lewd. One showed a woman from behind, leaning away from the camera; her bare bottom and thighs took up much of the picture. Over her shoulder, her eyes were saucily appraising. There were a dozen such pictures. Did Albert know these women? Would he aim to turn me into such a one?

I was appalled; yet a shred of me rose like some maggot from a rotting feast and said, *Why be ashamed? Why not love pleasure?*

As I observed these sensations, aware also of the swell of alcohol in my blood, Albert left the closet and exclaimed over the "dratted heat." He opened the main room's windows, then removed his jacket and vest and stood before me. His high-waisted pants were held up by red suspenders, and sweat marked his shirt. Soon I would be pressed against that body. This seemed less desirable than I'd imagined in those fleeting seconds at his office.

"It's nice no one can see in," he said, gesturing to the uncurtained windows. "We're the tallest building on the block." He spoke with an ease I hadn't seen in him before. "Make yourself at home! Put down your things." Taking note of the baby in my shawl, he grabbed a kitchen towel from a rail on the wall and laid it in the tub. "You can rest her here. Take off some clothing!"

"If thee would give me a moment." My voice was diminished by the strangeness. "I'll get her to sleep and clean myself."

I was grateful when Albert stretched his body upon the bed in the next room and turned his face away. I didn't want his eyes to watch — to corrupt the acts of caring for my baby.

I changed Charlotte's diaper and blanket, then fed her till she slept and placed her in the tub, hoping she'd rest through whatever would follow. Fetching a towel and filling a tin pan at the sink's faucet, I wiped all the places I could reach under my clothing, rinsing the towel several times. At last I stepped into the other room and stood before the bed.

Albert had removed every bit of his clothing. He turned to me on the bed and laughed. "You can't mean to stay dressed!"

Though I was frightened, the sight of his lithe and muscled form did send a jolt through the place between my thighs. I removed my skirt and bodice but kept on my chemise and corset, as well as the stockings suspended from them. I lay beside him.

In seconds he was looming over me, supported by his outstretched arms, his breath more alcohol than air. He accosted my mouth with his larger one, so that I moved my face backward to reduce the pressure. Then he raised my chemise upward and rubbed his stiffened — I'll have to write it — penis into my thighs.

"Have you ever put one of these in your mouth?" he asked.

I replied no and peered past him, searching the photographs to see if one depicted such an act; I'd have much to learn to suit my new employment. Some showed women seated atop men whose penises were visible where they entered the women; another showed several men and women joined in diverse manners through their mouths and private parts. So this was what he wanted.

"Open your lips," said Albert. He pulled himself forward till his pink staff approached my face. He halted his buttocks upon my ribs, limiting my space for breathing. "Lift your head," he instructed. And then, as my face came toward him, he pushed his choking length into my throat.

I did nothing but accept it. Several times he pulled his member outward, then pushed it to the back of my throat again. He laughed with pleasure. I struggled not to close my teeth or use my tongue to shove him away. *Ten dollars today and twenty dollars a month,* my mind intoned. I wanted to cry out. Each time my throat was hit, I fought against a retch.

He moaned, tilting his torso backward. "Ah! Marvelous!"

A bitter gorge rose from my stomach, tasting like beer. Suddenly it increased and poured over his swollen part.

He removed himself and huffed. "That's rather unexpected!" Grabbing his shirt from the floor, he wiped the vomit away from himself and from my wet neck. His face reddened, but his member neither shrank nor shriveled. "Let's try the usual way, then," he said optimistically. "I'll fetch a rubber."

Through my raw throat I thanked him. I'd never seen a rubber, but I knew what they were for, and knew he'd likely obtained his illegally. By the time he'd located one in the kitchen cupboard and brought it to the bedroom, he was trying to unfurl the sack over a flagging penis.

A moment of quiet followed. I lay on the bed; he stood at its foot, tilting slightly from inebriation. Gesturing with his head to his bowed member, he said, "Don't take this as an insult. You've got such creamy skin. Lovely hips. Nice full breasts poking from that contraption you insist on continuing to wear."

As if wounded vanity was my main concern. I sighed as he reached for a bottle beside the bed.

"A little brandy should help." He pulled out the cork and took one gulp and another, shook his head at the force of the liquor, then set down the bottle. He gave a snort at noticing his suspenders on the floor and lifted them. "Bondage always arouses me," he said convivially. "Let's get your arms above you."

How casually he would make me helpless! I shook my head. This I would not do.

"Your arms," he repeated. "Simply put them over your head. I'll manage the rest.

460

Have you tried this? It raises my fever, I'll tell you." He stepped around the bed frame toward its top, his red suspenders in his hands, his face bright with an energy I'd seen in it before. All at once I perceived it as a degree of selfishness that was verging on brutality.

The ribald nudes on the walls mocked my fear. But if I allowed him to fasten my arms to the bed frame, how would I get free? What if he decided to keep me tied there a good while, to maintain his ill-gotten arousal, and Charlotte woke and cried?

What might this person do to my baby, whether now or later, when she grew?

That was a price she would not pay.

I reached an arm to the floor, grabbed my skirt, and found my small penknife in the pocket. In seconds the blade was open in my hand.

"Do — not — dare," I intoned. I got to my knees and gestured with the knife while gathering clothes with my free arm. "Keep away. I'm leaving."

He gave a bark-like laugh and moved closer. "You're jesting! Give that knife over to me!" A line of sweat appeared above his upper lip. "You can't go. How else will you survive with your baby? It's true you're not much of a lover, but I'll train you!" His tone

461

was a sort of greedy pleading. His eyes focused on my breasts, and he reached a hand as if to pull one from my corset. "Gorgeous! And your tasty milk!"

In seconds my clothes were gathered. Into the kitchen I ran, gesturing behind me with my pointy knife. Dropping my clothes, I tried to pull on my skirt with one hand. My corset had vomit at its edge.

"Lilli! Come, Lilli." He couldn't see how serious were my fear and fury. He followed me.

My sleeping baby gave forth a snort and began to wriggle her limbs. In a glimmer of nightmarish hilarity, I perceived that *Charlotte* contains the word *harlot.* She opened her eyes slightly, then fully. She stared at me and Albert.

"Don't come closer," I warned, waving the penknife.

But Albert continued to approach. "Stop, stop!" he said. "This is all unnecessary."

He reached an arm to halt my waving one, and that was his mistake. For as I pulled my arm away, the knife's blade crossed his palm. A smear of blood appeared, ran down his raised forearm, and dripped from his elbow to the floor.

"My God! What have you done?"

He stood naked, a rubber dangling from

him. I stammered a moment as he grabbed a dishtowel from a hook and swabbed his palm. His face looked baffled, as if all had been good fun till this.

In those precious seconds, I got my skirt hooked and my bodice partly fastened. Then I scooped up my squalling baby and our valise and ran to the door, where I grabbed my boots from the rug and stepped into them. The door was easy to unlock. I thumped down flight after flight of stairs, clutching everything to me and praying not to trip on untied laces. Behind me he called, "But Miss de Jong! You can't leave!"

I did.

When my staccato steps finally reached the cobblestone street, Charlotte began to scream. She batted at her face, smearing it with tears and mucus. I straightened up our belongings, then walked from crowded streets to smaller and smaller ones, winding farther and farther north, leaving behind the main thoroughfares until I faced a narrow alley leading between two squat rowhouses. By this time, Charlotte had fallen asleep in my shawl from the strain of crying.

I followed the alley to an abandoned lot. It was bordered by the windowless, stuccoed walls of houses and overfilled by two enormous pear trees, long neglected, nearly as tall as the buildings. No doubt these were the remnants of an orchard. The trees were leafy and gnarled, their branches carrying hundreds of nascent fruits. I spread a cloth in their ample shade, noting with relief the maiden-hair ferns, periwinkle, and wild geranium that grew there — old acquaintances that had occupied swaths of Germantown in summer.

Charlotte remained sleeping when I placed her on a cloth. I sat blankly, unable to stay with any one thought. I reached to pick an unripe pear from the dirt and held it upright before me.

I wanted to see the star inside. My knife was in my pocket. After wiping its slight smear of blood onto a cloth, I cut the pear through its middle to make two pieces, top and bottom.

"What is an apple?" Johan had asked me in the kitchen as he'd cut open an apple in this way.

I'd shrugged. "A tasty fruit."

He shook his head. "A red house with no door and a star inside."

I pulled the top and bottom of my pear apart. In each portion spread a star of seeds. The wonder of that moment with Johan pierced me.

Love had seemed my birthright then. I had believed he loved me. With the slender knife in my hand, I thought of terrible things — of bringing Charlotte to the street, where someone would find her, then cutting myself — of how, under those pear trees, without impedance, I could bleed and die.

I stared at my small darling, considering.

But if I let us both live, I thought, then one day I could share with Charlotte this vision of a simple pear.

The notion had a startling relevance as I held my blade aloft, examining its sharpened edge, considering what force it had in my despairing hand.

I turned the knife back to the pear. With only my attachments to Charlotte and to this world's beauty as my reasons, I wrenched myself from thoughts of death and the relief it promised. I decided to slice the pear into bites and nourish myself with it, so that I would continue to produce milk for the bundled person asleep at my side.

I crunched. The unripe fruit offered a hint of its future sweetness. My chewing slowed until I lacked the strength for one more chew; I sank into a state of unawareness and then into a dreamless sleep.

Eventually, my eyes opened to the chattering of a pair of squirrels. The larger one was clutching the remains of my pear in its bony paws, gnawing at it with quick ferocity. A smaller squirrel lunged, intent on stealing the morsel, but the larger one leaped over the attacker's back and raced up a tree. It stopped at a nest where the trunks of the two trees met and intertwined, then disappeared inside.

I raised my eyes higher, seeing how the trunks and branches were so intermingled that the two trees lived as one. Having begun their lives so very close, their only way to continue upward had been to join. There was no dividing them.

A nerve twinged in my chest. I pictured Father, solemn Father, sitting half the night before the embers of a fading fire as Mother's condition worsened. By the time she'd died, his every movement pulled from a dwindling store of strength.

I'd blamed him for falling into his cousin's arms. Yet in a blink, I understood his reason — not that he hadn't truly loved Mother, but that they had loved each other so entirely that their trunks and branches had grown together. With her gone, he couldn't stand alone.

And I can't, either. I've clung to Charlotte.

We spent the hot afternoon hours in the shade, resting and recovering. I took that opportunity to change my clothing, since only blank walls overlooked us. But I had not one clean item for Charlotte, who was sweating in her blanket wrap. Then small red ants reached Charlotte's face and bit her, which made her scream; they climbed to attack the delicate flesh of my neck. This was no lasting refuge.

On our way back to the station, we passed a house on a quiet alley with its back shutters closed; on its clothesline hung three white baby gowns, embroidered by some mother's careful hand. A craving overtook me. While praying for forgiveness — though knowing this to be a specious and a cowardly prayer — I ran up and took the simplest gown, along with a pail that had clean water in it. Behind the woodpile I crouched to wash off Charlotte's squirming body. Then I covered my child with the raiment another woman had made for hers, as if that raiment could bring us the security we lacked. I nearly sobbed with relief when Charlotte patted my chest and grinned, more clean and comfortable in her purloined garment.

When I returned the pail, a woman coming out the back door saw me and hollered. I ran off, ashamed.

I'd stolen more than a gown. I'd made her clothesline into a place where she'd fear to hang good clothes for years to come.

This was two days ago, perhaps the day before that. Daily I grind away more dignity on the millstone I'm circling.

Against a station wall, I write a page, then bat away the flies. Their winged black bodies swarm Charlotte and me, feasting on our sweat and grime.

Leaning to kiss her scalp, I inhale the subtle fragrance of her being.

■ ■ ■ ■

NOTEBOOK NINE

■ ■ ■ ■

Sixth Month 18
It's late evening. I have a safe place to sleep and a thrilling plan!

Just hours ago I was seated on the Belgian block on Chestnut Street, alongside others without homes, chewing on a discarded sausage from a paper packet. I got out Albert's handkerchief and wiped my oily mouth. A large theater sat across the street, and on its marquis were the words SARAH BERNHARDT, *LA LIBERTÉ*. I was wondering who this free woman was when a police wagon pulled up!

Two policemen were instantly upon the crowd of vagrants, grabbing and shoving, pushing at us with sticks. I dropped my food and tucked the handkerchief into my pocket. Caught in a throng that moved toward the police wagon, I hung on with difficulty to Charlotte and the valise.

The big, blue-coated men pushed several

children and an inebriated man into their covered wagon. These unfortunate ones took spaces on the plank benches, skirting a woman's body that appeared unconscious. Others cried and pleaded, tried to run, or fought to free themselves from the policemen's grip. Then the hairy, sweating arm of a policeman yoked my neck. He pulled me toward the wagon's yawning entrance.

"What is thee doing?" I tried to pull away.

"Takin' ya to de station house," he growled. "A magistrate'll find work for ya."

"I have work!" I said. "I only stopped here for a rest!"

The man rolled his eyes. "Dat's what dey all say. If we took 'em at dere word, we'd have nuttin' but scum on de streets." He shoved me toward the wagon, then released me to slap his stick on the arms of children seeking to climb out. I tried to move away, but he grabbed me again. Charlotte squawked from within her shawl sling.

"Watch out for my baby!"

"Oh, ya got a bastard, heh?" He snickered.

I pulled against his force; he bent and put his arms behind my thighs, then lifted me. I struggled to keep hold of my valise. At that moment, an imperious voice rang across the street — and toward us came striding none other than Clementina, her shoulders thrust back, her head erect in a high-crowned hat. She must have come to see *la Liberté.*

"I asked you, sir, what are you doing to this woman?" she said.

"She'll be goin' to de almshouse or de workhouse, ma'am. Why, d'ya know 'er?"

"Certainly I know her." Clementina scowled. "She was in my employ. A good woman she is, with no business in your wagon."

Astounded, I gave her the nearest that a terrified person could to a grateful smile.

Another policeman replied, his spectacles halfway down his nose from his exertions. "If she's no longer in your employ," he observed, "then she's most likely a vagrant. We're bound by law to take her."

The burly man added, tightening his hold on me, "Fined if we don't, an' paid by de head if we do."

Clementina saw immediately what was necessary to free me. She reached into her purse, then held out two dollar bills. The big man released me to grab them. As I regained my footing, he pushed me toward Clementina, who raised her arms as shields.

Then piteous cries came from the wagon. Two boys called out to me: "Mama! Mama! Don't leave us!"

What was I to do? I nodded sympathetically toward the waifs. Amid their ongoing pleas, a policeman herded them out. The boys threw their thin, muscled limbs about me in a parody of affection. With my free hand I patted a tousled head.

A policeman stepped close to Clementina. "Ye gotta pay for dem."

She wore a look of deepest scorn as she addressed me. "*These* are your children, too?"

"No!" I flushed. "We've never met."

The boys disentangled themselves and ran rapidly away on bare, dirt-blackened feet.

"We'll catch more soon enough," said the other policeman. He climbed into the wagon to guard their remaining treasure. His compatriot climbed to the driver's seat, behind two powerful horses. At the whip's snap, the wagon lurched forward, leaving Clementina and me standing together.

"Thee saved us!" I reached to embrace her, but she stepped away and shook her coiled locks.

"Are you a vagrant?" Her clear green eyes took in my condition. "You look like one. And your breath is atrocious."

"No," I said hastily. "I'm just on my way to — to —"

"I suppose I ought to have given a thought to what might happen to you." Confusion

474

crossed her face. "Ah, there is something —" She turned her attention to her shoes, to coax a memory free. She raised her head. "I stopped in at Pine Street this morning. Our caretaker said a letter came for you."

I couldn't help but yell. "A letter? From whom?" Could it be from Johan or Peter? My veins streamed with optimism.

"I didn't see," she said, wincing. "But you can knock at the kitchen door. Mr. Mundy will fetch it."

"That's the best news thee could offer!" I said. "And how is Henry? I'm so terribly sorry for —"

"He's well," she snapped. "We've replaced you with a woman whose baby was stillborn. It's far simpler."

As I pondered how to answer this, Clementina stared strangely at my skirt pocket. She reached an arm and withdrew her husband's handkerchief.

It hung at arm's length in front of her, crinkled by dried splotches of milk and smeared with mouth wipings. I felt as if the handkerchief alone could reveal what had transpired between her husband and me. My face burned. Her expression was quiet and subtle, with much taking place beneath its surface; I understood from it that she'd seen evidence before of Albert's intimacies with other women.

"I'm sorry," I stammered, watching as red spots grew on her cheeks.

Clementina dropped the handkerchief and ground it with the toe of her shoe into the grimy cobblestones. "Vermin!" she hissed at me. I began to step away. Another voice shot across the street.

"Clementina!" Her friend Letitia — her dress a tall column of white, festooned with ribbons — dodged traffic to cross. She pulled at Clementina's arm. "Come! We have to claim our tickets!"

The lady whose son I'd nursed looked up at me then, and I perceived in her downward-curving mouth and eyes that I had wounded her. Shame made me shrink into myself as she allowed her baffled friend to take her arm and lead her toward the brightly painted theater.

Only a few seconds passed before a rustling arose at my side, and a sharp pain crossed my hand. Someone was yanking at my valise — the very boys who'd pretended to be my own!

The case fell to the sidewalk, and their fast hands undid its buckle. I yelled as they fell upon my goods, gathering clothing in their thieving arms, but no one heeded me. Heads down, the boys ran into the crowd, concealed in seconds.

I closed the valise to secure what little remained of our possessions. At least my notebooks were unharmed. For the sake of the baby at my chest, I avoided sobbing, but strong feelings pushed against my temples and made them throb. On the sidewalk around me, people with destinations pushed past and banged against my crouching body. Charlotte began to make her hungry noises and batted my neck with her hands, making milk rush to my breasts. And all at once I wanted to scream and throw off every encumbrance — Charlotte, the valise, my wrinkled clothing and filthy boots, the pins and combs in my hair, the purse at my throat — to fling them from my body and race away from all that chained me. My heart fluttered as I tried to draw air. Sweat trickled down my back. My brief pleasure with Johan had opened the door to a living hell! I stared into its blaze.

Horses stampeded by, raising dirt into our faces. Charlotte coughed as grit descended on us. My eyes filled with stinging bits.

I am nothing, I thought. I remembered Nancy, who'd said she wasn't worth saving.

I decided in that instant to get my letter immediately, before Clementina might take the chance to deprive me of it.

■ ■ ■ ■

The fetching of the letter from the Burnhams' caretaker occurred without incident.
But reading the contents of that single
sheet, forwarded from the Haven, was an
incident indeed. The letter was from the
Haven's Pittsburgh solicitor, who reported
locating a red-haired man named Johannes
Ernst. This man has lived in Pittsburgh
many years, is married to an Olivia Stone,
and denies knowing me.

There was apparently nothing true about
our contact, and Charlotte and I are the
castaway consequences of his lies.

But why should I be surprised at his
trickery? Think of all the ways the others
hiding at the Haven were betrayed.

I walked and walked. Charlotte was restive at my chest; she must have sensed my
distress through my nervous pulse, the
dampness of my skin, my sour odor. Then
hunger drew me toward the wafting scents
of a market building.

Putting aside caution, I entered and
stopped before the stall of a fishmonger. I
observed an oblong of smoked trout, imag-
ining how the flavors of fat, salt, fish, and
smoke would suffuse my tongue. The wom-

478

an's melodious voice startled me.

"What can I get you, miss?"

"What's the cost of two ounces of smoked trout?" My voice came out with a quaver.

"The least I sell is a half-pound." She watched me pleasantly.

I apologized and bade her good day.

She pressed her plump lips together as I left, then called me back. "I'd be glad to offer you a taste."

I nodded dumbly. With a long, slender knife, she cut a sliver of the fish and placed it on a paper, then reached it to me.

"You can sit there," she said, pointing her chin to a barrel beside her stall.

I sat and ate the gleaming morsel, trying to be slow.

"What's your name?" she asked.

I told her.

"Have you got a baby?" She gestured to my shawl.

I nodded again, not wanting to stop chewing.

"Have you anywhere to live?"

Wondering at her directness, I swallowed and replied that I'm a widow looking for work, with many hopeful prospects but nowhere to live at present. Her cheeks grew rosy with what appeared to be sympathy.

"You look awfully tired. I have an idea."

She turned to the bloody-aproned butcher at the next stall and asked him to tell potential customers that she'd return shortly. At her beckoning, I rose and followed her down a crowded row of stalls to the back doors of the market shed. She opened a door and directed me to follow further.

"What does thee want with me?" I asked. My chest constricted. Could she be aiming to trick me as Nancy was tricked?

"Oh, goodness." She allowed the door to close, straining to be audible amid the shouts of buyers and sellers that echoed off the metal roof. "Of course you're afraid." She reached and shook my hand; her shake was sturdy. "I'm Mrs. Bernstein. I'm a widow, too."

I still didn't understand her intentions.

"You can rest and nurse the baby in my wagon out back." She had to yell above the haggling, which rose louder as she gestured to the door. "Would you like to rest there?"

I examined her a moment, from her laced brown boots to the thick braids pinned in a crown about her head and then her genial face, which spoke of a person unaffected by the straining or pretensions of a liar. Her chestnut eyes compelled me.

"Come. There's nothing to fear." She

waved me toward her.

I followed through a shaded lot to her wagon. It was a fishy-smelling affair with a sagging horse at its helm. The safest place I'd seen in days. I thanked her and climbed to the bench.

She leaned her forearms on the wagon's side. "My husband died twenty years ago last spring. Like you, I had a baby to care for, and I lost our house."

"I see," I replied, glad to have an explanation for her kindness. How sad, that kindness should require an explanation in order to be trusted.

"I close my stall at three. That's when I'll load the wagon. Until then, you can rest here."

She departed. I changed Charlotte and took stock of her condition. The sore on her bottom had closed, and her cough was nearly gone. Nevertheless, I vacillated between worry and hope. Worry: Could malnutrition and neglect have stunted her for good? Hope: She flashed me a gummy smile, which my heart swelled to see, and turned up her eyes for a period of staring. Her soul ran like a river behind her eyes. I sensed two rivers joining in our gaze.

Then she attached her mouth firmly to my nipple, and my happiness soared. For

481

even in her weakened state, her body conveyed the force of a thousand sprouting seeds.

In time her lips parted and released me, and her weight grew heavier. I took that blessed chance to join her. Amid the sounds of mules and horses neighing softly, drinking from buckets at their feet, and shaking to find relief from the rub of harnesses, I fell into a fathomless sleep.

Some hours later, I opened my eyes with difficulty to Mrs. Bernstein's gentle nudging. My mind pulled free of sleep's grasping arms as she spoke.

"Would you be willing to stay the night on my back porch?" Over the edge of the wagon, she patted my knee. "You're welcome to it."

I accepted gladly. So Mrs. Bernstein loaded her wagon with the remaining fish and ice, then drove us south and east. The Hebrew lettering on the shops informed me that the area had many Jewish residents. I felt a thrill at the strangeness, as though I'd stepped into a nook of some far-off city.

She tied the horse to a post, then led us to the side door of a row-house and into a single room on the first story, at the back. As she passed inside, she kissed a totem that bore Hebrew lettering. She insisted that I sit in her one chair at a small table, which I did, with Charlotte at my chest. The room was clean, with whitewashed walls and a scratched pine floor. A narrow bed sat against a wall.

Somehow Mrs. Bernstein knew that I'd want most of all to wash myself and Charlotte. I helped her carry a large wooden washtub to the porch, which overlooked a shallow yard protected by a high stone wall. She poured hot water from the stove into the washtub, added cold water, gave me a bar of soap and towel, and drew a curtain across the porch.

Charlotte went in first. And oh, the glad sounds she made as I slid her naked form into the water! She even chuckled as I held her with one arm and scrubbed her. I kissed her belly, and she thrashed her legs, raising up water that spotted my clothes. She grabbed a lock of my hair and pulled, making me yelp. Then I dried her and left her naked, for the novelty of it.

How does a baby know to look its mother in the eyes? Charlotte looked eagerly, as if drinking in what she found. On a length of flannel she wriggled and cooed, gazing at me with an utter faith I don't deserve.

Our hostess had by then unloaded some fish for our supper and left to deliver the remainder to a relief society and to take the wagon and horse to a stable. Upon returning, so I could bathe, she brought a freshly diapered Charlotte into her room and amused her.

The pleasures of clean water cannot be overstated. I fairly melted as it flowed along my skin, taking off layers of dirt and sweat, and bringing on a state of newness and optimism. And my feet — oh! They shed layers of blistered skin and dirt, till only tenderness remained. When the water had cooled, I dried off and donned my Mother Hubbard dress, cherishing its looseness. Then I washed all my other clothes, as well as Charlotte's blanket, diaper, and gown. I cut a half-dozen more diapers, enough to last the night at least. I hung our wet things on the clothesline in the yard and lay my valise open in the slanting sun.

Mrs. Bernstein cooked up a heaping plate of fish. She said I must call her Vera. I ate with passion, continuing till I was over-stuffed. As we cleaned, I asked how she had gotten her start at fishmongering.

"My husband was a fisherman, and after his death, his friends began supplying me," she said. "For eighteen years I sold fish from a cart. By two years ago, I'd saved enough to pay the annual rent on a market stall."

Her son is now twenty-one and works as a fisherman, she said; he rents a room nearby with his wife and their baby. "I hope to find a little house for us before long," she said. "And what are your good prospects?"

"Good prospects?" I was taken off guard.

"The ones you mentioned at my stall."

I faltered a moment before admitting that I had no good ones, or truly, none at all.

"Why hasn't your husband's family helped you?" she asked.

Her gold-red braids shone in the light from the gas lamp behind her, and her manner was so endowed with sympathy that I couldn't lie. I told her he hadn't been my husband and apologized for my dishonesty. I recounted the rudiments of my story, concluding with the Pittsburgh solicitor's findings in the letter I'd fetched from Pine Street hours earlier. I told her that Johan had married in Pittsburgh before coming to Philadelphia, taken a lark with me, and constructed a ruse to get himself home. What had become of Peter, I had no guess.

"You've got to go to Pittsburgh and show Johan your baby," she told me. "Maybe he *was* married all along. But maybe he found himself a woman there and told lies to the solicitor at his door. You have to find out for yourself. Maybe he'll change his mind when he sees you both."

This was similar to what Frau V. had told me — advice I had avoided heeding. But finally I was freed of useless pride. Vera convinced me to call on Johan at the address the solicitor had sent and to demand restitution and support.

She even gave me twenty-five cents to help with my train fare.

As I write, Charlotte and I are resting on Vera's back porch. Darkness surrounds us, save for a candle's flickering beam. I've taken my locket from my purse and am rubbing its smooth gold surface.

Mother, can thee see us now? See the kindness, so like thine, that flows from human hearts?

I don't know where we'll sleep in Pittsburgh. I don't know how long we'll stay. But the only way to get us off the street is Johan.

Sixth Month 19

Excited birds woke me in the gray. Through the window shone a lantern from Vera's room. I dressed us in damp and wrinkled clothes; then Vera came out with a burlap bag and opened the porch curtain, as was apparently her daily habit. A hundred birds swooped in by air, and squirrels and chipmunks drew close. As she poured seeds and grains onto the ground, this winged and furred menagerie hopped and pranced, releasing a cacophony of cries. When she withdrew to the porch, they set upon her offerings, pecking and nibbling and competing.

"I'll have to leave soon to get fish at the dock," she said. But she invited me first to sit on her chair and eat a full bowl of porridge with milk and molasses. She served me coffee, too. Then she washed the cup, spoon, and bowl and served herself.

While Vera ate, I packed our things. Beside me Charlotte kicked her legs and worked to clasp her little hands above, then pulled to pry them apart. She even rocked over to one side, crowing with exultation. Amid all this mad achievement, I counted my begged-for coins and what was left of the money I'd been spared from paying at Blockley. Adding in the quarter dollar from Vera, with its image of Lady Liberty, I counted seven dollars and thirty-two cents — more than I'd expected, and probably enough to get us to Pittsburgh and lodge us there a night or two, if I found a place that would admit us.

Vera came out then. "I need to fetch the horse and wagon and buy my fish," she said.

"I wish I could offer you another night, but the walls have eyes." When her landlord learned of my presence, she explained, he might request more rent. "I know you'll have good luck in Pittsburgh," she told me.

I gave profuse thanks for her shelter, food, counsel, and coin. We walked to the cobblestone street, bowed, and parted ways.

I decided as I headed toward Broad Street Station that if Johan won't give aid when faced directly by his impoverished lover and baby, then I won't hesitate to visit the Pittsburgh solicitor and initiate a suit. With the money I win, I'll consign a sewing machine and rent a room in Pittsburgh. Perhaps I'll even hire the solicitor to locate Peter. It isn't possible that Peter is with Johan anymore, since Johan's deceit would have been all too clear.

After consulting tomorrow's train schedule, I bought a ticket for the first leg of our journey. Charlotte, being in arms, will ride for free. To build strength, I bought a small serving of pepper pot from a cart and savored its tripe and meat and vegetables. At a fruit cart I traded a precious coin for a pint of overripe raspberries from the damaged-fruit pile, which quelled my remaining hunger and my thirst.

All that's left is to spend one more night

on the station floor. The carved horse from Margaret is tucked into my pocket. Charlotte rests in my lap, growing ever stronger. A thrill runs through me to think of facing Johan with his crimes.

Sixth Month 20

Perhaps by now thee expects the unexpected.

I woke again to the policeman's boot, but on this morning I had the right to take the wide marble staircase to the second-story lobby. I showed my ticket and was admitted. A uniformed man at the door to the ladies' waiting room allowed us into the nearly empty, elegant space; we passed through and entered the ladies' toilet. I drank from a faucet, then washed all that I could reach and dried myself with a towel handed to me by a soft-spoken young attendant. Next I washed Charlotte's hands and face; she gurgled happily; the attendant smiled. Apparently our use of the place was not so unorthodox, and I figured that our baths and clothes-washing and one full night's rest at Vera's had rendered us less objectionable.

My clean face in the mirror looked swollen from the heat, however, and pasty with exhaustion. With my tortoise-shell comb I sorted out my hair and combed Charlotte's red-gold curls, which now rise an inch above her scalp. As I was admiring her, three women wearing lace gloves, feathered hats, and dresses with protruding bustles walked in. They stared with disgust — revealing the incompleteness of our transformation. The attendant told us gently to move along; I gave her a penny with my thanks.

Soon a loud voice announced our train's arrival. We were pulled in an excited horde to a train shed as the long black creature approached. In a deep baritone the conductor called out, "All abooooard!"

The train was filling quickly. I settled next to a man who'd nodded to sleep over his newspaper, tucking the valise beneath my feet. Charlotte sucked her fingers in my shawl and pressed her bare toes into me. I placed my lips on her forehead and felt the thrumming thrust of life inside. It seemed as if a fresh wind blew through my mind, clearing it of heavy clouds and making the air brighter, the contours of every object more delineated.

The conductor punched my ticket. I watched out the window as others filed onto our train. A train arrived on the opposite track, coming from the direction I was headed. Its doors opened. Then into the line descending its steps came someone startlingly familiar: my brother, looking sturdy and healthy, wearing a broad-brimmed hat and a drab, straight-cut suit.

Whatever grabs and squeezes one's heart did so to mine. *Act!* it screamed. I reached my free arm across the sleeping man and tried unsuccessfully to open the train window so I could call out. Peter was walking quickly toward the station building. I stood, pulled Charlotte close, stepped into the aisle with my valise, and ran to the nearest door. A porter stood in my way.

"Madam! This train is about to leave!"

"I must go out," I said, sliding past him down the steps. I jumped to the dirt and yelled after the retreating form: "Peter! Peter!"

How well I knew that gait, that plain gray coat Mother had sewed, that broad-brimmed hat and brown hair with its glints of yellow. My heart opened in anticipation of his embrace.

Peter had not yet turned around; he was forty feet or so ahead. I ran as hard as I could, weaving between the other people, squeezing Charlotte to my chest, the valise banging my leg. Charlotte began to protest.

"Peter de Jong!" I cried. "Thee in the gray coat! Stop!"

The man turned. "Is thee speaking to me?"

The face was narrower; the lips were too thin; the eyebrows arched above unfriendly eyes. The man was several inches shorter than Peter and some pounds heavier. In fact, he looked very little like my brother, save for his Friend's attire. My elation evaporated. I'd been overcome by a longing to know and be known, to see and be seen by just one face I'd cherished.

"I'm terribly sorry," I said. I turned away as he, with irritation, did the same.

I had to get back onto the train, but that very train was creaking into motion. Casting off my valise to free an arm, I ran along the track as the monster gathered speed, banging on its retreating side, a moan rising from my throat.

"Stop! Please stop!" I yelled, until a railroad worker clapped his hands on my shoulders and pulled me away.

"That's dangerous, ma'am," he scolded sharply. "Can't touch a moving train. Folks fall under that way."

I stumbled to find the valise where I'd abandoned it and sat upon its dirty side. Charlotte, no doubt afraid, was twisting in my shawl. I clutched her to me as she rooted at my bodice. She whined quietly. Oh, how

I detested myself and pitied her.

"Can't stop here, ma'am," the same worker admonished me. "Yer an obstruction."

I stood and returned to the grand second-story lobby, then down the stairs and out to the street, where I sit now against a station wall, my eyes stabbed by the early sun that shoots like an arrow between the buildings, as dry inside as a pile of sun-bleached bones.

■ ■ ■ ■

NOTEBOOK TEN

■ ■ ■ ■

Sixth Month 29

Charlotte was holding my hand to her chest as she nursed. Now she sleeps in my arms, and I've withdrawn my hand to write — slowly, so as not to rouse her. Her hands are still arched over the space that my hand occupied. As if my hand remains there. As if my pulse continues to beat against hers.

I pray that my love will continue to fill that space when I'm no longer near. I pray that whatever emptiness she feels will always be countered by my unseen love.

I've lit a candle by a window of our room and taken up a pencil. For I must tell how it is that four walls now contain us.

The night after I left the train — nine nights ago — I took a spot on the floor of Broad Street Station beneath a huge fan, near a shed where passengers debark, because the night was sweltering. Mosquitoes swarmed us; I slapped them on my flesh and clothes, leaving bloodstains behind. Charlotte's body was protected in a blanket, but her cheeks were dotted with bites. I held her hands in one of mine to stop her scratching.

We slept. In my dream, the time was dusk. I stood amid stunted spruce on the edge of a mountain. In awe I looked over an undulating spread of peaks and valleys; an emerald carpet of treetops covered every curve. This was a wilderness such as I'd never seen, where bears and mountain lions roamed, and people accustomed to shelter had better find their way out by nightfall.

But I had no idea which way would lead me out. I walked in one direction, another, and a third, finding no openings in the dense forest as the sky drained of daylight.

Then a voice yelled my name from an adjacent peak. It was the voice of my brother — he who has a virtual compass in his head! I tried to engage my faculties to reply, but my mouth wouldn't move. Against the downward drag of sleep, all I could force out was a moan. Yet he heard me and took a single step that crossed the intervening valley. He grabbed my shoulders, fingers digging in.

As if it lay beneath a pile of moss or dried leaves, my consciousness was dulled. But the pain those fingers caused in my sore muscles was real.

"Wake up!" said another voice, and then, "It's her, I'm sure of it."

Larger hands gripped and shook me. The heat of human breath came to my ear. My mind fought upward until I could open my eyes. Crouched over me were the two young men who'd left me behind.

"Can thee stand?" Peter's overgrown hair fell into his face as he bent close. "Is thee all right?" Then, to Johan: "It's a lucky thing thee noticed her."

I could neither stand nor answer. This was an outcome I'd long given up on praying for.

"What's thee doing here?" asked Johan sharply. I recoiled at his tone.

"Quiet!" someone shouted. A chorus of muttered complaints followed. The noises roused Charlotte, who stirred under my shawl, hands kneading my abdomen.

I stayed motionless to stall her awakening and gleaned what I could from the men's appearances. The weary leaning of their shoulders could be explained by the many trains they'd ridden from Pittsburgh, the transfers line to line. But the absence of any luggage, save one small satchel each; the grime on their gray suits and hats; their unkempt beards and strong odors — these spoke of a deprivation reaching well past one day's travel. Dust darkened Johan head to foot. The pencil tucked above his ear and the papers in his vest pocket told me his scribbling habit was ongoing. His brown eyes looked out guardedly above a scraggly beard that didn't suit him. Peter's face, though still inquisitive, held a hint of hardness. He had a beard, too, untrimmed and grimy. As I wondered what had become of these young men's scheme for success, Johan drew his hands together on his knees.

On his left hand, a scar shone where the pinkie and ring fingers should have been. I gasped.

Johan glanced at me, then averted his eyes. "My hand slipped. At the steel mill." He said this as if it hardly mattered.

"How terrible," I said, finally able to speak. He nodded impassively, looking at the far-off lobby wall.

Such coldness from a man who ought to beg my pardon. How did this injury figure into his return to Philadelphia? I wondered if Olivia had rejected him.

Peter put his face directly before mine. "Tell us! What is thee doing here?"

"There's nowhere else I can be," I replied. "Why has thee come?"

"But why can't thee be anywhere else?" asked Johan.

Beneath my shawl, I squeezed Charlotte gently. She gave out a string of peculiar sounds, kicked her legs, and wriggled. A puzzled Johan observed my moving shawl. I pulled the cloth away and our baby inclined her head toward the men, eyes blinking against the gaslight.

The whole truth penetrated Peter at once; the hue and curl of Charlotte's hair left little doubt as to her paternity. He dropped his face to his dirt-stained hands. But Johan stared at the baby, furrowing his brow.

"Whose child is this?"

"Can't thee tell?" I asked, offended.

Charlotte kicked her legs and expelled air in grunts, pleased with herself for existing.

"Why didn't thee answer my letters?" said Johan fiercely. "I went to the post office every day I could for the entire year."

He was going to lie? Gorge rose to my throat. "Letters? I received none."

"I sent them," he insisted. "I pleaded for letters back. Thee doubts my word?" He stood and dumped his satchel to the floor.

I took in a breath and prepared to tell him that I certainly did doubt his word. But Peter raised a hand to stop our argument. He moved closer, so that I smelled the sawdust that must be in his very veins.

"*I* got thy letter," he said. "We came right away."

"Right away? I wrote in Fourth Month! I worried and worried when I didn't hear."

"I wasn't expecting mail till I wrote Father for money. I only went to the post office this week." His color rose as Johan rolled his eyes. "The point is, Johan and I returned as soon as we learned thee wasn't well. To help thee."

To help thee! That precious sentiment. But Johan had already gotten that chance through the solicitor. I looked at him; his stiff face seemed to be holding back an unsorted mass of feeling. As I watched, he surrendered his weight to the cool marble floor, stretched his long legs forward, and stared at Charlotte. His expression moved from sorrow to confusion. The broad planes of his cheeks became mottled, and he turned to me.

"If this is our child," he demanded, "why didn't thee write to tell me?"

"I had no address!" Frustration tightened my throat. "Then a solicitor visited thee in Pittsburgh. But thee was married to Olivia Stone and denied knowing me!"

Johan snorted. "A solicitor? Found me married?"

"Why didn't Father help?" Peter asked. "Why not go home?"

"I couldn't, with a baby and no husband. Besides, Patience told me never to come back." I reached to my neck and fingered the scab from the rock she'd hurled.

"Get outta here!" called a deep voice. A hostile rumbling spread among the would-be sleepers. I struggled to my feet and pointed to an archway leading to a carriage bay.

Peter lifted my valise. Johan held my arm with his good hand. I tucked Charlotte close, and together we walked there and settled onto a set of moveable stairs.

We sat in silence, momentous concerns suspended between us like moisture after a heavy rain. To my one side, Peter turned his head so as not to be seen; the fall of his shoulders suggested grief. Charlotte settled in the shawl sling at my front, poking out her tiny toes and waggling them. To my other side sat Johan, who reached his unhurt hand forward to encompass Charlotte's feet. The shackles on my heart opened slightly, exposing wounded flesh.

What higher wisdom had lured me off that train toward Pittsburgh?

"I named her Charlotte, after my grandmother," I told him.

503

His eyes warmed in his dirt-streaked face. "She's truly ours?"

"There's no other possibility."

"Dearest," he said in a thick-throated voice. "I never should have left thee!" He bent his head and placed his lips over mine, then cupped his hands at my cheeks, framing our kiss.

The odors of his unwashed body were strong. His velvety mouth pressed mine with too much fervor. I disliked it until I smelled his breath — like fresh-shucked corn. His breath always had been sweet, as if it spoke more of his soul than of his body. But he seemed to have forgotten Peter beside us, the infant in my lap, our dirty and disheveled state, our year of separation. I pulled away to find Peter wiping his eyes and staring ahead. Johan stroked my cheek with a finger, watching our baby as she drifted toward sleep.

I sent two prayers into the ether: that Johan's claim of constancy would prove true, and that I could find a way to accept him back into my damaged heart. And in this odd configuration — or so I hoped — four outcasts began to assemble their souls into a little family.

The next morning, Peter and Johan got

their hair trimmed and beards shaved at a barber's, then rented us a room. They left me and Charlotte out of the story they told the property owner in her Market Street office. On the promise of two men's gainful employment, along with Peter's pocket watch for security and six dollars for the first month's rent, she was willing to lease them a large, third-story room in one of her many buildings. It's below Girard Avenue, a half-mile or so from the Schuylkill River — near to the noise and soot of the Baldwin Locomotive Works, but a thousand times better than the street.

The vigilance that kept me upright on the street burned out as soon as we had shelter. For days I had much trouble rising from a horizontal position. I did manage to write Father, telling him nothing but my new address and asking him to forward any letters that Johan might have sent to Germantown. I expressed the matter as urgently as I dared.

The days have passed with no word from Father, and keeping Johan at bay is difficult. On being anywhere near my body, he wants to touch. If Peter isn't in the room, and sometimes when he is, then to press against me, to stroke my neck, to smell and embrace me is Johan's main intent. He seems never to have left that place of naïve pleasure we occupied before he went away. In fact, during the hardships of Pittsburgh, he says he lived in a frenzy of desire, with its object being to hold me close, and its pain being . . . well, he claims he believed that a lack of love kept me from answering his letters.

Shortly after arriving in Pittsburgh, he found rich fodder in a tattered copy of a chapbook called *Leaves of Grass* by a man named Whitman, whom Johan called the Camden bard. "Listen," he said the first time we were alone, when Peter had gone out to buy food and furnishings. He read these lines and more from the book that lies beside me now:

I love you, oh you entirely possess me,
O that you and I escape from the rest and
     go utterly off, free and lawless,
Two hawks in the air, two fishes swimming
     in the sea. . . .
O you and I! what is it to us what the rest
     do or think?
What is all else to us? only that we enjoy
     each other and exhaust each other if it
     must be so.

But Whitman's lines did not enchant me. For such sentiments proclaim the glory of indulgence without a single glance at its dangers — its dangers to a woman, in particular, who believes the words of a quivering and openhearted man whose body lies naked over her. This sort of man is a hazard to womankind, for he departs with satisfaction, "free and lawless," yet leaves her paying, paying, all her life.

I've tried to explain to Johan my hard-won understandings. But he considers them "merely circumstantial"; if he'd known of my pregnancy, he says, he would have come to marry me, and I would have kept the faith he lives in. "There's nothing suspect," he told me, "in the passion that the Camden bard expresses."

But there is no such thing as merely circumstantial. Circumstances are all. What has occurred can't be undone. The chasm between us makes me lonely.

Will I ever tell Johan that I ate from sidewalks, took laudanum for dissolute days, begged for pennies, drugged babies through my breast? Will I confess to having earned a dollar of my purse by sexual congress, tried to become a man's paid strumpet, stolen a baby's gown, pondered taking my own life when the callous world piled insults upon me?

Will I one day tell our daughter that her

507

early months were lived in exile and deprivation — that she faced mortal hazards then?

Do secrets matter? No one life can be entirely shared by another.

Yet I'm marked by these trials, and he doesn't know why.

As he is marked by his trials.

He sleeps the sleep of the untroubled, however, even on the floor (for he and Peter gave the small mattress to Charlotte and me).

When I sleep, trouble dogs my dreams. I'm on the street again, with Charlotte dying or being taken from my arms; or I'm struggling to get her from the almshouse before she starves; or my breasts have turned to stone, when she needs my milk to live.

The sores on my feet have healed. I can tolerate the rub of stockings and shoes.

Sixth Month 30
Peter has finally found work, at a printer's. For six ten-hour days, he'll earn fourteen dollars a week — far more than the twenty-five a month I earned toiling day and night for the Burnhams. He despises working with enormous machines, but he says that a room of loud presses will be far better than

the open-hearth department at the steel mill, where he did common labor. He'd return to Father's workshop, he said, if he could.

For his part, Johan's had no luck at finding work because of his damaged hand and is spending less and less time trying. The good side of this is his increased time with Charlotte. She no longer cries when he holds her. The tenderness in his demeanor soothes her — and me, to watch it.

He seems an honest man. Did the solicitor find a different Johannes Ernst, another red-haired Pittsburgh resident? I must have evidence. I can't risk another fall.

Yesterday Charlotte was three months old. She shows so many skills. She laughs, squeals, and tries to lift her head while on her stomach. She clasps her sticky hands together and reaches for her feet. To know a thing, she opens her mouth to encompass it. Peter carved her a wooden rattle, and she clutches the handle in her fist, then crams its orb into her mouth as far as it can fit, licking. Into that cave she moves every item she can reach — the side of my hand, an edge of my shawl. All the while, she makes a clear, declarative sound: "Ah! Ah!"

As if to say, "I am! Look what I can do!"

Sometimes when the men talk, she becomes too distracted to continue nursing; she turns sideways to stare. She sends them the exploratory beginnings of letter sounds — a *v* and a *d*. Then, in place of feeding, she arches her back and pushes against me until I lay her on the ground. Her father and her uncle help her practice rolling over.

She seems so vital, yet I worry about the lasting effects of her hard weeks. No doubt there will be some. What indelible impressions have formed already in her?

The first time I saw a monarch butterfly and pointed, Mother told me, "Butterfly." I memorized the word, matching it to the tubular body, the antennae, the ochre and black wings. "Butterfly," I intoned with effort. Until one day another winged being flew by, clothed in different colors. Upon inquiring, I heard, "Butterfly."

Confusion beset me. How could it be?

By this I came to understand the notion of a category. Mother, Father, and brother are people; monarchs and other floating beings with chalky wings that land on flowers and suck their milk are butterflies. Yet the monarch remains my original butterfly. Every other seems a displacement.

What original butterflies have lodged themselves in Charlotte's brain? What representatives of categories are in permanent place? Might she, for instance, seek unsafe or chaotic streets in her future, or circumstances of privation, finding them to hold an oddly familiar comfort?

Oh, dear baby, flesh of my flesh . . . I want better for thee.

Seventh Month 2

Johan noticed the scar on Charlotte's bottom — the remnant of her sore — and wanted to know how she'd been injured. In halting sentences I told him of her confinement at the almshouse, then took us backward in time to Gina's, the Burnhams', Gerda's, the Haven, even to my months with Father and Patience. I spoke as sparely as I could, with subdued expression, because otherwise I might have been overcome. Then I brought him quickly past our homeless days, leaving out the incidents with Albert and the begging and the hunger and so much more, and commencing again with that afternoon before he and Peter found me, when I sat with Charlotte under the pear trees. I reminded Johan of what he'd showed me in an apple. I told him that wanting to show Charlotte the star inside a fruit had given me a reason not to die — as foolish as that sounded.

"So thee understands," he said, taking my

hand and squeezing.

"What?"

"How much the common beauty means."

"Of course. But not just beauty." I explained my notebooks, and how I'd survived by telling, held on through the daily increase of these pages.

"Held on? Survived? A reason not to die? What don't I know?"

I flushed.

"I'm sorry." He brought my hand toward his mouth and pressed the back of it to his lips. "I'll never read thy diaries. I owe thee that."

This made me lonelier. Can't I ever tell anyone all that happened? Not even Johan will insist upon it? If he had diaries, I would want to read them.

Seventh Month 3

Charlotte and I had a visitor this morning, shortly after Peter left for work and Johan went to offer himself at more shops and businesses. The visitor stomped up three flights of stairs and sent a strong knock through our room.

"Who is it?" I called. I had on my Mother Hubbard dress, and my hair was loose and frowsy.

"Thy father," came the low, stern voice.

Charlotte was napping on our mattress in a corner. I ran and propped a pillow to hide her, then moved a chair to block his view further, draping a skirt across it. I grabbed the drying diapers from the line that hangs wall to wall and stuffed them beneath the mattress.

His voice shot through the room: "Open the door, Lillian."

I did. Father strode in, dressed in his work clothes, sprinkled with sawdust and drops of shellac, glowing with exertion. The room shrank around his presence.

"Father," I said, offering my hand.

He stared as though seeing a ghost. The force of will that had propelled him across town dwindled and sputtered out. "Thee looks like thy mother. And as thin as she was before she died."

Couldn't he see the life surging in me? Or had I died for him when she did? That frightening thought clicked into place as I pointed to our small table and chairs, thankful that Johan had found them on the street and hauled them up. "Please sit," I offered. "I'll make tea."

He sat and looked dully at one of the walls I hadn't yet washed, with its grime and ripped paper. After removing his broad-brimmed hat to a chair, he rubbed his face with thick, muscled hands. I dipped our one pot into a water bucket — filled at the hydrant three stories down — and placed the pot on the stove. I stayed to let the stove's warm currents bathe me, despite the gathering heat. I looked at the chipped pottery upon the nearby shelf, the few rations, the painted horse that had passed from Margaret's father to Margaret to me, and wondered. What strangers occupied this space before us? A hook for a stirring spoon hung on the wall. Who'd put it there? At home I knew it was Mother, or Grandmother, or Great-grandmother. When I replaced a spoon on its hook, my hand and forearm moved in the layers of their similarly shaped hands and arms doing the very same. I was taking part in a palimpsest of gestures.

This was the modern way: my one hand, a new tin spoon, a hook put in by someone I would never know. Samuel de Jong in his daughter's apartment, waiting for tea.

"How is thy work as a governess?" he asked. "Does the family live in this building?"

I'd forgotten about that ruse. "I've — I've left that work."

My father nodded and waved his hand, urging me closer. "Come. I've brought things for thee."

I walked to him and sat, feeling the warmth emanating from his person and the anxiousness bubbling in mine. He reached inside his leather vest, then paused. "Am I too late to prevent thee from caring for this Johan fellow?"

"It depends on what thee has for me," I replied.

He withdrew a thin packet from his vest. Sighing, he laid it on the table and opened the paper wrap to reveal a short stack of envelopes. "I didn't want thee to be encouraged," he said.

I froze in place. The longed-for missives! Which Father had intentionally withheld!

"Here." He thrust the envelopes forward. I hesitated. "Take them," he demanded.

I did. The one on top had been much smudged and abused on its journey from Pittsburgh. I broke the seal and withdrew a single sheet written in Johan's loose and generous hand. He professed his ongoing love and his wish to marry as soon as he'd saved enough at the steel mill and located suitable chambers. The date was Eighth Month, Day 10, when I was two months along. He'd sent the address of their lodgings; I could have gone and married him before my pregnancy became evident. I glanced at the other postmarks: Tenth Month, Day 3, when I was still living at home, four months along; and Third Month, Day 30 — the day after I'd birthed our daughter.

"Does he ask for money, as thy brother did?" asked Father.

"No." I could hardly open my mouth.

"Does he tell where Peter is?"

"He's at work, in Philadelphia. They returned over a week ago. They leased this room."

Father raised his powerful arm and smashed his fist onto the table. A split appeared and widened between two boards; this evidence of shoddy craftsmanship further loosened his restraint. "How can thee care for that fool?" he yelled. "He lured thy brother from me and broke his promise to work five years in my shop. I work fourteen hours every day to fill my orders. And what does thee do? Thee loves the very man who sentenced me to this."

In her corner Charlotte began to whimper, but Father didn't notice. What had become of him? He was utterly lost without Mother. I'd never seen him strike anything. Tears dropped from my cheeks to my lap as he continued yelling.

"What kind of a life is thee going to have

with that" — and here he stood and scraped his chair back on the floor — "that *poet?*"

Charlotte increased her cries. Father turned toward the noise, brow creased, mouth frowning. I rushed over and lifted her. Her weight formed a reassuring anchor.

He pointed a thick finger. "Whose baby is that?"

I pointed to her red curls. She mouthed my dress frantically. Father couldn't speak but merely sputtered. Finally he asked, "How?"

"Didn't thee wonder why I left so suddenly?"

"No." He shook his head. "Becoming a governess was a sensible —"

"Thee should have wondered," I said amid my baby's wails. "I meant to go to Pittsburgh to marry Johan once I had their address. But I never had it! Then Patience discovered my condition and forced me out. I gave birth at a charity. We were living on the street when Johan and Peter found us in late Sixth Month."

Milk dripped to my abdomen. My father's face went blank, as if in search of an expression.

"If thee will excuse me," I said through a choked throat. "I need to feed my daughter."

I stepped to the chair by the mattress and

sat. I got Charlotte settled, then covered her with the shawl from Clementina. Two washings in soap and vinegar had returned the shawl to a glorious golden yellow.

To his credit, Father didn't leave. He occupied himself in trying to fit the pieces of the table back together, as if he were a human vise. He muttered with frustration, the chair creaking as he shifted his bulk. Then, reacting to my revelations, he huffed in disgust. "Disgracing the memory of thy mother," he said. If he'd been out of doors, I believe he would have spit.

I felt astonished. He'd withheld the letters that could have saved me from a year of grievous exercises and disgrace. Then he'd stood aside and asked no questions when I left home precipitously, forced to leave by the thief he'd married while Mother's dying breath hung close upon us.

And he dared to despise me.

Emotions roiled through my body and brought on a sweat. Charlotte pulled her mouth from me and began to cry, sensing my distress. For her sake, I closed my eyes and pulled her closer, concentrating only on her form against me. With surprising quickness, we both grew calm.

Within that calm, at long last, I no longer feared my father. I would say just who had done the worse disgracing. I looked at a grimy wall, at the torn shreds of paper dangling in the overheated air.

"And thee?" I asked. "How many weeks did thee wait after Mother's death before —" My voice caught and my stomach tightened. "Before taking up the bottle, and bedding thy cousin, and disgracing our family name?"

His silence told me I'd hit my mark. At last he said, "I followed my own way, the Discipline be damned."

"And thy children be damned? Did thee not guess that we'd all suffer, as occupants of thy house, and that I'd be suspended from my work?"

He sighed, as if my having a point of view inconvenienced him. "I did what I needed to do. I have the right to act as I wish."

"Regardless of the costs to others," I snapped. "Costs thee hasn't taken a moment to notice."

Eventually he replied. "I suppose I haven't." He sighed. "I suppose I haven't noticed much at all." His face grew soft and baffled, as it always had when he'd been faced with his own shortsightedness.

His apology went unspoken, but I relished it. He pushed his hand across the coarse surface of what had briefly been our table, then tried again to bring the parts together. "Piece of factory junk. Has thee got any glue?"

"Only flour and water." I leaned my lips to Charlotte's head, to her silken hair.

"No sense fixing this anyway. I'll bring a small table. It won't take but a day or two to make." He released the pieces to the floor, then pulled out his leather coin purse and opened its mouth. "Get a tea set, and some better tea." He laid two dollar coins on the floor beside him.

The tea! I stood and looked to the pot on the stove, where the water had boiled dry. I had been going to brew it in that very pot, and the tea in a paper box upon the shelf was the worst dust, left after others had paid good money for the leaves. I was moved that he'd noticed, though more pressing items than a tea set needed buying. His nurturance had often been that unpredictable, that random.

"Many thanks," I replied. I lowered my head to Charlotte and pulled the shawl back slightly to uncover her head as she nursed, watching her lips purse and listening to her gulp.

"My first grandchild." Father huffed. "A bastard."

I recognized in him the self-pity I'd seen

in some drunks on the street. "Her name is Charlotte."

"After my mother!" He stared in chagrin.

I was ready to tell him why I had every right to follow the naming pattern of our family, and how Charlotte had already survived much and proved worthy to be called after his mother, till I recalled old Hannah's exhortation at the meetinghouse burying ground: "Thy father needs thee!"

"Has thee been unwell?" My voice quavered with stifled feeling.

"There was trouble with my liver, but I'm recovered."

I waited to hear more. Through the opened window came the clarifying scents from our window box, where thyme, sage, and rosemary burst from the soil.

"We've got a baby coming very soon." Father reached his feet to the floor ahead of him to give room to his long legs. "It's difficult."

"I understand."

Did I? I knew there must be rancor in the house. I knew I wanted to get my private possessions away from his wife.

"When thee brings the table," I said, "could thee bring my trunk?" My diaries should still be in there, and the silver spoons, which I might pawn, and the wedding linens. The oldest linens were from Grandmother, fragile and stained; the next oldest, starched and neatly pressed, were those Mother had made while dreaming of her someday marriage; atop those emblems of hopeful longing lay my own handiwork.

"I'll try to bring it all within the week, unless the baby comes." Father cleared his throat and stood. Charlotte leaned from me, ready for the other side, so I shifted and settled her. Father watched, the muscles of his face slackening.

"I was wrong to hold the letters back," he said.

Tears clouded my vision as he stepped away; the door opened and clicked shut. His feet stomped down the stairs, growing ever farther and fainter.

I wondered if he would bring us a table. In the meantime, I supposed we'd eat off the floor.

I placed my sleeping baby down and put the two unopened letters on the shelf beside the stove. I craved them as keenly as if they were bread fresh from the oven, sliced and thickly buttered. But I also dreaded knowing their contents, which could just as well be like ice, or swords. Those letters would put some change in motion. They remained on the shelf all afternoon.

Near sunset, Johan returned from seeking work, hot and smelling of the street. He removed his jacket and stood before me, stains beneath the arms of his shirt, then pulled his suspenders over his shoulders. I had an unpleasant memory of Albert as Johan bent to kiss me. Still overheated, he removed his shoes and socks. On his long toes, gold-red hairs shone. He sat at one of our chairs, beside the pieces of our table.

"What happened here?" he asked. Like Father — like any craftsman, perhaps — he lifted the pieces and tried to fit them together.

I told him of Father's violence and pointed to the withheld letters. He strode to the shelf and grabbed the envelopes.

"Open them!" He thrust them at me. "That solicitor was a liar. He wanted to pretend he'd done something, to get his fee!"

My heart cramped as I took the two letters and sat on the mattress, thinking less of their contents than of his unexpected temper, so like Father's.

Yet on paper, my lover's words did more than soothe; they made me ashamed of how readily I'd believed him a betrayer. He wrote of longing for me; he sent again their first address, then the next one, when their location changed; he went most days to the post office to see if I'd replied. The letter he'd sent when I was four months along, his second, consisted chiefly of him begging me to reply, if only to explain the reason for my shunning of him. He asked whether I'd found another love. He'd matured, he said; he wanted me to travel there as soon as possible. He enclosed four dollars, hoping I could supplement them with my own, and saying he would keep me when I arrived. He quoted his favorite bard:

O to return to Paradise! O bashful and
    feminine!
O to draw you to me, to plant on you for
    the first time the lips of a determin'd
    man.

The one sent on the day after Charlotte was born, his final missive, went as follows:

1883. 3rd mo. 30

To Lilli,
"Brightest truth, purest trust in the universe — all were for me In the kiss of one girl."

Those words of Robert Browning's might as well be mine.

I'm puzzled at thy silence.

No, devastated. Did it mean nothing that I gave my word and body? That thee gave thine?

No matter; I have nothing for thee now. It doesn't matter why. There's only this: goodbye.

My mind filled in the gaps with images of what he'd told me — of the accident at the mill, and his selling pencils on the street, and Peter having to pay most costs for them; of how they'd stayed in a cheap lodging house until Peter was fired from the mill for protesting his rough treatment by the more skilled workers; then, for seven cents a night, they'd slept in a long room of beds made of fabric strips suspended between boards. To raise money for a better place, Peter joined a gang of day laborers from that lodging house, and Johan traveled farther on foot to buy his pencils at a discount, and spent more hours selling them each day.

By this time, Johan had seated himself beside me on the mattress, and Charlotte was asleep on a blanket. I joined my eyes to his.

"Now will thee marry me?" he said, leaning closer, so that I felt his warmth.

There had been no grand time in Pittsburgh of thriving and exploring, as I'd imagined. And Johan had been truthful about his letters. But I retained one stubborn reservation.

"Why did thee stay away? Thee should have returned to find out why I never answered."

Johan looked to his damaged hand, his expression not self-pitying but ashamed.

What lies at the root of a man's shame? Perhaps his failure to serve a cause, to perform the roles he's given.

He rubbed the scar as he spoke and shook his head side to side. "I had nothing to offer. I left to set things up for us, and all I could do was stand on the sidewalk and hawk pencils."

"So the will was sucked out of thee." I saw a strange picture. "By life's giant mouth!"

He smiled wanly. "That, and maybe — maybe I already doubted that thee could love me."

"Doubted? I would have married thee here," I said. "We should have gone to Pittsburgh together. Thee treated me as if I was baggage to send for."

But blame can often be justified only by a partial view. I'd permitted myself to be treated like baggage, as if I couldn't strike out on a journey without his consent.

"Thee could have written the truth to me," he replied, "instead of writing Peter. Why didn't thee?"

I searched his face. How certain I'd been that he'd tricked me. Or had I been certain? I recalled that vision I'd had of him, downcast and beseeching. I asked, "Would thee have come back?"

"Would I have — ?" His voice broke. "Without thy news, I didn't dare. But with it? If I'd known that thee needed me, that we had a *child*? Absolutely."

Look how our corresponding burdens of doubt and shame had kept us in our private hells. Father had set these wheels in motion by hiding Johan's letters, yes. But we'd continued their turning.

I wanted to weep. We might have embraced. But Peter came back then, walking through the door to our one room with an exhausted stoop, his hands and clothing stained with ink. He sank to the floor to remove his boots, and I apprised him of the day's occurrences.

"Did Father apologize for holding back the letters?" he asked.

527

"He admitted to doing wrong." A pang came as I said this. No matter that I craved his apology, to receive it was bittersweet. A giant of my younger years was proven, after all, a man.

"That hardly helps," said Johan. He stood up from the mattress. "He ruined our lives."

"No." Peter turned to Johan. "It was thy carelessness that caused the ruin. How could thee take liberties with my sister — and leave her behind?"

"I didn't think —"

"Thee didn't think."

"Neither did I," I argued. "The fault was both of ours." I said this, but I was glad when Peter pushed further.

"Whose idea was it, to draw so close" — Peter spit the next words — "to copulate before you parted, without marrying first?"

We all blushed pink.

"I suggested it," said Johan, his face downcast. "I invited her to my room. I pressed her."

"I refuse to regret it." I pointed at Charlotte on the blanket beside me.

Slowly Johan shook his head. "I don't regret her."

My brother couldn't bear us. "What's all this mawkishness?" He began to pace the painted wood floor. "From what I've heard, the baby almost died at the almshouse. Lilli could have perished with her on the street, even been murdered or badly abused." He lowered his tone. "I'm sure there's some abuse she isn't telling."

I shut my eyes briefly against their stinging. He knew me well.

"All because this fellow" — he jabbed toward Johan — "is too much of a dreamer to see the possible effects of his actions."

"Thee sounds like thy father," Johan observed.

"Well, in this case, Father's right." Peter stepped to his pile of belongings on the floor and pulled out an envelope, withdrawing a photograph and waving it before my face. "I left her behind to come find thee. Anyway, her mother wouldn't let her see me after I lost my work. But I'm going to visit once I'm good and settled here." He handed me the picture. "And we didn't do the careless thing that thee and Johan did."

I looked at the young woman. It appeared she had light brown hair. Her clothing and manner were free from vanity. There was a pleasant press to her lips, and her face held an eager, honest look. "What's her name?"

"Meredith Henson. I think thee will like her."

"I believe I will." I stood and kissed his

cheek. "This is happy news!"

Yet I couldn't help but feel stung at how easily my younger brother judged himself superior.

Seventh Month 5

Father sent a letter by post. "It's too late to defend against thy disgracing," he wrote. "But Peter mustn't live with thee and Johan. Tell him he's welcome here, and I'll employ him again. I need his help. Tell him."

Inside his letter was tucked something far sweeter, an envelope that bore these words in Mother's calligraphic hand: *For my daughter, to be opened on the occasion of her marriage.*

She must have written it a few days before her death, after receiving her leading that Johan and I should marry. With a shiver of joy and grief, I tucked the envelope into this notebook, until the time to read it should arrive.

"She wanted us together," Johan said. He leaned and kissed my forehead as I wept.

Seventh Month 7

Last evening brought a surfeit of sweetness.

After an early supper of millet and lentils cooked in beef juice, I nursed Charlotte and put her on a pile of clothes to sleep. There were several hours till Peter would return. Johan and I lay together on the mattress; I rested my head on his chest, relishing the steady beating of his heart, until our touching turned to passion. And although some fleeting images of Albert interfered, I was able to accept my lover's skin on mine, to turn my pliant lips to his. Within cautious bounds, we explored a realm of tenderness that desperate Albert might never know.

Afterward, my body vibrating, I listened to Johan read his newest poem. It was a tiny prescription, really, for how this bond of ours could last. He envisioned it — like metal — as being formed in the heat of our trials, pounded into shape on an anvil of awareness, and cooled and strengthened by the waters of time.

So his time at the steel mill had come to something.

We agreed that our wedding should be in five days, by which time we'll have made our simple arrangements. Sated by our closeness, we dozed. Peter returned; we all retired.

It's near dawn, and I've risen with Charlotte to nurse. My wedding day is planned. So I'll read Mother's letter before the street sounds rise to a cacophony and wake the men. Then, no matter how it may disassemble me, I'll transcribe the letter here.

My dearest Lillian,

In marriage as in all, moderation is key. Thee has a self-righteous disposition, not unlike thy mother's; but let it not loose against thy husband, who means thee well. Remain temperate with him in all things earthly.

Hold tight to the reins of thy disposition, but not to the reins of thy spirit. Let it roam to perceive God's wisdom. Know that to love thy husband truly, thee must remain sensible of thy Inward Light and share the knowledge that it brings. For secrets will corrode thy bonds.

Know, too, that no matter how dearly thee loves thy husband — and I hope it will be very dearly — it is as a mother that thee shapes the world to come.

Do not be surprised, when thee has children, to find what I have found: of all the kinds of love that bind, a mother's love for her offspring is the strongest imperative on earth. It is as common as sunlight, as all-penetrating, as necessary to life. Its strength will fill thee, and in time will grow large enough to extend to many others, friend and stranger.

Dearest daughter, my firstborn child, thee and thy brother gave me this knowledge. I hope at times thee saw my gratitude and joy.

Treasure thy days on earth, as I have treasured mine.

I love thy soul.

> With all blessings on
> thy coming union,
> Mother

I won't write another word till the twelfth. I want *her* words to echo in me.

Seventh Month 12

Dawn brings pink and yellow to our windows. Beyond them, a continual sheet of rain touches the street. Bending forward, I see a city worker extinguishing the lamps. Early-rising laborers pass, mostly hidden by umbrellas, and sodden rats and dogs run along the bricks, sniffing for tidbits dropped by the street cleaners. In my lap Charlotte is taking nourishment, while Johan and Peter sleep, their bodies stretched across the painted planks.

In several hours, Johan and I will wed at a justice of the peace. Besides Peter, Johan has no one attending; he wants to contact his family only after Charlotte's untimely birth is covered over by some months of marriage. Father declined my invitation, writing that Patience is too near delivery. But Margaret and Miss Baker have gotten leave on some pretext and will be with us; Margaret will hold Charlotte. After a civil ceremony, we'll come back to this room for tea and sweets. Then Peter will leave the apartment, as he's going home to work again in Father's shop.

Therefore we face an urgent need of funds. Johan will find work better than selling pencils, I'm sure of it, though his missing fingers *and* his melancholy do impede him. But I already have a plan for how we'll survive. It came to me while reading Margaret's reply to our invitation, which was written in her blockish letters. When Hannah Purdes gave me lessons in geometry ten years back, she'd charged twenty-five cents per lesson. I went to a newspaper office and placed this advertisement to run weekly:

Experienced teacher available to teach reading and writing to adults and children. 35 cents per lesson. Also, letters read and written. Inquire at 21xx Montpelier Street, 3rd Floor Left, Phila.

Even as I waited in line, speaking in a friendly way with others, a woman and a man said they would come to me for help with legal letters they need written, and pay a dollar each. It seems my former teaching of persuasion will find new purpose.

Then, taking two of the four dollars in Johan's letter, I found a rag-seller's shop and chose a pale yellow gown and cap, as well as a straw hat. At a jeweler's, I allowed myself a new clasp for my locket's chain. So the gold locket with its tintype of Mother rests once more above my heart.

In my silence since recording Mother's letter here, I've wondered why she knew the corrosive force of secrets — if her marriage, too, had a hidden rock at its center. Did she go to the grave with painful secrets? Must every woman? Will I?

Which brings me to this moment. My tenth notebook is nearly filled. I don't know what will become of the many pages I've covered with scrawling. Perhaps I'll burn them, or bury them, or hide them beneath the floorboards. Perhaps I'll let some dear person read them, in time. I know only this for certain: Words come to me.

I hope one day to have a voice as strong as a hand on a drum, a hand that pounds its urgent messages across a distance.

Johan says I've changed. He says I've grown less youthful in my spirit.

Of course I have. I'm no longer innocent — nor am I any longer ashamed of not being so.

For of what use is innocence? It delivers us to danger.

I think of innocence; I think of Eve, how she chose knowledge; and there I linger.

It's said that every woman's painful labor is God's punishment. Eve ate an apple, and God pours wrath on every mother. So the Bible tells it.

Yet in the quiet as my baby sucks, across the boundaries of time, Eve's story reaches like a hammer. It strikes the bedrock of my heart and cracks it in two. Up leaps a fountain of refreshment — of other meanings.

That the apple is the world of pleasure that impregnates us.

That a woman in labor is drenched in two worlds simultaneously — on the border of the eternal garden and the living-dying world.

That from this suffering she emerges far more knowing, holding the new life in her arms and her own changed self — delivered of her baby and her innocence.

That by passing through this suffering and

furthering our human race, she crosses to a land where pain and joy are ever mingled and where her every move has consequence.

That every mother follows Eve.

This knowledge is not a curse. Separation from the garden's innocence is not a sin.

It is a beginning.

Johan stirs; he lifts his head and sends a warming glance across the room.

My baby nestles in my arms.

The sun now shoots its rays above the buildings opposite and brings my wedding day.

Life holds so much and moves so quickly. One can at best convey a pinprick of its darkness, and of its light.

AUTHOR'S NOTE

This work of fiction began in the long days and nights of nursing and nurturing my baby. As I held her in my arms and listened to the ticking of a clock, a voice came now and then into my mind. It was the voice of an unwed mother from long ago.

Sometimes she railed against being cast out, with her life derailed for good, while her lover walked freely among respected persons. Sometimes my own moments merged with hers, as when I marveled at the calm that descended while nursing or felt a fatigue I could never before have imagined. After placing my sleeping infant down, I walked to my desk and jotted those words onto scraps of paper.

While pregnant, I was inclined to study. I followed the stages of a growing human. I looked into practices of labor and delivery and armed myself with all manner of ideas and stuff. I considered these acts to be preparatory, even protective. Yet for my own specific labor, and for the actuality of caring for the infant who emerged, I was utterly unprepared.

So perhaps this was when the door to Lilli's story opened: when I was stunned at being the basis of a newborn's survival and awed by how my body and heart changed in service of her. Becoming a mother was no small shift in identity. I would never see any aspect of living in the same way again.

One more ingredient was vital to the brewing story. When we were a few months into parenthood, my husband showed me a review by Joan Acocella of *The History of the European Family,* a multi-editor, three-volume work that includes much tragic information about families in the past. I read there of the prevalence of so-called illegitimate births in Europe, at times over 50 percent. I'd known that having a baby deemed fatherless meant shame for mother and child, but I hadn't fully considered the costs of such prejudice. Many mothers gave up their infants to institutions or alleyways or worse, or struggled hard to keep them, and those infants often died.

Then there was the abject poverty that led couples with too many mouths to feed to give up their new babies. When the price of bread rose, so did the numbers of abandoned infants. Many infants with wealthier parents also perished; out of tradition and preference, newborns were brought to the homes of wet nurses, often in the country, who cared for multiple babies at once and couldn't protect them from fast-circulating diseases and an insufficient diet.

I hadn't known this vast history of infant death. Bits of understanding began to germinate in my consciousness. As I nursed, the woman's voice continued to speak. A small pile of scraps formed. I began to research.

The tragedies observed in Europe also took place in the newer nation across the sea. Of foundlings, social-work pioneer Amos Warner noted in his 1894 book *American Charities,* it "can matter little to the individual infant whether it is murdered outright or is placed in a foundling hospital." And wet nursing, in its various settings, was also characterized by infant death.

Because babies had a too-great chance of dying while away "at nurse," urban families began bringing wet nurses as servants into their homes. Unwed mothers were a ready population to fill these positions, because they had fresh milk and, often, no place to live and no other decent work options. So at a time when character was believed to pass from nipple to mouth, mothers viewed as immoral were nevertheless invited into homes to nurse strangers' infants.

These women might have become pregnant by accident or by force. They might have found themselves unaided due to the father's desertion or death, due to rejection and expulsion by their families, or some combination. Regardless of the cause of their pregnancies and desperation, such women and their infants were — and in many places still are — separated and punished.

In order to become a live-in wet nurse, too, the unwed mother usually had to give up her infant or board it elsewhere. For if it stayed with her, she might have favored it — or she simply might not have had enough milk for two babies. But her infant, whether boarded with a woman feeding multiple infants or surrendered to an institution, had a small chance of surviving. As physician Charles West observed about this arrangement in his 1874 *Lectures on the Diseases of Infancy and Childhood,* "by the sacrifice of the infant of the poor woman, the offspring of the wealthy will be preserved."

Why was the separation of mother and

infant usually deadly? Because no safe substitute for human milk existed. Cow's milk, the usual substitute, was often problematic. It might have been thinned with unclean water or not kept cool on its trip from udder to household; it might have contained harmful bacteria, including those causing tuberculosis, typhoid, diphtheria, and diarrhea. Doctors of the nineteenth century and the early twentieth made note of the often revolting condition of milk, as here: "[W]hile mother's milk is free from germs, cow's milk, as ordinarily obtained, swarms with them, and often contains manure and other filth."* Bottles, too, were frequently contaminated, from inadequate cleaning.

In the United States, milk safety improved in the twentieth century with more oversight, more cooling to retard spoilage, and more effective pasteurization. But it is still true in many places on earth that the milk of human mothers is crucial to infants' survival.

I thought of my imaginary wet nurse, worrying about her baby from an intolerable

* Kenelm Winslow, *The Home Medical Library,* vol. III (New York: The Review of Reviews Company, 1908), pp. 119–20.

distance; I thought of her baby, whose life was threatened by the absence of her mother's milk and care. Could such a mother accomplish what many wet nurses intended? Could she find a situation that would keep her baby alive while she saved money by working as a servant, then reclaim her baby and create a better life?

In her definitive work *A Social History of Wet Nursing in America: From Breast to Bottle* (1996), Janet Golden notes that these women left no accounts of their experiences, stating that "wet nurses remain historically silent."

My narrator would tell her story.

But who was she? What sort of a person might have had the moral courage to do as she does and the education to write well and regularly in a diary? I decided that she would be a Quaker.

This choice allowed her to be well educated, since Quaker girls in late-nineteenth-century Philadelphia could receive strong educations at Friends' schools. It allowed her to be outspoken, too; some nineteenth-century Friends were principled fighters for social justice. Their numbers included the legendary reformers Lucretia Mott and Susan B. Anthony. Among Quakers, the keeping of intense and lengthy journals was not uncommon. And I was drawn to the Religious Society of Friends because of its founding principles: that everyone can have direct access to God, and that all carry the light of God within. The Friends' Meeting for Worship can be a time for cultivating a relationship with that Inner Light, an invitation to radical thinking and spiritual exploration. This milieu, and then an alienation from it, could have given rise to the woman who'd sprung up in my head.

As for that alienation, it was necessary for Lilli to be isolated in order for the plot to unfold as it does. But the interplay between her family and their Meeting is meant to serve the needs of the novel, not to show the history of any actual family or Meeting. Could such events have occurred? Perhaps. The Friends' Discipline of the Philadelphia Yearly Meeting — a set of principles and behavioral guidance that is referred to in the novel as the Discipline — gave stern instructions on how to deal with members who strayed. Yet some Friends would likely have reached out to sustain others who were struggling as Lilli's family was. As is true in fairy tales, however, the adventure can only begin in earnest when a character steps outside the zone of safety.

■ ■ ■ ■

The distinctive speech of Quakers (also called Friends) appearing in this novel may be of interest to readers. The Religious Society of Friends is a worldwide network of local meetings, or churches. When the religion began in seventeenth-century England, British people used the informal "thee" and "thou" when talking with peers, and they used the more formal "you" when talking with individuals of a higher social status. But Quakers, in keeping with their revolutionary position that all souls are equal before God, refused to follow this custom. When speaking to *any* individual, they used only "thou" and "thee."

Such choices in language — what Friends call *plain speech* — spread with the religion across the globe; some Friends today continue to speak in this way. By Lilli's time, in 1880s Philadelphia, the use of "thou" and "thee" was fading, although "thee" seems to have lasted longer. I chose for Lilli and her family to follow the custom of using "thee," both to reflect their greater observance and to be true to Lilli's role as a teacher (since teachers were charged with encouraging their students to use plain speech). When Lilli records what non-Quakers said, however, she records their use of "you."

Other features of Friends' speech that show up in Lilli's diary include the use of people's given names without titles (but only if she learns the person's first name) and the use of numbers to indicate days and months. This is done to avoid honoring the non-Christian gods that our usual days and months were named after.

As for Lilli's home, because of my interest in a storied and Quaker-influenced area called Germantown, I decided that Lilli and her family would live there. This former township became a part of Philadelphia in 1854. The first American document protesting against slavery was signed in 1688 by some of its Quaker settlers. To visit its sites is to encounter American history in a moving and genuine way. Germantown holds 579 properties within its National Historic Landmark and National Register of Historic Places designations, among them Johnson House, a station on the underground railroad; the birthplace of Louisa May Alcott, author of *Little Women;* and the Germantown White House, where George and Martha Washington and their household members lived and worked in 1793 and 1794.

I took small liberties in my depiction of 1880s Germantown. When Lilli passes along the main street in a carriage, for instance, the order of the streets she passes is not quite the actual order. The Appleton estate and Lilli's childhood home are invented, though they are in sections where such places could have been located. If one visited Germantown, one *would* find the meetinghouse, the burial ground, the school where my imaginary Lilli studied and taught, train tracks and stations, and other sites, but much in the environment (including waterways) has changed dramatically. In the case of Angela and Victor's home in an Italian enclave, Italian families did live in that area from about that time; the industriousness I report was apparently not unusual; the block on which I've placed them had no water lines or hydrants to help put out a fire; and a coal yard and train tracks sat close by.

The same combination of actual and fictional applies to the novel's scenes in downtown Philadelphia. Albert's office and apartment buildings are invented. Broad Street Station stood until 1953 by the still-standing and wondrous City Hall. The chapel in which Lilli considers the story of

Job was inspired by a small and stunning chapel in the First Unitarian Church of Philadelphia, in a building on Chestnut Street completed in 1885. Little remains of the vast public hospital and almshouse complex in West Philadelphia that was long called Old Blockley. The smells of Blockley's interiors are based partly on a doctor's recollections of the period. And while Blockley's practices regarding foundlings varied over time, and the appearance of its nursery is imagined, its dangers were all too real.

Between 1860 and 1864, nearly 82 percent of Blockley's foundlings died. In 1880, all foundlings died, per an investigative committee's 1882 report on rampant atrocities and thefts by those entrusted with running Blockley. One section of that report concluded that "the deaths of these infants was [*sic*] due to *ignorance* and *neglect*" and noted with horror the "barbarous cruelty" that allowed for "the abandonment of helpless infants to die for want of ordinary care." Fortunately, it appears that, in the month after the fictional Lilli rescued Charlotte, those responsible for foundlings at Blockley started boarding out the infants with nursing women, hoping for better outcomes.

As is depicted in the novel, corruption at

Blockley was extreme, per the vigorous 1882 investigation; in response to its findings, the superintendent fled to Canada and had to be brought back to face charges. And the unclaimed bodies of paupers were indeed ferried across the Schuylkill River and sold to medical students for dissection. (What changed, in time, was that this practice became legal.)

The maternity home that takes in Lilli is also based on a real institution — the State Hospital for Women and Infants. It opened in 1873 at its first home, at 1718 Filbert Street, through the efforts of doctors and residents who'd worked at Blockley and wanted to offer wronged women and their newborns an alternative to that site of disease and roughness. It had a Ladies' Committee, and its staff included a matron and, soon, a woman doctor. While by 1882 at least one other such institution had opened (contrary to the fictional Anne Pierce's claim of hers being the only one), I chose this place.

As I learned through records preserved at the archives of Pennsylvania Hospital, for its first sixteen years the refuge was desperately short of funds. Despite the hopeful inclusion of "State" in its name and its board's stirring annual appeals, it received no state funding until 1889. At the time when I've imagined Lilli there, it could house only an average of twelve women at once, couldn't shelter nursing mothers and infants long enough to give the infants a strong start, and had to turn most applicants away.

To read the records of this institution is to be struck by the difficulty of being a pregnant and abandoned woman in the late nineteenth century and of being in the position of trying to help her in a climate of hate. The primary factor that draws one to comprehend the difficulty — that paints a world startling and compelling — is that the charity had one or more impassioned writers at its helm. In annual reports of the 1880s, the condition of the arriving inmates is described as "depressed by the disgrace attaching to their situation; anxious through fear that their fall should become known to their friends; distressed by their inability to account satisfactorily for their enforced absence from home or from their places of labor; injured by tight lacing — done with a view of hiding their shame; suffering from attempts to produce abortion; unhappy in view of the necessity of separation from their children; and not infrequently, from exposure and insufficiency of food, on the verge of serious illness."

An 1878 report noted, "No other class of offenders has . . . been so left outside the pale of humanitarian and Christian helpfulness. . . . [E]xcept in the institution whose interests are represented by this board, no organized effort has been made, no hand has been outstretched, to save those who, but for one false step, were guiltless of offense."

If only it were possible to send gratitude into the past for the kind intentions of those who ran this charity. Clearly this good place would be Lilli's refuge.

Starting in the first annual report, in 1874, the writers refer to much "misapprehension" and prejudice against the institution by the public and the press. Once, the hospital had to be closed for a short while, and no other hospital in the city would take in the young women. The hospital was accused of caring for the "deliberately vicious" and was lambasted in the papers, including a Philadelphia newspaper called *The Day.* A scene in the novel — when Anne Pierce gathers the inmates to discuss a cruel article — was inspired by this. Anne's reply to the newspaper, which Lilli quotes, contains several lines modeled on lines in the annual reports.

■ ■ ■ ■

Historians and novelists have in common a love of reaching for the sinuous shapes that poke from the debris of history and of pulling them into sight. Though this novel is an imagined story that hangs itself on rudiments of history, innumerable details still had to be obtained — from city trash-collection practices to women's underwear to what words were in use; from the supervision of wet nurses' diets to hackney-carriage prices; from medicinal herbs to how toast could be made; from vagrancy laws and their irregular enforcement to malnourished infants and their recovery — and on and on, seemingly ad infinitum.

My larger aim was to create belief in lives that could have been lived and to bring the meaning of their struggles into the light of our day. I wanted to give voice to a deserted woman in 1883 who asserts the value of her bond with her infant — and to show how obstacles of prejudice and inequality littered their way.

The difficult work of mothers has long been drastically under-recognized. I wanted to tell a story in which women's strength was crucial to the world's surviving and thriving — as it truly is and always has been.

ACKNOWLEDGMENTS

This book is partly an homage to the city of Philadelphia, which enchants me with how visibly its past continues in its present, as well as by how humbly it contains this richness. I send much appreciation to the people who preserve and interpret this past.

I consulted many people and resources and explored many places while writing this novel. Any errors, elisions, or alterations are my own. I send special thanks to the following people and institutions.

To Janet Golden, whose book *A Social History of Wet Nursing in America: From Breast to Bottle* (1996) was vital to my understanding of urban wet nursing and more in the nineteenth century; her excellent references made it easy to choose further resources.

To Stacey Peeples at the Pennsylvania Hospital Archives, who warmly granted access to the invaluable records of the State Hospital for Women and Infants and other materials.

To Pendle Hill in Wallingford, Pennsylvania, where I took retreats, spoke with Friends, attended Meeting for Worship, and found print resources. Pendle Hill's publications include many gems I relied on, such as Howard H. Brinton's *Quaker Journals: Varieties of Religious Experience Among Friends* (1972).

To Anne D. and Stephen Burt, my aunt and uncle by marriage, who shared their collection of spiritual works by Friends and who live gently as environmentalists and lovers of peace.

To Sam Katz, who gave me the opportunity to learn documentary screenwriting and delve further into Philadelphia history.

To V. Chapman-Smith, Emma Lapsansky-Werner, Cynthia Little, Marion Roydhouse, and Anna Coxe Toogood. The hours I passed discussing women's history with these scholars were joyous.

To Ann Fessler, whose book *The Girls Who Went Away: The Hidden History of Women Who Surrendered Children for Adoption in the Decades Before Roe v. Wade* (2006) provides dramatic instances of the lifelong impacts of early pregnancy and of giving up a baby.

To those who sustain the area resources

that were of benefit to this book, including the sites of Historic Germantown, the Historical Society of Pennsylvania, the College of Physicians of Philadelphia, the Haverford College Libraries Quaker and Special Collections, the Encyclopedia of Greater Philadelphia, and the Germantown Historical Society.

To Alex Bartlett, Sid Cook, Kristina Haugland, Emma Lapsansky-Werner, Jonathan Maberry, Irv Miller, David Odell, Steven Peitzman, Lisa Pergolizzi-Brock, Suzanne Prigohzy, Lynn Rosen, Susan Gregory Thomas, Jacqueline Wolf, and Simone Zelitch for your time and guidance.

To Mary Bailey, Arnold Benton, Suzanne Benton, Jane Carroll, Stephen Frank, Lisa Kopel, Jennifer Lowman, Frances Nadel, Carol O'Donoghue, Suzanne Rotondo, Ilene Raymond Rush, Deborah Shaw, and David Updike for your valuable responses and support.

To Anne Dubuisson, Natasha Kassell, and the Spinners (Susan Martel, Ellen Murphey, and Lori Weinrott) for your sustaining input and motivating deadlines.

To the hundreds of writing students and clients who've entrusted me with your works in progress and taught me much about writing and life, and to my former teacher Valerie Martin, whose keen mind and example I've treasured.

To my wise and kind agent and editors, Jane von Mehren, Nan Talese, and Ronit Wagman, for loving Lilli's voice from the first sentence to the last and for giving this book a caring home.

To Carolyn Williams and Daniel Meyer, helpful, smart, and gracious; Pei Loi Koay, book designer; and Michael J. Windsor, book-jacket genie, as well as the many others at Doubleday and Penguin Random House who've moved this book into the world, including Todd Doughty, Victoria Chow, and Lauren Weber.

To Dori Ostermiller, gifted writer, for more than two decades of joyful and life-sustaining friendship, and to all my life-sustaining friends and family, whom I dearly love.

To my father, Arnold Benton, for your honesty and caring, and for teaching me that every phenomenon can be known from many points of view.

To my mother, Suzanne Benton, for raising and sustaining me in your loving and creative spirit, and for teaching me that one's understanding of history depends entirely on where one looks.

To my husband, David, and our daughter,

Dariel: Living with you and loving you are my greatest pleasures and sources of growth. My home is where you are.

Though writers work alone, we sit as if shoulder to shoulder with all who value stories, and aim our efforts toward those who might find value in them.

In other words, to you, reader.

ABOUT THE AUTHOR

Janet Benton's work has appeared in *The New York Times, The Philadelphia Inquirer, Glimmer Train,* and many other publications. She has cowritten and edited historical documentaries for television. She holds a B.A. in religious studies from Oberlin College and an M.F.A. in creative writing from the University of Massachusetts, Amherst, and for decades she has been an editor, taught writing, and helped individuals and organizations craft their stories. She lives in Philadelphia with her husband and daughter. *Lilli de Jong* is her first novel. Visit her at www.janetbentonauthor.com.